ABOUT THE AUTHOR

GREGORY MAGUIRE is the bestselling author of *Confessions of an Ugly Stepsister, Lost, Mirror Mirror,* and the Wicked Years, a series that includes *Wicked, Son of a Witch,* and *A Lion Among Men.* He is also the author of the acclaimed nonfiction work *Making Mischief: A Maurice Sendak Appreciation* and *Matchless,* an illustrated reimagining of the classic children's tale "The Little Match Girl." *Wicked,* now a beloved classic, is the basis for the Tony Award–winning Broadway musical of the same name. Maguire has lectured on art, literature, and culture both at home and abroad. He lives with his family near Boston, Massachusetts.

The Next Queen
of Heaven

The Next Queen of Heaven

A NOVEL

GREGORY MAGUIRE

HARPER

NEW YORK • LONDON • TORONTO • SYDNEY

HARPER

A limited edition paperback of this book was published in 2009 by Concord Free Press.

HarperCollins books may be purchased for educational, business, or sales promotional use. For information please write: Special Markets Department, HarperCollins Publishers, 10 East 53rd Street, New York, NY 10022.

FIRST HARPER paperback published 2010.

Library of Congress Cataloging-in-Publication Data

Maguire, Gregory.
    The next queen of heaven : a novel / by Gregory Maguire. — 1st Harper pbk. ed.
        p. cm.
    ISBN 978-0-06-199779-2 (pbk.)
    1. City and town life—New York (State)—Fiction. 2. Eccentrics and eccentricities—Fiction. 3. Mothers and daughters—Fiction. 4. Teenagers—Fiction. 5. New York (State)—Fiction. I. Title.
    PS3563.A3535N49 2010
    813'.54—dc22   2010019896

10 11 12 13 14   ETM/RRD   10 9 8 7 6 5 4 3 2 1

Author's Note

Thank you to early readers of *The Next Queen of Heaven*—Betty Levin, Andy Newman, William Reiss, and Maggie Stern Terris.

Special thanks are due to the heavenly beings behind Concord Free Press, a nonprofit publishing venture founded by Ann and Stona Fitch. (Check it out at www.concordfreepress.com.) Early editorial advice from Ann Fitch shaped the Concord Free Press edition, which is almost exactly reproduced in this HarperCollins edition but for some adjustments due to a few different house-style conventions and to even fewer second thoughts. Thanks to Concord Free Press for bringing this baby into the world, and to Cassie Jones and HarperCollins for providing it shelter and a permanent home once it had arrived.

For readers who know me primarily as a writer of fantasy, the setting and subject matter (and the vernacular spoken by characters herein) may come as a surprise. Forgive me my trespasses. It's my suspicion that heaven may be both more disguised and more accessible than any other fantastic locale I might choose to write about.

For those who keep singing
and
for those who keep silent.

1999

To Tabitha's remark that the town's first speed-trap camera was totally unfair and kind of kinky, Mrs. Scales replied, after a prayerful silence, "Why don't you think of it as the Eye of God?"

"God doesn't do three strikes you're out, last I heard," said Tabitha. "Or give tickets. Big Brother's more like it. I bet Jack Reeves sits in his mayor's spy room somewhere taking notes and feeling himself."

"I doubt it," said her mother. "But Big Brother, that's good. You're doing some reading."

"Don't count on it. It's just the forensic club is going Big Brother this, Big Brother that, at the No More Columbines pep rally."

"Well, you can relax about surveillance from anyone but me. Besides, they say the camera isn't hooked up yet. It doesn't see anything. So it can't do anything."

Tabitha inhaled around the gum she had tongued against the back of her front teeth. "Maybe you're right about it being, like, the Eye of God."

Praise you Jesus, thought her mother, she's coming around at last.

"Totally fucking blind."

They coasted past the hapless aperture, a heady four miles per hour over the limit. A little frostiness of mood, not so bad in itself. Union Street curved north into downtown Thebes—what passed for downtown—and the silence locked mother and daughter together. Better than the usual smackdown session, thought Mrs. Scales.

She took advantage of the time out to practice her Inner Breathing. Breathe east. She imagined, miles out of sight, the softwood heart of the Northeast, the Adirondacks.

Breathe west. In the slant light of dusk—daylight savings time taking its bite again—she glimpsed the first iteration of America's liquid prairie. It looked like chemical water on fire in the gloaming. The Lakes, the Lakes. Ontario, Huron, Superior, Erie. That other one. Not for the first time did *Erie* seem the word to cover them all.

Breathe north. Montreal (more or less). Breathe south. Syracuse. Compass rose breathing. Center yourself, for Christ's sake.

Mrs. Scales considered her dilemmas. Maybe this very moment, in the car hurrying past nasturtium-edged clouds, Tabitha was undergoing a conversion. Evolving from potty mouth to docile daughter. It could happen. Leontina was praying for it hard enough, wasn't she? Or did this mean that her prayer, like her backhand and also according to the dental technician the care of her gums, was sadly lacking?

At the light by Croton Drugs, old Mrs. Chanarinjee in her push-walker and sari paused in the crosswalk. She leaned down at the open passenger window and chuckled a hello across Tabitha to her mother. Tabitha, recoiling as if she were being nosed by a dog, muttered, "She has curry coming out of her cunt," and flipped her the bird. Mrs. Chanarinjee reached in and grabbed Tabitha's middle finger and squeezed it till she squealed. Inner breathing north east south west. Discernment, please. Was Mrs. Chanarinjee dispensing the wrath of a savage foreign god she'd never quite abandoned, or was she just unclear on the execution of the American handshake?

"Let the fuck go a me. Aren't you supposed to be like on some burning pile of furniture or something?"

"I'm supposed to be on Percoset for my hips," said Mrs. Chanarinjee. All business now. "This Sunday, Mrs. Leontina Scales. Is it your turn to do the milk or mine?"

"I think mine, Savitra. Better get to the curb before the light changes."

"Before the light changes, yes, yes."

"Stupid bitch." Tabitha exercised no volume control. "Stupid holy cow. Who wears tablecloths in fucking *October*?"

Breathe. The compass rose again. Inner Breathing of the spirit. "It wouldn't hurt you, Tabitha, to try to be nicer to people."

"It wouldn't hurt *me* if she fell down dead in that paisley bedsheet."

The next day Tabitha's mother met with Pastor Jakob Huyck and put it to him in hypothetical terms. If there was a child who had a mouth on her, who seemed determined to drive her single parent into an early grave, what would Pastor Huyck recommend? "Prayer," said Pastor Huyck promptly. He nodded his head and picked at his straw-colored goatee as if it had lice in it. He was about fifty-five, and Mrs. Scales thought the goatee seemed rather a loose-cannon approach to Modern Maturity. "Prayer, and a good example," said Pastor Huyck in his coming-attractions baritone. "Does she have a good example at home, Leontina?"

"An example of what?"

"I'll do the praying. You be the good example. Don't forget your Inner Breathing. Also your pocketbook, it's there by the plant."

On her way home, Mrs. Scales considered his advice. Be a good example? Had he meant her to be an example of goodness? She already had that one down cold, and it wasn't working. So he must mean be a good, effective example of badness. To show Tabitha how objectionable it was.

Centering herself by Inner Breathing and through flexing her rump muscles in rotation against the car seat, she veered off course and headed to the high school. "Thought I'd surprise you with a ride home," she called brightly into the clot of sullen teenagers loitering between parked cars.

"No way," said Tabitha, refusing to be separated from the human camouflage. "Caleb Briggs gets done at the plant at three, and he's taking me to the Ames in Cleary Corners. The new Boss Bitch CD is out."

"I'll take you. I have to get some milk for Sunday anyway."

"Shit," said Tabitha. She left her bosom companions without comment. They looked into middle distances, perhaps hoping for this charade of family life to conclude lest they became virally infected. Not for the first time, Mrs. Scales wondered if anyone actually liked her daughter. They didn't seem distressed to have her flushed out of their midst.

Leontina Scales used her blinker and peered both ways before inching out.

"This is so embarrassing," said Tabitha. "Nobody's mother has picked them up since like fourth grade. You're like demented. This is like Auschwitz."

"We're clear. You can sit up."

"I like it down here. I think I'll die down here."

"I have to go to the Grand Union first. Then to Maxy's Hardware. You want to come in?"

"What the fuck for? I'd rather squat here and read the Bible."

"Oh?" Mrs. Scales felt a pleasant shock. This was turning out better than she thought.

"Earth to Mom. *Only kidding.* I'm not a, you know. *Loser.*"

Mrs. Scales took her time in the Grand Union. She did Inner Breathing to steady her resolve as far as the fish aisle, but the ice smelled old. By the time she got back to the car, Tabitha was fake snoring, nasally sucking in the word "fuuuuuuuuuuuuuck" and exhaling on "shiiiiiiiiiiiiiiiiiiit."

"Very funny. Next stop, Maxy's."

"Can I get out there and walk home?"

"I thought I was taking you to the Ames to get that new CD. The Boss Lady."

"Boss Bitch, Mom. *Bitch.*" Apparently Tabitha liked the sound of that. "Bitch, Mom. Bitch, Mom."

"Tabitha."

Her daughter muttered a profanity so cutting-edge that Leontina couldn't place it as scatological, theological, sociological, or erotic. "That isn't very nice." She hoped a generic response wasn't too lame.

"Depends on who does it." A snort.

After Maxy's, Mrs. Scales steered the car over Irish Hollow Road and came the back way into the Crosswinds Shopping Center parking lot. Tabitha opened her eyes. "Look, that's Caleb's motorcycle? That one? I'll get out here and go with him? Caleb Briggs? He musta called in sick to work. I'll go home with him. You know. Caleb Briggs."

"Oh no you won't. Go in and pick up your new CD. I have to go to the ATM first. I'm all out. I'll meet you in a little while at the cashier."

Mrs. Scales sat in the car with her hands clenched on the steering wheel. The minute hand twitched seven times. Then she got out. It felt as if she were going to the doctor. All dry mouth and nervous stomach. She aimed the door-lock rays at one of her new bumper stickers. "I brake for Communion." When Leontina Scales had raised Tabitha in such decency, why was she so contrary? Why?

At the door of the Ames she looked in. This was the busy time. She saw Mrs. Prothero from church, with Mrs. Getchen and Mrs. Howe. Old Man Getchen was nodding off on a bench in the mold-blue light of fluorescence, trying to outlive his wife. Through the glass Mrs. Scales thought she could see Tabitha way down at the back. She didn't know if Tabitha had found her CD yet. A formation of teenagers dawdled in front of the checkout lines, apparently waiting for one of their herd to reappear. Great. An audience. This wouldn't work without an audience.

Mrs. Scales pushed the door open. "Afternoon, Vivian, hello there, Pauline. Mrs. Howe." This wasn't going to be easy. "Mind my language for a moment." She wasn't sure they had heard her. She took a deep Breath, Inner from all four quarters of the compass. Pastor Huyck recommended this, she reminded the Lord. "Tabitha! Tabitha Scales! Tabitha!"

The chattering yielded at once to an all-strings version of "Beauty and the Beast." Cashiers turned. Mrs. Prothero, Mrs. Getchen, Mrs. Howe turned. Mrs. Scales gave a wave and a bright-eyed smile that verged, she knew, on the hysterical. "Tabitha Scales," she yelled, a gritty, carrying, outdoorsy bray, "you get the hell over here, or I'll kick your ass so hard the shit is going to paralyze the fucking fan!" There. Four, count 'em, four Little Uglies in one sentence. Leontina had been good in English composition in her day.

Mr. Getchen stood up. "Pauline, get a move on if you know what's good for you." Mrs. Getchen gaped at him as if he'd orchestrated all this.

Picked out by perspective, Tabitha appeared at the far end of an aisle. Her hands theatrically up on either side of her head, a pantomimed shrug you could have read through a beer glass. "What's the matter, what are you *doing*?" she called. "I'm coming, okay?"

Mrs. Scales let it rip some more. "I don't know why in tarnation I put up with a bitch like you. Did you get your stupid music?" *Tarnation* was a choke cribbed out of her own mother's mouth; Mrs. Scales hoped no one noticed.

Tabitha was all but sprinting. "Chill! *Chill*, will you?" She breezed past the few customers in line.

Mrs. Scales waited until Tabitha was right in front of her. She used as ordinary a voice as she could manage. "What a shame. Didn't they carry the CD you wanted? Dear?"

"Forget it. I'm here. Let's go. Are you mental? Are you, like, having sudden onset industrial menopause? Why are you doing this?"

"For the love of Christ." Leontina passed her friends from church, who were staring palely at her. She hesitated. The teenagers had all clustered near the bottle deposit cash window as if ready to dive through it for safety in the event that Mrs. Scales was packing heat. Empowered, Mrs. Scales raised her voice to them. "A little demonstration of contemporary slang. Would you like to hear me improvise—?"

"*Mom.*"

Some store manager had just turned the Muzak up three notches and was probably calling Jack Reeves over at the police station. "Well, next time, then," said Mrs. Scales. She couldn't resist adding, "Thank you for not listening." She strode out across the mud mat. Tabitha skulked after.

The parking lot was a relief for them although, with her pulse racing, Mrs. Scales couldn't keep track of the order for Inner Breathing.

"I was, like, dying of embarrassment. What's the matter with you?"

"Well, honey." She made a show of gripping her car keys in a way that suggested she could use them to gouge out her own daughter's eyes if attacked. "Now you know how I feel when you use coarse language in front of my friends. It's not a whole lot of fun. Is it."

Total silence in the car on the way home, which these days was the only way to escape Tabitha's spontaneous profanity. But it was a start.

2

FOR THREE DAYS Tabitha managed a civil tongue, but the cease-fire failed on Saturday night. She went out and didn't come home till eight a.m. next morning. Welts on her arms, her clothes disheveled, a rubber Halloween mask of Richard Nixon slung onto the kitchen table like the head of John the Baptist or Holofernes. Its nose a half inch deep in margarine. "Where have you been, young lady?" asked Mrs. Scales, swallowing back her alternative opening gambit, *Has some pervert deflowered my firstborn because he was turned on by the thought of a cross-dressing Tricky Dick?*

When she was ready to reply, Tabitha managed, "Bliss *out*, life is adventure, and after all, Halloween's coming tonight, isn't it? So go to Sunday service, and trick or treat already."

"I need to talk to you about hymen integrity."

"Mom, I'm not talking about anything till I zone out for a while. I'm, like, so wasted."

Leontina moved the margarine away from the rubber mask. "And you know Pastor Jakob forbids the children of the Cliffs of Zion Radical Radiant Pentecostal Church plastic masks and costumes. Disguises of all kinds promote dishonesty, and dishonesty is an open invitation to You Know Who. A recipe for trouble and no mistake. Though I gather you've been experimenting with making mistakes."

Tabitha, letting out a laugh that yodeled into a shriek, impounded herself in the bathroom. The water ran suspiciously noisy. "Are you weeping in there?" said Mrs. Scales, ear against the door. Her sons emerged from their separate dens, blinking and scratching like the animals they were. "Tabitha's been out all night. I believe she's been drinking, or *something*," said their mother. "And I have to go to Meeting even if nobody else is, and I don't want to leave her in this condition without you boys knowing."

"She's drinking? At this hour? Attagirl," said Hogan, and went back to bed.

"I'll fix her some coffee and find some aspirin, Mom," said Kirk. "You go on to Meeting. Go. *Go*."

She left feeling that she was living and driving a lie, with her car sporting the other new bumper sticker that said "Grace Happens." Happens to whom? That's what she wanted to know. Maybe the bumper sticker was missing a line: GRACE HAPPENS TO VANISH.

Mrs. Scales tiptoed into Meeting with a red face. In this claustrophobic town, someone at Meeting would be ready to share new gossip about the Hussy of Thebes, Tabitha Scales. How much more shame could Tabitha heap upon her family? Was she aiming for an entry in *Guinness World Records*?

And—oh, but her mother could hardly tolerate thoughts at the clinical level—what yowls of pleasure or pain had Tabitha emitted at the infliction of those wounds? And that aroma of sex . . . soft baby asparagus cut with a weak solution of Clorox. Despite her own clammy celibacy in that regard, currently, Mrs. Scales remembered the characteristics of intercourse all too well.

Leontina found it hard to focus during Pastor Jakob Huyck's homily. She fretted with a frozen smile until the announcements, when Pastor Huyck reminded them, "The Radical Radiant Pentecostals and the Roman Catholics enjoy an unholy alliance. We share the parking lot between our buildings. And I've promised Father Mike Sheehy you won't mow down any Catholics today. Prove me prophetic."

Devotion yielded to committee sessions and study circles. Leontina Scales excused herself a few minutes early from the Inner Breathing class that Savitra Chanarinjee always called Remedial Prayer. She would set up the coffee for the break. She plugged in the twin Mister Coffees—or Misters Coffee, as Kirk would have it. (Mister Fastidious.)

Then Leontina realized that what with her rage and worry she'd forgotten to stop and get 2 percent milk from the Stewart's. What milk *did* lurk in the back of the Cliffs of Zion fridge was giving off an almighty odor. So Mrs. Scales prayed briefly for the courage to change the things she could, and she crossed the parking lot, weaving between Roman Catholic and Radical Radiant Pentecostal cars. She sneaked through the back door of the church of Our Lady Something or Other. (Our Ladies were like Barbies: new ones seemed to be issued annually.)

She couldn't find a light switch, but descended the stairs anyway. Overhead the folksy choir was insisting "All We Have We Give to You." Mrs. Scales hoped that the sentiment extended to nondairy creamer.

Mrs. Scales was a devout woman when the mood struck, and regularly on Sunday mornings the mood struck with some aggression. However, as she felt her way down to Our Lady's kitchenette, she found herself wincing. Wurlitzer piety it was not.

What a week. Ruefully she remembered a few days ago, Tabitha waffling on about an Eye of God that had accidentally gotten unplugged somehow. A God that had suffered some sort of seizure and was cognizant but paralyzed. It was hard to imagine His Eye following her down these dark steps.

The argument this morning with Tabitha has thrown every-thing awry, thought Leontina. I can't even begin to locate my In-ner Breathing. My mind's too worked up with Halloween images. A menace underneath the stairs. A creature in the dark. Slobber-ing its syllables together: OPEN YOUR MIND TO ME. Hackneyed, of course, B-movie quality at best, but better than OPEN YOUR LEGS.

But even that thought: a violation. She shuddered and wished she were the type to wear a Burberry scarf so she could clutch it now, but *uh-unh*. Not with the shoulders of a stevedore as her own mother, the redoubtable Ida Prelutski, used to point out. Honey, can't you hunch a little and try to appear normal?

Open the door to worry, and look what happens: a junior assis-tant of Beelzebub tempts you to abhor your own firstborn child. Turn her into an embodiment of one of the deadly sins. Plainly put—or in words that would have been plain enough in Ida Pre-lutski's mouth—a floozy. A strumpet. A tramp. A harlot. (Wasn't there an eatery in that Syracuse mall called Harlots? What were they thinking?)

Harsh words, these, but thinking them as she navigated the stairs of a Catholic church only made her descent the more alarm-ing, as Mrs. Scales didn't hold with religion of the Roman variety.

She paused for a minute in the dark. Halfway down and half-way up.

The stairwell proved exceedingly dark. There'd be a switch at the bottom, surely? Her thoughts returned to Halloween coming tonight—*your children will turn to beasts before your eyes*, was that le-gitimate Biblical prophecy or was it a movie trailer voice-over? She was beset by beasts, the nameless kind. They had waited all her life to get her. All she'd ever wanted was to be free. But free, free of what? If you couldn't name the beasts, see them, you couldn't process your prayer request with any accuracy. Being a devoted study circlist has never helped me much, she thought.

She imagined marching to Tabitha and saying, "No more, young lady; out of my house. In the sight of God I can be shamed by my own flesh and blood no longer. Get out. And take that severed head of Nixon with you." She knew Tabitha would only snort some lewd reply.

She drew herself together—this is what happened when you didn't sleep all night out of worry. You went stark raving un-Christian. And she a middle-aged pillar of the Radical Radiant Pentecostals. (Also Republican, with some standards.) Take a good look at yourself, she remonstrated. Behind enemy lines, sneaking into the Catholic stronghold. *During Mass.* Of course, I'll replace the milk.

At length she made it to the bottom of the stairs without twisting an ankle. She still couldn't find the switch, but the refrigerator—a Kelvinator dating to the last days of the Eisenhower administration, by the look of it—would probably feature a twenty-watt bulb in the ceiling panel inside the door. It did. The light came on just in time for Mrs. Leontina Scales to see a semi-retired statue of Our Lady with a Chip on Her Shoulder perched up top. It shifted, with a faint sound of grit giving way, and glissaded off the pockmarked appliance.

It was a heavy statue. It bounced against Mrs. Scales's skull and then smashed to the linoleum. She registered that the noise was substantial, even thunderous, but that was all.

3

UPSTAIRS, THE CHIEF of the collection basket brigade, Turk Schaeffer, heaved himself from his kneeling position, made a perfunctory genuflection, and trudged off to investigate. Father Mike sat in his chair, eyes closed in contemplation of austere mystery.

Nearing the end of the third chorus, the choir stumbled since the music director, Jeremy Carr, remained paused, his head cocked as if expecting further tympanic crashes. Should they wait for his cue? Or continue on as they'd rehearsed? Under the lead of the loudest soprano, Peggy Mueller, the choir charged into the fourth verse, reminding Jeremy of his obligations to his all-volunteer army of would-be soloists. His arm started wagging again.

Turk Schaeffer found Mrs. Leontina Scales out cold in a puddle of full cream milk. Shards of grayish porcelain were scattered around her. Turk, a retired lineman with Niagara Mohawk, had seen his share of accidents. He could tell that Mrs. Scales, whom he knew only to nod to when he ran into her at the Grand Union, wasn't hurt bad. She was breathing. No blood pinked up the milk. But a lump the size of an eggroll pushed up through her thinning hair.

"Mercy, Turk, what's up?" said Polly Osterhaus, an alto whom the choir director had sent downstairs, as backup. Altos were good in a crisis.

"I can take care of this," said Turk.

"Is that Mrs. Scales from over on Papermill Road? What happened to her?"

"Our Lady took her out, looks like," said Turk. "Polly, why'ncha go to the rectory and get the clinic to send someone over? And grab some ice from Father Mike's icebox—this freezer has been out of commission since before Vatican II. And bring a towel." He leaned and peered. "And if you see a quart of milk, better bring that too. There's nothing left for coffee hour, especially now that there's something for everyone to hang around and yak about."

Polly Osterhaus felt Mrs. Scales's wrist first. "Well, her pulse seems good. I guess she's okay. You better not move her till the experts get here. Should I run across and interrupt the Radiantics at their seance? You think?"

"Not that serious, I'm guessing."

Polly left. Turk mopped up the milk. When he took the woman's head into his lap, the bump was growing a yellowy mauve-brown like an onion found at the back of the cabinet. His stomach lurched.

A taciturn man can be an observant man. Turk knew a few things about Leontina Scales, a few things he would rather not say. He didn't want to wake up and find himself married to another Mrs. Turk Schaeffer anytime soon, though his first wife was dead these four years already. So with strictly charitable intentions he patted Leontina Scales's forehead and the stiff, Brillo-paddy structure of her hair (reinforced by strategies enacted at Linda Pearl's House of Beauty, no doubt; round this edge of Oswego County, women's hair didn't come by such an exoskeletal quality without the interventions of Linda Pearl). He hoped, for her sake, that Mrs.

Scales would recover quickly enough so that no one would need to send for her daughter. A piece of work, that one. But the apple didn't fall very far from the tree, in his humble opinion.

———————

LEONTINA SCALES BLINKED herself awake thinking, at first, that she had gotten drunk and passed out. So it was alarming to find the music ministry of Our Lady Comfort of the Concussed standing in a semi-circle around her. At least they weren't singing. Which was something of a blessing. As she emerged a bit further she realized that she couldn't have blacked out in an alcoholic haze as she didn't touch liquor any more.

She struggled to speak and couldn't. She thought of her second husband, Wally, and how he would grab the end of his necktie with one hand, stretch it out taut like a razor strop, and slide his whiskey sours along the incline, a runway directly to his mouth. Leontina had admired his ingenuity and then she had left him, because she'd hated his taste in ties, and ingenuity wasn't enough to sustain a marriage.

Due to Wally's example, she'd sworn off alcohol. So she couldn't be drunk. She had been attacked by a demon. Had something beneath the stairs gotten her? An eyeless Nixon? Or was this a stroke?

Jeremy Carr crouched down at her side and touched her hand. "Are you with us?" he said. For a minute Mrs. Scales thought the choir director meant was she joining his papist cowboy chorale. But perhaps he was being sympathetic in a sort of psychological way. Men are from Mars, women are from Venus, but Catholics are from another space-time continuum altogether. Mrs. Scales shook her head when she meant to nod, which confused herself as well as him.

"Don't crowd the lady," said Turk Schaeffer.

"The clinic's sending an ambulance over," said Polly Osterhaus.

"How're we feeling, eh there?" Turk bobbed his head down into Leontina's line of vision. Mrs. Scales was glad to see someone nearer her own generation hovering like an Old Testament patriarch or like Dan Conner on *Roseanne*. "You want we should call anyone? Tabitha? Hogan?"

"Oh," said Mrs. Leontina Scales, though she meant to say No. "Oh, oh." She sounded like a geriatric sequel to a kindergarten primer. *Dick and Jane Lose Their Marbles. The Second Childhood of Dick and Jane.* She nodded her head though she meant to shake it.

"Tabitha's home, I guess?" asked Turk.

"Yes again," she said, and nodded, though once more she had meant to shake her head, and say Guess again. Turk disappeared from view. The choir filled in. Starting to remember what had happened, she closed her eyes.

In vestments Father Mike came billowing by. "Forgive us our trespassers," he said. "It's Leontina Scales, isn't it? Well, the milk of human kindness isn't a bad thing to take a morning bath in, Mrs. Scales. Don't you worry, we'll have you up and out of here and back across the way before you can say—"

"Go to hell," said Leontina. Astounding herself as much as the others, she passed out again.

"Better call the family," said Father Mike. "Turk, you up to it?"

As he hauled himself up the basement steps, Turk found himself wishing he wasn't quite such a pillar of the church. The Scales family specialized in odd ducks as far as he was concerned. Small towns probably don't have more lunatics per capita than cities do, thought Turk, they just show up easier. And around here gossip was both a sin and a competitive pastime, the way bridge had been to his parents' generation.

Turk Schaeffer recalled some story about Tabitha Scales as a kid. Suggestible, as the young always are. At the age of seven she had spent three-quarters of a year with a clothespin on her nose, trying to keep witchcraft from winging itself through her nasal passages. That's what comes of naming your kids after TV characters, thought Turk.

Tabitha was now, what? Seventeen? As far as Turk knew she spent more time dawdling at home waiting for someone to offer her a job than she did going to school. Turk knew about Tabitha because he played cards with Jack Reeves every other Tuesday and Jack—the town's police chief, fire chief, and high school principal—had a habit of dishing the dirt after the third beer or so. Rumor had it that Tabitha was in and out of that police station so often that she had taken to decorating her own cell. Supposedly it was appointed with a Kurt Cobain poster and an old Aerosmith poster and a pink and black afghan that her mother had made.

Tabitha was too pretty for her own good. Anyone at all coming to town was of interest to her. Because Tabitha's prettiness attracted trouble in the form of roadies with motorbikes throbbing between their legs.

She was slender, pouting, wide of eye and glazed of skin, skin with a puddingy sheen that suggested intelligence when all other evidence pointed to the contrary. She was crowned with an airy storm of pale chestnut hair. Men tended to lose their center of gravity for a minute when she passed by. Back when Tabitha was all of twelve, she was already pungent as eucalyptus.

The middle child, Turk Schaeffer remembered, was Hogan. Hogan Hero Scales. There was something wrong with him, having to do with small animals and microwaves. Oswego Electronics had put their collective foot down and refused to repair another appliance at the Scales home. Warranty or no.

Turk didn't remember what the third kid was called. Probably Kermit or Fonzie or something.

———————

THE DEVOUT OF Cliffs of Zion Radical Radiant began to worry when they'd filed out of Meeting for Consanguinity Hour only to discover that the Mister Coffees (regular and decaf) were still cold and empty. Mrs. Scales usually took her Coffee Ministry seriously. She was nowhere to be found. So Pastor Jakob Huyck himself went sniffing about the back door of Our Lady's. "Jakob, we've landed one of yours," Father Mike Sheehy said, seeing him there. "What'll you give for her release?"

"Mike, she's a secret agent. You found her out, you keep her." But Pastor Huyck's tone changed when he saw Leontina stretched out on the daybed that the Catholic maintenance man used for his afternoon naps. "Leontina, what're you doing here?"

"Leaping a lot," she said.

"Beg pardon?"

"Leaping every now and then. Can't help it." She closed her eyes and began to snore.

"Goodness," said Pastor Huyck. "Now there's a hidden charism."

"Father Mike," said Turk Schaeffer, "the Scales kids are here."

"Have them come down."

"Hope your insurance is paid up, Father Mike," Pastor Huyck said.

"I'll call the clinic again," Polly Osterhaus said. "Where's that ambulance?"

"I was supposed to have a meeting with you, Father Mike," said Jeremy Carr, his arms full of sheet music.

"Can you chat with Sister Alice?" said Father Mike. He looked up the stairs.

Turk turned to see Tabitha Scales and the younger brother navigating through the coffee-and-doughnuts crowd. Kirk, he remembered now. Kirk had an airbrushed sort of anxiety about him, a pensive concern, almost saintly. The entire alto section and one of the tenors fell in love with him at once. Tabitha approached more reluctantly. Sheathed in shaggy mammoth-fur leggings over a tight-fitting leotard. Not quite Sunday school. "Our Lady in pieces on the ground?" said Tabitha Scales, glancing around. "I can't believe it. Ma, what are you doing in a Catholic church basement? Field trip?"

"Aching and leaping, aching and leaping," said Mrs. Scales, opening her eyes again.

"The leap of faith?" said Father Mike, though more from habit than humor.

He was feeling her forehead and she didn't like it. "Ooh, fuck you," she said.

"Not again with this language!" said Tabitha. "Are you possessed or what?"

"Am of God, who takes away the sins of the world," replied her mother. "So you: shut up."

4

HAD THE HOLY Spirit perfected its own Inner Breathing exercises and centered itself, using the Compass Rose method, right into the rectory of Our Lady's, its private Eye of God might have taken in a pair of parish employees in conversation.

Sister Alice Coyne. Mid forties. Radiated concern which, while genuine, was also a symptom of mild deafness. She strained to apprehend.

Pleasant enough to look at, by consensus of anyone who spent time considering the physical loveliness of nuns, admittedly a small pool. Her clothes sensible without being industrial. The pearly-gray rayon blouses looked closer to silk than to starched linen.

She bustled into Father Mike's study ahead of Jeremy Carr. "What a stir this morning. I'm off to Rochester shortly, Jeremy, but I'll do what I can if this is urgent."

"It isn't, and it is, kind of."

Jeremy Carr. Early thirties. Mess of brown hair, a bird's nest worn upside down. Dropped into the late nineties by way of the early seventies but, Sister Alice ventured to herself, not so much timeless as clueless. So often he seems to be partly ten years old.

Self-effacing, he threaded his way about the rectory and the church in a camouflage of piety. He favored cheap flannel shirts from Gopal's Army Navy Shop. Smears of robin's egg blue, cream, cranberry, foul brown. Sister Alice could sometimes smell engine grease on Jeremy, but it probably came from some fixative used in preparing the fabric. She suspected that Jeremy wasn't mechanically inclined.

"What's up in Rochester?" asked Jeremy.

"Chapter meeting of the Southern Province." Sister Alice didn't know Jeremy all that well; she'd been working at Our Lady's as a jack-of-all-trades only since the previous April and her purview didn't include the music ministry. "The Southern Province of the Sisters of the Sorrowful Mysteries," she continued, a touch more sharply. "We originated in France, but we're predominantly Canadian. The Northern Province is Quebec and Ontario; the Southern Province, New York and Pennsylvania. We now call France the Eastern Province, though I think that's affected us."

"And the West?"

"We're not in a position currently to open new markets." Jeremy didn't seem to realize she was joking. Sister Alice sighed. "Father Mike asked me to troubleshoot for him, Jeremy. He said you'd requested a meeting urgently—you've got some business matter on hand?"

She expected it might be a petty cash issue. Our Lady's wasn't exactly a tub on its own keel. Given that last year the parish had fallen 62 percent short of its assessment for the annual Bishop's Development Fund contributions, in conscience Sister Alice couldn't recommend an outlay for sheet music that the choir seemed incapable of putting to good use anyway. Father Mike, a softie, often used Sister Alice as a first line of defense against requests for funds. She set her jaw and smiled the company smile.

Jeremy shrugged. "Maybe this isn't the right time?"

Oh, Lord, he's not going to quit, thought Sister Alice. Out in the nowhere land between Syracuse and Watertown, music directors don't grow on trees. Especially music directors who will work for next to nothing. Even as it was, had Old Lady Donegan not died two years ago and left her small portfolio expressly to the cause of Honoring God with Music, Jeremy would've had to be let go. (There'd been some strong feeling in the Parish Council that Old Lady Donegan had intended the loyal parishioners to Honor God with Music by firing Jeremy Carr, dismissing the choir, and installing a tape deck from Radio Shack instead.) "If you're not sure, perhaps you need to think a bit more," said Sister Alice in her consoling tone. "Entirely understandable. No hasty decisions. Talk to Father Mike. He's good with the young."

Jeremy raised an eyebrow. "I'm not *that* young."

"Look, everyone loves the job you do, and nobody thinks it can be easy, not with Peggy Mueller and that vibrato she can bring down Canadian geese with. You do the Lord's own work, Jeremy—"

"It's not about the choir. I mean, not directly. Not really."

"A fine job, quite a wonderful job—" Sister Alice took a few seconds to climb down from the heights of platitude. "Well anyway, no one could do better with what you've got to work with."

Jeremy was laughing. "They're not *that* bad. You should have heard us seven years ago when I started. It was as if Vatican II had never happened. They were still singing 'Joy to the World' every week for recessional, because that was the only thing old Miss Trembly could play using foot pedals, and it eased the pain in her insteps."

Sister Alice permitted herself a wry hiss of air through nostrils. "Well, if you're not resigning or asking for a raise, maybe I can handle it. I can try. What's up?"

"The choir meets in the rectory every Thursday evening from

seven to nine. We use the meeting room next to the office. We have to be out by nine because Father Mike goes to bed early these days—he's saying the seven a.m. daily mass over in Cleary Corners ever since Father Giuseppe died."

"You need more time to practice? I shouldn't sound so surprised, of course—"

"It's not that. You and I both know that extra rehearsal isn't going to make much difference. The thing is, I'm working with another group, and I wanted to see if there was a night this other group could meet in the rectory for rehearsal. We're flexible and could manage whatever night is good—Monday, Tuesday, Wednesday. I know the Legion of Mary and the Holy Names Society alternate their meetings every other Friday night, so that's out."

"What's the group?"

"Some guys. Not a church group. Only three of us. We're rehearsing for a sort of show just after New Year's in New York. We need a piano."

"What sort of show?"

"It's an AIDS benefit." Jeremy's jaw worked back and forth; a tooth-grinder, noted Sister Alice. She bet he wore a retainer at night.

"You want to use Our Lady's rectory to practice for an AIDS charity?"

"One night a week? None of us have a piano. The church isn't heated during the week, and we need a warm place. So I thought, you know, the rectory."

"I see." Sister Alice put her file folders on Father Mike's desk with an airy flop. "This isn't a liturgical group, I take it?"

"Not exactly." Jeremy seemed to be reviewing the group's members in his mind. "In fact, not at all. I'm the only one who goes to church, and I get paid for it."

"Not very much," said Sister Alice. "Enough," she added, protective of the parish budget.

"I don't know what Father Mike would think. I was kind of hoping to talk to him about it."

"Can I take it that some of the members of your group have friends or relatives who are suffering with AIDS?"

Jeremy's hands played a scale on the arms of his chair. "Take it that way."

The late October light intensified as the wind moved the trees outside the study. It poured in more yellowly—special effects courtesy of the beeches, which were losing their leaves late this year.

"And your intention would be charity, I suppose," said Sister Alice.

"I don't want to misrepresent myself. There's a complexity of reasons." He didn't look at her.

Sister Alice saw that she was now on terrain over which she was not licensed to navigate. "Why don't you approach Father Mike with this yourself, once he's settled that Leontina Scales. He's a man of the world, Jeremy; there's no reason to be shy around him."

"Can you tell me whether or not you'll recommend it?" he said, as Sister Alice began to collect her files again and cram them into her briefcase.

"You credit me with influence. Thank you for the frisson. But really, I'm not authorized to recommend for or against a scheduling matter." Sister Alice avoided the question while implying that scheduling matters were far beneath her. "Still, I'll pass your concerns along. I'm sure Father Mike will want to have a heart-to-heart with you. And if that's that?" She stood up so fast the chair came an inch off the floor with her.

They left the rectory together. Jeremy was silent. He didn't think he'd done very well. Though he liked Sister Alice Coyne, he wished he'd just waited until Father Mike was available. But Our Lady's was a zoo this morning, and Jeremy wanted to get back to the boys with an answer as soon as possible. It seemed important—every minute was important.

Ahead, Sister Alice paused on the rectory sidewalk and Jeremy nearly bumped into her. An orderly was fussing at the open doors of an ambulance. They were getting that woman out of harm's way. She was half sitting up on the stretcher, waving her arms about, barking orders, and her kids looked fussed and flustered.

The parking lot was partially cleared of cars by now, so the ambulance could maneuver, but Sister Alice wanted to beat it to the driveway. She dug for her keys in the colorful peasant rucksack she carried, a souvenir of that summer holiday spent in Managua with Witness for Peace. "You celebrating Halloween night with your buddies?" she asked Jeremy.

He shrugged. "Not going out on the town. I'm not one for disguises. They give me the creeps."

"Well, look the other way, then. I'm about to become Sister Mary Leadfoot, scourge of the New York State Thruway." She jammed dark glasses on and jumped in her car.

That didn't go too poorly, thought Jeremy. Inconclusive, but nothing ruled out.

As he turned back to the church, to straighten up the sheet music and lock up the AV system, he pictured the night ahead. Halloween was for kids. He hated grown-ups in masks and always had.

He imagined himself tonight, upstairs in his flat, a back room on a dead-end street blunted by a hill beginning three lots on. Maybe with the guys, maybe not. Avoiding the monstrous crowds. Halloween seemed like Epiphany, the apostles all closeted away from the callous crowds and from the fear of the risen Jesus, too, about whom they'd been starting to hear. And He appeared to them in their midst. Through a locked door. Talk about your Stephen King scenario: they must have been scared witless. And then they devoted their lives to the church and died as martyrs, every last one of them as far as he knew. A haunting of sorts.

5

IF DYING WAS moving through a dark tunnel to the light, what happened if you got stuck? What did that do to you? How about to the people in the tunnel behind you who were trying to die? How come the study circles had never talked about *this*?

Leontina Scales couldn't quite identify the smeared landscape beyond the windows, nor could she pull into focus the face hovering above her. She suspected it to be that vengeful Virgin Mary, thundering down. "Point oh two five cc's," said the voice. "Relax your fists, Mrs. Scales. I only want to do this once."

Haven't you already done enough, thought Mrs. Scales. And what about that thing under the stairs, which you were in cahoots with and no denying? Like Claudette Colbert in *It Happened One Night*: the Virgin stops the traffic and then who-the-hell-knows-who jumps out. *Surprise*. It sure wasn't Clark Gable. Though didn't Clark Gable have a kind of Satanic perkiness to his eyebrows, come to think of it? Could it have been Salman Rushdie? Or did she have this straight?

Then a nip, a sting in her arm somewhere. A stitch, a spindle's prick. She struggled and cried out, and hit out; even endless vigilance wasn't enough.

"Is she normally agitated like this?" asked Our Lady.

"Is she normal, better question," said a voice that sounded like Tabitha.

"All will be well," said Our Lady, taking Leontina's pulse with a manner more practiced than motherly. Though perhaps that amounted to the same thing. "Jesus, she's strong. She's a pisser, she is." She looked over the horizon. "Takes all kinds to make a world."

Tabitha's voice said, "I don't suppose she's like, you know, dying or anything."

"Tabby!" Kirk poked her, hard.

"She's out," said the orderly, and sat back on a jump-seat. "Look, kids, I'm going to have to write up a report. Can you tell me if your mom has been acting strange in the past twenty-four hours or so?"

Tabitha felt Kirk glance at her. She wired her advice: Pin this on me and just wait to see what I'll do to you.

"Mom has an active emotional life," ventured Kirk.

"Any sign of increased stress? Or, um, mental breakdown?"

"She's raising three teenagers on her own. Does that count?"

"Fair enough."

"She always says we aggravate the hell out of her."

Tabitha winced. Oh God, Kirk taking it on himself. Here it comes, watch for it, people: the sniffle. The world's only living fifteen-year-old crybaby.

Damn. Tabitha wasn't going to let Mom do in an afternoon coma what she hadn't managed to do in her morning screech-a-thon: ruffle out of Tabitha that rich sense of well-being conferred upon her by sex with Caleb Briggs. The deeper Mom wanted to wipe it away, the more Tabitha would cling to that sense of invading glee. Caleb was tawny and twenty. He was a bolt in the belt region, tender as kittens in his nipples—who knew about that before last night? Just touching them had been like electroshock therapy and his voice had gone falsetto in a keen—and his thighs could bring down oak trees, or stampeding cattle, or her. Just seeing what she could do to him with a halt, a pulse, persistence, and a little dab of Crisco. I've become a living catalog of turn-ons.

"Who is the next of kin adult?"

"I'm almost eighteen," said Tabitha. "Keep her a week or two and I'm your gal."

"Yes, but next to you, I mean."

"There's three former husbands," said Kirk.

Tabitha yawned. "The was-bands, we call 'em. As in, you know. I saw your husband last night out with a blonde. Oh, you're so wrong: Phil isn't my husband any more, he's my was-band."

"None of them live nearby, anyway." Kirk leaned forward and put his male-model cuticles on display, softly touching their mother's wrist. "And Mom was an only child."

"Well, hmm. Her parents, then?"

Tabitha snorted. "Escaped through death."

The woman seemed either mollified or beaten, but had the gumption to add, "Don't worry about your mom following their example. She's going to be just fine."

"Thanks for the warning."

———

AT THE HOSPITAL, Mrs. Scales was rolled into the depths, and the double doors whooshed closed behind the stretcher. "It'll be at least an hour," said the intake nurse, apparently to her computer monitor. "But we gotta figure out this next of kin thing."

"How about Pastor Jakob?" Kirk said to Tabitha.

"How about Caleb Briggs?" said Tabitha. "He's twenty."

"Caleb? Mom's never even met him."

"She's out, what does she care?"

"We'll do your pastor, that sounds fine enough," said Nurse Typo, pecking away. "How do you spell Huyck?"

"He's her pastor, not ours," said Kirk. "Tabitha doesn't go and I only go sometimes. I haven't been Centered."

The nurse looked over the tops of her glasses at them, finally.

"That's like being caught in the crosshairs of a rifle, except the crosshairs are the crucifix."

"Are they now. How does h-i-k-e sound to you?"

"Close enough."

"We'll call it a wrap then. Café on the ground floor by the rear elevators. Someone will come find you in the waiting room in about an hour."

Kirk went to the men's room, probably to have a pretty little cry and admire himself in the mirror, and Tabitha headed for the cafeteria, but the gift shop appeared first, so she nipped inside to see if she could snag a pack of gum or something. She sidled around the shelving and just in time caught sight of Solange Lefebvre and Hannah Brewster from Math Reinforcement. Solange was an import from Paris, France, where they did math the French way, which is why she needed remedial, and Hannah's family was so old and highbrow that they hadn't had to produce a working brain cell in generations. Both girls sucked big time.

Their heads were snared in lunchroom lady hairnets. Their candy-striper aprons didn't close in the back and they must have made sure to wear their tightest fitting jeans so old men left in wheelchairs could sharpen their noses between blue-denimed cheeks.

"It is such a bore, it sweeps me with ennui," said Solange. Only it sounded like *Eet ees sush a bore, eet sweeps me with ennui.*

"*Je suis* pretty *fatigué* myself," said Hannah. "I hope we don't get

Pediatrics. Last time one of those little cancer kids almost broke my arm trying to make me drag him out of there. I nearly had to kick him."

"I prefer ze department of ze elderly madames. It is more easier there, because they never want to converse with any young and lovely girl."

You can't be talking about yourself, thought Tabitha. You could freeze-dry a croissant just by looking at it.

They wandered up the aisle. Tabitha didn't want to run into them, but they did provide a distraction of sorts. So she found herself following them one aisle over. She could always snub them in person if they turned a corner and caught her.

When she was within earshot again, she got an earful. "I do think Mr. Finn will give you a passing grade," Solange was saying. "He knows you will need ze maths in order to select a decent college. And he likes you. I see that he likes you."

"You're *dreadful*." Hannah was blushing. As if Hannah could even imagine what having someone like you could do to you, turning your spine to jelly, making of your vagina a sixth sense. She'd probably never kissed a boy. You could kind of tell.

"Anyway," continued Hannah, "Mom's family wanted me to go to Radcliffe only it's part of Harvard now, so we don't know about that."

Harvard? Fat chance. You get lost doing laps in the county pool, Hannah.

"I believe every scholar in Mr. Finn's class will achieve many diplomas and proceed toward university," said Solange. "Except for only one."

Here it comes, thought Tabitha.

Hannah grimaced. "Tabby's special."

"Special?" Solange didn't know the lingo.

"Special. Special needs, to start with. She'll be lucky if she graduates. And special because she sure acts like she thinks she's a hot ticket. Anyway I doubt she's doing college prep. She'll be married and pregnant before next year."

"Well, she can keep her special eyes off my little brioche."

"She's probably already taken a big bite out of your little brioche. Better check the goods before you buy." They laughed wickedly.

I hate them, thought Tabitha. What's a brioche?

"You're joking, though," said Solange. "Is she that bad?"

"She's so good, is the locker-room news, she's extra bad. She's done the whole football team in alphabetical order."

"She knows her alphabet that well?"

"Well, *le ordaire alphabétique* isn't the important part. She knows something." Hannah sounded a little wistful.

You bet the fuck I know something, thought Tabitha.

"I can't find it. We're going to be late. You got what you came for?"

"For my yeast infection, yes," said Solange. "Had we better depart?"

They left. Tabitha liberated a PowerBar on the way out. Lord, give me strength, she thought. On the silence of her rubber-soled Reeboks she followed her classmates twenty paces behind. They passed through a door propped open with a chair and Tabitha heard a sound of metal locker doors banging, and she saw her classmates continue through an interior door to some further station. Probably to get their assignments.

She hoped it wasn't the E.R.

None of the lockers had locks on them. By the third try Tabitha had found Solange's waxy white pharmaceutical bag and Hannah's funky little pink purse advertising *Cancun!* in rhinestones. So Tabitha went back to cruise the aisles of the shop until she found what she needed. Then at the locker room she replaced Solange Lefebvre's treatment for yeast fever with a cure for constipation. She hoped Solange's English wasn't so good that she'd strain to read the small print on ze package.

As for Hannah, Tabitha removed the thumbtack holding up a sign reminding volunteers to wash their hands whenever they got crap and stuff on them. With care she punctured the little flattish foil packet all the way through a half dozen times, at an angle so the little slits might not be visible in dim light. How providential, a gift from God: the condom that Tabitha hadn't had time to insist Caleb wear. Across the edge she scrawled, *U Go To Hell* and she drew a big heart around the words. She thought of writing "from a special friend" with the hopes that Hannah would give out to some unsuspecting boy, but she wasn't sure how to spell *special*. She slipped it into Hannah's purse and replaced the health advisory with the thumbtack.

On the way back to find Kirk and see what the doctors were going to say, Tabitha Scales passed through a corridor where light came in through the UV-glazed windows, picking out with punishing clarity the bad art that someone had forced the hospital to hang on display. Angels and little stupid flowers and, for some reason, a fire hydrant. The constant pinging of the hospital PA system paused for once, allowing airtime for a half-dozen measures of some weary song that had been played too often all year long. What was it? Oh, right. "Believe," by Cher.

Tabitha experienced a certain lift. Mom was comatose and Caleb was waiting offstage. For the last day of October, the sun was curiously strong. She thought that she might be blushing, though maybe that was the aftereffect of the idea of blowing the football team in alphabetical order. (*As if.* Not even close.)

She had all of her life ahead of her. She felt almost special.

6

A LATE OCTOBER sun can seem like a trawler seen from an undersea slope. The way it hovers in that cellophane blue, the way it drags shadows across the terrain like dark nets. This year the trees had husbanded their leaves with a kind of greediness, but their grip was slackening. Morse Hill Road felt like a sluice through brown rapids.

Jeremy pulled into the lot at Bozo Joe's, more colloquially called Unfriendly's after the fast-food franchise that, like so many other chains, had abandoned Thebes and unloaded the decommissioned building at a loss. Fixtures too: the mock Colonial-style booths upholstered in Wedgwood-blue vinyl, the ice cream flavors painted on the slats of a display panel shaped like a window shutter. But the unplugged freezers by the take-out windows now housed brown paper napkins. The menu featured your basic burgers and grease. Bozo Joe wasn't in the business of fulfilling anyone's culinary dreams. This was Thebes, New York, after all.

Jeremy sat in the car, fiddling with his car keys. He'd hoped the others would arrive earlier, so he could get away with ordering only a cheap coffee. But no sign of Marty's car—Babs, the Chariot of the Odds.

Irresolute, staying put until he got too chilly, he watched the late afternoon Sunday patrons come and go. He'd been in Thebes for how many years now, and still he felt he had only a feeble grasp of what made it tick—what made it refuse to die. Around here, most guys his age had been married a good decade. They were saddled with dead-end jobs in the sand and gravel industry or with failing family farms too far from anything to sell to developers. The men tended to drink themselves to sleep most nights. Their wives, according to the oracles of the faculty lounge, did the same. And to judge by Jeremy's own workload, their kids were prematurely soured underachievers, blanched and neutered by their daytime TV habit.

If only Jeremy were laid off from his part-time tutoring job, or fired, he'd have to quit choir directing because he couldn't afford to live on church income alone. And then something else would have to happen. A chain reaction knocking him toward good luck, maybe.

He caught himself stalling, avoiding even this little conflict of ordering ahead of the others. Acquiescence as a virtue? Hardly.

He settled in their regular booth, feeling like the first actor on the set for a gay knockoff of *Seinfeld*. Avoiding the waitress's eye, which suited her fine as she was avoiding his, Jeremy looked out the window, saw the guys arriving in the Dodge Dart with the push-button transmission. Marty Rothbard had bought it for ninety dollars from some old geezer over in North Derby. It was older than Marty. He called it Babs because its headlights were out of kilter and peered inward at each other.

He studied his friends as if he hadn't seen them before. This, he knew, was his songwriter's habit, a kind of voyeurism. The regular plundering of his friends' emotional lives to create something new because his own experience remained so slight these days.

Jeremy waved, but they didn't see him in the window.

Russet-cheeked, ferret-eyed Sean Riley had a long red scarf wrapped two or three times around his neck, and a bright blue knit cap with a white pompom. Marty Rothbard was trim and meticulous, in a leather bomber's jacket that emphasized his hard-kept waistline. Marty looked full of stage cheeriness and Sean withdrawn. A little more rawboned, maybe.

With fuss and fanfare they made their entrance. Sean sank onto the opposite bench, lounging, and Marty Rothbard slid in next to Jeremy. "I think you're nuts," said Marty. "Jeremy, he's nuts. I think he's got the deliriums already."

"I'm just saying," said Sean. "Think about it."

"Think about what you want, Svetty's on her way."

A hefty woman who looked about fifty or twenty years either side of that, Svetlana came pitching menus at them. "Boys." Her Slavic accent made the word a kind of sonic implosion. "Vhat'll you vant, boo-oys."

"Svetlana darling, we want you and only you. But fries on the side would cheer us up."

"Meck id sneppy. Boss in shit mood. Business dead." Svetlana Boyle—she had married the unlikely Finbar Boyle, probably to get her green card—scratched her ear with the rubbery end of her pencil and flicked a speck of Soviet-era earwax onto the floor. "Coffee?"

"Do you have something good for us?" asked Sean.

"You vait. Bozo Joe joost like KGB tonight. Mebbe if it get busy he help, he on floor, ve discuss. Or not. Coffee?"

Three coffees. Jeremy didn't order a burger. Svetty Boyle glared at him as if he must be responsible for everything wrong in her life. As if his buying one burger could improve the economy of Thebes, her marriage, and her accent. As she shuffled away, Sean yawned.

Marty lit right in. "Break up our tie vote. What do you think,

Jeremy? Instant death or long slow painful decline? Which would
you choose?"

"Are those the only choices?"

"I know you intend to be assumed bodily into heaven, but for
the sake of conversation."

"This is a cheery subject," Jeremy said. He dared to arch his
eyebrows questioningly at Marty, since Sean's head was lowered as
if he was studying the pattern in the Formica.

"That flight that went down last night. In the Atlantic," said
Marty.

"Egypt Air," intoned Sean. "990. This morning, actually."

"Oh," said Jeremy. "Yeah, we prayed about that in the petitions
today."

"Everyone dead in a matter of moments," said Sean. "A better
way to go, or not? You're off on a holiday, something goes wrong,
fifteen minutes later you're dead. No muss, no fuss, no endless
scenes, no long good-byes, no drawn out pain, no expensive thera-
pies."

"You're sick," said Marty.

"That's my point. Accident is preferable to sickness, as long as
it's quick and fatal."

"It's not all about you, though, is it?" said Jeremy. "I mean, even
your own death isn't only about you. It's about everyone else you
know, too. That airliner—can't even think about it. But what about
all those relatives today? In New York and Cairo? No one got to say
good-bye."

"I think *that's* sick," said Sean. "Prolong your suffering so you
can prolong their suffering? If they wanted to say good-bye they
coulda got their asses in the goddamn car and driven to the air-
port."

Some other patrons came in—several corpses in white powder and high collars, blood dripping from their mouths. They sat

across from the guys and grinned at them, as if newly emerged from graves to lend a fresh perspective to the discussion. Next, a mother with some kids dressed in prefab drugstore costumes, who sat as far away from the adult ghouls as they could. "We might be in luck after all," said Marty. "A couple more tables and Bozo will have to inch his butt off the stool and help, and we're cooking." But for the time being Svetlana traversed the floor on her own, a Volga tugboat in plimsolls.

Jeremy changed the subject. "Let's get down to business. Any luck?"

"If we could do without the piano," said Marty, "there's any number of choices."

"Well, that's the problem, isn't it. We need a piano. That's the point."

"We need a piano, Marty," echoed Sean. "We need to perfect our fatal harmonies. Hey, that's a good name for us. The Fatal Harmonies. Better than the Off Nights."

"I know it's Halloween," replied Marty, "but enough with the fatality tonight, will you? Just because you have the lowest T-cell count, you're claiming unfair advantage."

"You ever come to mass," said Jeremy, "I'll show you fatal harmonies. Peggy Mueller has a soprano voice like a short-range missile. When she turns devoutly to the figure of Jesus on the cross, singing to it, it looks like she's going to open her mouth and flay Jesus all over again using only her tremolo."

"See, Jeremy's showing his hand: he'd prefer a long drawn-out death, not instant annihilation," said Marty. "Flaying, Jeremy, please. Don't get me started."

"They'll have to augment the historic agony of Christ by inserting another Station of the Cross between numbers ten and eleven. Station Number Ten-A. Peggy Mueller Lacerates Jesus with an Obbligato."

"I stay away from church for ten commanding reasons, I don't need any new ones," said Sean. "You can't reconvert me."

"Convert me," said Marty to Jeremy. He stroked the lapels of his bomber jacket as if they were mink and then undid a top shirt button. "Maybe you can make me a Jew for Jesus if you're passionate enough about it. I'm open to try."

"I'll send you a pamphlet. Come on, guys. Focus. We can't hold our pitch well enough to work *a cappella*, and the guitar and bass just isn't varied enough." Jeremy was all business. "We need a place with a piano, and a place large enough for guitar and bass. Any other thoughts?"

Marty said, "There must be a piano in the Mildred Cleary Elementary Prison, isn't there?"

"Of course. A spinet about a thousand years old. It hasn't been tuned since the invention of central heating. But we couldn't get our foot in the door there. Three gay men in a grade school? There'd be a mob. There'd be a riot."

"Even after hours?"

"You come from some bizarre Jewish tradition where people regularly exercise the faculty of reason. This is upstate New York, Marty, not Park Slope. Children are our precious resource."

"We're not necessarily a gay group," said Sean, examining the bowl of his spoon as he spoke. "Couldn't we, like, just not mention we're a gay group?"

Jeremy and Marty glanced at each other. Sean hadn't come out to his family and he was still living with them, so his reticence was second nature by now. But really. With HIV and AIDS incubating right there in the booth with them, like holy ghosts—well, that kind of timidity just wasn't on any more. There was no time.

"You were going to look into the meeting room in the rectory, weren't you?" said Marty. "Weren't you going to ask your priest today?"

"I got sidetracked. Some woman from Cliffs of Zion fell down the stairs or something. I never got to see Father Mike."

"Suicide attempt? 'Fess up. Show and tell."

"Pretty much a non-story. Somebody named Scales."

"I know them," said Sean, who had grown up in Thebes. "I mean I know who they are. You mean the Scales family on Papermill Road? There's a mother with three kids, ages sort of straddling late-high school and early-career-in-fast-food?"

"Sounds like the one. Mrs. Scales came into Our Lady's and a statue fell on her head. There was a lot of to-do so I never got to see Father Mike."

"Well, let's keep looking," said Sean, "because I'd curl up my little leprechaun feet and wither if ever I set one of my ruby slippers in a Catholic church again."

"Oh come on. We're only talking the rectory. The church building isn't heated during the week and it's too cold at this time of year to practice there. Your T-cell count being what it is. No, I'm still waiting to hear from Father Mike about the rectory. I talked to Sister Alice, his staff assistant."

"The privacy of the confessional still applies, I hope." Sean's parents were staunch churchgoers.

"I wasn't confessing anything," said Jeremy. "Anyway, until Vatican III happens, you don't confess to nuns. It really *has* been a long time since you've made your Easter duty, Sean."

"When I'm on my deathbed I'll have Father Mike in for a highball and a Gitane. I'll renounce the world and transfer my assets into the heavenly portfolio. No need to rush things, though."

Sean drew heavily on the coffee stirrer. It was amazing he still needed his fix, since his lung lining had been described as quilted. How did his system process the smoke?

"Anyway, Sister Alice is nice enough. So is Father Mike. They'll help if they can. I was sort of hoping that we'd have some choices. Didn't anyone else come up with anything?"

"I do remember the Scales family." Sean sat up a little straighter. "Kirk Scales. He was in my brother's school play last year. He was the dead kid in *Our Town*. What a little godsend *that* one is!"

"Do tell," said Marty. "Start with his toes and work up."

"Guys," said Jeremy. "We've got a problem to solve here. We haven't found any other available piano? It's hard to believe."

"Look," said Sean. "Let's take care of business and get out of here, okay? I don't like the clientele tonight. Sitting across from the walking dead. They don't like sitting across from us either, by the look of things. Call me superstitious, but it creeps me out."

"I think you'll have to come back," said Jeremy in a softer voice. "Svetty Boyle can't slip away unnoticed. This place isn't going to get busy enough for Bozo Joe to shift his behind away from his throne back there and help her."

"Fuck," said Sean.

"Hey, leave it to me." Marty zipped up his jacket with a flourish and arranged the collar to stand at attention, emphasizing his strong chin. Jeremy gritted his teeth. "If I can get Bozo to come over, you skedaddle back to the bathroom hall. Svetty Boyle will see you. You have the cash, Sean?"

"Actually I'm a little short. I need to borrow twenty."

Marty shrugged. Jeremy shook his head and handed over his last twenty. "You're not going to—I hope you don't—" he said.

"Get moving," said Marty. Sean stood, caught Svetlana's eye, and began to meander toward the men's room. Marty reached out and grabbed Jeremy's wrist before he could withdraw it. Marty gave out a falsetto squeal that turned all heads except Sean's.

"Jesus, don't," begged Jeremy. Marty used his chest voice in a credible imitation of Dusty Springfield doing "You Don't Have to Say You Love Me."

"No, no, no." Jeremy tried to pull his hand away but Marty had both hands around Jeremy's wrist now.

"Believe me," he sang, letting out a little tremolo. The vampires giggled and hissed. He put on the volume. "Believe me." The diva belt. Oh God. Oh God.

"Shut up, you fag," said one of the vampires.

"It's a Halloween act, how's he doing?" said Jeremy to them. Here comes Bozo Joe.

"What the hell you think you're doing?" said the owner. But Marty's eyes were closed now and he was swaying, swept away by love. "You pay the bill and get out if you wanna sing. You're disturbing the customers."

Svetlana was off the floor, out doing the deal. It wouldn't take long. Marty began the second verse. "You want I should call the cops?" said Bozo Joe. "As if they don't have enough trouble on Halloween?"

"Sorry about this, he gets this way," said Jeremy between clenched teeth. "Marty, please!"

Then Sean was back, dropping into his seat, and Marty stopped as if unplugged. He blinked two or three times at the owner and said, as if waking up, "Oh, something just comes over me, this feeling I just can't hide. Inappropriate. I know."

"Svetlana," called Joe, "get the check. This table's done."

Sean patted his chest to show he had gotten the grass. Svetlana appeared in no special hurry, grumpy as ever. The Vampires had decided to retaliate with a performance of the Backstreet Boys' "I Want It That Way," only they weren't being nice about it.

"Let's get out of here before this turns into the story of Matthew Shepard," said Sean.

In the parking lot, Jeremy got into the backseat of Babs so they could finish the conversation. He rolled a joint but didn't smoke. Communion once a day was enough. Marty and Sean passed the roach back and forth. "Do you think Bozo Joe is calling the cops because we're still here?" asked Marty a few moments later.

"Nah. We make the place look popular if someone drives by," said Jeremy.

"Anyway this is medicinal pot," said Sean.

There was a moment of peace. The car began to fill with blue-brown fog; in the fading sunlight through the windshield, the Off Nights sang a little. If they could only do concerts in automobiles, they'd be bigger than the Backstreet Boys. Bigger than Monica ("Angel of Mine") and R. Kelly and Celine Dion ("I'm Your Angel") and Sarah McLachlan ("Angel") put together. They were angels in the smoke. Jeremy was getting a sympathetic buzz just from the fug. Bigger even than Mariah Carey ("I Still Believe"). A girl could hope.

Silence after the sound.

"Put another way," said Marty, "those folks on Egypt Air last night didn't have a chance to smoke a last joint."

"I'm going," said Jeremy. "You owe me twenty, Sean." He bumped his head as he got out.

He sauntered to the edge of the parking lot, where the sidewalk crept by, to clear his head. Breathed the real air deeply, feeling the giddiness ebb and return. Along came a pint-size Mr. Potato Head and a skeleton who was wearing his full-face mask backward so he could see where he was going. The skeleton said "Trick or treat?" in a perfunctory way, just in case.

"Sorry, I'm, uh, not supplied."

They passed without comment, looking for sweeter pastures. The Frankenstein face grinned its plastic rictus at Jeremy as the kids walked away. Jeremy found himself thinking, maybe Bozo Joe had something ripe enough for them. Or Svetty Boyle.

7

TABITHA SURPRISED HER brothers by choosing to go to school without being nagged into it. "Anyone ever needs proof that your circuits are fried, this is it," said Hogan, watching her dress. "Look: Kommandant Mom is off duty on account of a concussion, and for once she's not stationed at the bottom of the stairs with her arms folded and her foot tapping. And here you are like, like a bobby-soxer, all ponytails and kneesocks. Your tits are so prompt they're going to get to school ahead of you and erase the blackboard for which loser teacher? Is it Hess in science lab?"

"Don't be vulgar. I failed science lab last year and Hess won't let me back."

"You're *being* Mom. That's it. I get it. Why? Guilty conscience? I know you didn't push her down the stairs that day. You were home sleeping it off."

"Are you crazy? I'm just making the best of a bad situation. What if I'm not there, and some social worker snoops in at school? Mr. Reeves might say I'm playing hookey. The bad apple. Maybe they'll take Mom away to a rehab resettlement camp somewhere."

"Works for me. Works wonders for me."

"Right. Then they'll notice we're minors and you go to a foster home, Hog. Or given you're sixteen, to some sort of school more like a jail."

"They have juvenile delinquent girls in this jail you describe? Paradise."

"No. Only guys. Jerk-off smelly bullying morons."

Hogan glanced through the hall doorway into the kitchen, where Kirk was cleaning out the fridge and humming something from Mom's LP of *South Pacific*. "Wash That Man Right Out of My Hair." Hogan's voice lowered. "They'd have an awful lot of fun with My Little Pony in there."

"Exactly. So off I go to school." She added, "You gonna drive me or what?"

"Where's Caleb, your Mister Motorcycle Man?"

Tabitha pursed her lips, tamping her lipstick the way her mother always did. "Mmmm," she said, a beat too long. "Well, let's go, Hog."

Nice of Hogan not to press the issue, she thought. But where *was* Caleb Briggs? Had she been so very hot the night before Halloween that she had scared him off? Her mind went back to the time she'd seen his bike in the Ames parking lot—the time her mother had started cussing like a streetwalker who has run out of sidewalk. Tabitha hadn't caught sight of Caleb in the store that day. And those louts lounging around near the soda cans mounded by the front windows—she'd hurried past them in shame and mortification, without giving them a sideways look. But were they Caleb's friends? And if so, where was he? Not hiding behind shelving to avoid her, the way she had done to avoid Hannah and Solange?

It was all too confusing. Here she thought she'd convinced Caleb she was sexually provocative enough to last out a set of marriage vows, give good value for money, no prim virginal dope, and she'd quite possibly scared him off with her vigor and, um, imagination. Maybe that business with the chocolate-covered cherries and the jumper cables had been a bit too knowing.

She fingered her white collar into a more belligerent pertness. Hogan was wrong about her strategy. She missed Caleb, and he wasn't answering her phone calls. So she hoped at least to get some sympathy from someone. Some grown-up to crow, "Your mom has gone temporarily brain dead and here you are, just carrying on! You brave dear!" She imagined the words. She had practiced how she might drop her gaze to the floor and twist her hands together, maybe murmur and blush a little if she could manage it. The problem was that she couldn't imagine who would address her with such concern. Nobody liked her. Hess had thrown her out of the lab last year when her own personal breakage costs had topped two hundred bucks. That cow McTavish hated her guts. Mr. Abbott didn't know who she was since he was old enough to be senile and she'd only gone to Civilization Survey, like, twice.

And her so-called *classmates*. They were stuck living the lie that was high school. The boys all did sports as if they were NFL material. Except the nerds whom nobody bothered with, including themselves. And the girls were like Solange and Hannah. Guarded, that was the word. Guarded, because Tabitha was lusty and liberated and wore her reputation as a free girl the way others wore their alligator logos or the letter jackets of their boyfriends.

Thebes was so lame it might as well be amputated.

Tabitha wasn't going to make her mother's mistake and get stuck here. She and Caleb would light out for someplace better. But not until Tabitha had seen Mom safely home. And if that meant sucking up big time, well then, Hello there, Mrs. Prendergast, you're looking less smarmy than usual in that French-cut skirt—did you inherit it from your sister in Toronto after she died of liver failure? Hi, Mr. Hess! Remember me? Little Miss Crash-Crazy-Oopsy-Daisy? Morning, Mr. Reeves. *Principal* Reeves. Love the sideburns. I admire the man who can wear furry twin outlines of Florida below his ears. No, really.

"You're up to no good, I can smell it," said Hogan as he arrived at the curb of the high school.

"Coming in?" Her voice was sweet.

"Shit. Left my geometry homework on the kitchen table. And I pulled an all-nighter to finish it." Pausing. "Hell no."

"Right. Well, later."

Hogan started to ease away. Kirk was only halfway out of the car and he fell on the sidewalk, ripping a hole in his trouser knee. Hogan's laughter trailed out into the drop-off traffic.

"What?" Nice Kirk was nearly spitting. "He forgot I was in the backseat?"

"I have to admit, Kirk," ventured his sister, "you're *such* a spaz. Hog probably just couldn't help himself."

"I spent fifteen minutes pressing these trousers."

"Maybe today you'll meet someone who can press them for you. Maybe, Kirk, today is your big day for *love*." Oooh, she could be so mean. Good to know she hadn't lost it.

Kirk didn't reply. He just limped off. Tabitha considered saying a prayer for strength, but then thought, fuck it, and she marched into the fray.

———————

SCHOOL NOT HAVING worked out quite as well as she would have liked, Tabitha found herself somewhat relieved, if that was the word, to show up with Hogan and Kirk at the clinic for visiting hours at four so they could see their mother, decay and all.

They were huddled in the hallway, which smelled of disinfectant and pea soup. "Tell us what you know, über-nurse," said Hogan.

Nurse Marilee Gompers smiled hatefully and observed that

Mrs. Scales could sit up, brush her own hair, attend to her own toilet, and as of today when they took it away from her, walk without the aid of a walker. Her blood pressure was good, her vital signs what they should be. She looked brightly and with focus at whoever came in the room. None of the tests had shown signs of hemorrhaging. No evidence of a subdural hematoma. The staff could think of no reason to keep her under observation. Since their mother didn't have a regular physician with whom they could consult, the Scales kids took the nurse at her word when she said that the patient was fine.

"She can talk?" asked Tabitha.

"Go in and see for yourself. She's a great one for talking, a regular Chatty Cathy."

They loitered until Nurse Gompers pushed them through the door. "I'll shut this. For privacy," she said, with a wink.

Leontina Scales was sitting up in an ugly metal chair with one rectangular biscuit-colored cushion creased into the middle to provide both a seat and a back. Her spine sagged, her chin jutted forward, and she glowered at her children. "Outa here," she groused. "Now. Outa here."

"But you need their help, Mom." Kirk patted her wrist. She shrugged his hand off and he looked hurt, and tucked his hands in his armpits.

"We can bust her out, she don't have to stay if she don't want," said Hogan.

"Let's pretend to do this right," said Tabitha. "As the oldest I get to make the decisions, I think."

"Outa here," said Mrs. Scales, more forcefully

"Too bad," said Hogan, pretending to look, "there's no plug for us to pull."

"She's right to flee," said a voice. They had forgotten to notice that their mother didn't have a private room. In the next bed sat a wispy black woman with flyaway white hair. She wore a hospital gown and an IV bottle-feeder and a purple church hat with a little net veil lowered over her eyes.

"What you in for?" said Hogan.

"Life."

"Eww."

"As in livin' too hard and I see no shame in that."

"Ow. Outa here," said Mrs. Scales. "Ow."

"She's got the right notion," said the black woman. "In seven weeks and change Y-Two-Kay gonna kick some butt big time. I intend to be on the Other Side by the time it happens. You never seen the hell that's gonna erupt outa the broken pipes of those computers."

"We don't use computers much," said Tabitha. "Doubt you do, either."

"You might not, I might not, but the world does. I seen it in my visions. Planes crashing out of the sky. Bank accounts frying, money sizzling away like water on Bo'more sidewalks in August. Trains crash, cars crash, markets crash, war and pestilence and famine on all sides. Four horsemen of the Apocalypse my foot: they gonna need two, three dozen horsemen minimum, to mop us all up. That's why Jesus on His way again. What you think Y-Two-Kay mean, anyway?"

"It means Year Two Thousand," said Kirk. "The millennium."

"Millennium, my ass."

"Actually the millennium begins January 1, 2001, according to my math teacher."

"Your math teacher don't know how to squat in the fields when she has to go. Computers are taking over the world and destroying it big time in seven weeks. Y-Two-Kay don't stand for that, though. It stand for Yahweh-to-Come."

"I thought you said Jesus," said Hogan. "Get your facts straight, ma'am."

"Yahweh, Yehovah, Yesus, you think I write the name tag? Name don't signify. He can be Yolanda Christ this time around if he wants. I'm outa here. He ain't gonna be happy to see his world all broke."

"Haven't you got family?" asked Kirk. "Any visitors?"

"Kirk can be your little boy." Tabitha pushed him forward. "We don't need him any more."

"I thought Jesus gonna come from that Monica Jewinsky and Bill Clinton, but she'd a born him by now, unless the baby's been holdin' out till Y-Two-Kay midnight. One thing I'll tell you right now, you can't impeach God. Ain't gonna happen."

Hogan sounded delighted. "The second coming—a bastard son of Slick Willy? I love it."

The woman nodded grimly. "The first black president, they call him. First and last, by the look of it."

By now Mrs. Scales had her hand around her ears, so Tabitha went to the nurses' station. Nurse Gompers faked being busy over someone dying or something, but Tabitha wouldn't leave. She didn't want to go back in her mother's room, even with the consolation that there was someone on earth more screwy than her own mother.

Eventually Nurse Gompers condescended to recognize Tabitha, and she expounded on Mrs. Scales's situation in maddeningly medical language. Despite that, Tabitha picked up that the clinic intended to release her mother into Tabitha's own care.

"Is that legal?" said Tabitha, losing track of her own intentions and her strategies.

"The next of kin your family provided, Pastor Huyck called up this morning and I gave him my recommendation, and he approved it and faxed over a waiver. Close enough, he said."

"But Mom doesn't talk like she used to. She's not herself."

"I don't know what you mean," said Nurse Gompers. She strode down the hall whacking the wall with her clipboard. Tabitha followed her into the room.

"Well." Tabitha knew this sounded lame. "Look. I mean, she won't eat her Jell-O."

"Odd damned Jell-O." Mrs. Scales knocked the dish on the floor.

"They all do that," said Nurse Gompers. "I would too. What's your point?"

"Oh I walk through the valley of darkness," said Mrs. Scales. "Oh, evil shall I fear."

"You said she was religious. She's always quoting something," said the nurse.

"The devil can quote scripture for his own purpose. And she the devil's secretary, in my humble opinion," said the woman from the next bed. "She works for the Big Snake. Watch your back, Nurse Gompers. She evil."

"Marilee, I say unto you," said Mrs. Scales, "get lost." She turned to the woman in the bed near the window. "Oh to hell, you."

"I call that a sense of humor," said Nurse Gompers. "I'm not retracting the doctor's discharge order because you don't like your mother's funnybone. Shame on you. How's tomorrow, when school gets out?"

"I'm busy," said Hogan. "I could do two weeks from Thursday."

"Have mercy on me, a sinner, and get this vamp of Satan outa my sight," said the older woman beneath the going-to-church hat. "My eyes sting in their sockets just lookin' at her."

The next day Tabitha and Hogan came to pick their mother up. Pushing Mrs. Scales in a wheelchair out to the curb, Nurse Gompers seemed a bit harried. "Someone's in rare form. Someone wants to go home in a big way."

"I kingdom come," said Leontina Scales, hitting Nurse Gompers's fingers with a complimentary satchel of aspirin, plastic shower cap, and thermometer. "I will be done!"

Tabitha knew that her mother didn't like her to drive since, among other reasons, Tabitha didn't even have a learner's permit. But Tabitha's driving seemed of minor concern to Mrs. Scales today.

"It's so good she has an outlet in her church interests." Settling her patient into the passenger seat, Nurse Gompers looked more than grateful. "She's got a lot to offer, I can see that. Now make sure she takes her meals regularly. She seems to be hungry. But she wouldn't touch her lunch."

"Eat us not into temptation." Mrs. Scales spat on the sidewalk. Her children stared.

"You're talking about her as if she's not here," said Tabitha.

"One more moment." The nurse gritted her teeth. "I'm working to overcome my separation anxiety." She narrowly avoided getting jabbed in the stomach by the handle of the wheelchair as Mrs. Scales kicked it backward from her place in the passenger's seat.

"Don't be a stranger, dear," said Marilee Gompers. She appeared to be talking to the wheelchair. "We're always here for you."

"Oh, oh, for Christ's sake, go," said Mrs. Leontina Scales, "home, will you? Ill the Nazi bitch."

"Learning some new words, Mom," said Hogan. "Hey lady, you done her some good."

"We do our best." Nurse Gompers sat down in the vacated wheelchair, shooing the car away, away.

"To hell!" cried Mrs. Scales, waving her hand at Nurse Gompers.

"Mom," said Tabitha, "are you trying to like make some kind of point again?"

Mrs. Scales spread her hands out wide. She almost knocked

Tabitha in the chin. "Ever again. Oh more doctors. Ever again, do you hear me? Odd can take care of me. Odd is my physician, and I'll *kill* myself if you take me back there, do you hear me? Ooh you *hear* me? Abby, I'll kill myself. At's a promise. Odd is my managed care, no one else. Eave me alone."

"You're talking crazy," said Tabitha. "What're you now, nuts? You're on your way home. This isn't the time for a tantrum."

"I'm to be born!" she cried. "I'm to die! I'm to plant! I'm to pluck up that which is planted! I'm to kill! I'm to heal!"

"You're to go home and get some supper, there's Spaghetti-O's," said Tabitha.

"I'm to get, and I'm to lose," said Leontina Scales in a smaller voice. "I'm to keep silence."

She kept silence then. There was nothing to do but look at the town as they drove through. Concentrate on it, because it was hard to figure out what kind of thing was sitting there in the front seat where their mother should be.

Thebes wasn't a place that the Scales kids had ever given much thought to. Except for the occasional shopping trip to Syracuse or Watertown, and a tour of Boston once, Thebes was all they knew other than TV. But things aged in Thebes faster than on TV. More graffiti on the overpasses, more houses that had run out of money before the siding had gotten all the way around.

"Repair ye the way of the Lord," murmured Mrs. Scales, pointing at a road crew from the highway department drinking from Thermoses. They were taking a break from repaving the northbound lanes of I-81.

Tabitha's eyes veered over to the road crew, checking them out. Two studly, three dudly.

Mrs. Leontina Scales hit the dashboard with her hand. "Odd, odd, why hast Thou forsaken me?" she cried.

"Momster." Hogan leaned forward from the backseat. "Take a chill pill. What's the matter? You're going home."

She closed her eyes and put her hands up to her face. "Ow, the serpent was more subtle than any beast of the field," she muttered. Tabitha glanced in the rearview mirror. After his demonstration of concern, Hogan was sinking back into his doldrums. He had pulled a small drum of dental floss from his shirt pocket and was twining a green strand around his fingers. Maybe he was going to try to strangle Mom from behind. He'd have to yank pretty hard.

"Look," said Tabitha, trying to be a TV daughter, "the colors are really late this year. Look, Mom, the reds over there behind Maxy's Hardware. You don't see reds like that often, even on cable." Mrs. Scales didn't look up.

Maybe, thought Tabitha, she'll be better when she gets home. Her things around her. Her friends to come calling. But what friends would those be? Hogan was a handful and so, Tabitha knew, was she, and her mother hadn't had much in the way of friends since divorcing her third husband, Kirk's dad. Too many wives scared she'd steal their husbands? Too many husbands scared they'd be stolen? Who knew? Maybe Tabitha could get Kirk to drop by Cliffs of Zion and put out a call for help. People must have heard what had happened. Pastor Huyck, that terminally perky sack of wind, must be spreading the word.

Surely her mother would get better. But for now she looked a mess. Her hair was all wrong, for one thing. Some fool had combed it up and you could see the thinning patches. Well, Tabitha wasn't going to start grooming her mother. It was hard enough to get a half hour in the bathroom for herself every morning, what with Kirk busy plucking every hair in his nostrils and who knew where else, for that matter.

Tabitha rolled her eyes when she pulled up in the driveway.

Kirk had made a sign. It was hung over the front door and was hand lettered to say WELCOME HOME!! Kirk was waiting by the door with his best Bride of Christ expression on.

Mrs. Scales seemed to be making an effort to pull herself together. She got out of the car without comment. She stopped a few steps short of the aluminum storm door that was still shy of a lower panel of glass since the time, three years ago, that Hogan had drop-kicked the old cat through it. She looked up at her youngest son. Her face seemed to screw in and out as if she was struggling for depth of field. "A sight for sore eyes, Captain Kirky," she managed.

"Peace to all who enter here," said Kirk, giving the Vulcan sign for something obscure and, thought Tabitha wistfully, with any luck obscene. "Seek and ye shall find rest."

"Am right I will," said Mrs. Scales.

"Be it ever so humble, there's no place like home," said Kirk.

"Can the crap and let us through," said Tabitha.

Kirk steered Mrs. Scales into the living room and Tabitha and Hogan, no more than ghost images once Kirk was involved, followed bitterly.

The house looked pretty good, Tabitha had to admit. She had collected the newspapers and the laundry, the empty glasses and dirty plates. Once she had put the new cat safely in a bedroom closet with the door closed, she had made Hogan vacuum the whole place. Kirk, on his own, had piled some pumpkins and leaves and sheaves of wheat into a kind of Harvest Home assemblage, like a picture on the front of a menu. The TV was on, companionably; everyone's eyes slid over there to check what was on—as much a way of telling the time as anything else. Commercial break; must be about quarter past four.

Mrs. Scales detached herself from her younger son and stood in the middle of the Colonial-style braided rug. She looked about her, and turned around with her arms out. "Mom, it's not *that* clean that you don't recognize it!" said Tabitha.

"See, I told you vacuuming was a waste of time," muttered Hogan. "You're such a nag, Tabbers."

"You're home," said Tabitha, "this is home, your home, and you're home!"

Mrs. Scales shook her head and pursed her lips. She began to tap one shoulder as if looking for a pocketbook strap, then she patted her trouser pockets for car keys.

"Sit down and put your feet up," said Kirk. "We'll get some supper on the table. You're just worn out. Come, here's your chair." He rubbed the velour upholstery of the recliner. "You want this or the Shopping Channel?"

Mrs. Leontina Scales made a gesture like the casting of a fly fisherman. They all understood it: Turn it off with the remote. Hogan did.

The house seemed quieter with the TV off and Mom home than it had seemed with her gone. Weird, thought Tabitha. "I'm going to start supper," she said. She had been hoping for a cry of delight from Mom. Tabitha's not learning to cook had been another cause of friction between them. But Mom was busy scrabbling with the old *Parade* magazines and the outdated *TV Guides* on the half-barrel side table. "Suppertime," said Tabitha, louder.

"Upper time, don't bother."

"She's lost the beginning part," said Kirk. "She's not saying the start of the sentence. That's what's so odd. Mom, what's going on?"

She had found the worn out paperback Bible, bound in black faux leather. "Ache me home," she said to Kirk. "Ache me home this minute, you bastard."

Tears stood thickly in Kirk's eyes. "You are home, Mom."

Hogan said, "Fuck this crazy shit," and disappeared into the garage.

In the kitchen Tabitha began to smash pots around, maybe to drown out the sound of Kirk's analysis, his girlie whimpers. "Spaghetti-O's, frozen green beans, chow mein noodles, how does that sound?" she called. "All I gotta do is find the can opener. Do we have one?" No answer. She came to the door to shrug her question again, louder.

"Izzy," said Mrs. Scales in a dismissive voice. She laid her hands on the book and closed her eyes.

"Dizzy?" said Kirk. "Should I get you something—"

"Izzy," said their mother. "Izzy."

"Busy?"

She nodded.

"Now what are you doing that you're too busy for supper?" said Tabitha in a false high voice.

"Eating the Bible," said Mrs. Leontina Scales. Her well-chewed fingernails began to twist at the book's cover, as if she had forgotten which way to open a book.

8

ON THE WHOLE, Jeremy liked Father Mike Sheehy. Our Lady's needed someone with common sense, and for that they had Sister Alice Coyne. But Father Mike was a burly sort of ordinary guy. When he wore his short-sleeved black cotton shirts in the summertime, Jeremy half expected to see the holy initials JMJ tattooed on his forearms. He wasn't doughy, he wasn't especially bookish. His sermons tended to be powered by scraps of science trivia popularized by Carl Sagan or Lewis Thomas.

Jeremy suspected that parishioners of a certain age who had been trained actually to listen to sermons couldn't fathom Father Mike's streamy bio-faith. By the time he finished, their minds were filled with stars and grains of sand and even the tiniest sparrow and the inside and the outside of the curve of eternity. It was probably the closest many of them came to mystical thought or a good marijuana buzz.

Jeremy found Father Mike in the food pantry. He and Peggy Mueller were stacking industrial-size drums of no-name chicken stock. "We had an appointment," said Jeremy.

Father Mike brushed back the forelock of his thinning, sandy hair, and replied, "Oh, right. I was in the office but then Peggy came by and she had these donations from Job Lot Circus. And they're awfully heavy."

"You need more help?"

"This is the last of them; I can finish stacking," said Peggy Mueller. "I'll type up directions on how to make vegetable soup and divide it for freezing. Our regular clients aren't going to know what to do with so much chicken stock. I'd hate to see it go to waste." She blinked at Jeremy and put a finger out desultorily. "Would you, for instance, know what to do with a gallon can of chicken stock? Jeremy?"

"Is this an essay question or multiple choice?"

"I don't know how you get by," said Peggy Mueller. "Artists. Musicians. The world could blow up and you'd be thinking your thoughts. You need a wife, Jeremy." She primped a bit as if she weren't already married. She probably knew that Jeremy was gay. This could be one of those social farces, acted out for the benefit of Father Mike. In fact Jeremy wasn't much of a cook, though. So point taken.

Peggy Mueller was well into her forties. She had a bad back. Stacking cans of chicken stock was penance, a nod to the ancient beloved convention of martyrdom. She drew her sweater about her bony shoulders and elevated her chin and said, "Go on, Father Mike; I'll finish up here."

"Don't forget to enter everything in the green book," said Father Mike. "The federal regulations are so strict, you can't even give food to the hungry without filing forms in triplicate." He finished stamping on the edges of the cardboard boxes, breaking them down for the recycling bin, and nodded to Jeremy. "Come on, Sister Alice is still upstairs, I think."

Sister Alice was lambasting someone at the phone company about erroneous charges. Jeremy, who liked Sister Alice too, felt sorry for the person on the other end of the line.

Father Mike and Jeremy crowded in the doorway ostentatiously.

The main office of the rectory was a study in early 1970s office decor. A lime green shag carpet had been tramped into submission by parishioners coming to conduct the business part of being Catholic. Some suspiciously artsy seminarian who had preceded him in parish employment, Jeremy guessed, had color-coordinated the three metal filing cabinets with a shade of green that had aged differently, in splotches, so the cabinets were deteriorating into camouflage. The desk weighed about a thousand pounds and featured rubber molding as if it had been designed for a ride in an executive amusement park. Bumper desks. The top of the desk, covered with paperwork, hadn't been seen since Father Mike's investiture as pastor.

Father Mike tapped his watch crystal. "This is not worth the time it's taking, good-bye," said Sister Alice, and hung up.

"Mrs. Castaneda making calls to her sister in Chiapas again?" asked Father Mike. Mrs. Castaneda was the cleaning lady.

"Mistake on the Motherhouse bill, I'm afraid," said Sister Alice. "Four calls to Kuala Lumpur, an obvious mistake. No rest for the weary."

She followed Father Mike and Jeremy into the staff room and, unusually, closed the door.

"It was quite a do last week, wasn't it?" said Father Mike. "That statue. I still don't know why it took it into its head to skip off the top of the refrigerator just then. Our Lady had been very happy there for decades."

"Perhaps a truck went by," said Sister Alice. "Vibrations, you know. They better get that speed trap thingy hooked up soon. What with I-81 northbound down to one lane, all that traffic slipping off and cutting through Thebes is making Union Street into Trampoline Alley."

"I called Pastor Huyck about the patient. Her name is Leontina

Scales," said Father Mike. "He hasn't had the chance to see her yet, but he's been told by the clinic that she's recovering nicely, and has gone home. No harm done, thank goodness. So that's why I was tied up a good part of Sunday afternoon. Jeremy, Sister Alice tells me about your request for rehearsal space in the rectory."

"Sister Alice gave you all the particulars?"

"Your friends—being sick, you mean."

"Both of them." He considered. "Not so bad yet, but I only know what I know by made-for-TV movies on Lifetime. These are the first cases in Thebes."

"That we're aware of," said Father Mike, but he wouldn't say more on that.

"We're rehearsing for a cabaret spot in Manhattan. In January. That's what, eight, ten weeks from now. It's an AIDS benefit, a showcase for singer-songwriters, and somehow I qualified for a slot. We're doing a short set of my own music. There's going to be judges. People with connections. Some executives from recording studios. Stephen Sondheim is on the panel."

Father Mike looked puzzled. "Father Mike wouldn't know him," intoned Sister Alice, "Sondheim's not Catholic." She began to hum "Send in the Clowns."

"Oh, him," said Father Mike. "I like that song. Well, isn't that grand. So, if you win, will you become the next Saint Louis Jesuits? Catholic megastars?"

"We're not doing religious music. Sometimes I write other stuff."

"Secular? Like the Clancy Brothers?"

"It's not very cutting edge, but it's beyond the Clancy Brothers."

Father Mike looked put out. "I still have that eight-track tape of the Carpenters. I love how they sounded. I wish they'd done an album of religious music. Maybe that anorectic one would have gotten faith and trusted God enough to eat a decent breakfast every now and then."

"You should get a new tape deck," said Jeremy. "The eight-track keeps you in the past, Father Mike."

"When I get a new car. But so many devout mechanics around here who all want to fix my old car for free—never going to happen. Anyway, cutting to the chase, Jeremy. We can't give you a room in the rectory for eight weeks. I'm sorry."

Jeremy turned his head and looked at Father Mike out of the corner of his eyes. "What's the problem?" His voice sounded more brittle than he intended.

"Now, none of that. It's not the AIDS issue or the gay issue either, Jeremy. True, the Parish Council deludes itself into thinking it has jurisdiction over pastoral decisions, but in fact it's a matter of simple logistics. As you know, Thursday is choir night. Friday alternates between Legion of Mary and Holy Names. Monday night I do couples counseling, and since the office is right next door to the meeting room, music is out of the question. And we've made a commitment for every second Tuesday from now through Easter for adult education of the catechumens. So that leaves us Wednesdays, Jeremy, or Saturdays. And with the vigil mass, Saturdays aren't workable."

"Saturdays are out for us too. Sean is still able to work, and he works a shift and a half on Saturday, because it's time-and-a-half."

"Sean Riley? Not Sean Riley," said Father Mike. "Oh, Jesus."

Shoot. Big mouth big mistake. "I hadn't meant to say that."

"Lips are sealed," said Father Mike. Sister Alice trained her eyes on the floor.

"But Wednesdays?" said Jeremy.

"Not on," said Father Mike. "Nothing regular, but the room is already booked in mid-November for two successive weeks, the

Cub Scout planning sessions. Then in early December the ladies come in and do that flurry of potholders for the jumble sale. That already knocks out four weeks, and there will be emergency meetings of the Parish Council when the boiler bursts, or there's some heated reaction to the next Letter of the Bishop or something. The odd spiritual crisis. The church has to serve the whole community. If we had more space—"

Jeremy tried to sound disgusted. "I could be the one with AIDS, you know."

"I never assumed you weren't. It's a matter of space and need."

"It's a matter of priorities."

"Church work comes first in a church, actually. But I've shared all this with Sister Alice—you did yourself—and so she's got the floor now."

Sister Alice said, "Jeremy, do you know the Motherhouse of the Sisters of the Sorrowful Mysteries? Out on Slopemeadow Road?"

"No. Is it the place beyond the Kmart?"

"No, that's an old waterworks. The Motherhouse is this side of Kmart—in that uphill wooded stretch, on the left as you're going east. Two stone pillars and an old wrought-iron sign arching overhead."

"Oh right. I thought that was some kind of private cemetery or something."

"Too near the truth." Sister Alice sighed. "That's why I'm here talking to you with Father Mike. I was discussing my religious order the other day, wasn't I? The headquarters are still in Canada, but with real estate prices what they are up there—I mean out of this world—the Order has put some of its Montreal property on the market. Retrenching, I think the word is. Downsizing."

"What, they're firing nuns?" said Jeremy.

"There aren't any nuns to fire. Though believe me in my day I would have been glad of the blessed opportunity in the case of

Sister . . . but never mind that. Listen, the Order still maintains, at considerable cost, this behemoth of a convent out on Slopemeadow Road. It was built in a faux-Gothic style in the 1920s, when vocations were up. Can't unload the property; there's no demand for a seventy-room complex eight miles out of Thebes, New York."

"A ghost convent," said Jeremy.

"Almost. The thing is this. Though the presence of Sisters of the Sorrowful Mysteries has dwindled in this part of New York, the Order maintains the property as a kind of retirement home for the elderly nuns. There are seventeen women out there now. Sisters between the ages of seventy and ninety-eight. Their health is not universally good, but they are in a lot better shape, physically, than most of their peers who are not in the religious life."

"Oh? How do they deserve that?"

"Think about it. They all lived lives of hard work and prayer, some of them for most of the century. Back before the craze for fresh fruits and vegetables, the Sisters were eating lean cuisine because that was all they could afford. Back before the days of the Exercycle, the Sisters walked everywhere they needed to go, and got better exercise than most. More than you."

"No doubt about that. I'm allergic to exercise."

"The Sisters never smoked. We ate low-fat before it became popular. We were always good at penitence."

"Did you do those 'Buns of Steel' videos?"

"Jeremy," intoned Father Mike, leafing through a catalog of vestments.

Sister Alice plunged on. "The old nuns are built like powerhouses and they take forever to die. I do mean *forever*. I am the only member of the Order in this Province under the age of seventy. My contemporaries—the women I entered with—are either serving in Montreal or, regrettably, have left the religious life."

"These nuns have a piano?" Jeremy began to get the point.

"They have a piano. The whole place is heated like a green-house because, of course, they're old women with poor circulation. You might be able to go there once a week for ten weeks or so, and have a place to practice. I think it could probably be arranged. How are Tuesdays?"

He didn't want to sound too eager. It sounded perfect. "I'd have to run it by the guys. But I don't see why not—"

"Not so fast. There's a cost here."

"We're not in a position to rent the space, Sister Alice. We don't have any money, either singly or as a group—"

"I'm talking barter. There are seventeen old nuns out there, in varying degrees of physical health. But their mental health is my concern, too. They are woefully secluded. They are too infirm to get out often, and yet too healthy to die. They are women with a wide variety of interests and also, I might add, a considerable amount of education, in some cases. But they suffer from being isolated out there. Not enough going on for them. The word I'm trying to avoid is . . ."

"Lunacy?"

"Depression. This is a group of seriously depressed older women, able to take care of themselves but not much more than that. They can manage the running of the building, the cooking, the laundry, the nursing of the sick among them—more or less—while I handle the finances and so on. My Abbess in Montreal approves my administrative work here at Our Lady's, but requires that I look in on the Motherhouse and try to provide what they need. And I feel that what they need is some human contact."

"Oh." Jeremy felt conflicted. "Some say gay men aren't fully human."

"They say that about women who live in community, too," snapped Sister Alice. "Look, I think I could persuade them to open up their parlor to you boys, if you agreed to spend some time chatting with them each time you went. You would get your rehearsal space and you'd be doing a service to them as well. What do you think?"

"Sister Alice." Jeremy rubbed his hands together. It must look like avarice, he thought, and that's what I feel, but can I make this work? "I don't want to be rude, but we're talking about men who don't all have as easygoing an attitude toward the Church as I do. We're talking about a couple of gay men with HIV. One of them isn't Catholic. And the Catholic one hates organized religion with a passion."

"There's a Bechstein."

"Oooh, you're good." Jeremy turned to Father Mike. "Are you sure that Wednesday nights are out—?"

"Isn't she a miracle worker?" Father Mike beamed at Sister Alice.

"Flattery, flattery; more welcome than accurate. Still, I'll take what I can get." Sister Alice picked up a motorcycle helmet from behind the plastic tub of a dying ficus. Jeremy raised his eyebrows. "I did a mischief to the car's rotator cuff, or whatever it's called," she said as they walked out together. "I talked the garage into loaning me a bike for the duration."

"Don't you need a special license to drive a motorcycle?"

"Jeremy. Come on. No highway trooper in upstate New York is going to ask to see a nun's driver's license."

He didn't know if she was joking or not, but a bike waited in the parking lot, next to the St. Vincent de Paul Society drop-off bin. "Want to take a spin around the block?"

"No. No thanks."

She looked at him with a shake of her head. "You know, I hate to fall back on stereotypes, Jeremy, but isn't a handsome young buck like you supposed to have a more heightened sense of adventure than a middle-aged nun? You should get out more."

He thought she'd stepped across the line. He tried for a neutral tone, maybe mocking, maybe aggressive: "You want to get me a hooker? Or some Ecstasy? Or a new job that actually pays real money?"

She wasn't one to back down. "A new boyfriend, maybe. Someone who could make you a little cheerier. Don't look so shocked. I told you I know depression when I see it. Here, would you pin my veil to my backpack? It tends to whip about." She handed him an old Clinton/Gore button and turned her back to him.

"Are you allowed to do political advertising? Aren't you avowedly neutral according to the tax code?"

"If they can catch up with me, they can sue me. Hey, Jeremy, think about what I said."

"About the convent?"

She was revving the motor. She mouthed "Think about it," and gave a thumbs-up as she pulled the visor down.

9

HAVING FINISHED MARKING the sockets of empty egg cartons with digits, one through six, so his preschoolers could wrestle with the concept of one-to-one correspondence, Jeremy was tucking them in a grocery bag for school tomorrow when he saw Babs pull up at the curb. The parking was diagonal here to accommodate patrons of Getchen's Market downstairs, so Jeremy had a cameraman's angle above Sean as he emerged from the passenger's seat. What a gauntness in Sean these days. A paperiness not always obvious face on. Still, by habit perhaps, Sean tucked his shirt in and then puffed it out a little over the belt in the back, that useful practice to make the waist look thinner so the bum was more shapely.

If Sean's waist gets any thinner, though, thought Jeremy, he's going to be a walking emblem of eternity—that mathematical symbol called the lazy eight, the bow-tie loop that crosses in the middle and returns the way it came, all the while lying on its side like road kill.

More to the point, even at this stage in his illness Sean is still angling for me, or at any rate he hasn't gotten out of the habit of trying.

Problematic though that was for Jeremy, he had to concede that by focusing such keen attention to old habits did Sean keep himself together.

While for me? Old habits are my death trap.

Another conundrum. Still, despite the mixed signals it might give, he found himself straightening his own clothes. Old habits do die hard. He went to open the stair door.

Mounting the outside steps, Sean and Marty were still nattering about, it seemed, some hunky Central American kid newly staffing the produce aisle of the Price Chopper. Sean was narrating and Marty salivating. "But you'll never guess what his name was," said Sean.

"Pablo? Pedro? I know: Emmanuel."

"God with us," sang Sean, from *Messiah*. "I wish. No. *Hector*. Who names an Ecuadoran kid Hector?"

Jeremy beamed, feeling a false sort of liveliness on his face. "Fresh love. Come in, tell all." Oh, that someone might step in and displace himself in Sean's affections.

Sean handed Jeremy a six-pack. "Sadly, more fresh than love. I fluttered around the vegetable bin, pretending clumsiness, asking for help at dropping spinach leaves into my plastic bag. I didn't even have to pretend I was shaking; I *was* shaking. His forearms seizing out from under his rolled-up dirty white grocer's jacket, two sizes too big for him—they were parsnip-brown and smelled like garden soil. I wanted to push him backward into the greens bin and make a mixed salad of him, to go."

Marty whistled. "Ravishment in the radishes. Wish I'd been there."

"A little olive oil applied judiciously does wonders."

"Myself, I prefer a creamy Italian. The creamier the—"

"Stop." Jeremy, ever the killjoy. But this time for good reason, to keep Sean on the subject of real life, not this capering into whispery fantasies that dulled the senses—as he well knew. "You've a live prospect then. Get his phone number?"

"Hardly." Sean busied himself with his fingernails. "Believe me, I batted my eyelashes till they were flaking off into the spinach. But his face had that hollow look, as if there was something gone . . . you know that look. The inward focus. Distantly attentive to the home you're missing, or the someone you're missing. Somewhere in Central America, probably. That look that a bird has when it turns its dry reptilian eye on you. That look that doesn't see you, because the mind is filled up with someone it would rather see."

"Loneliness." Jeremy felt like a walking book of adages culled from the *Farmer's Almanac*. "The perfect precondition for a new romance—"

Sean raised his eyebrows. "Peddling false hope is not only cowardly, but vicious. Besides, I'm waiting for you to wake up and notice I'm here in your apartment. Wearing a fabulous shirt, by the way."

"Yeah, suits you."

"I put it on for Hector but he doesn't know I exist. So you might as well."

"Down to business," said Jeremy, and they collapsed onto what passed for furniture, some old nylon-webbed lawn chairs that his father had intended to drag to the dump. Jeremy started to explain the situation proposed by Sister Alice Coyne, but only got a few sentences out before Sean interrupted.

"Absolutely not. I'd rather kill myself."

"It's not such a bad idea," said Jeremy. "I mean, who would know, for one thing? These aren't even local nuns, they're all transplanted here to retire. They don't get out. Who's going to tell your parents? Sean, get over yourself." As if he were one to talk.

"The smell of ripe baloney is stronger today than usual. Does it come in a can so you can touch up the soiled atmosphere?" Marty as usual trying to broker a truce.

"Let's stick this subject out," said Jeremy. "We don't have all day."

"I'm not doing it," said Sean. "Don't waste your breath."

"Sean, how can you turn your back on the Church and still be so scared of some dumb old nuns?" said Marty.

"You didn't go to Catholic school. Recovery is not an option."

"So I hear, but these nuns didn't inflict any damage on you. For one thing, they're too old to have taught you."

"Hah!" Sean pretended to hawk and spit. "There's no such thing as a too-old nun. They're like the Pope. The older they get, the more infallible. Anyway, they might not have ruined my life, but they did their dirty business to other poor souls. When does the statute of limitations run out on psychotic abusive grade school nuns?"

"It's not as if we have other choices," said Jeremy.

"Look. Our Lady's gives you a paycheck, and so you feel obligated to comfort the enemy. That's your weirdness. That doesn't mean *we* have to. If the Church hadn't so roundly announced that we were in a state of mortal sin these last, oh, two thousand years or so, we wouldn't be in the mess we're in."

"The mess of needing a rehearsal space?" asked Jeremy.

"Western governments emerged out of the ashes of the collapsed Church oligarchy and they appropriated the same oppressive cultural norms. Still no women priests in the Catholic Church, Jeremy, or haven't you noticed? Fags still have to ride in the third-class car if they want to get on the Gospel Train. I know: God loves us and will forgive us our sins so long as we don't sin in any really interesting way. Don't get me started. It's a no go, Jeremy."

"You're talking about your parents, I think."

"And so what if I am? Where do you think they got it from? Fucked up as they are, I don't blame them for inventing churchy shit, just for swallowing it. Let others be bad that we, O Lord— that's Deirdre and Paddy Riley, R-I-L-E-Y—might be good. I hate the whole stupid thing. If I didn't have the hots for you, Jeremy, I'd be walking out of here in a snit." He arched his feet in Jeremy's direction and opened his legs.

Jeremy looked the other way. "Marty? The voice of Jewish reason here?"

"On the one hand, he has a point," said Marty. "The norm that says it's okay to kill Matthew Shepard is constantly endorsed and reinforced by good people keeping silent. Hey, did you hear the second attacker got convicted today?"

"Good news like that still doesn't have the capacity to make anyone happy," said Sean. "Or maybe I've just forgotten what happiness is."

"Playing devil's advocate, then, I also say: How bad could it be?" continued Marty. "I mean, we go in there and do our work, we say hi to the old penguins for ten minutes. Big deal. Do we have much choice?"

"I'm not chatting up any old nun," said Sean, "who is breathing down her desiccated sinuses in disapproval of me."

"What if you brought the choir out there to rehearse?" asked Marty. "Then we could use the parish house meeting room freed up on Thursday nights."

"I already thought of that. Peggy Mueller can't change her night. Leonard's bowling night is Thursday, so that's the only night she gets to go out. Come on, guys, a little flexibility here. I'm trying to work this out for all of us."

"Well," said Marty, "I'm game. I'm immune to nuns. I'll smear myself with cream cheese and lox and rub gefilte fish into my hair.

We're only talking a ten-week commitment. The time it takes to argue about it we could be rehearsing, you know."

Jeremy released some beers from the cardboard sleeve and held them out, a kind of peace offering. "Unless we get a place to practice, there's no point carrying on. We can't tiptoe into the Manhattan big time without shaping up our act. I won't do it. It's not just that my career might be on the line: it's that I will be petrified and not able to open my mouth."

Sean put his hands over his eyes. "Does this constitute an artistic tantrum? At least be honest about *that*. You don't have a career yet, Jeremy, unless you think singing in church qualifies. If I'm going to go along with this, let's be clear about why. No false pretenses."

Was Sean ready to admit Jeremy and Marty were doing this partly for him: to keep him going, keep him singing while he could still sing, keep him thinking forward—into the next century, and as beyond into it as he could imagine? Jeremy summoned up a high-toned look of umbrage he hardly felt. "It is my career. You think I work so hard on my music for—"

"It's not your career on the line." Sean leaned one elbow on the aluminum arm of the chair till it squeaked. "You want to get out of Thebes and escape your glamorous *bête noire*, and since they don't take fags in the Foreign Legion, this is the only thing that you can think of. Fair enough. Okay, you win. I'll help you on this, even though I can tell your little trial shot in New York City is an exercise to escape from the toxic radiation of your college heartthrob. You think I can't tell that? I should have my head examined to be helping."

"You'll come too," said Jeremy. "The symposium is only a weekend, for crying out loud."

"Give it a rest, and stop looking so self-righteous at me. It's not your career on the line, Jeremy. It's your heart on the line. If you're going to drag me into that nunnery warehouse, at least be an honest man about it."

Sean shook the can of beer just a little and set it on his zipper, and flipped the pull tab. The golden spume rose six inches and fizzed on his lap. "You wish I didn't know you so well," said Sean, "don't you. You wish you hadn't told me so much." Then, in a nicer voice, "Here, have a brew. No strings attached."

10

In an excess of nervous energy Tabitha had gotten out some of the Christmas ornaments and hung them up on the hooks in the bay window that used to hold planters before all the plants crisped and flaked to death. A little fringe of hard plastic angels with vacant expressions, twisting in the currents from the floor heaters. She hoped they might make her mother happy, but in fact only the new cat seemed to notice. Meanwhile Tabitha and her mother, and for that matter Hogan and Kirk, seemed all twisted themselves, unsettled and airborne and unfocussed, each in a different way. A change of situation like this was hard to negotiate.

As far as Tabitha could tell, for the first couple of days at home, Mrs. Leontina Scales did nothing but finger the pages of the Bible. She didn't seem to be reading it, exactly; she felt the margins and ran her hands over the columns of type as if admiring the weave and nubble of a nice piece of cloth. She would take cups of black tea and a slice of toast every now and then. But Tabitha could rarely get her to engage in conversation.

Tabitha played Christmas music on the CD player until Mrs. Scales said, "Leap in heavenly peace, my ass," and snapped the CD in the garbage disposal and turned it on. Tabitha had to admire her gumption. If only her mother could learn to use her lunatic superpowers for goodness.

On Monday morning Mr. Reeves called and asked to speak to Mrs. Scales. "She can't come to the phone right now," said Tabitha. "I'll take a message."

"I've called and left three messages," said Mr. Reeves. "You're not giving them to her."

"Says who? I am too. I can't make her call you back if she doesn't want to." The phrase came to her too fast to hold it back. "Am I my mother's keeper?"

"Well." An intake of breath from the principal. "That's a good question. I am giving you the benefit of the doubt and assuming your absence from school is because of your mother's accident. But I better not find out you're milking this, Tabitha."

"Don't worry. You won't."

"If you can't bring your mother to the phone I'm going to have to stop by, or get Social Services involved."

"She's deep in prayer, but when she comes up to room temperature again I'll tell her you called."

"I need to know how to reach your father, Tabitha. The forms we have on file here don't give a current phone number—"

"Oh my mistake she's on the toilet and needs a little attention. She'll call you back, Mr. Reeves. Promise." Tabitha hung up so hard the mute plastic angels swayed in consternation.

I hate this prison. Where is Caleb hanging out these days? Why doesn't he answer my messages? How dare he abandon me when my mom is on the fritz?

Tabitha had gotten tired of driving by the trailer Caleb shared with his older brother. There'd been no lights on for a week. She didn't dare ask Hogan to keep an eye out for him, because Hogan could take a request like that too far and she didn't want Caleb to get hurt. And she had all too few girlfriends from school left, not after making cozy with their personal jackhammers. Her only confidant was Linda Pearl at the beauty salon. So she'd have to set Linda Pearl on the job of sleuthing out the dirt about Caleb.

The principal's remark about her father brought back a conversation with Caleb Briggs a month ago or so. Generally Tabitha wasn't the reflective sort, so she didn't step outside her own skin to look back in. But Caleb had asked a question about Mrs. Scales, and Tabitha had found herself foaming to pin down for him the contradictions about her mother.

Mrs. Scales. Admired for a lot of good reasons. A pillar of the community, salt of the earth, steady as the Rock of Jehovah or whatever that insurance company was. Yet she had been married three times. Tabitha, Hogan, and Kirk had sprung from different dads. So as far as Tabitha was concerned, her own adventures in the vans and backseats and pool rooms (and once even in her cell at the jail) were in line with the standards of the Scales family.

No, she hadn't ever wanted to talk to her mother about men. Tabitha had prepared a rejoinder in case her mom ever got on her case about it. If you know so much, Tabitha would bark, how come you botched up three marriages in a row? Where's your next husband coming from? And don't you get any big ideas, she had joked to Caleb Briggs, who had kissed her dirty and changed the subject.

Later, lingering, unwilling to let him off and away on his bike too soon, she'd continued rehashing the family bio. The first husband was the Scales, and the Scales name had dribbled down over Tabitha's half brothers even though they weren't his kids. Casey Scales, purveyor of flooring materials. Ya gotcher linoleum, your Congoleum, your rush matting, your simulated pine planking in three-and-a-half and five-inch widths. You name it.

Casey Scales had come home from Vietnam and found Leontina Prelutski where he had left her, behind the goldfish counter at Woolworth's, back when Thebes still had a Woolworth's (now it was the Budget Five and Dime). Scales had thought Tina Prelutski was still there because she was faithful. More likely she'd been batting her eyes at every connoisseur of goldfish to come along, but since goldfish customers tended to be boys under the age of ten she hadn't gotten very far.

The wedding pictures, in Tabitha's humble opinion, were vomitrocious. In his tuxedo with a lime-green ruffled shirt her father looked like a percussionist escaped from the *Lawrence Welk Show*. And Tina Prelutski had been photographed tipped into a wedding dress designed for someone willowy. Leontina was more like a box hedge than a willow. You could see a tummy bulge that even studio lighting couldn't erase. She must have been lowered feet-first into that dress by a crane. And Farrah Fawcett-Majors's hair. What was everyone *thinking* of in those days?

The mothers-in-law, Mrs. Prelutski and Mrs. Scales, two attendants who looked like Soviet aerospace mathematicians, stood grimly on the side, flabby arms folded. Twin widows old enough to guess, accurately, that no good would come of this union. And along comes Tabitha to prove their point.

Describing her two grandmothers, now decently dead where they belonged, she'd laughed and laughed, but Caleb had not found her as amusing as she intended. He had disentangled himself and wiped up the beaded spill on his thigh and gone off to do something else he had to do. She had tidied up the trailer when he was gone, and in an excess of trust and confidence she hadn't even thrown out the well-thumbed dirty magazines she'd found under his mattress. And except for the night in the Nixon mask, that was the last she'd seen of him.

She'd given Caleb every chance. Every chance and, God knows, every liberty. Where was her fucking payback? No phone call, no help with Mom, no nothing.

She didn't want Mr. Reeves bringing the county authorities down on her. So Tabitha found her father's phone number scribbled in the back of the NYNEX yellow pages. He lived with his new wife down in Vestal, near Binghamton. Flooring was big down there, apparently. "Hold the line, Tabitha, he's on his way," said his new wife, who wasn't very new even when he'd married her.

Tabitha didn't bother to grunt a thank-you. She didn't like the second Mrs. Scales very much. Maybe if she ever met her she might change her mind, but till then, forget it.

"Howcha doin', Tabbles?" said her dad. He was always coming up with new childish nicknames to disguise the fact that he had cut out when she was two.

"Good. You okay?"

"Things are great. Never better. Getting into indoor-outdoor carpeting. All over again. The new thing. You'd be surprised. Consumers fickle? Whatcha gonna do. Wait and see attitude. The grass is always greener when it's Astroturf. Butcha never know. Still, imagine vacuuming your lawn. No dandelions. Whatcha say?"

"I'm calling about Mom."

"What's that?"

"She had an accident. Not a car accident, no, a church accident, I guess. The nurse and doctors say she's fine, but she's not very much like normal."

"Nurses and doctors? *That'll* be the day. She was never much like *normal*, Tabinetta. You want I should what? Talk to her? Put her on."

"I'm not sure she'd talk to you."

"She sounds her old self to me. Cooking with gas. Try her and see, Tabbles."

"Mom." Tabitha held out the receiver. "Guess who. It's the Dad behind Door Number One."

Mrs. Scales didn't look at Tabitha. "Eek and ye shall find."

"It's Daddy Casey. He wants to talk to you."

Her mother just shook her head.

"See?" said Tabitha to her father. "She won't come to the phone."

"Tell you what," said Daddy Casey. "Try Daddy Wally and then try Daddy Booth. If she won't talk to anyone, call me back. But I'm probably not going to be here. A trade fair. Floor show. I'm the opening number. Ha ha!"

Tabitha didn't laugh, just hung up. Men. Daddy Casey on one hand, Caleb Briggs on the other. Unreliable. Caleb would be laying somebody else soon if Tabitha dropped out of sight entirely.

She perked up though. Maybe he'd been too drunk to remember what he'd done so *right* that wild session on Halloween night. That miraculous spree, from which she'd come home masked, stoned, and elated from the orgasm so intense she hadn't even been able to lie about it to her mother. Prompting the fight that had forced Mrs. Scales into seeking solace in a Catholic church, of all godforsaken places. So it was sort of Caleb's fault. In a way. She hadn't really put it to herself like that before. He owed her.

"Gotta go shopping, Mom." Tabitha noticed she was talking more loudly, as if her mom had gone deaf, though there wasn't any real sign of that. Her mom had just lost interest in her kids, that's all. She seemed to take no notice of Tabitha's walking around, jangling the car keys. Ordinarily Tabitha wasn't allowed to drive after that incident with the state trooper in the rest stop. But Mrs. Scales showed no sign of objecting this morning. She was cuddling the Bible and glancing every now and then at some talk show in which they appeared, at quick glance, to be stir-frying a dozen or so severed human ears. Maybe they were oysters.

Caleb Briggs wasn't to be found, which wasn't such a problem except that Tabitha also wasn't running into Stephanie Getchen, either, that whore. That slut waiting for an opportunity. Neither Caleb nor Stephanie were hanging around the soda machine behind Scarcese's Budget Gas, not loitering at the low-budget KFC knockoff, Tennessee Fried Chicken. (*Visit the Corporal*, said their menu, after which wags always scrawled *Punishment*.) Nor were Caleb or Stephanie anywhere near the Crosswinds Shopping Center at Cleary Corners, which was the closest to an honest-to-God mall that Thebes could manage.

Whatever. Tabitha would find that cockteasing bitch and tear her limb from limb. But what if it wasn't Stephanie? How embarrassing to trash the wrong girl.

She thought of driving out to Caleb's trailer and breaking in. She knew she could. But then what? She couldn't envision herself draped in Caleb's big shirts just sitting around the way her own abandoned mother sat. After all the times Caleb nudged Tabitha through the trailer's flimsy tin-can door in a whimpering, desperate kind of way, like a dog who needed a walk, bad? What a comedown.

Tabitha didn't believe she had much of a sense of pride. I don't know the meaning of the word, she thought of saying aloud, with her chin up and a bright spark in her eye. Still, she wasn't going to stoop to ambushing Caleb in his infidelity. She wasn't going to give him the satisfaction. Or Stephanie Getchen, or whoever else it might be.

So why don't I feel better about myself?

When she got home, Hogan was in his room, blasting some toxic talk radio thing on his speakers the size of Stonehenge. Kirk was making cookies. "So how's it going, Suzy Homewrecker?"

"I hate being a sophomore," said Kirk. "Everybody's so juvenile. Hey, do you think I'm supposed to grease this cookie sheet? I thought maybe Mom would like something fresh baked."

"Freihofer's not good enough for her now?"

"I finished the box when I got home."

"What? And ruin that girlish figure?"

"Tabitha, cut it out, will you? Mom's in her room with the lights off and a pound of bacon on her eyes. Don't ask me why. I'm just trying to do something nice for her."

"Suck-up." Still, the phone was free and not under surveillance, so Tabitha decided to call Hogan's dad. His name was Wally Hauenstein and he lived in Drexel Hill, Pennsylvania. Or, apparently, he used to. The phone was disconnected and there was no Wally Hauenstein listed, not in the whole greater Philadelphia metropolitan area.

Tabitha considered sauntering by Hogan's room and letting him know this interesting piece of news. But that could wait; she didn't have the time to be nasty. She just continued down the list of her mother's former husbands to Booth Garrison. A long phone message listed all sorts of fax numbers and beeper numbers and weekend cottage numbers. She maintained a steady hand on the receiver until the ping sounded. "Daddy Booth, this is Tabitha, would you call us, thanks," and she heard his voice say "Hello?" just as she was about to hang up.

"You want me to come out to Thebes?" said Daddy Booth. "Is that what you're asking me to do?"

"I don't know," said Tabitha. "I'm asking you to do something."

"Put Kirk on the line."

"He's making cookies. It'll take him a minute to fold up his frilly apron." She wasn't fond of Daddy Booth, and she hadn't been fond of him during the nineteen months of his marriage to their mother. He'd coddled baby Kirk, he'd been wary of Hogan even as a toddler, and he'd considered Tabitha moronic. But he'd been marginally more involved in the upbringing of his son and stepkids, even after the divorce, than either Daddy Casey or Daddy Wally. He alone sent a check once in a while. And if his work took him into the vicinity he would stop by for a meal.

He had a real love-hate thing for Kirk, Kirk being his only son but so disappointing. He knew that Kirk was bright even if he was probably going to be a faggot someday. Booth Garrison liked bright people; he liked himself in that regard, too. All the more reason for Tabitha to sneer at Kirk as he came up and took the phone receiver. "Hi," said Kirk, noncommittal with his dad as always.

Tabitha listened to the conversation for a while, and then lost track. She wandered down the hall and pushed her mother's bedroom door open an inch or two. Her mother had fallen asleep on her bed. A red lacy shawl was draped over the bedside lamp and rosy patterns, like cells in bio lab, spiderwebbed the walls. It was less like a bordello than a trip into someone's large intestine. The packet of bacon had slipped to one side and lay halfway across an inert Bible.

Her mother looked like an old woman, though she was a pert late fortysomething; Tabitha could never remember the age exactly. Her mother's mouth drooped a bit, and Tabitha noticed creases in the skin around the jaw. Interesting, when her mother believed in being not just active but *active*: She liked to move. She liked to swing from room to room and do things, to run from place to place, to guide that car along the roads. She was supposed to be full of zeal and criticism. But asleep in the late afternoon? She was a picture of someone's grandmother.

That, Tabitha realized, is part of the problem. It's hard enough to deal with a mother, especially an annoying mom like a Leontina Scales. But to have her promoted with no advance warning into grandmotherliness—well, it's shocking. And she's not taking care of her hair at all. She looks like Albert Einstein when he was discovering electricity

"What'd he say?" asked Tabitha, when Kirk had hung up with that irritating gentility he showed to inanimate objects.

"Basically, he reminded us that he had divorced her thirteen and a half years ago and it was our turn."

"To take care of her?" Tabitha was shocked.

"To divorce her."

"And you said?"

"I said, Screw you, Daddy Booth."

"Screw you? Gee whillikers, Boy Wonderpants, don't be so Fifties! I mean, for God's sake, can't you even say *fuck you* when it's the right time to say fuck you? What do you think, you're on some kind of a—a cruise? Screw you, in your white tuxedo? Do you need to take Cursing for Dummies? It's *fuck you*. Listen and learn. Repeat after me. Fuck *you*."

"Fuck you."

"No, fuck *you*."

"No, fuck you."

"A little enthusiasm. Say it as if you mean it. You sound like you're asking to borrow someone's cell phone. Put some feeling into it. Poke your clenched hand in my face. Like so. Fuck you."

"Fuck *you*."

From behind the slightly ajar door, their mother's voice ventured. "Otherfuckers! Ill you otherfuckers shut the fuck up?"

"Motherfuckers," Hogan interpreted as the talk radio host paused to grab a breath. "Now that notion is seriously creepy."

The doorbell rang. Kirk went to answer it. "Say it to whoever it is, Kirk, say it say it say it. I dare you. It's practice," said Tabitha, pirouetting close behind him. He opened the door and muttered, "Hellotherefuckyou," under his breath. Mrs. Chanarinjee handed him a casserole covered with tin foil and fled.

JEREMY WAS LATE. He'd been gathering his papers, the photo-copied lyric sheets and pencil-corrected vocal parts (working at sparer harmonies, more Brian Eno, less Crosby, Stills and Nash), and he remembered a half-song scribbled late last night, at one of those testing moments of loneliness. It must have fallen to the floor by the side of his narrow bed. In lurching to grab it he knocked over the stack on the bedside table. Including the paperback Bible he used for his church work.

Exhibit A slid from its sacred keep between the pages of Kings. That snapshot. The only one Jeremy had. The sole material evidence of his own private David and Jonathan story only without, so far, the death in battle. It might have had the decency to land face-down on the floor, but it didn't. Two abashed but undaunted faces caught in a half kiss courtesy of someone's archaic black and white film stock. Familiar as myth and just as distant.

Jeremy could hardly imagine he'd ever been capable of glowing like a Three Mile Island meltdown. Unsettling, the way the effect of an insubstantial kiss lingered through time, a harmonic just beyond the capacity of the ear to apprehend, but not of the memory to register and to twist, once again, between poles pulling either grateful or sour.

He stuffed the photo back in the Bible without being sure of its precise address. Let it spend some time away from "Thy love for me was greater than that of a woman." Perhaps the cold shower of "My God, my God, why hast thou forsaken me?" No surprise that David the buff savior of the nation calling Jonathan to his tent for figs and wine and torchlit sex on the sheepskin had become, when older and wiser, David the disconsolate psalmist. Hadn't David also written musical settings to which his psalms should be sung? Opinions were divided, though it was easier to imagine a Brian Eno treatment of De Profundis than, say, the surfer-dude chorale of the Beach Boys.

The matter of Willem, so volatile maybe because so suppressed, was hard to tamp down once it emerged. On the way to the first session on Slopemeadow Road, Jeremy tried to divert himself from the sting of it. Rehearsing a tenor glissando, a swooping sixth, he thought mostly of the barn swallows, the parabolic loops they used to make from the eaves of the lake house where he had spent summers with his parents back when they were still easy with him. The swallows came and went in couples. On any given summer morning, one was never more than moments away from the other; you hardly had to turn your head to find the mate. What if one died, victim of some kind of avian heart attack? The other one seemed to disappear. Jeremy had never seen a barn swallow on its own.

Not as if he hadn't tried to leave, he talked to himself. That terrible aborted campaign to relocate himself in California. Peggy Mueller had a sister who worked as an executive assistant for a music producer and everyone did what Peggy Mueller said, including her siblings. So five years ago Jeremy hadn't renewed his lease on his apartment in Thebes, and had resigned from his church job, and with a lump in his throat that proved such symptoms were not merely figures of speech he'd tried to escape. Survived the flight from Albany to Chicago, and the flight from Chicago to LAX in alternating paroxysms of pride and terror. Eileen, Peggy's sister, had made up the foldout sofa in the condo's low narrow living room. It looked out on a view of the San Bernardino Mountains, sere and brown as Mount Sinai for all Jeremy could tell. Not quite the land of milk and honey, despite its reputation.

She'd brought him to a dinner party that first Saturday. He still cringed at the thought of it. Six or eight people. Had Eileen been trying to see if she could flush his possible gay identity out into the public by observing him in the company of the L.A. ambisexual elite? If so, she'd failed. (Only after he'd fled had he realized how single she had seemed, and that her hopes of his romantic availability must have been attached to her welcome.)

The guests were all roughly his age—mid twenties cresting at or just across the threshold of their thirties. Jeremy had been unable to pick up the simplest cues as to their makeup or character. The women posed brittle and laconic in over-large, candy-colored plastic eyeglass frames and wry expressive earrings; the men glistened sleek as pumas in their nylon dance-competition shirts and smart linen slacks that were in fact disappointingly slack. The dinner party had been rife with the cabbalistic mysteries of foreign society; the horde of guests and Eileen, too, spoke in L.A. code.

Jeremy couldn't guess if they were anything but asexual until he was emerging from a bathroom, where he'd gone to splash water on his face. One of them—probably one of the men, though everyone's voice seemed coolly inflectionless and on the same pitch, or was that something wrong with his ears due to the air pressure of the transcontinental flights?—one of them said something like, "How public-spirited of you to bring him out to play, Eileen."

"Shh," she had said; the "shhh" had cut through him. He strained more keenly. "Eileen, are you sure he's house trained?

Devon, you're very brave to let him sit on your Ernardo Praxis leopards-and-lilies without a splat mat. Or are you about to have it re-upholstered again? He's a gorgeous house present; they can be cute when they're stupid, and he's *very* cute." A hiss of suppressed mirth—not so much a laugh-track as a sneer-track.

He didn't remember much about how he'd explained his change of heart to Eileen. It had cost all he had left to convert the return ticket he'd intended to use at Christmas into flights the following Tuesday morning. And, injury piled upon insult, in the weeks that followed, no one from the agencies he'd rung ever answered his call. Only one of the nine demo tapes he'd sent out came back, and that one was "return to sender" because the agency had closed or moved.

No childhood nook in his parents' home to which he could crawl—not welcome there—and no other ideas. Ashamed at his public humiliation—Jeremy Carr, off to make his career in the L.A. big time!—he'd commandeered a corner of Marty's living room floor until he'd gotten the job at the school, and then the parish council offered him his old job back. The single barn swallow had tried to leave, but had had to loop back.

How much of his failure to escape was due to Willem? How much of his attachment to Willem was due to his parents' polite lack of interest in his affairs? The parabolic loops were endless, but he swooped about Thebes year after year, unable to untie the knots. Only music seemed to help. It hardly mattered whether he was steeped in his own compositions or some saccharine late-nineteenth-century hymn tune. Any time he opened his mouth to sing, the lump in his throat dissolved and a single barn swallow escaped for a certain number of bars, until the bars closed in again.

———

JEREMY ARRIVED FIRST. No other cars in the circular drive. Sister Alice pulled up next, in a new car. "You don't use the motorcycle at night?" he asked.

"This is a rental," she replied. "Little incident with a brain-dead driver passing on a stretch of the Syracuse road where the shoulder was torn up for repair."

"Nobody hurt, I hope."

"Only the bike."

As Jeremy began to suspect that Sister Alice was naming herself as the brain-dead driver, Babs showed up, her headlights raking the dark drive askance, braiding the surface in a nubble of gravel. "My comrades at arms," said Jeremy.

Sister Alice was brusque and friendly in about equal proportions. She shook their hands and bustled about the trunk of the car, hoisting a couple of bags of groceries. Sean shuffled forward to help her. "That's a good lad. Thanks. Mind the pears, they'll bruise."

"And so it starts," mumbled Sean in a low voice.

"And so it does. Right this way, fellows. I have a key this time, but next week you'll have to ring the bell. I'd call ahead and remind Sister Jaundice you're coming; she's the most ambulatory and she mans the door in the evening."

"Sister Jaundice?" said Jeremy.

"Oh, now that's a slip. Can you tell I'm a tad overworked? Sister Jeanne d'Arc, I mean. My my." Her face was red. "Sister Jaundice was a pet term from when Sister Jeanne d'Arc spent a couple of years as head of the infirmary at the convent in Waterbury, Connecticut. Tending the sick was not her strong suit. But don't call her Sister Jaundice if you know what's good for you."

"I have a bad feeling about all this," said Sean. "Is this the Sisters of the Order of Frankenstein?"

Jeremy had to concede it: the place had a Gothic aspect. Three stories of ivy-clutched gray stone, rusticated blocks with beveled edges, were capped with a roof of iron-brown slates and multiple gables and eaves. Forsythia planted on either side of the front door had gone mad and overgrown; the bare hoops of it looked like giant spider legs in the shadows. The granite steps were littered with leaves. "I ring," said Sister Alice, "so as not to startle Sister Igor, and I enter." It wasn't nice to hear her join their mocking, which made them drop it; perhaps, thought Jeremy as they followed her in, that was her strategy.

The place had clearly been built as a convent. Instead of an imposing reception hall with black-and-white marble floors and a sweeping staircase—no Mother Superior would ever allow herself to make that grand an entrance—visitors came immediately upon a second door. A screened window was inset at face height. "Another time, Sister Jeanne d'Arc will meet you here," said Sister Alice, "but today we pass on." She unlocked the barricade and led them through into a modest, walnut-paneled chamber. A few wooden chairs, an umbrella stand, and a painting of the Virgin looking gripped with a case of cramps. A sweet smell of a generic floor wax was fletched with tones of rising damp and stewing celery. Sister Alice groped for a light switch, but the wall sconces were fitted with electric bulbs whose wattage barely made it into the double digits. Very Eastern Europe, thought Jeremy. He didn't look at his friends.

The colored glass looked encrusted with bird shit. Sean said, "It all falls in place. The Addams family were lapsed Catholics. McAddams originally. Yes, that makes a lot of sense."

"And then Sister Jeanne d'Arc will lead you through here." Sister Alice pushed at a swinging door, revealing a long corridor that ran the width of the building. "The chapel is straight ahead—I'd

show you but I think the Sisters are waiting—the kitchens and dining areas down to the right, but we head here. Ow." She had walked
into a bicycle parked in the gloom. "Sister Clothilde and her weight
problem. We can't afford an Exercycle so she uses the real thing.
She's supposed to keep it in the laundry. Mind your way, fellows.
We're going to the sunroom at the end of the corridor."

At 7:30 p.m. the sunroom was, of course, devoid of daylight.
The furniture seemed to be shrouded in dust cloths, but when
Sister Alice pressed the push-button light switch, the dust cloths
turned out to be nuns.

"Holy Jesus," murmured Sean. "They're *baaaaaack*."

"You're sitting here in the dark?" said Sister Alice.

"Sister Felicity was saving electricity," said a voice from behind
the piano. "She was leading us in a guided meditation." Eyes were
blinking, chins were lifting. Nuns were coming around.

"Sisters, Sisters," said Sister Alice, "God be with you and good
evening and what are you thinking of? Where's Mother Clare du
Plessix?"

Some yellowing ferns in a pot waved and swayed, and an old
face appeared behind them.

Sister Alice Coyne went and extended her hand. After a few
moments, Mother Clare du Plessix brought her own hand forward,
and Sister Alice kissed it. "Have you brought the Cinnamon Cheerios?" said Mother Clare du Plessix.

"Yes, yes, and the Saran Wrap. It was a deal, two for one. I
bought twelve."

"We'll be dead and buried, the lot of us, before we use up twelve
rolls of Saran Wrap."

"Well, what about see-through shrouds?" murmured Sean.

The nuns were leaning forward. A half dozen of them, maybe?
In the dark, their faces looked almost as if done up in mime's

greasepaint. Sister Alice said, "Sisters, may I present my young friends from Our Lady's parish in Thebes; Jeremy Carr, and Sean, and—and—"

"Marty," Jeremy intoned.

"Young friends from *church?*" said Sean in a shocked voice.

"Marty," said Sister Alice. "Right. And boys, this is Mother Clare du Plessix, the ringleader of this crew of cutthroats and brigands."

"Sister Alice," said Mother Clare du Plessix in a tired voice.

"Yes, yes, well, I'm just excited, excuse me, please. I've been looking forward to this, you see. And, going round the room, here's Sister Perpetua, and Sister Felicity, and there is Sister Jeanne d'Arc. On the pew by the windows—"

"You have pews in a sunroom?" said Marty Rothbard. "This is a stricter life than I thought."

"They came out of the chapel after Vatican II made us turn the altar around. The new altar takes up a lot more space," said Mother Clare du Plessix. "The sun isn't good for the pews, but it isn't good for us, either, so we don't come in here much except at night."

"That's, left to right, Sisters Clothilde, Magdalene, and Maria Goretti," said Sister Alice. "Is that it? Where's the rest?"

"They've taken a vow of deafness." Sister Clothilde's face looked like one of those dolls made out of old stockings, all smooth-skinned but pouchy. She was leaning forward as if with some spiritual form of scoliosis.

"They weren't feeling well tonight?" said Sister Alice.

"Celery soup. It goes right through you," said Sister Jeanne d'Arc. "They didn't want to be up and down, up and down during the show."

"Show?" Sean used a raised-eyebrow tone of voice.

"There's not going to be a show. Actually." Jeremy was polite but terse.

Sister Alice was hardly listening. "But that's only—only seven of you. Ten sisters are upstairs?"

"All tucked in and saying their prayers," said Mother Clare du Plessix.

"I'll go upstairs and see if they don't want to come down—"

"Sister Alice," said Mother Clare du Plessix, "they are more eager for our report tomorrow than they are to experience the concert for themselves tonight." She smiled at the men; at least they thought it was a smile. "But may I say that we're all ears." She gestured to the piano.

"Do you take requests?" said Sister Magdalene.

"How about a nice round of *Pange Lingua*?" said Sister Maria Goretti.

"We're not a church choir," said Jeremy. Sister Alice Coyne was suddenly busy with the paper bags of Saran Wrap and Cheerios. "Sister Alice, I hope you haven't misled anyone—"

"I certainly hope so, too," said Sister Clothilde. "We're missing a rerun of *The Sound of Music* for this. How *do* you handle a novice like Maria? If you ask me, arsenic in her pitch pipe."

"Sister Clothilde," said Mother Clare du Plessix. "Custody of the senses—"

"All those musicals set in World War II, they all came out just when we got permission to go to films," said Sister Clothilde. "I always get them mixed up. *Cabaret* and *The Sound of Music*. I keep remembering Maria Von Trapp bringing those kids onto the stage in that Berlin beer cellar with the underdressed female orchestra. But I must be wrong."

"Please," said Jeremy. This was becoming a nightmare. "I'm not sure how this is going to work. Maybe it's a bad idea."

"*Maybe?*" Sean's voice was incredulous: part David Niven, part Dana Carvey as the Church Lady.

"We weren't intending to sing publicly for anyone," said Jeremy.

"They'll just listen," said Sister Alice.

"No harm to anyone," said Sister Felicity. She had a kind of palsy that made her look like a blur in the dim light.

"We won't even hum along," said Sister Perpetua.

"We can hardly hum any more without passing out," said Sister Clothilde, who, being sizable, was given to wheezing.

"No," said Jeremy. "No, Sister Alice. I don't want to be rude, but this is a no go. We're pleased to meet your colleagues and all that—and glad to chat with them, as I said, but we have to do our rehearsal in privacy. That's just a given. We're trying to thrash out arrangements for half a dozen numbers. No way is this a concert situation."

"Think of it as an offering—"

"It's just not possible." His friends weren't used to hearing him be so forceful. He didn't feel forceful. "If it's too much to clear the room tonight, then we'll just chat a little and begin singing next week."

"No, no, we know when we're not wanted," said Mother Clare du Plessix. "No harm done. Frankly, I would have expected the same if I were leading a chorus. Sisters, shall we repair to the lounge upstairs?"

"We'll make it in time for the wedding scene between Maria and the Captain," said Sister Clothilde. "As far as I'm concerned, the convent was better off without her. And whatever happened to that jilted Baroness? You can bet *she* never retired to a cloister to improve her pitch."

A small silence as they all—nuns and men alike—considered their own lives in light of the Baroness.

"She went on the stage at that Berlin beer hall, probably," said Sister Clothilde decisively. "A moral decline."

"I always hated that movie," said Sister Jeanne d'Arc. "Singing nuns. As if nuns have nothing better to do. Cheap sentiment, if you ask me."

"All sentiment is cheap to you." Sister Clothilde's scorn was faint but definite.

"Sisters," said Mother Clare du Plessix. "Sisters."

Sister Alice said, "I must not have been clear in my expectations of this arrangement. This is my fault and I'm very sorry. Assuming we can get our signals straight next week, Jeremy, how best should we proceed tonight?"

"I think we should just leave," said Sean. "We can't practice in public, and we don't sing religious music, and since we can get up and vacate the room faster than your sisterly sisters can, I say let's just get out of here."

"I can give you a run for your money on my bike," said Sister Clothilde. "Oh, I left it down by the front parlor. Well, next time."

———

"There isn't going to be a next time," said Sean, as they convened in the parking circle. "They're all lunatics."

"Oh, come on," said Jeremy. "They might be a bit talky, but they're not—"

"Talky? Talky? What, are we the first men they've seen since they entered puberty? That's not talky, that's compulsive. I'm not coming back."

But Marty was laughing. "They're not so bad," he said.

"So the lines got crossed," said Jeremy. "Big deal. They were probably babbling because they were nervous. It looked like a good piano, did you notice? I think it was a Bechstein."

Sister Alice came down the front steps. "Well, it's three to three, with Sister Clothilde sitting on the fence."

"Pity the fence," murmured Sean.

"What do you mean?" said Jeremy.

"As to whether to have you back," said Sister Alice. "This wasn't really what they'd been expecting either, frankly."

"Ooh, the nails come out," said Marty. "And what had you led them to expect? Pray tell?"

"At the very least," said Sister Alice, "courtesy, and perhaps as a bonus a little genuine interest in them. They are people, you know"—she whirled and pointed a finger at Sean Riley—"they are real people, even if they are nuns."

"Well, they used to be real people," he said.

"Watch your tongue," said Sister Alice.

"We're not in school, Sis-*tah*."

"You're guests in my home. I expected more of you. The singing, okay; they understand that. But to come and go in fifteen minutes? You're not high school freshmen. You ought to be able to converse with some elderly women. That was the deal."

Jeremy interrupted them. "Sister Alice, I'll call you. We'll need to talk. But it's a cold night, and I don't want Sean standing out getting the shivers. Do you mind?"

"Well sure, make me out to be the baby," muttered Sean, but he got in the car, and Marty gave a little wave to Jeremy as Babs growled to life. Having nothing to add, Jeremy got in his own car and followed them. At the end of the circular drive, looking back at Sister Alice, he noticed a few dark shapes in the windows of the sunroom watching them go.

By Friday Tabitha thought she might be going nuts. Was insanity contagious?

Her mother's unrelenting cursing, strengthened by a display of the fervor she had more commonly husbanded, seemed to be leeching into the paisley wall-to-wall. The house felt gummy. "Am right! Am straight!" over and over again. When Tabitha realized Leontina Scales was meaning "Damn right" and "Damn straight," she hadn't been able to resist shouting "Am mother!" when she served the supper, tater tots and American cheese. Her mother draped the cheese slices over the arms of her chair and then pitched the food projectiles at the enlarged photograph of the family that hung over the mantel, where they bounced back and landed in various paisley zones, like breaded fetuses floating in orange-and-purple wombs. Kirk fluttered about with a pair of hot-dog tongs, picking them up.

When Linda Pearl Wasserman rang to ask if Tabitha could open up the House of Beauty the next morning, since Linda Pearl had an emergency meeting with her accountant due to an IRS audit, Tabitha had leapt to agree.

"You'll be all right then," said Tabitha over breakfast. She was getting used to tooling around in her mother's car without aggravation, since Mrs. Scales didn't express any interest in going out.

"Eeking in tongues, on fire for the Lord," said Mrs. Scales. Which was about as good as it got these days, so Tabitha left in a decent mood. Between the Bible and reruns of *Scooby Doo*, there ought to be enough for Mom to suck on.

Linda Pearl's House of Beauty was midway on Niagara Street, stuck between the Dunkin' Donuts and a storefront that became H&R Block for twelve weeks a year and was otherwise a dive where flies went to commit suicide. A supply of available parking spaces suggested there'd be no opening rush at the appointment desk.

Tabitha pretended that it was her own salon. She dialed the thermostat up and tipped the blinds so that the sun could come shadow-striping the linoleum. She put the kettle on and turned the TV on but kept the sound low; Linda Pearl's set was old and could only get public television, and Bert and Ernie first thing in the morning was a little much. They made her feel stupid.

She set out the scissors and the gels. She folded the plastic capes and set them in the basket. Then she remembered to open the side door, the men's entrance. Tabitha knew this moronic necessity was Linda Pearl's nod to reality. When Eli Briggs had died two years ago and his barbershop over on Monument Street closed down, Linda Pearl had readied herself for an onslaught of male customers. She had someone in the high school art department make a new sign that said UNISEX and hung it from HOUSE OF BEAUTY. (One afternoon the middle school kids started chanting "Linda Pearl, Unisex," and that became "Linda Pearl, you need sex," so she had had to take the sign down. Too close to the truth.)

For a time Linda Pearl Wasserman was stumped, thinking that she'd blown her chance of cornering the shave-and-a-haircut market. The guys were going to drive all the way over to Cleary Corners rather than walk in a place that said "House of Beauty" over the door? That was guys for you. Then Linda Pearl had got Tabitha to get Caleb Briggs to come over and bust a hole in the side wall, and Turk Schaeffer had put in a door. A new sign said "Men Only: Barber Services." It stuck out on a pole from a corner of her building. Linda Pearl had stacked up a couple of empty six-packs of Bud on the sidewalk to get their attention, and she'd subscribed to *American Rifle* and *Sports Illustrated*. The men of Thebes were appeased. They could bring themselves to get their haircuts at Linda Pearl's salon as long as they entered through a side door that made no mention of beauty.

So when Tabitha opened the side door, she wasn't entirely surprised to see that governmental Jack-of-all-trades-Reeves waiting to have his sideburns trimmed. But she wasn't pleased, either.

"Well, well," said Jack. "You're looking pretty sprightly this morning, Tabitha."

"Morning, Mr. Reeves."

"What's the news on your mom? They say she had a run-in with the Roman Catholics. She feeling more like herself?"

"Beats me." Tabitha was used to being evasive, but in this instance was—somewhat accidentally—telling the truth. She didn't know how her mother felt normally, so it was hard to say whether she was feeling more or less like herself since this fit had come over her.

"She sitting up and taking nourishment?"

"She's home, resting up. And she prays a lot."

"That's our Leontina. But it's not like her to miss a PTA meeting. She wasn't there to take the minutes, and didn't call to get a substitute."

"She was—I don't know, watching something on TV, I think."

"Well, give her my best, and can you put me in the book for a trim at eleven?"

"I can give you a trim right now."

"You think I trust you near my jugular with a razor? Just kidding. No, I have to go check in City Hall and answer the phone emergencies."

"Linda Pearl is free at eleven. I'll put you down."

"You seem a little, I don't know. Everything *is* okay at home, isn't it?"

"Oh, just fine," said Tabitha. She said it again in a higher voice. "Yes, just fine."

"Hogan's been absent a lot this week. Flu?"

She wasn't overly fond of Hogan but she wasn't going to be used as a stooge against him. "Kirk is shaping up to be a good student, isn't he?" she said. "You must be surprised after me and Hog."

"Kirk's okay," said Jack Reeves noncommittally. "But I was asking about Hogan."

Suddenly she felt tired, though it was still so early in the day. She couldn't run interference for her mom and Hogan both; it was too much for her. "Mom needs looking after for a while," she said, as guardedly as she could manage. "It's kind of strange," she found herself saying. "We're not really sure what she wants."

Jack Reeves began to back away as if he suspected Tabitha was about to ask him to come over and give an opinion. "What you should do is go see Jakob Huyck. Pastor Huyck. He knows your mom as well as anyone, doesn't he? He'd be a good one to talk to."

She had almost thought of this herself, but the thought hadn't quite made it into words yet. She allowed herself to smile at Mr. Reeves for completing her idea.

When Linda Pearl came in, Tabitha was all ready to ask to be excused the rest of the morning. But Linda Pearl didn't wait even for the end of the hellos. "I heard the news," she said, throwing her Windbreaker on a chair and ruffling her hair to allow perspiration on her neck to dry. "You must be a basket case. You must be out of your mind."

"What news?" said Tabitha.

"Don't tell me you don't *know*?" Her pause was magnificently timed; her lobstery Bea Arthur voice dropped to a crawl. "Oh Lordy. Don't let me be the one to tell you."

"What?"

"Sit down."

"I don't need to sit down. What?"

Linda Pearl shook her head. "Do as I say."

Tabitha sat down. Linda Pearl drew in a deep breath. "Now don't blame me, I'm only telling you what I heard."

"Linda Pearl, if you milk this any longer it'll curdle."

Linda Pearl made the sign of the cross as if she were about to meet martyrdom face on. "Caleb Briggs is engaged."

Tabitha hadn't heard correctly. Had she? For a moment she thought, Did we get engaged that night? I was too wasted to notice? "Say what?"

"Your Caleb. Caleb Briggs is going to get married. Right after Christmas. I heard it at Bingo last night. It's all over town. Oh, Lord, don't cry, Tabitha."

But Tabitha was nowhere near crying, yet. "That's the stupidest thing I ever heard. He doesn't have a job. He doesn't want a wife. He told me that a hundred times. That was fine with me because I don't want a husband. Half the time I don't even want a boyfriend."

"Well, that's good, because now—"

"What are you *saying*?" Tabitha shook Linda Pearl's shoulders so hard that her retro flip nearly flipped out.

"Don't go postal on me, don't go nutso, it's not my fault." For strength, she unpacked an éclair from a Dunkin' Donuts sack.

"Linda Pearl Wasserman, you may be twelve years older than

me and maybe you are a little bit overweight and have given up getting married, but if an éclair means more to you right now when my life is like nuclear bombing all around . . ." She ran out of steam and couldn't think of a suitable consequence. "Well, you know what you can do with that éclair."

Linda Pearl put the pastry carefully back on its square of translucent paper. "Tabitha honey, I'm sorry. I just never did know how to break rotten news to people. When my aunt died by driving off that Thruway bridge that wasn't there any more, I mean the one that collapsed, I didn't know what to say to my dad except 'Female drivers.' Which was kind of stupid because female drivers are statistically less likely to drive off bridges that aren't there, I mean if they have a choice. My point is I didn't know how to be kind and I was nervous. I don't remember what I said next. I probably went and had an éclair."

She approached Tabitha gingerly as if trying to figure out the proper holds for being kind. "Forget it," said Tabitha, "I don't need a hug, thank you very much. Will you just tell me what you know? If you don't mind? If it's not too much to *ask*?"

"Sarcasm. I deserve it. Heap it on." Tabitha stayed silent. "Well, according to what I heard—Old Lady Scarcese at the Knights of Columbus Bingo night—he's marrying someone from over by the Glory of God Retirement Home. You know, that failed little set of townhouses that went into receivership and sold for thirty-nine-five each? The bitch lives there. She's some sort of a freelance attorney or something—"

"She has a *job*?" Tabitha was outraged. "You mean it's not some loser like Stephanie Getchen? You mean it's some real person? How dare he?"

"She owns her own home, Tabitha. She must be doing something right."

"What's her name?"

"Now, don't you get started—"

"I'm not going to ice her, Linda Pearl, I just want to find out what she looks like. They must know her name."

"I don't know if I should tell you." Linda Pearl's eyelids slitted almost shut, which was their natural station; it made Tabitha realize Linda Pearl had been staring wide-eyed at Tabitha since she'd arrived. "Tabby-cat, what if weeks from now Chief Jack Reeves walks in here and says to me, 'What do you know about Tabitha Scales and a bloody act of vengeance against the woman engaged to that sweetheart, Caleb Briggs?' It gives me chills thinking about it."

"For one thing, if Jack Reeves starts calling Caleb Briggs a sweetheart, you'll have a lot more to talk about at Knights of Columbus Bingo night than me. For another, Reeves is coming back in at eleven for a trim. I forgot to tell you."

"I shouldn't say. I never should. Polly Osterhaus. And God have mercy on my soul." She looked around at the razors that Tabitha had laid out on the counter near the men's side. "I'm going to count those babies every night, Tabitha, and if one is missing I'll know where to look for it."

"You didn't get enough sleep, Linda Pearl, you're wacko. And take it from me, I'm an expert on wacko these days."

"I was too excited. I couldn't wait to tell you, but I didn't want to call. How's your mom, by the way?"

"I need to go see—" But Tabitha couldn't finish. She slumped down on the stool suddenly and threw her head in her arms and began to wail. She knocked the éclair off the counter and since it landed gooey-side up—amazingly—through her cold hot cold tears she watched as Linda Pearl struggled with the temptation to rescue it for later.

I3

GINNIE PRESLEY, BOTH squint-eyed and dyslexic, needed Jeremy's full attention, and today he was more than glad to stay after school was released to give it to her. His part-time tutoring job was allowing him to duck the convent debacle for a while. He hoped that Sean would come around—and that the nuns would, too—but Jeremy knew that nudging Sean wouldn't work. Sean's loyalty would reassert itself without Jeremy's needing to go seductive. That he couldn't do, for the reason that he also had to leave Thebes—the reason that was just now pausing in the doorway of Mrs. Doorneweerd's room, and now speaking.

"Jeremy—what do you know. I wondered if you'd be here."

Jeremy blinked. Ginnie Presley took advantage of the diversion to shunt herself a bit deeper into his lap. From where Jeremy was sprawled in the antique beanbag chair, he looked up through the fish tank to see a wavery Willem Handelaers. The fish scrolled back and forth like a screensaver; the bubbles from the aerator stitched silver chains across Willem's face. Damn him, thought Jeremy, he still looks like a Greek warrior statue in mint condition—a Praxiteles clothed in L.L. Bean millennial fall fashions. The light through the fish tank gave Willem's blond voltage a kind of oxidized look. He took a step through the door. He was carrying one of his kids.

"Oh," said Jeremy. "Hi."

Ginnie said, "Hi," too, in a dubious voice, meaning, Jeremy inferred, *Get lost*. Willem took no notice and came around the fish tank, and Jeremy had to dump Ginnie off his lap and scramble to his feet. They shook hands as if they were concluding a deal in life insurance.

"This is Charlotte," said Willem to Ginnie, who scowled. To Jeremy, Willem said, "Her big brother Bartholomew is going to come to Mildred Cleary next year, and since I was in town I thought I'd stop and pick up the application for kindergarten. Charlotte, do you remember Jeremy?"

Charlotte Handelaers buried her face in her father's neck, just as Jeremy would have been inclined to do if Charlotte and Ginnie were suddenly struck blind. Charlotte rubbed her shyness deeper. Ginnie Presley, seeing her chance for escape—younger children always demanded more attention—said, "So I can go now?"

"You're going to take *Hop on Pop* home and read it to your mother tonight, right?" said Jeremy.

"If my pop lived with us, I could read it to him," said Ginnie.

"You read it once to yourself and once to your Mom, and next week you'll read it to me," said Jeremy, "and maybe we'll get to *One Fish Two Fish Black Fish Blue Fish*."

"*Red Fish Blue Fish*," said Ginnie witheringly.

"See, I told you you can read," said Jeremy. "So long now."

Ginnie hulked away like an eight-year-old factory worker after a day on the assembly line: shoulders down, head to one side as if too exhausted to hold it erect. "We know *Hop on Pop*, don't we?" said Willem, nuzzling into Charlotte. "Daddy knows it by heart. Didn't he read it to Bartholomew four thousand times this year?"

"Barty," murmured Charlotte, looking around for her brother.

"It's a good book," said Jeremy.

"But enough is enough," said Willem. "The simplest Seuss for youngest use now requires a good belt of Jack Daniel's. I was reading it to Charlotte the other day for the eighth time and got to the page about Red in bed, and found myself improvising. Rob, Rob, he likes his job. He does his job with the knob of Bob."

"So how's Francesca?" said Jeremy.

"He makes Bob bob, and throb, and sob."

"Your wife," said Jeremy.

"Before a mob."

"Francesca? Though not too much rhymes with Francesca. Except Fresca."

"Don't you remember Jeremy?" said Willem to his daughter. "Don't be shy, Charlotte. Look, he likes you. He remembers you. He's Daddy's old friend. Give Jeremy a kiss."

"Don't make her, it's okay. She doesn't have to like me. I generally don't even like myself the first half hour of every day, either, so no reason she should—"

But this must be a game that the Handelaers family played, for after Willem kissed his daughter on the beautiful round bulge of her left cheek, she turned with eyes down and pouted her lips incrementally in Jeremy's direction. "See, she will; she trusts you if I trust you," said Willem.

"She shouldn't, you shouldn't." Jeremy moved closer and Charlotte leaned out to graze his face with her lips. Then she arched her neck and turned her right cheek to Jeremy for a return kiss. He put his hand on the back of her corduroy overalls and came in a little nearer again, and kissed her. She wriggled a bit, but returned the kiss to her dad. Willem shifted his stance, flexing that marmoreal thigh under the chinos, closing the distance, and he kissed Charlotte on the lips.

"Willem, don't."

"This is how the game goes," said Willem, and Charlotte swiveled to pass the kiss on. Jeremy took in a sweep of breath, and then kissed Charlotte lightly, an airbrushed kiss. More of a graze, really. Charlotte delivered it back to Willem, who by now had circled his free hand around to rest lightly on Jeremy's hip. Some fingers migrated across Jeremy's bum, one of them stroking the top of the crease. "Mmm," said Willem. "Who's my baby? Who's my precious sweetheart?"

Jeremy knew that three seconds of this was about all he could stand. He closed his eyes for one moment, letting Willem and Charlotte both bow their heads into the hollows under his uplifted jaw. Charlotte smelled of the dust of dried cereal. Willem had a distant streak of vetiver laced beneath his toasty smoker's breath and the Saab-interior smell of his leather jacket. There were the memories of other, richer smells, hidden but implied, but Jeremy pulled away before allowing himself to itemize them and need them. "Really," he said coldly, "Mrs. Doorneweerd goes off to a staff meeting and look what the classroom aide gets up to."

"Gives a whole new set of possibilities to the idea of a Parent-Teacher Association," said Willem, but he moved away too, and jiggled Charlotte, who wasn't ready yet to stop this fun, either. "Hey diddle diddle, the girl's in the middle; Jeremy's over the moon," said Willem.

"Stop," said Jeremy, laughing. Out of tension. He knew how this went well enough to know that it *would* stop, just now; and it did. Charlotte let out a spiraling chortle, and kicked her feet to be let down.

"I hoped I'd find you here, actually," said Willem. He lowered his rump onto the radiator that ran beneath the windowsill. "How are you doing?"

"Oh, well. You know me." Jeremy picked up some papers and shuffled them without glancing at them. "I need to have myself arrested for abusing my own inner child."

"You're looking good. Health still okay?"

"Believe me, Willem, if the test comes back positive I'm not going to spare you the responsibility to comfort me." Here it is, right on schedule, always blurting out proof of my continuing need and regret. "I feel better and more guilty with each six-month period that I come away clean from the clinic. Though it's not as if I'm putting myself at any kind of risk any more. Thebes isn't exactly the Mecca for hot guys on the prowl for repressed liturgical musicians of the Catholic persuasion."

"Oh, Mr. Right, well, who's he?" said Mr. Right, grinning at his daughter, who had found some building blocks on a shelf.

"Ask Mrs. Right. How *is* Francesca?"

"She's doing great. Very involved last summer getting a new porch put on the house. She designed a pattern of brick and of ceramic tiles that was a real bitch to lay; they had to rip the whole thing up once because the footing was uneven. We were sorry you didn't get there for the harvest party we had; it was warm enough to be out on the porch a good part of the evening, even with the lake wind. Her latest obsession has something to do with stenciling the fireplace surrounds on the second floor, in order not to freak out over the coming global computer collapse."

"Well, tell her hi."

"She says hi. She knew I was going to look for you."

Well, of course; she wasn't an idiot.

"It's partly for her that I've come, in fact, to ask you a favor."

Jeremy sensed an easing of pressure, and an elevating of the usual sadness. Willem hadn't sought him out because of sentiment or bittersweet memory. Francesca had sent Willem here on a mission. So now I can be colder and more immune to Willem's charm. Whoopee. "Anything. What's up?"

"A friend of Francesca's sister Irene is getting married in a couple of months." Jeremy thought, Of course, he could always have just phoned me; and he felt cheap at his instinct to identify the escape clause, but grateful.

"I lost you," said Jeremy suddenly, "what's this?"

"Francesca and Irene's friend. I think you know her—Polly Osterhaus."

"Right, she's in my choir. She's an alto."

"Well, Polly's getting married. Just after New Year's, I think. And it seems you're not being invited to do the music."

"Why do you say that?" Jeremy was miffed. Polly should have told him her plans. It was embarrassing to hear depressing marriage news through the grapevine.

"Jeremy, are you listening? Polly is friends with Irene."

"Irene?"

"Irene Menengest, Francesca's younger sister. Polly has asked Irene to sing something at the wedding, and Irene needs some coaching and maybe an accompanist, and Francesca thought of you."

"Polly could have thought of me."

"Polly might not know how nervous Irene is about this. Or maybe Polly's, um, conflicted because she's not asking you to sing at her wedding."

"She should be. I'm her choir director. I intend to sulk the rest of the month."

"Will you help Irene? You know her, don't you?—didn't you meet her at the house last year? Bartholomew's birthday party?"

How touching, how stupid. Did Willem expect Jeremy to remember incidental friends and family members when he was visiting Willem's beautiful 1840s home, making steady and difficult peace with Willem's perfect 1990s wife, enjoying and being jealous of Willem's irreplaceable kids, his hilltop view out over Lake Ontario? Even his Irish setter, Clay, was sexy with that recherché bandanna around his neck.

"Oh, yeah," said Jeremy, "Irene. Is she the plump one with the beautiful dimples and the Guatemalan shawls and all? Sort of testy?"

"She's got a decent voice, but she's nervous."

"I could probably meet her a couple of times and give her some pointers, but I don't know about the actual wedding. Depends on when it is. I have some other plans for early January."

"She'll be awfully glad, and so will Francesca. I knew you'd do it; I told Francesca you would."

"I can do the rehearsal. I can't say I can make the wedding," said Jeremy, more pointedly this time. "Irene might have to get another accompanist, someone down from Watertown maybe, depending on what the piece is. I might not be here."

But Willem was already busy collecting Charlotte, helping her put the blocks away. He didn't hear Jeremy's announcement, and didn't ask what Jeremy was going to do, and why. Willem squatted in such a way that his knees angled out, and his shoulders hunched in, and his daughter was caught and giggling, encircled by his warm fatherliness. Together they put the blocks back on the shelf. Jeremy let himself notice the pull of stonewashed cotton trousers along the top of Willem's buttocks, the arch of spine underneath the leather jacket. He had all he could do to keep from going over and crouching behind Willem, burying his mouth in Willem's hair, slipping his hands into the pockets of Willem's bomber jacket.

But steady, steady now. Willem hadn't picked up on Jeremy's

cues. He hadn't flinched in alarm at the notion that Jeremy might actually be going somewhere else. Willem's not flinching was why Jeremy had to try again to get outa here. After a while, even a brave solitary barn swallow is fed up with its matchmaking kin, and either has to leave or else dive-bomb itself into the side of the barn.

14

JEREMY ON THE road, car doing the speed limit, or thereabouts. Car behaving. Car responding. Jeremy's tax dollars at work—as if I earn enough to pay taxes, he thought.

Car yielding to the driver's masterful touch, angling obliquely to avoid the work-zone cones. Then the car entering a lateral swerve, very minor but unsettling; maybe the slope of gravel making a temporary shoulder has been improperly graded, or it has slipped in wet weather. Or am I going faster than I thought? What is the speed limit on an escape route?

Losing my grip, he thought, in the endless instant in which the car and the ground refused to cooperate. As he recovered from the fishtailing and the car returned to firmer road surface, the flush of relief came first. The nervous system's response to rattle-scarum panic, the gin-fizz of natural opiates.

Calm first. Weird, welcome calm. A James Bond sort of insouciance, fingers rolling on the wheel even more lightly than before. (How against type for a Jeremy Carr. There's no such creature as a gay James Bond.) A mile or two later, he grew aware of a bitter after-odor, an oily residue rising to his skin, extruded damp, drying itchy. While the car purred homeward as if nothing had happened to it, Jeremy's palms sweated, his eyes refused to blink as if he might miss the next danger waiting to snare him. Unwilling now, or unable after his scare, to duck the memory one more time. The roadworks had flushed it front and center.

The Sad Affair of Willem Handelaers and Jeremy Carr. (Interesting how even in his own memories he took second billing.) An obsession? He had worried about that for a while. He had gone for several outpatient therapy sessions with a counselor down in Utica. The counselor had said, "There's always electroshock, you know," but Jeremy had decided to take that as a joke. Father Mike Sheehy, who had not been told the particulars of Willem's name or gender, had listened once to Jeremy and said gingerly, "Jesus said that we were to love one another as He loved us. Jeremy, what you need to remember is that love as a policy is stronger than love as an emotion. Perhaps this person needs you to be loving in a more distant way, so that this person's life can continue to unfold according to God's plan. Perhaps this is what you need, too." He had smiled at Jeremy through a kindly avuncular distance that was heartbreaking in and of itself.

But distance can be a kind of aphrodisiac, too, Jeremy had thought; absence makes the heart grow fonder, and foolish, and forgiving. He had thanked Father Mike for his thoughts and for the blessing, and he had said some Hail Marys like a small boy wobbling to stay up on the kneeler. And he had thought that love as a policy made a lot of sense for those who could manage it, and anyone who could manage it belonged in religious life. The rest of us have to struggle with the more ordinary love, the common or garden variety: love as a crippling condition. Love as a syndrome.

Transferring, after his second year at Lemoyne in Syracuse, to the SUNY Albany campus. A regimented forest of attenuated concrete pillars, three stories high, holding up a single perforated canopy that roofed the entire suite of academic buildings. The music department had murmured insincere enthusiasm for his soft-pop compositions. Well, not being lieder, or motets, or twelve-tone histrionics, or jazz: what could they say? But already worried about a tendency to duck and run from difficult situations, Jeremy decided to stick it out.

Late 1991—eight years ago almost exactly. Jeremy is twenty-one. Sees a note posted on one of those pillars advertising a get-together for students from the Thousand Islands region of New York State. Wanders over. Meets Sean Riley. Sean from Thebes, New York, a couple of hours west of the Carr family summer place on Larch Lake, the Adirondacks. Jeremy, who never trusts his reading of anyone's sexuality, hasn't guessed that Sean is gay, for all Sean's primping and camping it up. Jeremy has assumed it to be a takeoff on some sitcom character he's unaware of. Being unaware is a chronic condition for Jeremy, and he knows it. But Jeremy likes Sean, sort of, and if Willem hadn't shown up at the meeting too, maybe Jeremy would have succumbed to Sean's overtures. Once he'd recognized them for what they were. In 1991 he isn't, after all, wholly clueless, nor entirely virginal. Depending on the definitions.

And then what? Might Jeremy have been infected by Sean, or might Jeremy have kept Sean headlocked in a monogamous relationship and helped Sean maintain his health?

Love as a policy. Love as a syndrome.

But along comes Willem, showing up in the doorway the first time as vividly as he had done today. Willem entering the room, forced by the throng to back up almost immediately against the black lacquered door opened ajar against the wall. Some smitten track lighting manages to find him and turn him into a contemporary Renaissance ikon, with Rembrandt golden skin and a Memling-like acuity of expression. Almost a devotional portrait. A local saint. So this is what it felt like for knees to go weak. Where is a kneeler when you most need one.

Takes twenty minutes to get up the nerve to wander over. The opening sentences are lost to time; Jeremy hasn't been able to understand his own words even as he speaks them, or comprehend Willem's soft under-chuckle of a reply.

Willem is about five years older than Jeremy. A grad student in library science. Already developing an expertise in Internet connections for research libraries. Though his family has legitimate roots in the upper Hudson River Valley, *Willem* instead of *William* on anyone else would be risible. But no one cries *pretentious*; not at a legacy part Yankee, part Godsend. Those cheekbones, the swarthy Dutch lips, that jovial, mica-glinted sideways glance.

What do we talk about? Kuwait; Baghdad; Bush. World affairs, subjects as far away as we can get from me, standing here, and you, standing there. Previous flirtations and regrettable dalliances aside, this is the real thing. Jeremy knows it at once. What is Colin Powell's future? Is this the start of an Arab-American alliance? Someone turns up the sound; George Michael's "Freedom" is too loud. They begin to bellow, to no avail. The Mother of All Battles, you said? Hah. Push over the line. Invade me. Occupy me, you lovely swaggering bastard. Willem shrugs, can't fight over the noise. They stand shoulder to shoulder for a few minutes, almost touching, surveying the crowd as if looking for their future together.

The crowd eddies. A program begins. Jeremy mentions a bar across Western Avenue. Willem begs off. Disappears before Jeremy can even ask where he lives.

For the next six weeks Jeremy prowls the academic podium, trying to run into him again. He takes his sandwich in the lobby of the basement air well near Library Science, hoping their paths half-accidentally will cross.

But by now Sean has become a friend and has done some sleuthing, too. Willem is spoken for. "There's a *girl* in his life," Sean confides to Jeremy, a cautionary remark that also serves as Sean's coming-out flare.

Briefly Jeremy wonders if Sean is lying, in order to release Jeremy from the phantom graduate school librarian. To turn Jeremy toward his own arms. Months go by; Jeremy resists Sean, but he's almost given up on Willem. Spring arrives, becomes late spring. Forsythia yields to lilacs. A dreadful local weather hangs over campus, the stench of roasting animal remains from some nearby meat processing plant. One day when for once he has forgotten to keep his eyes open, Jeremy runs into Willem at the bus stop at the circle. Willem has a gown and graduate hood slung over one arm, and a girlfriend on the other.

"Already?" is all Jeremy can say, realizing: it's not meat, it's the smell of the future roasting. Someone has turned up the dial on the Whitney Houston power ballad: "I Will Always Love You" goes sonic. How can you already love someone if you have never loved him yet?

Willem's nonchalance unsettles Jeremy—has he misread all this? "I'm sure our paths will cross. We're from the same time zone, aren't we?" The girlfriend smiles with champion cheer; Jeremy wants to punch her lights out. "You're south of Watertown, is it—?"

"Utica," says Jeremy, "but I'll be in the Adirondacks this summer."

Lost, lost at sea, at night, in the woods, in the ocean depths, lost in space: but Jeremy wanders into the Library Science reception area. He knows he is good-looking enough to flirt successfully with the female assistant clerk, who against school policy releases Willem's home address. A Handelaer family address outside of

Antwerp, New York. He sends a postcard, includes his own home address in Utica and summer phone number at the lake. A message in a bottle flung into the abyss.

He is at the lake alone, spending his days playing his guitar and scribbling lyrics. He is twenty-two but having lost some credits in transferring from Lemoyne he has a semester left. It's slightly shaming still to be doing the Six Nations Ice Cream shack four evenings a week, but it allows him to sunbathe during the day and write music late at night. The lake house stands on a pretty parcel about eighty feet wide and six hundred feet deep: it was sold off from a big house next door in the thirties when the crash beggared even Manhattan magnates with summer estates in the mountains. The roadside chalet is shingled with cedar and roofed with copper, which makes the upstairs unbearably hot. Beyond, on a spit of land lined with poplars, the property points itself peninsular toward the two-story boathouse. His parents have a boat they rarely use any more, and the watery downstairs is spider-dense and full of mold.

The upper floor—Jeremy's domain—is reached by an outdoor staircase, and the single room is paneled in tongue-and-groove pine with walnut trim. There's the guitar, the desk, dirty clothes strewn among the fresh, a narrow single bed with high turned posts, liquid light rippling up through the floorboards along with the occasional spider. Two gabled windows on each side, and double doors at the far end opening out to a balcony overlooking the lake. Sometimes—the water is deep enough—when Jeremy comes home so late no neighbors could possibly be out in boats (and no one could see from their recessed houses anyway) he peels off his ice-cream crusted regulation Six Nations shirt and dives naked into the black relief.

He is about to reverse out of the driveway one afternoon when a car he doesn't recognize pulls in, blocking him. He's almost late.

Gets out to see what's what, and behind those sunglasses, hair a bit longer and blonder from the summer, lo and behold. "Tried to ring several times to say I was passing through," says Willem. "No answer, no machine."

"I, um, stay in the boathouse except for, um, coffee and the bathroom. So I don't hear the phone. And the machine's broken."

"The lady at the post office told me where to find the house."

Jeremy calls in sick. There's nothing in the kitchen, since Jeremy's parents aren't up till next week and Jeremy usually eats Six Nations tuna salad. They go get some ground meat and onions and a six-pack and some ice cream. They walk a bit around the lake. They talk like young nobles in German novels, they talk like Keats or Emily Dickinson or Blake, with what (in retrospect) seems embarrassing familiarity, about Liberty, and Honesty, and the Accidental Valor of the Heart. Jeremy feels himself to be home, in the way he feels at home in church. They talk the big stuff and nothing about the Girlfriend, or where Willem is driving to, and why his route takes him so out of the way past this obscure lake. And when he might need to get back on the road.

He likes the boathouse. He wants to canoe. Jeremy hasn't bothered to canoe in four or five years. They get it off the sawhorses and thwump it into the water and go out like Native American brothers at sunset. Willem sits fore, and the water kicked up from his paddle dots Jeremy's shirt, making it wet and cling to him; spurts into Jeremy's face; behind Willem's back he opens his mouth and drinks what is offered.

Willem says, swim? Jeremy won't swim. He invents a knee injury. Scooping ice cream too vigorously, wounded in the service of Six Nations. Jeremy knows he can't risk showing himself in a bathing suit: the only suit is a Seventies relic of his dad's that now fits Jeremy, a lemon colored Speedo that would hide too little of

Jeremy's enthusiasm. He hopes Willem will drop the subject, and he does.

They fry up burgers. Willem eats two. Jeremy pushes his around the melmac plate. They pull a single beer from the plastic grip of the sixpack, and sit outside until almost dark, but the bugs come up and they retreat to the lakehouse.

Willem hadn't known Jeremy was a music student. How could he? He cracks another beer and pops open one for Jeremy, too. Eventually Jeremy sings, knowing the songs are all wrong, not ready, but at least the pronouns are suitably vague. Two of these songs are about Willem and he doesn't even know it.

The dark deepens. The Harringtons in the big house, apparently launching a weekend house party, start blaring Depeche Mode. "Personal Jesus." Jeremy has to stop singing; he can't do battle of the bands with Depeche Mode.

He is twenty-two, and a young twenty-two. Ready now either to age, to move on, or to get stuck here, depending on what happens next. But he doesn't see that immediately. He only sees Willem's golden head as the sky in the screen doors behind him goes from electric violet to black. The light through the yellow lamp shade on the dresser bathes them in afterglow before the fact, and the warm paneling glows as if the boathouse were made of skin.

But he blathers, worse and worse as the minutes pass. Then Willem has to pee. A pee before getting back on the road? Jeremy directs him to the balcony. Easier than sending him to the house—what if he grabs his car keys, which are still on the kitchen table in there, and takes off? Jeremy looks the other way, fiddles with the guitar tuning before hanging it back up on the wall by its leather strap.

They trade places; Jeremy pees. Prepares something to say when he comes back in, because the conversation has been loping

in circles for a while as if searching for a campsite. When he comes
back in, he says, "I'm so glad you caught me before I—" but Willem is gone.

No, not gone. Sitting cross-legged on the bed with the last two
beers. He beckons. "I had to catch you; you sent me a postcard inviting me to."

Jeremy had said *Keep in touch*, true, but he hadn't expected Willem to get it. He approaches the bed as if the mattress is stuffed
with live grenades.

"Don't sing any more," says Willem.

"I should go, um, lock the front door."

"There are two cars in the driveway. No one will come and steal
the broken phone machine. Take a rest. You've been entertaining
for hours."

He can hardly stand it; he starts to pop up. Willem makes a
shushing sign with his finger and then he takes the last two beers
from the plastic webbing.

Opens one, opens the other.

"Usually, I don't actually drink much," says Jeremy, which is
true.

"Shhh." Willem takes the webbing and reaches for Jeremy's
hands, which he yields up in a state of disbelief. The first touch
of Willem's beer-cold fingertips almost severs Jeremy's spine. Willem says, "I've caught you, so I'm not going to throw you back.
I'm going to keep you." He feeds Jeremy's hands one at a time
through adjacent circles of the plastic webbing, yoking them like
handcuffs. Jeremy can't speak. Willem lifts Jeremy's hands gently
over his head, and pulls the webbing—through a third hole—over
the farther bedpost, so Jeremy has to lean back against the pillows.
His hands over his head, palms together like a dancer from Cal-
cutta. Like a boy in prayer.

"Now let's see about that bad knee of yours, shall we?" He gives Jeremy a sip of beer and lets froth foam down the buttons of the Six Nations ice cream shack uniform shirt. He undoes the buttons and his face comes near as one hand runs across electrified skin. Then he puts the beer aside and more or less tears off their clothes. How do they come off over the yoke? Jeremy can't remember. Maybe Willem rips them. Or do the very stitches come out of their own accord? The seams unravel? The shorts and shirts, blasted to the edges of the room by the force of their collision?

Later that night—midnight, 2, 4 A.M., they hardly sleep—they drop naked into the water to soothe their rosy rawness, inside and out. They swim and wrestle and fetch up upon the rocks like shipwreck victims clutching each other for life. A loon sends its serrated complaint out against the warning of morning, coyotes on a far hillside bay for forty minutes or so, and it seems they never sleep.

But they must do, for the next morning just before dawn they make love again, and leap from the balcony railing to wash the spume off their chests and legs and mouths, and when they emerge around the corner of the birches, Mr. Carr is standing at the steps with a plate of doughnuts and a Thermos of coffee.

"I was just going to leave these on the bottom step," he says, averting his eyes, but his voice is *indictment trial conviction* all at once. "We couldn't sleep last night and we thought we'd surprise you."

"Guess you did," says Jeremy, and that is all that passes between them on the subject. Ever. Willem leaves fifteen minutes later. Jeremy walks him to the edge of the road. Jeremy's parents' car is pulled onto the lawn since there has been no room in the driveway. His mother never appears at the porch or the door or even, as far as Jeremy can tell, a window.

What follows deteriorates in a half-life that runs on fast forward.

Jeremy and Willem send cryptic postcards with the beginnings of a private language that never has a full chance to develop. They meet ten, fifteen times. Until recently Jeremy has been able to catalog in sequence every one of their trysts, each conversation, each novelty of lovemaking, each panic at separation, each lunging reunion, at times so hot and eager as to appear, if someone from a distance were actually watching, as if they were in hand-to-hand combat. Face to face combat.

It is a whole life to Jeremy, and more than adequately compensates for the frondeur that his parents show. He knows, later on when his parents separate, that his being caught *in flagrante* has had nothing to do with it. Years later he thinks: but we might have only been being guy-sy guys, skinny-dipping like, like soldiers in Iraq. When at last this occurs to him, though, it is too late.

Jeremy doesn't go to his own graduation; by the following May, when he would have received his diploma, Jeremy's friends have already matriculated. And he can't bear to put his parents through a charade of family togetherness on his behalf. Besides, two weeks after the ceremony he skips, when he is back at the lake doing Six Nations Ice Cream one final summer since he has no job after college, a postcard comes from Willem saying they need to talk, but Jeremy should meet him someplace other than the lake. At a restaurant in Watertown. During regular dining hours. So there'll be no combustion of romance, apparently. Jeremy has seen this coming but denied his own eyes.

It is a difficult breakup. Willem requests it. When Jeremy balks, Willem insists. To this day, this very today in the classroom, Willem has never been able to say that he doesn't love Jeremy. That would have been so kind, if he'd only said it. But Willem has a weird code of honor that elevates truth over charity. Willem has said, over and over, "It's not what I want, not really; you're not who

I want." Giving Jeremy the obvious rejoinder, "I am who you want, it's just that you just want something else more." This Willem has never been able to deny.

He has, though, been able to say with honesty that he loves Francesca; he has loved her before laying eyes on Jeremy that day in the Student Union; he loves her still, and even more than before. He wants children. He wants a home. He wants her. "Shouldn't you understand this," he says to Jeremy, "you who believe in the holiness of the heart's affections?"

Since Jeremy's home life has imploded as well as his fantasy romance, he hardly feels in a position to argue. Miserably, Jeremy does understand it. He tries to hate Francesca Menengest, and he puts off meeting her. He won't go to their wedding, and he has to work as hard as he can not to send some dark reminder of Willem's past—a plastic grip from a six-pack, say, or a copy of *Personal Jesus* shattered into pieces with a hammer. Truthfully, he doesn't blame Francesca for loving Willem. How could Jeremy do that? Nor, when in the first of many attempts to put this behind him, he actually brings himself to meet her, does Jeremy find her despicable. She isn't conniving, proprietary, or superior. (She also isn't the blonde Willem was with that day in spring.) Francesca greets him, first and every time afterward, as if he is a distant and welcome member of their family. She seems a good partner, if obsessively alert to her House Beautiful and her Children First. She seems to know that hers is a Husband Interesting—of course she knows!—and with a thoughtfulness Jeremy has to admire, she even finds a way to absent herself when Jeremy makes himself come to visit them in Syracuse.

The past, an eternal force, always abuts the present, making of it a sort of wave of perpetual anguish that never finds anything to break itself against, and so keeps searching.

But why Willem, among all the possibilities? Jeremy knew his own native reticence was compensated, in the natural order biology and God decreed, by a winning enough form, face, manner. If he'd never been drop-dead gorgeous, he'd turned some heads, attracted attention he'd not intended to seek. And nice guys, most of them. So why hadn't he contracted the virus of first love with say, Gorgeous Gus, the gay volleyball T.A. at LeMoyne, who used to make the men's team do calisthenics in their jockstraps? Why not the guy in *Celtic Revival: Romance and Revolution,* who read Yeats aloud to Jeremy as if he were Maude Gonne? Or any of the mostly straight guys in the dorm who got tanked enough to accidentally bump into him at beerkeg blasts and not stop quickly enough, signaling curiosity, a willingness to be seduced? One of them even crawled into Jeremy's bed. Sex, maybe, but romance, the meaning of it: null and void.

Never any of them, never even close. *Willem, Willem.* Maybe only because of that mutuality: that he had shown up at the lake with his sudden lust timed to match Jeremy's own, before his own had faded. The combustible romance, prominent experience as it was of sexual ingenuity and risk and thrill and playpen wrestling, had served primarily as an armature on which, for a time, something else, love valid enough to deserve the term even when sex was removed from the equation, could climb, espaliered. Could root, flower.

They'd gone to a concert once. A chorale doing R. Vaughan Williams's *Five Mystical Songs.* The lyrics about the efflorescence of God's love cut and soothed at the same time. If God's love was eternal, then anytime anyone turned to pray, the attention was mutual. Willem, who did not indulge in the lingo of faith, seemed to feel something in the lyrics too, squeezing Jeremy's hand and stroking it until, in the auditorium, Jeremy's tears surged first and, wondrous shame, his come soon after.

How do you recover from that? Move on? Consign it to the Saint Vincent de Paul bin for recycled experience? Cherry-pick from its remains for song lyrics, for evidence of mistakes made, for clues to survival?

But *I moved to Thebes first*, Jeremy reminded himself. Sean Riley had grown up there, and Jeremy visited a couple of times. Seven years ago, when Sean rang to say his parents had heard there was a church musician's job open in their parish, Jeremy had applied— auditioned, really—and he'd been happy to go there from his father's new, cold condo in Utica. "Now there's two of us," Sean had said, "a town the size of Thebes, can you believe it?" And two became three, when Sean got a job in the paper mill and chatted up Marty Rothbard at a company pork roast one summer day.

Jeremy had dutifully met and joked and then sung with these guys, and he had tried to imagine a romance with either of them. Sean Riley was ready, always ready, and always would be; but Sean had never been a romantic interest of Jeremy's. He couldn't be. Sometimes Jeremy wished he hadn't been raised on the concept of romantic love; Sean looked as if he'd be great in bed. But Jeremy's heart was stopped: a rare condition among men, he deduced, being unable to care about sleeping with someone with whom I'm not in love.

When Francesca and Willem Handelaers decided to move to Monroe, north of Thebes, Willem had called Jeremy to ask if it was okay. "Of all the places in New York State, you have to move a dozen miles away from me?" said Jeremy. "I am supposed to believe this is just coincidence?"

But that, it seemed, was the truth. Francesca had inherited a great-aunt's home. They had come up to clean it out before putting it on the market, and had fallen in love with it. Willem was self-employed as an indexer and, with fax modem and the Internet, could work from anywhere in New York State. Francesca was pregnant with Bartholomew. They wouldn't do it, of course, if Jeremy was unsettled. "Of course I'm unsettled," Jeremy had said. "I've spent years trying to convince myself that I always despised you. You want me to regress?"

"I don't make demands of you," said Willem. This was true only up to a point. Without spelling them out, Willem made demands that Jeremy restrain himself, adopt a phony breeziness, endure casual encounters like the one in school today without complaining.

Willem kept a kind of distance, but his expression remained warm and confidential. Remembering how Willem liked to talk after sex, Jeremy suspected that Francesca knew most of the story. Willem's little *tendresse*—how sweet, and Jeremy such a funny puppy! Maybe it stoked some curious fires of their own marriage. But Jeremy hoped and believed that Willem had banked the richer memories of their affair in some corner that even industrious Francesca couldn't redecorate.

So the happy Handelaers had moved dangerously near, and Jeremy had stayed out of their way, and had kept waiting all this time for the abatement of need, of grief, of the sting of rejection. As Jeremy had grown more confident as a man, as a gay man, he had at least been able to laugh at himself. Was I that lousy a lover, technically, that I lost Willem not just for myself but for all of the gay brotherhood? And once in a while Jeremy had accepted an invitation to a party at the Handelaers, but always when there would be a dozen or more people around, so that when Willem failed to corner him in the pantry and attack him with whiskery rough kisses, it wouldn't seem too personal a slight. Willem was warm to everyone, as Jeremy was: that was always part of the attraction. But to see Willem with his arms around his wife and kids, or his sister-in-law or upscale

Monroe friends—it took all the juice out of the memory of their passion.

Yes, passion; the word that neither Sean nor Marty could bring himself to say without using the shackling quotes of irony. And Jeremy just couldn't bear to be another one of Willem's hail-fellow-well-met yuppie buddies. He didn't make enough money, for one thing, and for another he and Willem had burnished each other bright with coconut-scented massage oil and taken each other in every wrestling hold possible, and that still had to count for something, even though it was now almost a decade later.

His hands still stung; his underarms reeked. But he had returned to the present, however sorry it was. The involuntary reprise of the mothballed memory was done. For now.

As he pulled into the parking lot between Our Lady's and the Radical Radiants, he almost ran into someone pulling out from the other direction. A young woman—he recognized her—a girl, really. That daughter of the Pentecostal woman who got bonked on the head. The girl looked angry. She jerked on the wheel and gave Jeremy the finger. He sighed, and thought, if only.

He got out his keys and went into the church. It would be too cold for Sean here, and too cold for Jeremy after a few minutes, but the surprise visit from Willem still unsettled him. He folded back the piano lid and sat down, and put his head against the music rack for a minute. Then he flexed his hands a couple of times and began to play one of his own songs. He sang quietly, not so much a performance as a confession.

"There were lilacs by the side of the lake,
And the lake was silky steel.
One can be anesthetized by beauty,
Or one can remember how to feel.
You were sitting on the floor with your head in my lap

Which you had not done before.

There were lakeside lilacs nodding from a jar.

Sometimes I do not feel you any more."

It was the best he could do with what he had. It wasn't Whitney Houston, but at least it was his. The only thing he had been able to salvage out of all that wreckage.

15

ABOUT CALEB, TABITHA neither knew how to believe Linda Pearl Wasserman nor how to doubt her. Linda Pearl was a true friend, as true as they came, but how true was that? Tabitha had to admit that in tenth grade she herself had counted Gemma D'Agastino as a true friend. But then Gemma started ignoring Tabitha for that stringbean transfer student, Jayden Moody, and then got all emotional and distant and maybe got pregnant and maybe had an abortion (who knew because she wasn't talking to Tabitha any more) so the following May Tabitha had sent her a Happy Mother's Day card. Anonymously.

Tabitha had still liked Gemma, kind of, and it had seemed funny at the time. But on reflection, what kind of true friend would behave like either Gemma or Tabitha? What did Tabitha know about true friendliness? Could Linda Pearl Wasserman be trusted? Hogan's Magic 8-Ball said ASK AGAIN LATER four times in a row and the fifth time came out, exhaustedly, with MAYBE. So that was no help.

Still, Caleb was weirdly absent from his usual haunts and hideouts. Maybe this Polly person had had sex with him and then had to kill him before anyone found out. Tabitha knew the feeling.

Hogan and Kirk were no help, each of them mired in some

stupid high-school trauma she could care less about. Tabitha was on her own. Considering that Mom and her dissolving brain were parked in the living room and the world outside the house seemed tainted with millennial anxiety, the century was coming to a close with all the relish of a great big fart in a freezer bag.

Tabitha had taken to showing up for school long enough to be counted present by the homeroom monitor. But she skipped out before second period every day through the cafeteria's loading dock door. She drove to Thebes's sorry excuse for a downtown and pretended to be on errands for her mother. Shoplifting things like hairnets and rolls of chewable heartburn tablets that no teenager could possibly want. Just for practice. But really she was prowling for Caleb, store by store.

At night she walked the sidewalks. She felt she might break into every house in Thebes and find him in someone's bed, maybe everyone's bed. And then she might do that Polly person a favor and kill him herself. But how? Strangle him with an old lady's hairnet?

———

ON TUESDAY MORNING she found herself on the block of Union Street where the two churches on separate street corners squeezed the parking lot between them. The Catholic church was bolted but the Radical Radiant Pentecostal church was open, or at least not securely locked. She hardly expected to find Caleb in a church but what the hell, miracles happen. She was rooting through the lost-and-found box looking for something peppy to spruce herself up with in case she actually ever found Caleb, and whirled about when she heard someone approaching.

"Well, then, a lost sheep rather eager to get back into the fold."

Pastor Jakob Huyck wasn't expecting Tabitha Scales, but he wasn't too taken aback when he found her in the vestibule of Cliffs of Zion. He hadn't seen her since the day her mother had gone roamin' with the Romans—should look in on that poor deluded woman—and he had forgotten how beautiful the daughter was.

"Hi, Pastor Jake," she said.

"Stopped by for a little private prayer, maybe?—"

As if she'd just recognized the need, she said, "Can I talk to you?"

"I live to serve." He ushered her into his office. Huyck didn't have a wife who lived to serve him as a secretary/receptionist. So, though none of the good ladies of the church were around yet to tut at him, he left the door of the chamber open just in case someone came along. Propriety in the eyes of the Good Lord, he reminded himself, though he knew that the Good Lord's eyes weren't stopped by plywood doors from Iroquois Lumber.

He was proud of his consulting room. Unlike Father Mike's office around the corner, Huyck's walls sported no religious posters or offensive bloody art crucifixes that made Jesus look like a poster boy for Benetton. Instead, a slim anodized aluminum cross floated ethereally on a panel of black Chinese silk that itself floated against Benjamin Moore's Paul Revere Pewter, matte finish. A box of Kleenex was tucked behind a display of asparagus ferns that, he noted, were on their way out. Ah well. Ashes to ashes, dust to dust; it applied to houseplants as well as the baggage of the human body.

Though baggage was not quite the thing that sprang to mind when Huyck watched Tabitha fling her human body into the Danish Modern chair opposite him. She was at that early moment in the body's hurtle toward corruption when even dandruff and peeling sunburns seem attributes of mortal beauty. She'd make such a pretty addition to his congregation. Not for the first time, Huyck wondered why a tendency to faith wasn't transferred genetically along with snub noses and splayed feet. For Tabitha Scales, he knew to her mother's dismay, wasn't what you could call a devoted Christian.

Though she seemed to be trying to behave. He was touched. "Please tell me how I can help."

As she struggled to put her thoughts into words—perhaps she'd never been asked a kind question before—he rehearsed what he knew of the family. Dear Leontina Scales, that timid good woman. A divorcée, with this girl and two or three younger sons. The kids didn't come to service. Then Huyck remembered that for a while one kid, Kirk, had thrown himself into things. He'd taken part in the Christmas pageants for four or five years, starting as a bush and advancing through the roles of a star, a sheep with measles, a shepherd boy. The last time he had wanted to be the Little Drummer Boy and wear a ripped shirt open to the waist. "It shows my poverty," he'd argued. In nixing that, Huyck hadn't corrected him about what it really showed, but Kirk hadn't come back.

Tabitha said to him, "You know Mom. You know she had that hit on the head, and she was in the clinic over on Morse Hill Road. I think you signed for her release."

"Yes, well. Without a secretary things get in quite a muddle. I should come by."

"She just isn't herself, and the goons over at the clinic don't seem to get it."

"What do you mean?"

"She's just weird. I mean she does nothing but look at the Bible or TV all day long. She doesn't go out. She hasn't been back to church, have you noticed? And she's mean. She didn't used to be mean. She used to be, I don't know, kind of sickly normal. Now she's just sick. I have stopped by here a couple of times when I had to get out, but you're not here at night too often. You should come and see for yourself."

"I'll come over. Remember, Mother is recovering; probably just needs a little time out, too. Are you able to be there for her?"

"I'm not able to get *away* from her. Mostly I'm scared to leave her alone. She made me promise not to bring her back to the doctor. She's always been against doctors—says they interfere with the will of God or something. But she's not herself. It's spooky. You don't know what she's going to do next."

Huyck remembered that Leontina Scales had always had a tough time when the unscripted Glory and Praise segment began in the church hall. She fanned herself with the music booklet and closed her eyes and moved her lips, but nothing came out, and she had never gotten up to Sway in the Spirit. But he did wonder if her current ailment was a variety of conversion experience. The TV part was perplexing. Huyck had no use for what he called *the devil's electronic moving postcard from hell*. But when someone like Mrs. Scales threw herself into the Bible even more vigorously than usual, how could he be alarmed? "I will come and see her," he told Tabitha. "I should have before. Do you forgive me?"

Tabitha looked out at him from under a bush of airy bangs. He suspected she was raising her eyebrows in disbelief, though he couldn't see them. Then he caught it. "You've got something else on your mind."

"Look, Mom is more than enough on my mind."

"No. The sin of pride is my downfall, but I know my strengths, and I can see it in your need. Something else is going on that you're upset about. Do you want to talk about it?"

"Look. Pastor Huyck, I just came here to tell you about Mom. She's flaky. Kirk says she's lost the beginning part, I mean the front of her words. She calls us Abitha and Ogan and Irk. And she's taken to saying the Ail Mary, which I think isn't very Radical Radiant of her. Kirk goes, like, she's lost the beginning part in a different way. He says she doesn't know where to start, so she can't move. She opens the Bible and who can tell if she reads it."

Huyck closed his eyes. "I think it's you who don't know how to start. You need to tell me what's on your mind. I'm all yours, Tabitha." He had to look over at the anodized aluminum cross to assure Jesus and Tabitha both that he was speaking in a strictly pastoral way.

"Don't bother about me. I'm talking about Mom, and asking for your help. Isn't Mom one of your herd?"

"Cows make up a herd. Sheep make up a flock. Mother is not one of my cows."

"Well, I don't want her as one of my cows, either. Can't you do something? Nobody listens to me, I'm a stupid teenager."

"I'm sure you're not stupid. God gave you many gifts—"

"I came in last in my class." She folded her arms across that heavenly bosom, as if pleased to have given an undeniable proof of idiocy. "I've come to you for, um. Help. Isn't that your job?"

"It's not a job, it's a calling." This girl wasn't stupid, but she was no Miss Teen Challenge, either. "Look, Tabitha, I'd be remiss if I didn't say that I can tell you are upset. Something else is plaguing you. It's normal for a teenage girl to be resentful of Mother from time to time. You'll get over it, because you know the Commandment to honor your father and mother, and the Commandments demand obedience. I had a youth ministry in Little Falls and I know. There's another bee in your bonnet, and you can either tell me what it is or you can go away and regret that you didn't get it off your chest."

Her arms pressed that very chest even more tightly; the breasts nudged upward like water balloons caught in a pressure cooker.

He felt sad and old. "It's about a man, isn't it?"

"How would you know?" She sounded so wary that he knew he was right.

"Who is it? Not the name, I mean, but the circumstance."

"I'll tell you the name." She gripped the sides of the Danish Modern chair and leaned forward. "It's Caleb Briggs, and my friend Linda Pearl says he's engaged to some Catholic girl who has a job and a condo. And so what if I'm underage. I'm going to grow. How can he dump me without even telling me and get engaged to somebody, when my stupid mother is falling apart?"

"Do you love him?"

"I hate his guts. How could he do this to me?"

"Hey, let's put the brakes on. Love is gentle, love is kind."

"Love sucks. And Caleb has no business getting engaged to somebody without even telling me. Without even telling me, do you know what that means?"

"Calm down. Would you care for a soft drink? A Kleenex?"

"I'm not crying," said Tabitha, groping through the asparagus fern.

"Let it all out." Huyck handed her the tissues. "Love in its strongest form is a raw and powerful thing."

"Are you for real?" Tabitha sniffled percussively in several registers. "You're not even married, are you? What do you know about love? Caleb is a stud machine. And sometimes he's funny and he doesn't run over squirrels on purpose. He's the only thing that makes this stupid life bearable, and what did I ever do to him?"

"Did you give yourself to him?" He realized she wasn't sure what he meant. "Did you sleep with him?"

"Oh well, are you supposed to know about that? It's not like this is the police station, you're not Jack Reeves. I don't have to prove anything one way or the other, do I?"

"I'm not asking out of . . . I mean, it just helps to know how to guide and counsel you."

"It's none of your business. You're being creepy."

"The moral implications aside for a moment—and not far aside, mind you, we'll get back to them—are you adequately protected? I mean *birth control?* I mean condoms? There are all sorts of nasty infections out there, communicable in the most tempting of ways . . ."

"Pastor Huyck, you're very nice to be so nosy. But I have Linda Pearl Wasserman to advise me on all that stuff, and she's the county expert. I'm sorry I came here. I'm going to kill him, by the way, and then you can forgive me my sins before Jack Reeves throws the switch on the electric chair. It'll be a day of celebration in this damn town." She began to cry again.

"Are you pregnant?"

"Oh, wouldn't that be the last straw." She began to laugh. "I gotta get outa here. Pregnant! As if."

"The door is always open, Miss Scales. Miss Scales. Tabitha. Sit down for a moment. We're not done."

Tabitha didn't obey him. What a handful for her poor mother. "If you can come and see Mom, we'll forget about the rest of this. And if you tell Caleb Briggs I said anything, I'll run over you next. I'm a really bad driver. You should see my insurance rates."

"Tabitha," said Huyck. "I know the breakup of your romance with Caleb Briggs is awful for you. But you mustn't avoid it. You should go to him and release him. If he is engaged, he should enter into marriage with a clean slate. Go and finish things."

"Are you giving me permission to murder him because he's marrying a Catholic?"

Huyck became the tiniest bit fed up. "You must face your demons down, young lady. Embrace your mother, and face your demons down. That's my charge to you."

Tabitha considered Caleb, hunky tattooed Caleb naked in bed, laughing so hard that he snorted Genesee beer through his nose.

Frankly, she would rather embrace her demon and face her mother down. But Pastor Huyck clearly wasn't going to be much help in adding that crime to her list of civil infractions.

As she left, she dropped a couple of hairnets in the box of clothes for the poor. She found herself thinking. "Peace on earth, goodwill toward men." Maybe she'd try the Salvation Army next.

Pastor Huyck watched her out his window. The shoulders were down as if Tabitha Scales were a niece of Job, but her little Christian bottom maintained a definite sashay to it almost despite itself. He would have to stop by and check in on that Mother Job herself. Charity required it.

16

JEREMY HAD LEARNED not to mention Willem sightings to Sean. Some things were better left unheralded. Sean had enough on his plate without being reminded about Jeremy's obsessions. Once or twice, when Jeremy's reticence had slipped, Sean's affection for Jeremy took a turn for the sour. "Don't go looking for sympathy from me. That Willem plays you like a violin. You deserve what you get. That cock-tease. You slut." Sean's ire tended to ruin the mood, which was maybe what he intended. And maybe what Jeremy needed.

Luckily the next evening, on their second trip to the convent, Marty kept the news on, so Jeremy more easily avoided discussing the events of the week. When Marty finally turned it off, he said, "Did you hear they think that some relief pilot on that Egypt Air flight might have grabbed the controls and plunged the plane into Paradise?"

"Save us from holiness of every stripe and savor," intoned Sean. "Amen."

As Jeremy had been told to expect, Sister Jeanne d'Arc answered the door. "Who is it?" she called out. Scoliosis prevented her from being able to peer through the security screen.

"What, they're expecting the Chippendales?" murmured Sean.

"It's Jeremy Carr?" said Jeremy in a carrying voice. "Sister Alice said . . . ?"

The door swung open. "Fellows with cellos," said the nun, noting the bass that Marty was draped around. "A return engagement."

"Sorry about the misunderstanding last time," said Jeremy. "Glad your colleagues approved the idea of our making a second go of it. A quick hello, then we're off to rehearse."

"And we're not performing a concert," added Sean. "Not a note of it."

"Don't mind Sister Alice," replied Sister Jeanne d'Arc. "She gets in a muddle; she's young. Can't help it. Too much on her mind. Come along."

"Don't forget we also elected to return," said Sean. "By a slim margin."

Sister Jeanne d'Arc made a face at that, and considering the face she started out with—a kind of pouchy, plastic turnip with a high sheen—the effect was startlingly lively. "So we're truced then." She locked the door behind them with a key large enough to serve as a stage prop in a theater for the nearsighted.

The boys followed her. "We're obedient this week," she informed them. "We've vacated the sunroom for you. Those sisters who can tolerate a social life are finishing up some light housecleaning. Would you like to see the chapel while I signal your arrival?"

"Rather late in the day for housecleaning, isn't it?" asked Marty.

"At this hour we're usually in bed with lamps lowered. Those of us who decided to stay up and have a glass of milk with our guests, well, we needed to do something to keep ourselves alert. So we're Murphy-soaping the pews. Idle hands are the Devil's workshop, or so it was once thought."

"I don't need to see the chapel," said Sean.

"You know it then?" Sister Jeanne d'Arc's eyes brightened.

"I know chapels well enough to know I'm not going to no chapel of love."

"Don't deprive yourself. Ours is the most beautiful chapel in the province. The ceiling is covered with carved angels with spread wings. Copied from some parish church in East Anglia, we're told. We have the reference somewhere in the archives. Over a hundred angels hovering. You'll come see it, won't you." Not a question.

She arrived at the double doors of the chapel and glazed herself with holy water, and then began to tug with both hands at the right-hand iron doorknob. Her muttered "I can do it," prevented Jeremy from helping. Maybe getting the heavy door open was an act of corporal mortification, or served as physical therapy.

The chapel was dimly lit with light fixtures that reminded Jeremy of a Frank Lloyd Wright bank lobby. They hung from the ceiling like citronella candles, dark blue glass cylinders set in bronze cups. When their eyes became accustomed to the gloom, the guys could see some of the old nuns bobbing up and down along the pews, left to right and right to left, like mechanical targets in a shooting gallery. There was a mumble of prayer that died away as the sisters noticed the visitors.

"*Voilà, je vous présente* the Chapel of the Sacred Heart." Committing the sin of pride, old Sister Jeanne d'Arc, Jeremy was tickled to notice.

The room was a good size; it could hold several hundred. The walls were paneled halfway up in oak or walnut, interrupted by pilasters and heavy mosaic entablatures of the Stations of the Cross. Above the walls ran Palladian window frames with colored glass showing the Life of Christ in a fashion evoking late Victorian illustration, right down to the crosshatching on Pre-Raphaelite faces, though at this hour on a November evening the colors were flat and oily. A choir loft ran along the back, and the altar area was fitted with white and green marble fixtures and walls that made Jeremy think of an expensive Hollywood bathroom. The style was less Gothic than he had expected, except for the Crucifix on chains over the altar. Spanish baroque? The Christ in torment looked like something done by an artisan in the West Village.

"Holy Je-*sus*," mumbled Sean.

"Pray for us," intoned Sister Jeanne d'Arc. "Note the ceiling, now."

There it was, an entirely improbable flock of angels, all sprung from the same nest, of the same parentage. Divine replicands, spored or cloned or multiplied in the Highest sort of mathematics. The whole ceiling was a rookery for angels. Their chins sported an acorn rotundity, and the noses a knobbiness, but the angel eyes were painted instead of carved. The heads bobbed at intervals like the knots in a chenille spread. The wingspans, oddly flat, looked as if carved out of sheets of balsawood, but the wingtips met each other like ducks in formation in an Escher print. Ducks flying to be angels, and back again.

The angels were set at on a bias, so that their heads all faced the center seam of the pitched roof and slightly forward, altar-ward. It gave the grandeur of the room an angularity that seemed modern, surprising; it made the room appear to be suspended in motion, as if the angels were dragging the space beneath them toward the sanctuary.

"How many of you are there?" Marty sounded as much in awe as Jeremy had ever heard him.

"Depends on which you're counting. One hundred and four-teen angels, and seventeen nuns. Back in the old days, the hey-day of the Order, this chapel wasn't even big enough; we had to seat the postulants and novices in the crypt. Do you want to have a look-see?"

"I'm definitely not for crypts." Sean sat in a pew and lowered his head. Jeremy knew it to be a parody of being lost in prayer and hoped the nuns couldn't tell.

"As you wish." Sister Jeanne d'Arc led Jeremy and Marty up the central aisle. The other nuns bobbed their heads in silent greeting as the guys passed, but kept on with their labors. The smell of lemon wax surged with almost medicinal urgency. Jeremy guessed that they would return to find Sean waiting in the hall. His lungs weren't all that forgiving these days.

Sister Jeanne d'Arc pointed to the terrazzo floor. "Beneath the chapel on the left side is the boiler room," she said in a whisper, "but beneath, on this side, runs the oratory and crypt. Partly for heat conservation and partly, I think, due to sensible planning for the future, the Superior General approved this scheme of floor grilles at intervals along the side corridor." Sister Jeanne d'Arc pointed to a perforated iron panel set flush in the floor. About the dimensions of a coffin cover. Through the ornamental fretwork, the light fell on some sort of a sarcophagus in the crypt. "Seating for an additional forty-five below," said Sister Jeanne d'Arc. "When we were at peak numbers, we had dispensation from Rome to house the overflow down there, and thanks to the grilles the community technically could still attend Mass as a single body. Come down; this is where we stockpile the Mother of our community, Mother Regina Sainte-Foi."

Jeremy thought, why do the living adopt such a giddy tone when referring to the dead? As if there's escape for any of us. Is it anything other than black humor, the glib callow relief of being alive still?

The stone steps dropped into a musty, ill-lit area that seemed more like a wine cellar than an auxiliary chapel.

"Mother Regina, *requiescat in pace*." Sister Jeanne d'Arc blessed herself with two fingers and tapped the lid of the sarcophagus with two fingers as if requesting Mother Regina's attention. "No one is sure if she's actually buried here, and we daren't ask for permission to look. There was a confusion when she died about whether she'd intended the Order to have its primary headquarters in Canada or in the States, and there were Sisters on both sides of the border who had strong opinions about it. The pertinent paperwork that verifies Mother Regina's exact spot of final rest has gone walking, as they say in the video rentals. But we believe she must be here, for she helps keep the roof over our heads."

"Nuns rent videos?" Marty put his hand on his chest as if suffering a touch of angina.

The sarcophagus stood on a stone dais directly beneath the foremost grille. The spiky remains of some wildflowers littered a nearby plinth, and soft damp dust felted the horizontals. The sisters upstairs had resumed their prayers, and Jeremy guessed it was the rosary in Latin. Through one of the grilles he could hear Sean clear his throat and cough ostentatiously and get up to leave.

"It's almost an ossuary," said Sister Jeanne d'Arc. "A chapel of bones. A charnel house. Isn't it wonderful?"

Marty said, "You have black Masses down here?"

She shot him a look. "That's not even funny, young man."

"This place is seriously clammy. You've got some standing water over here," Jeremy pointed out.

"Even sanctuaries require maintenance," said Sister Jeanne d'Arc, "more's the pity. Alas, thanks to the lake effect, lots of rain and snow dumps on the chapel roof above those precious angels. We've never been entirely watertight. Sister Maria Goretti had to squirm out the window from the side of the choir loft and climb up there recently with another stretch of tarpaulin we got from the Army-Navy shop."

From his childhood Jeremy recalled reruns of *The Flying Nun*, that paper airplane of a religious woman, but if he remembered correctly, Sister Maria Goretti was shaped more like a giraffe. "Sister Maria Goretti goes out on the chapel roof? No way."

"Not till there's no other choice," admitted Sister Jeanne d'Arc. "But we can't let the angels get water-damaged; they're irreplaceable."

"So, I assume, is Sister Maria Goretti."

"She caught a tickle; it was a blowy day." Sister Jeanne d'Arc made a dismissive motion with her hand. "She's offering it up. She's in bed tonight, feeling lowly. Anyway, we've done what we can for the time being. I'll have to come down here with a mop and bucket and get this puddle. Keeps you hopping. Shall we?" Suddenly she seemed tired of the tour guide business and she genuflected at the edge of the crypt as if considering just staying behind and saving herself the trip up the stairs.

Having collected their rags and supplies and returned them to a rolling cart in the hallway, the other nuns were already leading Sean toward the refectory, which was at the opposite end of the first floor corridor from the sunroom. Jeremy found himself struggling to remember which nun was which. The oldest seemed to be Sister Perpetua, who looked like a rag doll in her black serge habit. Her eyes were rheumy and her upper lip creased, and she had a weedy little chin like a catfish. For all that, her step was more sprightly than Sister Jeanne d'Arc's, and her head jerked about to follow what was being said the way a parrot's head moves, in sharp, offended gestures.

Mother Clare du Plessix was not large the way Sister Clothilde was large—Sister Clothilde was flabby; Mother Clare more like a Mission-style hutch, broad and square and airy-looking. Mother Clare seemed silent; one eye strayed outward from time to time. She hunched her shoulders up and dropped them regularly;

perhaps she was engaged in a Socratic dialogue with herself, or perhaps her camisole straps were binding. She was heavy in the front.

Sister Felicity, all aborted cartwheels and hesitant *bourrées*, seemed to have been given the wrong name. She proved to be the worrier among them; she scurried back to make sure they'd turned off the light switches; then she scurried forward as if scared of the dark. "Oh, the milk, the hot water, and so on," she said, and plowed ahead with her head down, disappearing behind a swinging door. "The kitchen," said Sister Jeanne d'Arc. "Sister Felicity's special charge."

"Sister Felicity's penance," said Sister Perpetua.

"No, our penance," said Sister Clothilde, huffing. Her hugeness was sweet, like a puff pastry, and she turned to grin at the visitors. She might just be an airhead, thought Jeremy; with the constitutionally cloistered, it's so hard to make a judgment about normalcy. As he knew from personal experience.

In admonition Mother Clare du Plessix said softly, "Sisters," and they passed the kitchen, from which issued the sounds of a kettle smashing on a stovetop.

Sister Magdalene came the closest to the kind of nun who inspired holy terror in schoolchildren. She had a backbone like a coatrack, and long skeletal fingers. She was the tallest of the lot. Her bones creaked audibly. Alone of the old nuns, she eschewed the veil; her hair was silvery and sparse, and close-cropped like a crusty old City Desk man in a Fifties newspaper drama.

Sister Magdalene and Sister Clothilde opened the doors to the refectory and tucked their heads down, tacitly inviting the guys in. After the grandeur of the chapel, the refectory was plain as pudding. Extra tables were piled two deep, tops together, so half the room seemed a forest of table legs. At the other end, the walls were kitted out with long aluminum counters bare of anything but boxes of dried cereal. The effect was a little clinical.

On one table the nuns had laid out a repast. Some white plates thick as dinnerware, some heavy, well-polished silver knives and spoons. Cups and saucers, a little wicker basket of Celestial Seasonings teas, and a pound cake squatting unceremoniously on a platter too big for it.

"Bless us, Jesus, and in Your Holy Name may we be nourished so that we may nourish others," intoned Mother Clare, at a clip. Even before the perfunctory "Amens" the boys were being pushed to take sections of yellow cake with marmalade spooned on the side. Sister Felicity came barreling through with another metal tray on wheels—not unlike a hospital cart—and provided hot water and milk for the tea. The noise of stirring teaspoons echoing about the high-ceilinged space made Jeremy feel he was a thug in a warehouse conspiring with hit men.

"If we could sell it as a retreat center or a retirement home and move ourselves into a little ranch house without all these stairs, we'd be a lot better off," said Mother Clare, regarding the bowl of her spoon with some dismay. "I fear the tarnish has caught up with us again."

"We are none of us what we once were, alas," proposed Sister Clothilde.

Mother Clare looked a bit chagrined, but she turned and said to Jeremy, "Please tell us something about yourselves. Let me get your names straight. I know you're Jeremy, Sister Alice Coyne does nothing but sing your praises. Jeremy Carr, is it? And the others— if you would be so kind?"

"My short-term memory's so unreliable, I sometimes can't even remember what . . ." said Sister Clothilde. Her voice trailed off and she stared into the middle distance.

"Sister!" said Mother Clare. Sister Clothilde jumped. So did the guys, but then they realized Sister Clothilde wasn't being startled out of vagueness, she was being chastised for being flip.

"Well, my apologies," she said, in an unrepentant tone, "but in fact I *can't* remember their names."

Jeremy said, "Jeremy Carr. Sean Riley here, and this is Marty Rothbard."

"That's a mouthful," said Sister Perpetua. She glowered warmly at Marty Rothbard. "Were you named after Saint Martin of Tours?"

"I was named after Herman Martin Lefkowicz of Flatbush."

"I never heard of that saint, but they're letting anyone in these days. You used to have to suffer to be a saint. Now it's good works, good works, good works till the cows come home."

"He's my uncle, and a devout Orthodox Jew."

"I don't hold with Orthodoxy," said Sister Perpetua. "All that chanting and incense, and black-robed ladies ironing in the back of the basilica. The things they get up to. You can't fool me."

"Sister Perpetua," said Mother Clare, "our young friend isn't Catholic."

"Oh well," said Sister Perpetua, "neither was Saul till he got a yen to see Damascus. I guess there's time."

"I'm actually not shopping for a religion," said Marty.

"Tell us something about the Order," said Jeremy. "Sister Alice Coyne told us the name and the address, not much more. You're not the hermit kind of nuns, I take it."

"We are cloistered only by circumstances," said Mother Clare du Plessix.

"Come again?" said Marty.

"I don't mean to confuse. There are several types of religious orders. The Sisters of the Sorrowful Mysteries are an active order; we work largely in teaching. It's only in this extended old age that we verge, willy-nilly, on the contemplative. By which I mean that, by the default of our age, we confine ourselves to prayer and meditation and silence, as some sisters in other orders do from the moment they enter as young postulants. Aiming for the Grand, or Profound Silence."

"Not us. We were active. So we're not freaks," said Sister Clothilde, helping herself to another slice of pound cake. "We know the world in all its modern ways. Though we reserve the right to disapprove."

"In actual fact," said Mother Clare—it was as if she were speaking to herself; that wandering eye gave her an even more ethereal aspect—"the Sisters of the Sorrowful Mysteries, though an active order, were never as well integrated into the modern world as many other orders. Though we weren't cloistered, our missions tended to be boarding schools for girls, and our Superiors General usually chose to locate us remotely. Hence this upstate plantation out in the middle of nowhere."

"But was there a school you taught at around here?" said Jeremy. "I grew up in Utica; I don't know the history of Thebes well—"

"This was the New York Motherhouse," said Mother Clare, "and it still is, though the Montreal house has superseded it in worldly vigor. Which is to say that young girls came and studied here as postulants and novices before taking their final vows. They were then assigned to one of five schools we maintained in New York and Pennsylvania. Since the closing of the last school a decade ago, we've had no place to send new sisters. But then, we have no new sisters to send. It's been twelve years since we welcomed a sister into our community."

"That's why Sister Alice is allowed to work at Our Lady's?" said Jeremy. "There's nothing for her to do here?"

"Oh," said Sister Clothilde, pointing to the tarnished spoon that

Mother Clare du Plessix had criticized, "there's plenty for her to do. But Vatican II encouraged individual preferences and professional callings among the members of the community, and then, I can't tell you—"

"—all hell broke loose?" That was Marty; he couldn't help it. But the sisters smiled.

Mother Clare du Plessix finished Sister Clothilde's remark for her. "Some of us took to the new liberties with aplomb. Some did not."

"I'll never forget my first cup of decaf coffee," said Sister Perpetua. "I'd never been able to manage caffeine—it gives me the jumps—but if you couldn't manage caffeine you did without, and were grateful for the opportunity for humility. As far as I'm concerned, the best thing Vatican II did was decaf. All the rest of it, those fashionable veils and attractive skirts, and doing away with the *serre-tête*, it seemed dubious to me then and dubious to me it continues to seem, thirty years later."

"Then there was *The Nun in the World*, by Cardinal Suenens, that groundbreaking book." Mother Clare looked with raised eyebrows, clearly expecting recognition in the faces of her visitors.

"Perhaps," said Sister Felicity, overturning the sugar bowl as she reached to dab some crumbs off the Formica tabletop, "perhaps our young friends still think that The Nun in the World is a contradiction in terms."

"Of course not," said Jeremy. "Sister Alice is a wonderful example. She zips about in her own little car; she knows a lot of people in the parish. She has a good sense of humor. She can balance the books better than Father Mike. She's good with kids. She's not too holier-than-thou—"

"Not by quite a long shot," said Sister Clothilde.

"She is a fine example of the nun in the modern world," said

Mother Clare du Plessix with a firmness of tone, as if this were the vestige of an old argument. "We are all proud of her."

"But really," said Marty, "the stuff of being a nun is pretty archaic, you got to admit it. I mean, I'm not Catholic, but all those vows. It isn't what you'd call natural."

"Vows of poverty, chastity, and obedience," said Mother Clare. "The easiest vows to take. What could be more natural than to focus your attention on overcoming—"

"Vows of *poverty* and *chastity*?" said Sean. "This is really beyond the pale, don't you think? Guys? Though vows of obedience could be fun. Depending."

"We're going on," said Mother Clare suddenly. She turned and smiled at Sean; at least they guessed she was directing her smile at him. "We have so few people to talk to. It's why we're so pleased you've come. Tell us about yourself, dear boy."

Jeremy could see what was coming; Jeremy could see Sean itching to erupt with an in-your-face routine like some outtake of *The Birdcage*. He was chewing the corner of his lip for a cigarette, though he'd given them up after the first pneumonia scare. And this is my cross to bear, thought Jeremy, that I can't stand to see this collision about to happen.

But Sean only said, "If you want to hear confessions, let's start with Jeremy, shall we. Something's going on with him. He thinks we don't notice. Maybe you can ferret it out of him."

Damn Sean, damn him. Eyes like a hawk, like Joan Rivers. Jeremy bounded to his feet. "We *will* sing for you; we need to warm up," he declared. "Tea's done, and many thanks. Then we're off down the hall for our rehearsal. This has been great. Will you tell the others we missed them? Come on, guys. Something *a cappella*—" But he wasn't about to suggest one of his own pieces. Even as dry cuttings of the full people they might once have been, the nuns were too attentive. And his songs were too, well, confessional. "That Haydn round," he decided. They'd heard it at an AIDS memorial service in Little Falls a few months earlier, and it was easy to pick up. "The words are by Galileo, or reputed to be," he told the sisters.

"Well, he's been forgiven by Rome, so go on," said Mother Clare.

Sean was looking at him with curiosity, contempt, weariness. "Jeremy. I hate to bring up dementia, but the deal was we weren't going to sing. Can you possibly have forgotten?"

"We forget things all the time," said Sister Perpetua. "More tea?"

"I just thought," said Jeremy.

Sean was livid. "What's up with you today? You can keep to your half of the bargain, Jeremy. We're doing this whole thing for you. The music thing, the convent thing, the whole shit-and-shebang of it."

"Now there's a phrase I never saw in my breviary," said Sister Clothilde, as Sean glared at Jeremy and he shrugged. Sister Clothilde went on. "We know a Haydn round. Is it the same one? Do you mean the Star Carol? We can sing it to *you*. And then you can be dismissed to rehearse."

"I'll go tune up," said Sean, "on my own," and he stood to leave.

Sister Clothilde, on a watery little note, began. "Though my soul may set in darkness, it will rise in perfect light."

"I definitely don't need this. Deal-breaker, Jeremy," said Sean.

"Chill, Sean," said Marty.

Jeremy closed his eyes and started in at the third repeat, as Sisters Felicity and Perpetua joined their voices to Sister Clothilde. "I have loved the stars too fondly to be fearful of the night—fearful of the night."

"You owe me," said Sean, as the nuns began the round again.

The sisters sat with their hands in their laps and their eyes cast down at first, as if they were hostages testifying to their abductors. Mother Clare du Plessix looked up, her wild eye gleaming. Members of one flock, the other nuns allowed themselves to lift their eyes as well. Sister Perpetua ticked her forefinger back and forth like a metronome. Sister Clothilde grinned. Sister Felicity pursed her lips and her eyes teared. Sister Magdalene, who had not spoken all evening, was the only one not singing. Sister Jeanne d'Arc folded her arms about her habit and mouthed the words, though no sound came out. When the round had dribbled to a close, there was silence in the refectory for a moment.

Then Mother Clare du Plessix said, "Saint Cecilia, patron saint of music, you must be looking down on us tonight."

"That wasn't so bad," said Sister Perpetua, "given that I wandered off pitch in 1966 and I've never found my way back."

"Good night, ladies," said Sean. He was paler than he'd been, and Jeremy thought the vast icy room with its yards and yards of stainless steel counters had taken on the feel of a mortuary. "I hardly have to say I don't believe in anything like 'perfect light,' and I find it offensive."

"Mr. Riley," said Sister Jeanne d'Arc, "you're a singer, I'm told. And what we were singing, or pretending to sing, was a song."

"Souls setting in darkness," said Sean. "Puh-lease."

"We're closer to that particular darkness that you are, actuarially speaking," posited Sister Jeanne d'Arc. "Cut us some slack, brother."

Sean didn't bother to argue with them, but a fermata of unsaid ripostes hung in the air among them all, until Sister Clothilde said, "Isn't it nice to have a good look at some men?

"Well, you know what I mean," she continued, when all the sisters gaped at her.

17

Pastor Jakob Huyck studied the house on Papermill Road for a moment from his safe haven in the sad little Volkswagen Rabbit from which, at this stage in his life and in its, he would have preferred to be parted. The passenger door was kept closed with a bungee cord. The thoughtful brethren who had donated it for his use had been more kind than tidy. Something powerfully dairy had spilled into the upholstery once upon a time. Huyck had shampooed the carpet and the backseat, to no avail.

No crying over spilt milk. For his own spiritual integrity Pastor Jakob Huyck demanded that he consider this proverb whenever eyeing a comely young maiden out and about in the streets of Thebes, or any other streets or rest stops on the highways and byways of the Empire State, for that matter. He hadn't taken a vow of chastity himself, as it wasn't a condition of ordination for the Cliffs of Zion Radical Radiant Pentecostals; but he was expected to comport himself with dignity as befitting his station. Meaning—to spell it out, as he did frequently—that the sins of the flesh were forbidden him outside the bounds of holy matrimony, in which case presumably they were no longer sins and therefore, paradoxically, no longer quite as interesting.

He had been afraid to be married to check out his theory, for marriage was everlasting in this business, and that was a risk he wasn't prepared to take. Not that he didn't indulge in the odd fantasy from time to time. He wasn't perfect, and that was why Christ had died on the cross, for the forgiveness of his sins. And Huyck was a red-blooded man who knew the difference between satisfying a biological urge in the privacy of his own home and a crime against femininity and God and, quite likely, the laws of the State of New York.

But he did require of himself honesty. He admitted that it wasn't concern for Mrs. Scales but the allure of Tabitha Scales that had brought him to this curb of a Friday morning. He would know this and guard against it, and concentrate on the matter at hand. In the name of the great Eighteenth-Century German Pietists. In the name of all that was true and upright and free of idolatry. In Jesus's name.

The house was hardly more than a bungalow. It crouched behind overgrown arborvitae with a self-loathing air. Leaf-clogged gutters, rain stains on the siding, which was that rippled, ridged kind of prefabricated shingle, once painted a caboose red though now sadly faded to bloodstain. A TV antenna tilted against the cement-block chimney. Trees in the backyard—white pines—rose ominously, separating the house from the line of Adirondack foothills he suspected would otherwise be apparent.

The trees seemed to crowd the house even lower, divorcing it from its context of neighborhood; not unlike a stage set, actually. What play was about to unfold? A salvation play, he told himself, trying to avoid the thought of a shaming little farce featuring himself as the silly and unfulfilled gentleman caller. Oh yes, he knew pastors were figures of fun, even in this largely devout rural outback in the luff of the Tug Hill Plateau. Such was the curse of television, demoting and defrocking and defiling every last vestige of authority left to America. He only tried, and prayed, to be good despite it, a blameless example of Radical Radiant Pentecostal charity and steadfastness for the heathen, which he was always tempted to call the heathren.

And Tabitha Scales as the heathen sacrifice. Or, better yet, the pagan princess ripe for conversion. Downright moistened for conversion.

No doubt about it, he had to toss out those Bill Moyers tapes on Joseph Campbell; it was clouding his thinking. He threw open the door of the car and marched up to the house and rang the doorbell.

"Pastor Huyck, here to see your mother," he said to the shadowy figure who answered. Huyck smiled against temptation and despair.

"Lucky you." An unreliable teenage voice trying to be growly. "Just a mo."

The door closed and it reopened a moment later. Tabitha, pouty and perfect.

"Oh, it is you," she said. "I thought Hog was pulling my chain."

"Hog. Your brother," he ventured. If that was her boyfriend he feared the worst.

"Yeah, till I can figure out how you can divorce a brother. Come on in."

"Call me Pastor Huyck." He sucked in a breath and his stomach, too, as he had to brush past her in the doorway. *She didn't move to make room for me; she let my belly graze her forearm.*

"It's an interesting day for you to come," said Tabitha. "She's up and out of her chair today, in and out of every room, like a cat in heat. She's down in the basement now. I don't know what she's looking for down there. She's into all the old boxes and stuff. Photos, maybe, or her divorce decrees."

"Will you tell her I've come to call?"

"Well yeah, sure. Hogan? *Hog.* Go get Ma."

The boy who'd growled at him emerged from the kitchen doorway where, Huyck suspected, he'd been standing just out of view, listening. Hogan was one of those kids who look middle-aged before they finish adolescence, as much in the lost, unexpectant look in their faces as in the way they've already let their bodies go. Hogan Scales; Huyck remembered him now, though like his older sister he rarely darkened the door of Cliffs of Zion. He had a gas station attendant's shirt on with the red letters of his name picked out on the blue cotton. His stomach bulged sloppily. What a brooding, bitten-off expression under those simian eyebrows! "You won't remember me," began Huyck, holding out his hand.

"No, I probably won't." Hogan turned back into the kitchen and disappeared down a flight of steps to the basement, saying, "Ma, pull your clothes on, the minister's here."

"Kirk isn't home," said Tabitha. "He's at school. He's usually back by now, though; any minute, I guess."

"Shouldn't Hogan be at school too?"

"Another month and he's old enough to be a legal dropout. I think he's practicing."

"I'm sure he's helping take care of Mother."

"Well, duh. I can't hang around here all the time. I got things to do. Saturday mornings I got Linda Pearl's House of Beauty to open up. Mom is a basket case but Linda Pearl needs help, too. Act of charity, Pastor Huyck."

So she remembered his name; that was good.

"While we're waiting for Mother, can I ask you if you are all right?" He pitched his voice soft so she would have to lean in to him to hear.

She put her hair in her mouth and twined one leg around the other like an eight-year-old. Since she was wearing running shorts, it gave Huyck an impression of female calf and thigh more intensely athletic and—*particular*—than he'd experienced in some time. He almost lost his faith right then and there. Why didn't anyone ever talk about the bright night of the soul? Cheap strawberry shampoo.

"If you mean have I managed to find forgiveness in my soul for Caleb Shit-hole Briggs, the answer is *no*. But I have to admit I keep forgetting to look for it."

"Have you seen the lad?" The lad? The *lad*? Mercy, he was talking more and more like a Merchant-Ivory film. Thebes might be a bit out of the loop but this wasn't a time warp, for crying out loud. Beauty was doing it, beauty was turning him into an archetype. Only he wasn't sure which one. He hoped it wasn't the trickster, the minotaur, the fool. He couldn't remember the others. Except for the hero. He was pretty sure he wasn't the hero. "Have you seen your boyfriend?"

"I haven't had the time," said Tabitha, with a little spark of something that Pastor Huyck admired—was it maybe pride? Stubbornness? "When Mom gets up here you'll see; she's not herself, but figuring out who else she might be, and where her real self is—well, maybe you can. You're the God guy."

For an instant Huyck only heard her say "You're the god—" and he felt his vocation crumble in flames; then he took the whole thing in and behaved himself accordingly. "You must face your demons down," he reminded her. "Don't carry around your love for this man; it'll fester and metastasize and make you crazy. Go to him, dismiss him from your life, give him room to grow and change. It's not just a kindness to him, you know. It's what you need, too."

"So you said, but how the hell do you know what I need?"

"The charism of discernment," he replied, but she seemed to dismiss that as a topic beyond her ken or her interest, and anyway here was Mrs. Scales, clutching the arm of that homely bear-son of hers.

"Leontina. My word. How are you." He went forward to give her a pastoral embrace. She recoiled so fast that she knocked the toaster off the metal folding table.

It was a shock; Tabitha's words of warning hadn't been sufficient. Mrs. S. looked—well, grotesque. It wasn't the muscle-slackening that attended a stroke, was it?—no—and it wasn't that she looked as if she'd been groomed by a gorilla, her hair all on end like a fright wig. It had something to do with the hollows behind her eyes, as if—though Huyck prided himself at trying to avoid distracting poetic metaphors. So never mind.

But that foul and brilliant light in Mrs. Scales's eyes. That, and why didn't her children see to her clothing better. The striped trousers and flowered blouse and free-ranging goosey hair made her look like a circus clown on crack.

"I ought to have come to see you sooner," said Huyck. "I have been remiss. How are you doing, Leontina?"

"Ooo are you?" she said. "Ooh is this?" she asked her children.

"God," said Tabitha in disgust, "see what we mean?"

"Odd?" said Mrs. Scales. "In this house?" She curtseyed at Huyck in a mocking way.

"Ooh, she's on a roll today," said Hogan. "She thinks you're God. Want to work some miracle and make her better, God?"

"Shall we sit down?" said Huyck. This was far worse than he had expected. "May I?" He moved aside a pile of newspapers and some paper plates with pizza crusts stuck on them, and sat down. Tabitha laid a strong hand on her mother's shoulder and pushed her into the Colonial-style rocker-recliner with field and stream upholstery. There was a noise from the kitchen, and the other child came in, home from school, apparently.

"We have company," called Tabitha. "The pastor."

"The exorcist," said Hogan.

"I don't think so," said Pastor Huyck.

The returning student came in and kissed his mother, who received his peck without acknowledgment. Kirk. Yes, a bit of a wuss, as Huyck had remembered him, but now that he saw his brother Hogan at close range, he understood Kirk a little better and forgave him his lisp.

"I can see that things are in a state," said Huyck. "Perhaps I should talk to your mother alone for a few moments."

"Ooh has the time?" said Mrs. Scales. "Eave me be. Too busy to flap my lips at you." She clawed her hands over a Bible standing on the metal tray; it was covered in toast crumbs. "Eating the Bible, that's the only nourishment I get."

"Eating the Bible?" said Huyck.

"I told you, aren't you listening?" said Tabitha. "She's lost the front part of her sentences. She doesn't mean eating the Bible, she means reading it."

"Oh." Then he laughed. "Well, but that's a good sign! Man does not live by toast alone, but by every word that comes from the mouth of God! She knows where sustenance lies."

"That's not much help when she won't go out of the house any more," said Tabitha. "I've tried to get her to go back to the doctor but she won't budge."

"If you've got a doctor who's not being helpful, we can get Joanie Buselle in here," said Huyck. "She's not a Radical Radiant Pentecostal but she's a good solid nurse. She's the only one that Herm Mendoza allows to take the stitches out of his toes when he sews them up to make webbed feet. She's good with people. And with ducks." Suddenly he felt there was some room to be hopeful. "I like the idea of eating the Bible. Something so good, something so rich and rewarding, why wouldn't you want to eat it all up?"

"I used to eat the Hardy Boys," said Kirk helpfully.

They all stared at him. Leontina Scales went, "*Pfffff*," like a balloon venting.

"Daddy Wally gave us a whole set of Hardy Boys from way long ago, like World War II days," Kirk explained. "In a box, about thirty of them. Printed on this rich, creamy, thick cheap paper that had gone all yellow, and the edges didn't line up neatly like in modern books. Every page was a different width. When I used to read them at night—since Hogan doesn't like to read, and Tabitha doesn't either—"

"Tabitha *can't* read," said Hogan.

Behind her mother's back she gave Hogan the finger. "Oh, my," said Huyck, but it came out sounding admiring.

Kirk was oblivious. "Well, I used to rip a strip off the margin of the paper and wad it up like a piece of gum and chew it while I was reading. When the paper had lost its taste I'd flick it out onto the wall behind the radiator. There's still a huge clump of dried spitballs, clutching like a coral reef. I ate my way through the entire Hardy Boys."

"You would," snickered Hogan. "Who'd you enjoy more, Frank or Joe? Or could you manage to take them together?"

"You're so lame," sputtered Kirk, but the presence of a minister in the house apparently aborted any other response. The boy turned scarlet.

"At least if I was going to eat books, I'd eat Nancy Drew. I'd eat her and eat her—"

"You perv." Tabitha landed a backhand slap on Hogan's crown. "You're sick."

"Hey Kirk, did you ever try eating Tom Sawyer? How about, um, Hamlet. Since you're into meat. Or, no, I know, I know: I know what I'll get you for Christmas! A copy of *Moby Dick*! I'd like to see you try to swallow—" He howled with dry fake laughter. Kirk got up and—well, Huyck would have liked to think that he stalked out of the room, but the pastor was afraid that, technically, it was a flounce. The boy needed someone to slip him a copy of *Playboy* before it was too late, but this was outside the arena in which Huyck could sensibly work. He sighed, and thought: Mother married three times and no husband around now; the daughter has a reputation that verges on slutdom, the older son is a bully, the younger son a sissy. What a holy little family.

"I do think I should talk to your mother alone," said Huyck. He had allowed himself to neglect his duties and to abandon his authority in the face of Tabitha's biscuity appeal. It was time to do his work. "Tabitha, Hogan—"

But Mrs. Scales seemed to have had enough, too, even before they'd started. She dumped the Bible onto the folding table and wheeled her arms about, signaling that she wanted to be pulled to her feet. "Air is the house of God!" she cried. "Air! Air!"

The others looked around themselves. Did she want the front door open? It was a bit stuffy, but that was the heady strawberry lotion.

She lurched across the braided rug to the bedrooms that opened off the other end of the room. "Air is it!" she wailed. She pushed open a door. Tabitha and Hogan stayed still, looking defeated.

"Now she's back to stalking, great," said Hogan. "What, we gotta get a leash?"

Huyck told himself to be the adult these children sorely needed, and he followed Mrs. Scales. "Air is the house of the Lord!" she said, through clenched teeth, standing in the middle of a bedroom. Huyck guessed it was Hogan's room. A bank of black-sheathed stereo equipment flashed more colored lights than the cockpit of a 747. Posters showing some pretty athletic-looking women alternated with posters of Megadeth. A mound of clean laundry was dumped on the unmade bed, and a pile of paperbacks was topped with a pamphlet that said "So You Want to Join the Army." Half hidden under the pillow was a dog-eared copy of one of the Narnia books. *The Last Battle*, it looked like.

Mrs. Scales turned and passed by Huyck as if he were part of the ugly furnishings of the room. He felt cheapened. He followed her.

"Air is the house of the Lord!" she said again, only more to herself, and shoved through the second bedroom door.

"Mom," said Kirk, and turned his head to the wall. He'd been having a little cry for himself. Jesus, in your infinite mercy help these people, said Huyck to himself. Kirk's room was Spartan compared to the mess in the rest of the place. There was a Save the Whales poster showing a whale arcing through outer space. Shoes were lined up punctiliously on the closet floor, and on the radiator cover, clusters of plastic ivy leaves surrounded an eight-and-a-half-by-eleven color photocopy of one of those Renaissance paintings of Saint Sebastian looking just a hair-trigger short of sexual ecstasy—oh, the handwriting was on the wall here.

"Do you *mind*?" said Kirk in a fawningly polite voice. At least the kid was capable of sarcasm, that primary tool of adolescents everywhere.

"Air is the house of God!" Mrs. Scales pointed her index finger upward.

"Do you mean *there* it is?" said Kirk matter-of-factly. "Up there, there it is? Or do you mean *where* is it?"

"*Air* is it?" she jabbered, excited.

At once Huyck was able to recognize the challenge of the moment. This was the skill that made him such an effective minister. "I shall take you there; that's why I've come," he said. "I shall take you home. You are looking for your true home, not your earthly home; and I shall show it to you. Come with me."

"Actually, she was looking for something in the basement," said Hogan loudly, from the other room.

"It's okay, Mom," said Kirk, sighing. "We'll go with you."

"I'm not going nowhere," called Hogan.

"Go to hell," said Tabitha.

"Not there either."

"Get your mother her coat," said Huyck. "Tabitha, will you join us? We're off to the church. Your mother is looking for her beginning, for where she starts; she wants to eat the Bible, she needs to be where it's baked. Come on. Her true home is in the house of God. Isn't she saying so? Come *on*."

"God, another boss," muttered Tabitha. "Three daddies aren't enough, we gotta have Daddy Pastor too?"

They had to tilt Mrs. Scales into the backseat of Huyck's Rabbit, because he was afraid she would forget about having to hold the bungee cord and then she might go bouncing out onto the road. Kirk climbed into the back with her and held her hand when she would let him. Tabitha got in front and folded her beautiful bare legs—they must be icy cold!—into the space as best she could. The knees angled toward the shift, and every time Huyck went into fourth his knuckles grazed her knees. "It's November, you're crazy to go out like that," he told her.

"Put on the heat, why don't you."

He put on the heat and the speed, and they were pulling into the parking lot in less than twenty minutes.

Leontina Scales swiveled her head around with a wary look. "You know where you are now, Mom, don't you?" said Kirk. "Look, Cliffs of Zion. You want to go in?" Her children scrambled out of the car and tugged her out of the backseat. She seemed uncertain again. A cold wind arose, ripping the brown leaves from around the roots of the lilac hedge, tossing them over the parking lot.

"We'll enter God's house, and pray for mercy," said Huyck. He was back on home turf now. Even Tabitha's leggy splendor seemed muted here. In fact, he should probably advise her that she was not properly attired for the circumstances, but in the light of the needs of her mother perhaps he would let it go. Huyck put an arm around Leontina's waist, and pivoted her toward Cliffs of Zion. Just as neatly she slipped her waist out from beneath his arm, somehow, and she hurried in a determined, animal-like way in the other direction, across to the side door of Our Lady's.

"Oh Lordy," said Huyck. "Don't tell me we've lost her to Rome."

She flung the door open and hurtled herself inside. The Scales children and Huyck followed a few steps behind. Mrs. Scales stood poised on the landing for a moment, then plunged down the stairs. Huyck prayed that Father Mike Sheehy had locked the door to the kitchen, but his prayers apparently didn't have much currency in a Catholic church, for the door to the kitchen was easily flung wide, and Mrs. Scales barreled through.

Following, they found her on the floor beside the refrigerator, lying like a corpse, hands folded over her breast, eyes open. She was training her gaze on the top of the Kelvinator where, if Huyck had the story straight, a crappy old statue of Our Lady had been lurking, waiting for its victim. "Other of God, pray for us sinners," said Mrs. Scales.

18

CLOUDS FROM ONTARIO dredged the lake, dragging meat-locker air across apple orchards and gravel pits and spurs of abandoned railroad lines, up the sloping plain to Thebes. On his way from the grade school—Jeremy took a half-day's sick leave so he could pick Sean up at the mill—he passed three buggies, their bearded drivers and bonneted wives looking as if they'd been driving toward a funeral since the Nineteenth century. Amish from up near Morristown, probably; you rarely saw them down this far. Jeremy decided not to mention them to Sean.

"The saintly Jeremy doing his duty of charity again." Only Sean could sound put out at being catered to. He all but fell into the front seat. "Fuck, it's icy. Is your thermostat broken or what?"

Sean kept cranking the heat up, but every time he closed his eyes and leaned against the headrest, Jeremy twiddled the knob back down. He was afraid he'd doze in the coziness and crash on I-81.

He trotted out a couple of limp remarks—"Can't believe they've still got those north-bound lanes closed; it's gonna take us hours to get home" and "Don't suppose you've managed to hook up with your Hector at some salad bar"—to which Sean only grunted in reply. They lapsed into silence; this had become part of the routine.

On the way to the outpatient clinic at Saint Joseph's Hospital in Syracuse, Jeremy had learned not to probe about Sean's blood profile. They pretended they were going to some concert out of town. Right in step with Sean's knee-jerk denial instincts: Jeremy knew that Sean hauled his ass off to Syracuse instead of to the clinic on Morse Hill Road so no one in any blood lab there might recognize him and blab to his folks about it. "In my own time," he'd once barked at Jeremy. But would the time still be his own when, at last, Sean had to let them know?

Sometimes they sang, and that was useful as well as fun. Sean's Irish tenor could improvise complementary harmonies and counterpoints to lend character to Jeremy's melody. Later, Jeremy often found himself rewriting lyrics to reflect Sean's more oblique take on the straightforward sentiments he tended to produce on his own. The numbers still essentially Jeremy's, but as fed through Sean's more wily sensibility.

But though Jeremy began to hum some of the pieces they had worked on at the convent last week, after the nunaholic love-fest, Sean didn't rise to the bait today. Jeremy hoped this didn't mean Sean had even weightier concerns. He could be so contemptuous when you asked a question that sounded too Miss Manners. Yet if you treated the thing openly—T-cell counts, bogs of depression, breathing problems, the protease inhibitor cocktail still not quite taking?—that tetchy streak of Sean's kicked in too. Though Jeremy hated to think of it in these terms, it was as if Sean were saying, You avoided being intimate with me in any of the ways that were attractive, Jeremy, so you've forfeited the right to be intimate with my dying.

Fifteen minutes before they reached the Syracuse city lines, Sean roused himself a little. "What kind of plans do you have for Thursday, by the way?"

"The usual somewhat chill invitation from Dad to come home. I told him I can't. It would be a kindness, but he gets in this weepy limbo of missing Mom and I can't deal."

"I don't follow. They got divorced, and he goes to pieces when she dies?"

"It's called the mystery of human misery. But he's got his brother and ninety thousand nieces and nephews, every one of them straight and functioning. He can focus on them. I just remind him of Mom. I look like her too much."

"So what are you doing by way of our annual feast of gluttony?"

"Church in the morning, then I don't know what. Father Mike invited me to join him and Sister Alice. Going out. Olive Garden maybe."

"You haven't said yes?" Sean cracked his knuckles. "You're waiting to see if sweet Willem calls?"

But Jeremy had been expecting this and he blatted out a Phyllis Diller horseshit laugh. Unconvincing, but useful as a segue to his own question about Sean's plans.

In brogue. "Oh, laddie, it's the purgat'ry of home agin, for me sins don't you know. Sure and doesn't himself deserve it." Sigh. "It'll be Thanksgiving by the numbers. Macy's Thanksgiving Day Parade, Super Bowl, Norman Rockwell's recipe for stuffing, the whole nine yards. I'll put myself on autopilot and aim for the post-turkey L-tryptophan slump."

"Big crowd of relatives coming?"

"Connie, Maura, Mike and Siobhan, Uncle Finny and Aunt Chieko. Uncle Francis and Aunt Mary Pat, Uncle Pat and Aunt Mary Frances. Dad will be half crocked by halftime and Mam will burn at least one hand and probably two by forgetting the potholders. If we're lucky the dog won't throw up on the sofa before the scorched pies are served."

Jeremy's laughing was a little forced. "Why do you go? You could come to my place and have spaghetti and tuna fish with me. Or you could join Sister Alice and Father—"

"I'm not that prodigal. The convent life once a week is enough for this little lapsi-daisy, thank you for asking."

"Well, offer's open if, in the next coupla days, you happen to have a conversion experience and want to dine with the professed—"

"That's what I'm afraid of. Some conversion experience waiting up ahead to ambush me when my defenses are down. I'm trying to make it out of this life alive, if you know what I mean." But that was too direct, so Sean muted it, blunted it, by beginning to warble a troublesome bridge they'd been working on, and Jeremy joined in.

When the song faltered, Sean looked out the window at trash blowing out of wire baskets and said, "And don't think you're going to sit on my deathbed and pray me into submission, either."

"*Moi?* I'm the soul of probity. I do my best to keep my faith in the closet along with my red satin pumps."

"Hah. The original exhibitionist, more like it. I never saw anyone wear their convictions more ostentatiously. You might as well have a scapula over your sweatshirt and a rope of rosary beads swishing from your belt loop."

"I did that in grade school, don't remind me. In fourth grade when we had to write essays about what we wanted to be when we grew up, I wrote that it was a cross between a fireman and a saint."

"You just wanted to sleep in a room with a bunch of guys and get to slide down that pole in a state of excitement—"

"I wanted to be martyred by the Iroquois like Saint Isaac Jogues, assuming that there must be some Iroquois left here somewhere, like dinosaurs in the lost valley or fairies at the bottom of the garden."

"Yeah, fairies at the bottom of the garden, I'll bet. How your dad must've loved you. Did you envision being tortured for your faith first?"

"You mean by the fairies or the Iroquois? Well, a little. But not very painfully. I thought they would admire the strength of my faith."

"You'll never make it in this world, Jeremy. They talk about re-covering Catholics, but you're beyond recovery."

But *beyond recovery* was a phrase too near. They both shut up as Jeremy hunted for parking. All too soon: the antiseptic air of Saint Joe's, the whoosh of the door as they pushed through, the ping of secret codes sounding over the public address system, the air of muted courage and desperation, the breezy way the nurses avoided too close contact, and who could blame them?

It was a ninety-minute process, and they were used to it. Jeremy got a coffee down the street at Trini's Taco Palace—the coffee tasted of cumin powder, which was surprising since the tacos never did. He sipped slowly, to make it last. Funny thing about avoidance: everyone indulges in it one way or the other. Sean doesn't tell his family about the virus, but he manages to live at home and put up with his parents' own domestic brand of homophobia.

But why should Jeremy berate Sean for avoidance? Isn't that what I'm working my ass off to overcome, too? It's a long shot, sure, this competition in New York City. But there is never going to be an easy way out of Thebes. Away from Willem. Toward something fresh and vital and—and nutritious.

Jeremy had a thousand images of what could go wrong. Like L.A. only worse, now that he had applied for a slot and been accepted. Their instruments could sag out of tune, their voices slip out of pitch. The jaded Manhattan audience might sit there stunned at the earnestness of these rubes from upstate. What if Stephen

Sondheim stands up in the front row to hunt for earplugs in his pockets?

What could go wrong. His imagination far too clever and tireless. But what happens after the competition—the next day, and the day after that? With luck, the days will unfold, horribly empty or horribly full, on a city stage too crowded to admit thoughts of Willem. Well, thoughts, maybe, but in time those thoughts might lose their strength, their frequency. Jeremy would be reborn. Smaller, perhaps, more cagey, more cautious. He'd kind of like that. Or maybe not; maybe he'd be reborn free, released, exhilarated. Either way it would be something *other*; he'd have successfully escaped from this dead-end zone.

Please God.

When Jeremy made his way back to the clinic, Sean was already in the waiting room, a few minutes ahead of schedule. He sat as if, slip of a thing though he already was, he'd been further deflated. His eyes were closed and his head back, and a *Newsweek* had slid onto the floor between his feet.

"Hey," said Jeremy softly. Sean's eyes were moist and unfocussed at first. He stood quickly, with a deliberate jolt; it reminded Jeremy of some old District Commissioner in a men's club in Dar es Salaam or somewhere, jumping to attention to prove he wasn't beyond it. Jeremy knew enough not to ask for the blood profile till they were in the car. But when they had settled in, and Jeremy had maneuvered to the ramp heading up for the first reach of I-81 North, the stretch not closed for construction, Sean was diddling with the dial of the radio. "Where the fuck is your reception?"

"That radio has been on the fritz for a hundred years now."

Sean knew this, but he slapped at the dial as if he could make it behave. "At the least you should get the stupid thing fixed."

"I take it things aren't great."

"Oh, things are just fine, swimmingly normal, what do you expect?"

"T-cells?"

Jeremy could tell that Sean was struggling to keep from throttling him verbally. "The T-cells," Sean said, "are back down in the low single digits. What is the point of talking about this? Are you expecting perhaps a miracle cure? Why do you make me plow through this stuff for you?"

"You shouldn't have to keep it all—"

"That's my business—"

"—well, then, because I want to know, that's all."

"Call my hematologist if you're so fucking curious."

They drove in silence for a while. Jeremy wasn't above being pissed at this, even though he guessed Sean couldn't help it.

Look at the world outside Sean, not in him. The sprawl around Syracuse was bright in the sun; prefabricated warehouses, half-hearted little strip malls with Laundromats and CVS's. Without talking, they barreled past an IGA-Plus, and a couple of mobile home encampments. Parka-stout kids let out of school early were shrieking after a beach ball bouncing around in the frigid gale. When Jeremy got to the detour where all the lanes of the northbound section of the highway were closed, it was a relief if for no other reason than the view slowed down, became more rural and particular, took them further from hospital realities.

The county road was congested. Thanksgiving traffic on Tuesday evening already? Maybe. Jeremy decided to cut across through Colosse and head west on Route 69, which was windswept but largely untraveled this afternoon.

Falsely casual, Jeremy ventured, "The landscape's arresting as always but don't you want to say anything?"

"They told me to save my breath."

"—meaning?—"

"They said I should stop singing, for one thing."

Jeremy could sense Sean's head turning to look at him at last, but just at that moment he couldn't return the glance, as a farm truck was swinging wide into a dirt drive up ahead where the road swerved left. "They said," Sean continued, "that's too much effort for my lungs in the shape they're in."

"Oh." He wasn't sure how to say "Oh hell" or "Oh damn" without it sounding like he was mostly disgruntled about losing a good tenor. Sean would know what he meant but in this mood he'd take it the wrong way on purpose.

"They also said I should avoid telling long stories or getting in heated arguments. I told them, with Thanksgiving coming up, are they crazy? Don't they know of Mr. and Mrs. Riley, undisputed champions of Couples Confrontation? Some Catholic couples do Marriage Renewal; my folks do Marriage Revenge—" He began to wheeze, which he hadn't done on the way down. Power of suggestion, or was he worn out from the physical exam?

"All the more reason you should come to my place for Thanksgiving. We can rent a video or think of something."

"The something I can think of requires too much panting, even if I had the strength to catch you, pluck you, and truss you like a turkey. They say I'm beyond that, too. As if I couldn't tell."

"What about the T-cells. If you're going to talk. I'd rather know. Sean."

"Here's the order of business on Thursday. Up around seven when me mam starts clattering around in the kitchen, trying to multiply the number of pounds of turkey by twenty minutes per pound and then figure out how that translates into hours. She'll have the whole family up by seven-thirty doing extremely creative math, and in the end she'll shove the bird in around noontime and say, 'Bejazus, we'll eat when the blessed thing sees fit to finish cooking itself.' The kitchen will look like an Ulster Constabulary reprisal on the Shankill Road. Four pies with collapsed crusts and the extra filling dumped in the dog's dish, where it will be ignored for several days until it begins to smell, when the dog will eat it and throw up—"

Jeremy was laughing. "No long stories, they said—"

"I'm just getting started. I haven't told you about Connie's clairvoyant parlor games, in which she'll try to name who I'm going to marry. Or about Maura's anorexic sulks, and how she'll dump her plate of food in the toilet without even bothering to close the door. Or Mike and Siobhan's mind games, trying to figure out who is the ripest to be touched for a small loan, or Aunt Mary Frances's barbaric curried mango dip, or Uncle Frank's Indefatigable Flatulence, or Uncle Pat's raving republicanism—the Irish kind, not the GOP kind—nor, best of all, Aunt Bridget's holiday prayer, where she reminds God to touch each one of us in His special way, which always makes my Aunt Mary Ellen look as if she's going to cream on command, and makes Mam try to appear humble as if she doesn't really believe she's the only one in the room who's already been touched by God in His own special way—"

"Stop," said Jeremy, "stop—"

"And where am I in all this? Dying of AIDS, waiting for lesions to announce themselves—Connie would think they were hickeys—waiting for the lungs to deflate and not reinflate, as little saclet by saclet they give up the ghost."

"And there's not air, can't they give you air?"

"Air, that's all I need, sure!" cried Sean, smacking the window. He rolled it down and the air rushed in, filled with the smell of mowed wet fields, full of the cinnamon chill of the grave.

"You want pneumonia before we even get home? Stop—"

"No, you stop. Look, there. Where we did before. Look."

It was a farm stand on Route 3. They'd come this way the last time, just before Halloween, and they'd pulled up to buy a couple of pumpkins.

The stand was closed now. The windows that in season hung open, latching to hooks in the ceiling, were dropped and padlocked. Jeremy drew up anyway, not sure what Sean wanted, or why. The lake, stretching west as far as they could see, was an uneven silver color, showing streaks of tarnish where the wind ran firmly atop it. Trees thrashed their empty fingers in the sunlight; leaves eddied and flicked off the slope, and settled again. Sean threw the door open and said, "Wind, and air, if there was enough of it, there'd be enough time—" He pitched out of the car and galloped away as if trying to protect some injury inside that he couldn't feel. He was stiff and loose all at once.

"This is the perfect way to take care of yourself, of course it is, you asshole," shouted Jeremy, but turned the car off and went after him.

Sean wheeled, with his hands over his ears and his head up. His eyes were squinched, his heels thudding on the gravelly patch in front of the stand. A paper sign, flat against the boarded-up windows, said, CLOSED TILL IMMAC. CONCEPTION DAY, (DEC 8), X-MAS TREES SOLD THAN. Beyond the farm shed a crop of Christmas trees stood, five feet high in even ranks, uniformly shuddering in the wind.

Below the shed loitered a row of pumpkins left over from Halloween. Instead of being uniform like the Christmas trees, each one had been individuated by scars and time. A knife had sliced the scalp open, scooped the brains out, dug a leering expression into each bulbous canoodle, but age and weather had done the rest. The heads sank in on themselves, were overrun with ants; the eye sockets caved, the gums fell, the nostrils closed. The faces were in the act of giving up the ghost. It was impossible to tell if some of the mouths had been smiles, some of the eyes huge with surprise and delight; in decay all the countenances maintained a mutual close-lipped secrecy.

Sean whirled his hands at them as if they were a crucial part of his argument, but he didn't speak. From behind the farm stand protruded the edge of a ladder lying on its side. He went to that and kicked it, then hauled it off the ground. "What, what?" said Jeremy, grabbing the other side of it, "what are you up to?" The ladder clattered against the side of the stand, and Sean bolted up, Jeremy hoisting himself after him.

The roof, one plane, raked shallowly to follow the slope of the hill. They looked down the deteriorating tarpaper and saw the backs of the heads of pumpkins, the car in the pull-off, the gray-red tarmac, the pitch of two fields, one after the other, and the skidding surface of Lake Ontario aiming toward invisible Toronto. The wind was stronger up here, the air even colder, Alaska colder, the sunlight more obviously an attachable effect, draped from above and, at this time of day in late November, from the west. The shadows puddled eastward of everything; Sean and Jeremy huddled on their blue bases like plastic cowboy figures in perpetual crouch.

Jeremy put his arm around Sean, which was a comfort Sean rarely accepted, or maybe was no comfort at all, Jeremy realized. He waited to see if Sean would cry, or would say something more precise about his condition, but Sean merely drank the air deeply and chewed on his lip. Then, giving Jeremy a quizzical look, squinting his close-set eyes, he said, "As if I could stop singing with you, when that's all I have."

They didn't sing. They crouched there as if for the applause that didn't come, but accepted the light in its stead, until the light fell.

19

TABITHA'S MOTHER PRESENTED herself on Thanksgiving morning ready for church. She had draped a lacy bureau scarf over her head and attached it with plastic clothespins, and she carried her Bible in a plastic Price Chopper bag. Around her neck hung a homemade lei: strung popcorn interspersed with the occasional pitted black olive. Tabitha guessed this must be an imitation rosary, since a cross cut out of a Visa card dangled down the front.

"Can you do this run?" asked Tabitha of Hogan.

"No. Why don't we give Kirk the keys and tell him to teach himself to drive? With luck he'll have a fatal crash and solve two problems at once."

"Exceedingly funny," called Kirk from the bathroom where he appeared to be flossing his eyelashes. "I'm not going to church either."

"Hell in a haltertop," said Tabitha, which had been her mother's worst expression up until this month. It sounded corrupt coming out of her own mouth. "Okay, Mom, I'll take you, but I'm waiting in the car. You're on your own."

The parking lot between the churches was full to overflowing this morning. Radical Radiant Pentecostals and Roman Catholics alike needed to get the worship business over with early so they could go home to shove turkeys into the oven. Who knows what anyone had to be grateful for in November 1999, with Y2K and the end of days on its way?

Mrs. Scales needed help getting to the church door. But which one? Tabitha couldn't advise, though she hadn't given up on some sort of a holy miracle to knock some sense back into her mother. The Radical Radiants? Tabitha didn't think much of Pastor Jakob Huyck; he seemed hard to read. Then again, she'd never been much of a reader. The Catholics? At least the vestments of the Catholic priests were outward signs of their inner weirdness. They were like grown-up Goths.

Mrs. Scales twisted her elbow and led Tabitha toward the Catholic door. Tabitha pulled away until she remembered that Caleb's fiancée was Catholic, and what if she was dragging Caleb here and trying to convert him? If they were going to get married, Caleb must be spending time at the brainwashing sessions. He was probably in there right now, gargling some archaic oath to dead popes or dead Kennedys, or both.

Mrs. Scales apparently didn't want to attend mass. She went back downstairs and found her favorite spot at the foot of the old Kelvinator. It was the one place that she seemed at peace. Whatever depths of hatred and disgust Tabitha was finding within herself, she was glad to see her mother calm for a few minutes. Mrs. Scales closed her eyes and folded her hands on her bosom as if she expected someone to place a lily there. She looked like she was practicing to be a corpse. "Violent night, holy night," sang Mrs. Scales, rather tunelessly but at least softly. "Falling bombs, all is bright. Disney version, other and child."

"You've been practicing in your head," said Tabitha. "Nice."

"Holy infant so mental and wild."

"Don't leave until I come back to get you."

"Leap in heavenly peace." Mrs. Scales seemed happy enough.

The service was starting; Tabitha could hear the music. She closed the door to the Catholic kitchen but left the light on, as she didn't want anyone trampling on her mother. Then she made her way upstairs and found herself in a vestibule in the back of the church. She had a good view of the altar and of a small singing group. They could see her if they turned to look, but they had their eyes trained forward. Maybe a half dozen worshippers were singing along with the hymn, while the rest—forty or so—hunted through the hymnals as if unable to locate the song, or made a show of blowing their noses or suffering headaches.

The priest was singing, swinging his shoulders back and forth in time to the music, his head lifted but his eyes trained on the hymnal. The music leader played a guitar and looked like some escapee from a Grits and Granola checkout counter. A couple of women chirruped along behind him, and one shook a tambourine in a desultory fashion whenever she remembered she had it. And in a pew, third row back, eyes closed as if in pain or deep prayer, was Caleb, her own Caleb.

She hadn't seen him since the night before Halloween. They'd had a fight and made love, though whether the making love was making up or continuing the fight had been interestingly confusing. He had accused her of sleeping around, to which there was no sensible answer. It didn't mean she didn't love him. And so look what happens next? *He* immediately sleeps around. And gets caught. Though any girl who could get Caleb into a church and pretend to convert, well that was someone to notice. Tabitha had to admit it, even if she did hate the bitch. What was her name again? Polly something.

Caleb should look up and see her.

He should, but he didn't. He just stared down at his knees.

When the congregation stood to pray, he knelt on the little padded shelf they provided and he looked down. She would put dollars to doughnuts he was drooling over the behind of the pretty girl standing in the pew in front of him. Somehow, Tabitha felt consoled. He hadn't changed all that much. She could get him back. It was just a matter of planning. Pastor Huyck had said she should confront him, and maybe that was sound spiritual advice. But where? And when? She doubted that now was the appropriate moment.

The prayers concluded. As people settled back to listen to a reading, Tabitha Scales slipped up the aisle and found a seat a couple of rows behind Caleb. When he stood to drone out some cluster of semi-musical Alleluias with the rest of them, she had a good view of *his* ass. She'd had better views, of course, and given the churchy environment she took pleasure in remembering the particulars. But her pleasure waned the moment the song was done, and the choir disbanded from its position at the side altar. The shabby leader found a folding chair and the blond woolly mammoth of a soprano perched next to him. The other singer, a first-grade Brownie type, tippy-tippy-toed down the aisle and made her way into the pew where Caleb Briggs was waiting. She nudged up against him and Tabitha could tell by the pull of her sweater that they were gripping hands in some sort of lovelock.

She couldn't stand it. That Polly, that thing, that Bambi, standing up in front of a church and singing hymns, when she was an out-and-out thief! There is a name for this kind of thing, thought Tabitha. A sacrilege, that's it. A sacrilege. Or a fucking outrage. Furthermore, that hair. Tabitha could diagnose split ends from three pews back. What kind of a cushy job could this gal possibly have, to drag Caleb to the altar like this?

Somehow, though, Tabitha couldn't get up to leave; maybe she was afraid that they would see her. Everyone else was staring at the priest, who was standing in the aisle with a microphone. Caleb was laughing, and so was that Polly; the priest must be doing a stand-up routine. Partly to avoid everything else in her life, Tabitha began to listen.

He wasn't bad. It was some story about a kid and a cat that had gotten run over. The cat was in heaven, said the mom. With God. But Mommy, said the grieving child, What does God want with a dead cat?

Ha ha ha. Everyone laughed. Tabitha waited to hear how the mom would answer that, but the priest went on to talk about something else.

God's plans. God's plans. God was sure some sort of busybody in this church. There was that Old Lady Scarcese, nodding righteously as if she was sure God had personally approved of her outfit, a nylon Windbreaker that said Costco on the sleeve.

Did God plan for Caleb Briggs to sniff up the skirts of some overeducated Catholic girl? Did God hit her mother on the head with a statue just so that Tabitha could sit here and be insulted by the sight of Caleb snaking his arm around Polly as if they were at the Cineplex? Was God out to get Tabitha Scales? He'd better not try. Who said God had a plan for Tabitha? Maybe Tabitha had a plan for God. Ever think of that? Huh? Mister?

She liked the thought. Perhaps this was the consolation of prayer.

When she got back to listening to the priest, she was lost. Pilgrims, religious freedom, bountiful harvests, God's grace from sea to shining sea. Everything in the hands of God. What this had to do with Caleb was beyond Tabitha. The guitar guy was now at a piano, picking out the melody of "America the Beautiful." "As Jesus said: Where two or three are gathered in My name . . ." said the priest, in a dire tone as if a threat was to follow. Everyone looked

peaceful. What did he mean? Did this apply to all of America? Or
only the Catholics in Thebes? The Radical Radiant Pentecostals
were gathered in Jesus's holy name right now; you could hear them
shrieking even though the windows were closed. But none of the
Catholics looked alarmed. They must be used to it.

She tried to focus. God—well, God's mother, the statue—had
hit her mother on the head. Who was going to hit God on the head
to pay him back? To divert his attention from Leontina Scales? She
needed to get back to her ordinary inept motherliness. Let her go,
God. Time for the hostage crisis to be over.

Later, Tabitha wondered if she had had a little religious experience, or if maybe she just fell asleep for a moment. But all she
could recall was the sudden thought, delivered as if a Thanksgiving present from the Mind of God to Tabitha's mind, that maybe,
just maybe, her mom could be kind of nudged back to reality by
a little clonk on the head. A little tap, a little bonk, a careful little
swat with something heavy enough to register but padded enough
not to hurt. Like, say, a wrench wrapped in a couple of tea towels.
Why not?

Music. Prayers. Some bullshit Catholic calisthenics, up and
down, up and down, kneel and stand and sit. Tabitha did it without thinking. She just kept marveling: Did the Mind of God plan
to have me come in here and get enlightenment from, *who knew*,
a Roman Catholic father? I don't even believe in God. But maybe
He believes in me, she thought, blushing at the novelty of it. She
felt even faintly undressed, as if God could see all through her, and
had known what she needed. Just a little divine inspiration. Maybe
a wrench would be too heavy. An ice cream scoop? A steam iron?
Secateurs?

Then the whole crowd began twisting about and shaking hands
and saying "Piece of cake" or something—no, "Peace of Christ."

She was caught off guard, and Caleb was staring at her, turning peach colored and probably getting hard. "Tabitha," he said, stretching his hand out, heaving himself over two full pews, almost levitating toward her, "what the—" He caught himself. "What're you doing here?"

"Hi." She took his hand limply and let it go. The Polly girl looked astonished at Caleb's gymnastics.

"I've got so much news," he said.

"Piece of ass," she said. "Peace of Christ, I mean."

"Well, yeah," he said, as if that was pretty obvious.

"Caleb," said Polly, tugging at the waistband of his jeans.

"Later, girl," said Caleb.

"Later, my eye," muttered Tabitha. She wanted to leave right then but she didn't want to make a scene. At communion, folks shuffled forward and then made a dash for the side door, probably to avoid the traffic tie-up with the Radical Radiants. Like people darting out before the credits. Caleb seemed to be staying put, though, for his perky little Polly had gone forward and was whining some sort of show-tune chorus about shepherds and grapes and the cup of love. When she thought she could leave with her dignity intact, Tabitha slipped out and went downstairs to wake her mom out of the occasional coma that continued to pester her.

It took a few minutes. "Mom. Mom." Tabitha was afraid that the service would end and all the Catholics would flee and lock the church, so she hung around the base of the cellar steps until she was sure Polly and Caleb must have left, and then she went upstairs again. Except for Old Lady Scarcese, who was whipping herself into a devotional froth at the side altar, the church was empty. The boss people—the priest, a nun, and the music guy—were chortling away in a side room that had long flat drawers and a lot of golden tchotchkes. She stood in the doorway.

"Excuse me," she said, "I'm the one whose Mom is having this love affair with your refrigerator downstairs. She's still there, and I just don't want you to lock up—"

"Tabitha, isn't it," said the nun. "I'm Sister Alice Coyne. May I come down and talk to her?"

"She isn't herself," said Tabitha.

"Who is," said Sister Alice. "May I?"

TO TABITHA'S MORTIFICATION, the Catholics decided to come back to the house. They'd learned that Tabitha hadn't remembered about a turkey or anything, and that her brothers were next to useless. Rising to a challenge, the Catholics bustled about ready to do works of mercy like there was no tomorrow. Tabitha had to run her mother home at a clip far exceeding the speed limit, but when Jack Reeves pulled her over on Morse Hill Road to admonish her, she explained the situation and he didn't ticket her.

She shoved Hogan into his room and made him promise not to come out, and she got Kirk to run the vacuum up and down the most public parts of the room, but somehow the vacuum caught up a Kleenex and shredded it into little disgusting balls of paper that spewed all over the sofa, and she was on her hands and knees trying to pick them off when the doorbell rang and the Catholics arrived.

"Nothing like a little holiday togetherness," said the priest, who called himself Father Mike. "From the food pantry," explained Sister Alice, lugging a turkey the size of a woodchuck in a blackened baking pan. The music guy, Jeremy Carr, juggled some paper bags filled with Tupperware, salad dressing, cartons of eggnog, and rolls of paper towels, as if they expected to be coming to some trailer where paper towels were in short supply. Which, alas, was true, about the paper towels.

Mrs. Scales, settled in her own chair, frowned at the newcomers and nibbled at her rosary. Sister Alice and Jeremy bustled into the kitchen, and Tabitha followed. "I never heard of such a thing," said Sister Alice. "You with your poor mother still recovering, and your brothers, and no one to help you out! The idea!" She flung open cabinets like she lived there and piled up spoons and spices. That the turkey was too large for the oven didn't perturb her; she hacked it in half with a cleaver and arranged the sides in the pan to splay efficiently about each other. It looked as if it had exploded.

Jeremy was setting the table with Kirk. Kirk looked all bright and fizzy, like the time she'd surprised him standing up naked in the bathtub, shaping a kind of loincloth made out of bath bubbles around his groin. At least that's what it looked like. Maybe since Jeremy seemed soft-spoken for a guy, Kirk was lathering up with instant devotion. *That kind of sucks,* Tabitha thought, *but I can't manage Kirk's and Hog's disasters while I'm trying to oversee the old bitch.* So she only went through the dining room and said, "Don't fuss so, Kirk, you're like that little old lady who owns Tweetie Pie," and she hit him on the wrist with the gravy ladle. He made a dismissive little pout at her and kept yammering at Jeremy about some goop on Masterpiece Theatre, trying to impress the guy. She escaped into the living room.

Father Mike was reading the Bible out loud. Her mother had her eyes closed and her head back. Tabitha dropped onto the sofa for a minute, letting her eyes slide around the room, checking to make sure that she had already jettisoned into the bedrooms anything horrible.

When Father Mike paused for breath, Tabitha began to speak, but Father Mike held up one finger, silencing her. He kept reading.

So Tabitha went back to the kitchen, where Sister Alice was boiling up the neck and innards of the turkey and slicing an onion and melting some butter in a pan and running some water over some yams, all at once.

"He's got a very good bedside manner," said Sister Alice confidentially. "He brings comfort to the afflicted. What I want to know is, what do they say the affliction is?"

"The clinic says she's fine," said Tabitha. "But she's gone downhill since she got home."

"Someone should bring that clinic to task. I look in on a dozen and a half old sisters every week. I've spent my time doing infirmary work. Trust me. What's the therapy?"

"No therapy. Are you kidding? She won't let us bring her back."

"She should go back."

"You try it. Your funeral. I wouldn't touch it."

Sister Alice clucked as she rooted through the grocery bags. "Clearly your mother's suffering the aftereffects of some trauma. It's a kind of aphasia, isn't it? That biting off of words? And she can't seem to focus on where she is?"

"She doesn't say much except in holy language or swearing. There's not a whole lot of middle ground."

"Unusual case. Look, you fry these onions in this butter till they're transparent, but don't let them brown. No, stir them, don't you know how to sauté onions? Dear Lord. I thought some things were innate. Let me just spice up this . . . with a little of this . . . ooh, this is old, no flavor at all . . ." She dumped the dill weed into the trash can without asking if she could. "One suspects a stroke, of course."

"They tested for a stroke. No stroke."

"Well, they can't always tell so definitely—"

"No stroke. That's what they said."

"A blow to the head. I hardly think that statue could have picked up enough speed or momentum to do this much damage. Was there a prior cause?"

"What do you mean?"

"Had she had some sort of shock that morning? Was she in distress? In anxiety?"

"Oh. Oh."

"Good child," said Sister Alice in a soft voice, "whatever is it? What happened?"

"The onions. They're browning."

"Something happened and you blame yourself."

"Not till you started talking."

"It's sheer biology, it's mechanics in the brain, it's blood vessels and tension, nothing more. Whatever it is, you're not to blame. What happened? Did you hit her?"

"Could hitting her do it?" asked Tabitha, sullen but eager to know.

"Could quite possibly do it. A blow to the head can change everything."

So there was the answer. For sure. It was now merely a question of how and when. But the nun wouldn't let go; gosh, the Catholics really did love their guilt, just like everyone said. "You must not hold onto this," said Sister Alice. "You must tell me, or tell someone. You've taken on far more than you need to, and you're just a young thing. Believe me, I know."

"Get off my case." Tabitha suddenly had to wipe her face on the dishcloth. Onions and steam and salty condensation. "Enough of this stupid Bible reading, it's time for the parade." Sister Alice, her mitts in the oven rearranging the turkey because it was smoking, just clucked her tongue. Kirk was giggling in the dining room, and Jeremy had sat down on a dining room chair and was telling some story with both his hands in the air. The doorbell rang. Kirk was too wound up to get it, and Father Mike was in the middle of a psalm. The doorbell rang again, drawing Hogan from his room at last to answer it.

"Well, what have we here." The newcomer's voice was frosty and familiar.

"A convocation of ministers," said Father Mike, allowing himself to be interrupted.

"And Sister Alice in the kitchen?" said Pastor Huyck. "You're going ecumenical by stealth, Mike?"

"Feel free to mash the potatoes, Jakob."

Tabitha came to the door of the dining room, sneaking a peak at the religious men bunched uneasily together on the sofa. Pastor Huyck didn't ask after Tabitha. Hogan hulked back to his room and cranked up the stereo; "Burn the Priest" blared through the thin walls. Mrs. Scales seemed to come around for a minute, and she blinked at the pair of preachers in her living room.

"Happy Turkey Day," said Pastor Huyck.

"Praise God to whom all turkeys go," said Mrs. Scales, and waved back and forth in a big fanning gesture. Tabitha gritted her teeth and went back to stand next to Sister Alice at the stove. They worked quietly, listening to the big boys duke it out.

"Doing a little missionary work, Father Mike?" said Pastor Huyck. "Horning in on my territory?"

"Charity begins at home," replied Father Mike. "Since Mrs. Scales seems to find it homey in the basement of Our Lady's, I can but oblige."

"I suspect she's possessed."

"I suspect she's converting."

"Same thing." Pastor Huyck's joke didn't provoke so much as a chuckle from Father Mike.

"I suspect she's in a post-traumatic waking coma," called Sister Alice from the kitchen, "and my experience says that she'll come around."

"She needs some sense knocked into her," said Pastor Huyck.

Tabitha picked up the cast-iron skillet with the onions and weighed it in her hand. Not now, of course. But it was nice to know everyone seemed to agree on the right corrective measure. It made her feel a little less alone.

She put it down and went and said, "Anyone want some water with real ice in it?"

"Ah, there you are," said Pastor Huyck, all *brightly brightly* like a kindergarten teacher. Father Mike raised his eyebrows across the room at Sister Alice standing in the doorway behind Tabitha. From the dining room, Kirk launched into yet another flutter of story, something about some fool in a Shakespeare play. His voice fluted, even more highly pitched than before.

Hogan came to the kitchen door from the bathroom hall. "Gobble gobble," he said, rolling a finger in Kirk's direction.

"Eating any available Hardy boy," said Tabitha in a sing-song voice.

"For what he is about to receive, may the Lord make him truly grateful," said Hog, the most religious thing Tabitha had ever heard him say.

20

ON THE SUNDAY after Thanksgiving, Polly Osterhaus helped Jeremy Carr gather up the choir's photocopied sheet music. A few parishioners, passing the musicians on their way to the side door, felt free to comment. "Great music, Jer," said one. "Too loud," said another. "*Cocktail lounge music,*" hissed an old woman. Can't please everyone. When Jeremy had first started at this job seven years ago, some parishioner had sent Father Mike an unsigned check made out for a thousand dollars. Attached was a Post-It note saying, "You get the signature when you fire the choirmaster." Father Mike had never told Jeremy which parishioner it was.

Polly, straightening a stack of doxologies, said, "I don't know if you've heard the news, Germy. I'm getting married in the New Year."

"I wasn't going to believe it until you told me," he replied. "Was that the guy in the pew on Thursday? I guess it better have been. Hey, congratulations."

"I should've introduced you but I was embarrassed I hadn't told you yet. It's all been so fast. I mean, what if we broke off before it, like, gelled, and I had told everyone. Total shamefest. But so far so good."

"He's the Briggs guy, whose dad owned that barbershop—?"

"Um-hmm. Caleb Briggs. The thing is, I've asked my friend Irene Menengest to sing. Caleb doesn't like choirs and stuff, and I don't want to offend"—she looked around her shoulder but Peggy Mueller, the chief soprano, had already cut out—"anyone in our group. Better to use someone from outside than hurt anyone's feelings, don't you think?"

"You could've asked me."

"Caleb's the jealous type. He'd think I had a crush on you." Her unspoken *as if* hung between them; Jeremy had to duck his head to pick up a guitar pick.

"Actually, I know Irene. I met her at a party last year."

"Right. She said she thought she had met you. Her sister is Francesca Handelaers, and she tells me you're friends with Francesca's husband—"

"—I'm friends with all of them—"

"—was hoping you could accompany Irene at the wedding—piano music mostly, with an organ prelude and processional."

"Yeah, I heard about it already. I'd be happy to pitch in if the dates work. But I have to go out of town shortly after New Year's myself, and I'm taking a couple of weeks off following the Christmas rush."

"Well, if you can't make the actual wedding, can you help her rehearse once or twice? Irene is quite good but she's a sack of jitters over this."

"Rehearsals I can do. Is the wedding here?"

"Of course. Caleb's pretty vague about church, but he's willing to give in and convert. Not that he's converting from anything special. I think maybe the Church of the Rod and Gun Club." She couldn't suppress a tell-tale grin about sex that Jeremy had never seen on her face before, and that he was both embarrassed by and slightly jealous of. "But I know the drill."

"I hope we'll do a whole lot of pop music during the service," said Jeremy, and they both laughed. The number of weddings he'd played that the brides had wanted to walk down the aisle to Carly Simon's "That's the Way I've Always Heard It Should Be." To expedite things Jeremy had finally printed up a statement that said no Billy Joel, no Paul McCartney, no Whitney Houston or Celine Dion, no love themes from any Barbra Streisand movies. Save that stuff for the first dance at the wedding reception. If it was nothing else, church was the last bastion of church music, and needed to be protected as such.

———————

WHEN JEREMY PULLED up in front of the rectory on Tuesday night, he saw Willem's car there. Willem sat hunched over the steering column, arms laced around the wheel, head turned to address his sister-in-law with that kind of easy intensity for which Jeremy had no natural immunity. A Thirties aviator scarf of ivory linen was tucked into his University of Albany hooded sweatshirt. He saw Jeremy and waved, and he and Irene got out of the car.

"Sorry I'm late," said Jeremy. "You should've gone in. Chilly as hell." Oh, how wilting his inner butch could be.

Willem hunched his shoulders several times at Jeremy and grinned like a buffoon. His greenish Gaultier glasses glinted in the streetlight, so his eyes disappeared. "We did, but the priest seemed to think there wasn't any rehearsal there tonight, and I didn't want to leave Irene stranded in case you didn't show up. Her car's in the shop."

"Hi, Jeremy, nice of you to do this." Irene. She was a sour-sass soul with a rubbery face. None of her sister's zeal or compulsiveness, none of Francesca's watercolor blushes, either. Irene was just this side of stout, solid as a mailbox, and her hands dug deep into the pockets of her loden-green cape. "Your man in there said there was a conflict tonight and he tried to reach you but you were gone."

"Oh, great. Well, let me go see."

He let himself in the rectory and, hearing a noise in the kitchen, called out, "Hi, Father Mike, it's me," but it was Peggy Mueller who stuck her head out of the kitchen doorway. "He's upstairs, be right down, he said." Her eyes looked red-rimmed, and Jeremy's heart sank. Clearly Father Mike was needing the consultation room tonight for some emergency. "The kettle," mumbled Peggy, and disappeared with a little flutter of downcast lashes, as if she wanted Jeremy to follow her and ask her what was wrong. But he just waited for Father Mike to come heaving himself down the stairs.

"Oh, Jeremy, there you are. Some client of yours showed up, some music thing, but something's come up and I'm afraid—"

"I heard. I'll change my plans."

"A bit of counseling," said Father Mike, in the sanctity-of-the-confessional voice he had that, Jeremy always thought, was a trifle wistful, as if it was a burden not to be able to complain about Peggy Mueller just a little. Jeremy patted him on the shoulder and said, "Better you than me. See you later."

"Will we call it off?" asked Irene. "I hate to miss the opportunity. With Christmas coming everything will get so crazy."

"It's all piano stuff, isn't it," said Jeremy. "Sheez. Now that it's getting on to winter, it's too cold to hang out in the church except on Sunday when the heat's on. Look, I've got an idea. Why don't you jump into my car and we'll go see if we can barge in to this other rehearsal space I've been using lately. I can run you back to Monroe afterward, or wherever."

"I can hang around and wait," said Willem. "I don't mind."

"You have little kids you need to read Dr. Seuss to." Jeremy's voice was firmer than he expected. What a jolt, to be the one calling quits to an unanticipated rendezvous. He watched Willem shrug and touch a pair of fingers to his heart as if crushed.

"Suit yourself. See you later, Irene." Was it only Jeremy's imagination that Willem drove away looking the tiniest bit chagrined?

Probably. But Irene chattered, banal and personable, so Jeremy was spared the chance to obsess about it.

They pulled up in the drive of the convent of the Sisters of the Sorrowful Mysteries. "Ghoul Central," said Irene. "Are we going to practice wedding marches or wedding dirges?"

"Hold your fire," said Jeremy. He should have called first, but an acid light seethed in the kitchen and since it was only 7:15 he decided to risk a little wrath and ring the bell. The small window in the vestibule door opened only after a considerable pause, and anxious Sister Felicity stood there, peering over the bottom of the window. "Mercy, is that you?" Jeremy doubted she recognized him.

"Jeremy Carr, from the church. I know I said we weren't coming because Sean is under the weather, but it's our regular night and I had another thought, so I thought—"

"In for a penny, in for a pound," muttered Sister Felicity, and went to work on the bolts. "What's all this about, then?" she said, when the door swung open.

Jeremy introduced Irene Menengest and explained the situation. Sister Felicity looked dubious. "I'm just burning a little toast and scalding a little milk for the insomniacs among us," she said, implying that the nuns had been abed for hours already. "I hardly think I have the liberty to admit you, Jeremy, without Mother Clare du Plessix's permission."

"I could call Sister Alice, perhaps?—"

"Sister Alice would be too busy to answer the phone. And she may have a lot of responsibility for us decaying old things, but she doesn't have much authority, I'm afraid. That's her cross." She looked as if she thought Sister Alice's cross not quite crushing enough. "Oh come in, it's just us chickens and if you kill us all in our beds, we're one night closer to Jesus, that's all I can say."

"Did you have a good Thanksgiving, Sister Felicity?" said Jeremy.

"Are you talking spiritual nourishment or corporal cuisine? I don't do the holidays well, I get a string of migraines from the strain. Sister Alice might have seen fit to join her community on that day of gratitude, but she apparently had commitments elsewhere." Jeremy didn't let on that he'd seen Sister Alice cook for the needy; he guessed that Sister Felicity wouldn't know how to interpret his favorite bumper sticker, "Put the fun back in dysfunctional."

"There was some light meat and dark," said the nun, "there was squash and a pie and some real half-and-half for our decaf, and we considered ourselves lucky for it."

Irene Menengest gave Jeremy a look that said, Oooh, what a bitter little ferret. Jeremy pretended not to comprehend. "We need maybe forty minutes or an hour, if you don't mind," he said. "I won't make a practice of this, but we've a kind of emergency. Irene is a soprano—"

"—mezzo—" supplied Irene.

"I see," said Sister Felicity. Was the old nun irritated about Irene's being a woman instead of one of the guys? Maybe Sister Felicity felt upstaged by a fat strawberry blond in a thick coat with peasant stitching and buttons made out of hack-sawed slices of deer antlers. Jeremy supposed even old nuns could succumb to the temptation of regret about their lost looks. Everyone else did.

"Sing away, don't mind if I ignore you," continued Sister

Felicity. "I'll have to go up to tell Mother Clare so that nobody thinks they're hallucinating Joan-of-Arc voices. But frankly there's enough rampant loss of hearing among us that people will probably assume you're the radiator clanking. Let's try it and see." She allowed herself a wintry smirk as she closed them into the sunroom.

"Wow, that's some welcome," said Irene.

"Shall we get started? What have you got?"

They had gone through several hymns, with Jeremy transposing everything into B flat as Irene's pleasant voice had a limited register, when Sister Felicity reappeared with the rolling cart and a small treat laid out on a paper towel. She'd folded the edges of the towel and cut it with a scissors to make a design, as if Jeremy and Irene were second grade children having a party to celebrate making it through the primer. "Oh, you needn't have done this," said Irene. "My figure."

"I can see you don't worry much about that. Just a little shortbread and some of that zinger tea. Mother Clare said to." Sister Felicity looked as if she doubted Mother Clare's mental competence, but obedience was obedience. "I can't stay and chat, I'm afraid; I'm behind in my evening devotions. Jeremy, Mother Clare said I may allow you this once to let yourself out when you're done. She hopes you will conclude by nine."

"Oh, for sure," said Jeremy. "I've got to pick up Marty Rothbard at the Craftique at nine, and get Irene home before that. No problem."

When Sister Felicity had gone, Irene said, "She looks like Cloris Leachman in *Young Frankenstein*. Who are these strange creatures? Where do they come from? What do they want?"

"They want company. She's secretly devoted to me, I'm guessing. She's just skilled at not showing it after so many decades of denial."

"Oh, her too?" said Irene.

Jeremy stifled a fake yawn. He hoped it wasn't common knowledge in the Handelaers' extended family that he was Willem's cast-off everybody-tries-it-once-in-college gay fling. "I don't know much about Polly's boyfriend, have you met him? Caleb Briggs?"

"He's a bit backwoods, I think. I met him once or twice. It's a little sudden and I hope Polly doesn't regret it, but she is *such* a Catholic, you know. Don't you find being religious a tremendous liability? I mean, it's almost 2000. We have civil liberties these days."

He shuffled some music. "Frankly, the worst part of being a church musician is you have to talk about it all the time. Everybody treats you like you're some sort of pariah. For me being Catholic is just like being—well—an upstate New Yorker, or a college graduate, or a musician. It's just one of those things."

"And all these women here buying into the patriarchal hogwash." Irene made a motion with her hand. "Talk about the snow job of the millennium."

"Well now, that's a little harsh. You going to dismiss all the lives of all these women, and all the women in their communities in all those different countries over all those different centuries, just because you don't happen to like the pope? How many of them over the centuries had much in the way of choices? When really, think about it—proto-feminists, kind of—living in community, sharing everything they had, living simply and off the land—"

Irene was looking at him dubiously. "You really belong in the Nineteenth century," she said. "Can we take that from the top, or do you feel the need to do some more defending of the faith?"

"You brought it up. I get tired of my own personal beliefs being everybody's business," he snapped.

"You're in the business," she reminded him. "They pay you."

"You object so much, you could refuse to sing in a church wedding."

"And you're accompanying me—how cheerful would the Church have been if anything had ever come of you and W—"

He slammed the lid to the piano keys down and counted to ten, then opened it again. "I'm at measure 18. One and two and breathe and—"

"Don't take it personally," she said in outrageous calm.

"Yeah, religion's not personal at all. Remember to breathe. We modulate at measure forty-two." His hands capered. The F above C2 rang sharp as tarnish. The tang of red zinger tea was being subsumed into an older, resentful smell of cabbage. Willem hadn't needed to cave so easily when Jeremy told him to leave. He could've insisted on coming along. I could have shown him off to Sister Felicity. I hadn't gotten to show him off to anyone except my father, that one time, by accident, and that gay waiter at the Polish café in Watertown who insisted on snapping our picture.

At measure forty-two Irene remembered to modulate but Jeremy didn't.

21

TABITHA WAS IN the back room rinsing out the combs in blue sterilizing fluid. She always felt she was on some Saturday morning science show with organs in bottles, or little fetuses in formaldehyde, especially when she remembered to wear the white coat. A standard sucky early December day; the spitting wet might have been snow, but wasn't. Still, at least the place was quiet. What old witch was going to pay to have her hair done only to have it get rained on or blown out as she hobbled back to her car where her dead husband sat turning the pages of the free classifieds, waiting for her?

When Linda Pearl Wasserman came into the back room and slapped the door closed, a moldy clamminess seemed to follow in her wake. She looked at Tabitha with alarm verging on glee. "Oh God, what do I do now."

"What do you mean?" asked Tabitha.

"She's out there. The one. Your enemy. Caleb's fiancée."

"Linda Pearl. I know I'm a basket case but I'm actually trying to get over this and you're not making it any easier."

"Easy for you to say. *I've* got the girl in the front chair. She just wants a quick wash and set today, and is asking for advice on a hairdo for early January. *For her wedding.*"

Tabitha began to get interested despite herself. "What, you're going to sabotage her? Make her look like a concentration camp survivor?"

"Do I have to spell everything in capital letters? She's there in the chair, she's trapped like a—like a gerbil—what do you want to know? Girl, I'm here for you." She grabbed Tabitha's hands. "I live to help those in agony. Put me to work. I could wheedle state secrets out of, um, any big shot who came in here for a blow-dry." She tried again. "Mrs. Hilarious Clinton, for one. Now that she says she's going to run for senator from New York, if she campaigns around here and comes in for a photo-op I'll find out the truth about what she really puts in Bill's home-baked cookies."

"Well." Tabitha drew her hands back and made a show of drying them on the towel. She didn't like Linda Pearl to touch her. It was like shaking hands with a blob of defrosting pizza dough. "I guess you could find out how Caleb and her got engaged?"

"I'm all over it." She paused. "*Tabitha*. Do I have to do everything? I have a career in hair management, and I have to be an advice columnist too? You cretin. Listen: I'll find out where your Caleb is and I'll keep this Polly dolly in the chair and *you can go get him*. Thought you'd put up more of a fight. Frankly."

"I've had the fight knocked out of me by my mother." But was Linda Pearl on to something? Pastor Huyck had told Tabitha to face her demons down, to find Caleb and release him to his future, and liberate herself to her own. Or something like that. So maybe Linda Pearl, twitching with zeal at espionage of the heart, was being a messenger of God. The Angel of the House of Beauty.

Tabitha sighed. "Well, leave the door open and I'll come out behind the screen and listen. But Linda Pearl, don't slit her throat or do a buzz cut or anything. Not yet. If we want to do that it'd be better when she comes in the day before the wedding. Right?"

"The soul of normalness," said Linda Pearl in a testifying way. She locked eyes with Tabitha, sisters together on the Bitch Brigade, and she coursed out of the back room, fluting, "Coffee? Tea? Diet Shasta Cola?"

It didn't seem right to Tabitha that she should feel older than Linda Pearl when she was twelve years younger. But since she now felt older than her mother, maybe this was turning into a permanent condition. She hoped not. Lately her mother had taken to lying on top of her bed every night in her coat and boots, clutching the only pocketbook she had that would accommodate the Bible. She slept with all the lights on and woke herself every three hours, crying. Tabitha was reduced to dozing on the sofa so that she could leap to her mother's doorway and say coldly, "It's just a dream, Ma, wake up and go to sleep," which seemed to help.

But Tabitha wasn't getting a whole lot of rest, which made the world go streaky from time to time, as if it had been Windexed and not dried properly.

Bleary or no, it was still the world, and it harbored Caleb out there—that oak-necked traitor, that turncoat. The second Catholic wannabe of the season. It was funny how the world seemed smaller and less deliberately set on its pilings these days. How quickly things could change. One moment, Mom could be her old salt-of-the-earth self, Leontina Scales, running up potholders on her faithful Singer sewing machine with the treadle and the wheel to raise money for the Pentecostal missionaries in Ecuador or Peru or some other part of Africa. The next moment she was no better than a crazy Catholic lady escaped from the loony bin. How the world could shiver when it wanted. All the earthquakes weren't on the West Coast. Linda Pearl put her faith in hair fashions but Tabitha was finding this wasn't quite enough. Nothing was quite enough.

But she opened the door to the back room a few inches and stood behind it, listening. From the angled mirror in the corner she could see a white vinyl raincoat dripping from a hook, and back of that Polly's dust-colored douche-bag of a hairdo.

Linda Pearl was in her element. She went tripping lightly around the chair with a comb and the number seven scissors, gassing up a storm. "It all depends on the fall of the veil, brides never take that into consideration. They don't. They think it all has to do with how the veil is mounted. But different materials fall differently, fold differently. I've seen bouffants upwards a two hundred dollars flattened into classic Cherokee Cher before the minister even gets to say, 'If there's anyone here who knows anything juicy, speak now or forever hold your peace.' Is that something you worry about, by the way?"

"It's a very light veil, light as mosquito netting," said Polly Osterhaus.

"I mean anyone speaking up to protest your sacred union with your loved one."

"Oh, Catholics don't do that. They print the wedding plans in the parish bulletin for three weeks ahead of time in order to allow folks time to object, as if anyone would. It's called publishing the banns. Which is very old-fashioned, I think, but Father Mike says we still have to do it."

"Hardly seems like a wedding without that touch of drama." Linda Pearl grew sulky. She let the frond of hair drop as if offended. "Not that anyone would object in your case. What's the name of your sweetie?"

"Caleb." Polly shook out her hair as if to draw Linda Pearl back to the matter at hand. She ran one hand down from the central part to about four inches below the ear and said, "I was thinking maybe about this long in back, and layered forward to take a reverse curl?"

"He's not coming in here, is he?" Linda Pearl crossed to the window and looked over toward the Dunkin' Donuts.

"Of course not," said Polly shortly. "Why ever would he?"

"It's bad luck, from a hairdresser's point of view, for the husband-to-be to look in on the fiancée settling her hair concerns. Is he in the neighborhood?"

"He's getting the tires rotated over at Scarcese's. Is that far enough away for you?"

"Don't mess with custom, or custom messes with you," said Linda Pearl darkly. She flashed Tabitha a look in the mirror and gestured with her comb: Go on, go on. Tabitha hated to leave this scene; she could hardly imagine what Linda Pearl would say next. But Tabitha backed up and grabbed her anorak from the hook in the back room and nipped out the back door. In the strong wind the door slammed, and she wished she could hear what fib Linda Pearl would come up with to explain the noise. But there was no telling how long Caleb would be loitering around Scarcese's Budget Gas, and Tabitha had to take the opportunity while it presented itself.

She had left Kirk to babysit Mom that morning. He was doing some kind of school project, making a brightly colored tunic, and he had popped a cassette of some sickly high-sugar-content religious pop music into the boombox to keep Mom happy. It kept her quiet, anyway; happiness was harder to quantify these days. Tabitha had had to be content with that. She hadn't seen Hogan, however, before leaving the house. Since it was Saturday, Hogan might actually be in the middle of a shift; she couldn't remember. As she drove over to Scarcese's, she wondered if she would rather Hog be there or not. If she had a big square-off with Caleb, would Hog be a liability? Well, stupid question: Hog was always a liability. She sighed.

She pulled into the station and ran over some little girl's bicycle. How was she supposed to know it was there? She could see the girl inside buying ice cream, a dumb thing to buy at a gas station. The ice cream was probably polluted with gasoline fumes. And in December? What was wrong with everyone in Thebes anyway? Tabitha jumped out of the car and popped into the store section and said loudly, "I almost killed myself, I almost crashed into the pump swerving to avoid that bicycle, I almost blew this place up to kingdom come, who left their bicycle out there and almost caused a major *death*?"

The girl looked terrified and ran out, and wheeled her bike away, wailing to beat the band. Hogan looked in from the repair bay. "What're you doing here, Mom go and set herself on fire or something?"

"No, that's your job. Where's Caleb Briggs?"

"Mr. Can't-Tell-His-Cock-From-His-Carburetor?"

"You know who Caleb is." Tabitha wasn't exactly sure how much Hogan knew about her and Caleb. For just a moment, the whole *idea* of her-and-Caleb came sweeping in again, gathering her up; how could the idea have such force if it didn't have some possibility of being true?

"We needed some head gaskets and we ran out and I couldn't fix his car today except we get some. So he offered to go over to Bijou Motor Supply and pick some up. He just left. What you want with him?"

"None of your beeswax."

"Did you run over that girl's bike on purpose?" said Hogan. She looked at him and didn't answer. "Cool," he said.

Bijou Motor Supply was a few blocks away on Union. It used to be Thebes's only movie theater, back in the dark ages, and the marquee that looked like the prow of a ship still came jutting out over the sidewalk. The marquee read AUTO AND APPLIANCE PARTS POWER MOWER SKIDOO SNOWBLOW TRACTOR in plastic letters of different sizes. Tabitha didn't go in Bijou Motor Supply often. Last time was when her mom, rustling up those potholders-for-peasants, had needed a new belt for the sewing machine. But Tabitha liked this place in the way that she suspected some people liked church. The rows of seats had all been taken out but the graduated levels, arranged in soft terraced curves facing the stage area, were lined with long reaches of metal shelving. Above the stage the screen still hung, from whose bottom edge dangled a fringe of several dozen ancient yellow curling fly-strips. The stage—because the Bijou had been some sort of opera or vaudeville house even before the movies came in—housed the office area, and Tabitha could see Stephanie Getchen stuffing some papers in a file cabinet as if she were playing the role of a boring secretary in some boring play.

Caleb was here somewhere, for sure, wandering up and down one tiered row or another. Tabitha had a momentary panic, and resented Stephanie's public preening and twisting as she talked on the phone, so the phone cord wrapped around her bosom and down along her waistline in a telling spiral. But she couldn't let old anxieties about Stephanie flare up now. This might be Tabitha's only chance to get Caleb back. Hey, wait, was that what she was doing? She didn't have time to remember.

For a while she wandered up and down the rows as if in a maze. She came across a couple of customers in gray fedoras and mothbally coats who looked as if they might have been hunting for a certain kind of grommet for the better part of the century. Then she realized that if she went up to the balcony she'd be able to spot Caleb at once if he was still here. So she hopped over the velvet cord that still sported a CLOSED FOR THIS SHOW sign, and picked her way up the steps, on which boxes of outdated gidgets and widgets were carefully set, awaiting the second coming of their usefulness.

She stumbled over a dark something at the top of the stairs. Stephanie Getchen heard her swear, and put her hand above her eyes and peered as if looking out through stage lights, a supremely phony gesture since the stage was as dimly lit as the rest of the place. But that didn't matter; Tabitha had spied Caleb, pawing through some drawers in a display down in Row D, just off the center aisle on the left. Tabitha power-walked toward her future, not caring if Stephanie heard her. This was no time for delicacy.

Caleb turned as Tabitha approached. He was husked in a lumberjack's overshirt, big red-and-black squares, and his hands paused. One palm held a series of washers of various sizes and with the other hand he fingered a rusty four-inch bolt. "Hey, look who's playing at the Bijou," he said softly.

"Hey, Caleb." She hadn't planned much beyond this.

"What're you looking for? Can I help?"

"Wonder if you can." Tabitha was inclined to swirl her head around and make her hair roll; it was an undeniably terrific effect. But somehow, though she didn't trust words, she also didn't want to get in their way right now; she wanted to be able to hear them clearly, and to be heard. So she stood her ground with ordinary legs, instead of slinking her weight onto one leg and exaggerating the curve of her hip. She did not roll her hair as if it were a performing pet. She said, "You mentioned you got news for me."

"Oh, yeah." He went back to matching the bolt to the washers. "You'll never guess. You want to go somewhere, I can tell you?"

"We're already somewhere, I guess."

"Well, it's kind of—" He gestured to the stage, where Stephanie Getchen was making a big show of paying no attention, a scant thirty feet away.

"News is news."

"I guess I'm sorry to tell you like this." He seemed to give up on the washers and he pocketed the bolt. "I guess I should've come over or called you up or something. I heard about your ma."

"Was that what kept you from calling me?"

"Well, you sounded like you had your hands full."

"A little help might've helped." But she caught that this was sounding too *over*. "A little help could still be a big help."

He squirmed. Not an attractive thing to watch. Not very Caleb, either. Was he hexed? "I guess if I am such a useless shithead, you're better off without me."

"You're not talking about that fight we had just before Halloween? Caleb, come on. Couples fight. What's the big deal. Besides, it was kind of great." She lowered her voice. She didn't have much capacity for shame, but Stephanie Getchen was right there onstage behind her. For all Tabitha knew Stephanie was holding the phone receiver at arm's length to pick this up and broadcast it live.

"I'm not good enough for you."

"Well, that's okay, I'll make an exception."

"Don't kid, sweetie. This is serious. You know it is. That was not a good scene. I scared myself. I scared you."

"I can take care of myself—"

"I know you can, that's what I'm counting on. Look, you're going to make me say this out loud, aren't you? So I'll say it. I'm engaged to someone else. Tabs. It just happened."

Tabitha realized that she had never quite believed the rumors, not even when she'd seen Caleb and Polly together in church. Without saying so to herself, she'd lived in the snare of an impossible hope. There could've been any number of reasons he hadn't called her. He'd have to have been embarrassed with that scene in his trailer; he'd never mentioned sex toys before, and coupled with his anger, and her wearing that rubber Nixon mask—well, no wonder he'd been keeping his distance. And, for all anyone knew, Polly could have been his cousin or something. Thebes was small enough that there was a certain amount of inbreeding around that nobody much mentioned. Tabitha had thought that this disaster would just jigsaw itself solved. That it wasn't about to—did this mean she was, at last, grown up? Grown up in a way that sex and the dog leash and a little bit of Ecstasy had never meant?

"Glory be," she said.

"It's that girl you saw me with at the Catholic church. Polly Osterhaus's her name. Polly."

"You said you loved me," she said, shortly, quietly.

"I did," he said. "I do," he said. "What're ya gonna do?" he added.

"It isn't even Christmas yet. It's only five, six weeks since Halloween. We have one wild night, you're too embarrassed to apologize, and so you get engaged to get married after New Year's? To *somebody else*? You who were afraid of commitment, *you*?"

"It's more complicated than that."

"Well, I'm smarter than I used to be, tell me."

"She's pregnant."

Tabitha looked up. She saw the little windows in the projection booth that had been jerry-rigged up in the middle of the balcony. They were suddenly filled with light. Maybe someone had gone to lock some cash in the safe up there. The light came streaming out, a mocking soft echo of the once strong beam of the projectors. "So am I," she said.

22

SINCE ONLY OLD-SCHOOL Catholics paid attention to the concept of a Holy Day of Obligation, the church was almost empty on December 8, the Feast of the Immaculate Conception. And most of the worshippers were frail women, looking to Jeremy like character actresses trying out for the part of Elizabeth the cousin of Mary, in whose desiccated womb John the Baptist would flourish.

Old Lady Scarcese knelt, surrounded by her bodyguards, the Officers of the Sodality, all of them telling their beads with a frenzied hissle of lips, in competition with Father Mike Sheehy's sermon on (what was it now?) Mary and her courage. "You good faithful people know the Immaculate Conception doesn't describe Mary's conception of Jesus. How could that be—with Christmas only seventeen days away! She'd have had the fastest gestation in history, blowing up like special effects in a nature film." But Jeremy's mind wandered then toward the Annunciation, Mary's apprehension of her pregnancy. Gabriel the Archangel was probably gay. Unmarried virgins destined to give birth to God didn't have the leeway in public opinion to spend time cloistered with angelic male youths unless they were gay. Gay, and clad only in suggestive cotton percale bedsheets with a count of 400 tpi minimum.

But this wasn't exactly devotional reflection. "God created all things, including Mary conceived without sin, so then Mary gave birth to God," Father Mike said, interrupting Jeremy's reveries. "Think about it."

At communion, Jeremy noticed that girl, Tabitha Scales, sitting three-quarters of the way down the church, her head in her hands. His first thought was that Mrs. Scales must be downstairs prostrate before the refrigerator again. The girl looked wiped; after a few minutes he realized it was because she hadn't italicized her face with eyeliner and the like. She looked younger, more sodden, more confused. Though Jeremy wasn't above admiring from a safe distance the tender limbs and bruised-gazelle expression of her brother, Kirk, he also wasn't blind to Tabitha's porcelain features. Her improbable gravity.

He was packing up his guitar after mass when Tabitha approached him.

"Jeremy? You know if Father Sheehy's around?"

"Father Mike? You can go back to the sacristy and see."

"I can't go there." Her head was down.

"You want me to find him?"

"Please?"

He went back, but Father Mike had ducked out, late for his morning coffee-and-doughnuts with Jack Reeves and Turk Schaeffer. Sister Alice Coyne, busy folding up vestments, sported an expression on her face that said volumes about the nature of the feast day, the fallacies in the sermon, the drawbacks to an all-male priesthood, and her own commitment to stick it out and make the whole damn faith work anyway, sooner or later, as God was her witness. Jeremy hated to interrupt, for an expression like that was, he felt, the backbone of the Church. But so too was interrupting that expression when someone needed help, and Tabitha had seemed needy. "Sister Alice," he murmured. "S.O.S."

She took one look at Tabitha and dismissed Jeremy with a flip of her hand. "I'll lock up," she said.

Mrs. Katje Doorneweerd met him at the grade school door and said, "We're not going out at recess, Jeremy; the winds are too strong. Almost gale force, some cold front moving down across the Great Lakes." Jeremy sighed. This meant he'd have to attempt remedial work with the slow kids while the others, who badly needed exercise, shrieked through Simon Says in the same room. So he was initially glad when the school secretary called him to the office to take a phone call, until he realized the only call he could imagine was the one he was dreading: It would be from Sean, and it would be bad.

It wasn't Sean. It was a creaky old voice that was talking away before he got there. He listened until an interruption and he said, "Is that Mother Clare du Plessix?"

"It is she," said Mother Clare. "Do you think you can come?"

The wind; the rain; Sister Maria Goretti's cold had become pneumonia; the chapel roof leaking, and something about tarpaulins; and Sister Alice Coyne wasn't available at the parish offices of Our Lady's. Would Jeremy come, and bring some of those nice boys?

There was no way to decline, although Jeremy wouldn't think of coercing Sean Riley up onto any roof, gale wind or no. Mrs. Doorneweerd said, "I didn't even know there were any old nuns out that way; talk about your secret cults. Well, Wednesdays are the worst for indoor recess, and today's a lost cause anyway, so you might as well go. Though it does seem to me you've been a little less committed than last year. Word to the wise."

Sure, thought Jeremy. I'm angling to be fired, so my best strategy is befriending a coven of pickled nuns?

Marty Rothbard was available if not quite willing, and Jeremy swung by and picked him up at his apartment. They made it out to the convent within the hour. Dressed in a yellow raincoat that was so old that the plastic had cracked, Sister Jeanne d'Arc was working out front. She was trying to clear several decades' worth of dead leaves by poking a broom handle into the rainspout. In the mounting wind she didn't hear them approach, but she wasn't startled when they appeared beside her.

"The Cavalry arrives," she said. "What a mess it is up there. Mother Clare du Plessix has had physically to restrain Sister Clothilde from climbing that stepladder in the choir loft. Sister Clothilde, we fear, might not be appreciated by the roof beams. You boys are to the person a good deal slimmer, and stronger to boot."

"We're certainly not roofers," said Jeremy.

"Well, nor are we," said Sister Jeanne d'Arc, grunting with the force of her broom thrusting, "so it's a perfect match and no wonder we get on so well."

She led them inside, straight into the chapel. She pointed out the left portion of the ceiling where the wooden angels looked as if batiked with dark moisture. They've gone Indonesian, thought Jeremy.

Mother Clare du Plessix drifted in. "The roof won't make it through another winter like last year's. We thought we'd conquered the problem, but perhaps Sister Maria Goretti didn't have the strength in her forearms to tack down that tarpaulin sufficiently." Mother Clare's trust in God's providence, thought Jeremy, seemed insufficient. "From the window of the third floor dormitory one can see the far corner of the tarp flapping like a sail. In this wind the whole thing is likely to be torn away. You would be so good to have a go at it."

"Did she tack it down with a hem, or leave it open?" said Marty.

"She?" Mother Clare du Plessix's frostiness—aha, thought

Jeremy. The improper use of a pronoun without its antecedent could not be condoned, even if the roof was about to fall in.

"Sister Maria Goretti," replied Marty. "Did she fold a flap and tack down two thicknesses? That would prevent the wind catching it. Or help anyway."

"She's indisposed with a sad set of lungs and I couldn't put the question to her. Do you think you can set it to rights if she made a little mistake?"

"I'm a musician and a special ed teacher." Jeremy shrugged. "Musicians are hopeless, but special ed teachers, now—"

"We'll do what we can," said Marty, adding under his breath, "Germy, this is so butch, I think I'm going to come."

"We're very glad of that," said the nun. "Sister Felicity will show you the way. She's the best with stairs, being equipped with both of her natural hips."

Sister Felicity led them up the steps to the choir loft. Several choir chairs weighed down with hymnals had been arranged around the ladder to keep it from sliding on the oak flooring. Hardly comforting. Anyone might easily tumble off the top of the ladder, clear the choir loft railing, and land on the stone floor of the chapel, a healthy forty or fifty foot drop. "Mother Mary, keep them safe," said Sister Felicity.

"Mother Mary, this is scary," said Jeremy, halfway up.

"Mother Mary, quite contrary," said Marty from below. "Gee, for a fag your arms are hairy."

"This is a chapel," said Jeremy. "You want this ladder to shake with the wrath of God even before we get out the window?"

"You mean God would flounce her wrath around in a chapel? I thought there was such a thing as sanctuary. Believe me, I haven't felt so reverential in quite a while, what with the view I have of your butt."

They were out the window then, in a flourish of crosswinds and spikes of rain.

But it was beautiful up there, beautiful and terrible. The roof, more steeply pitched than it seemed from the inside, had been sheathed with an elegant kind of greenish-gold metal shingle, scalloped at the end. It felt soft and warm, even under the cold rain that coursed along it in rivulets. At four-foot intervals the original roofers had provided iron prongs, suitable for resting a heel or a palm. This was convenient for the guys, though Jeremy couldn't imagine how Sister Maria Goretti had managed in her old-fashioned long skirts and veils.

The tarpaulin was about twelve feet square and, indeed, it hadn't been tacked down with a hem, nor with much force, apparently; the nails were hammered in only to a half-inch depth, and they were too widely spaced. Marty called over his shoulder, "If I crash through the roof and fly with those artsy-craftsy angels, be sure nobody reads it as a deathbed conversion." He took the more treacherous route above the rotten section, clinging to the wrought-iron spikes along the roof ridge when he could. Jeremy, scrambling below, had a sick moment when one of the prong supports snapped under Marty's weight, but Marty rolled onto his back and grabbed above his head for another, and Jeremy watched the rain splashing into his open, terrified face. How strange that everything, everything, was beautiful, even terror.

The funny thing was that singing together proved, once again, to be the proper preparation for any other kind of collaborative effort. The wind was too strong and their fear too great to do much talking, but they understood each other's expressions and body language, and Jeremy managed to fold the seam of the tarpaulin under and stretch the tarpaulin tight while Marty removed the nails—he could do it with his hand—and then with the hammer drive them in again, right to the head. This wasn't going to be any kind of permanent improvement, but perhaps the roof would hold until the spring when it could be fixed by someone other than retired nuns or gay cabaret song stylists.

Sister Felicity was praying out loud as they descended the ladder, but she broke off to give them a grin when they were safely on the floor of the choir loft.

"A touch of tea to warm you up, you brave boys."

"Would love to, but the time—"

"You must. I'd never forgive myself if you came down with pneumonia like Sister Maria Goretti. Tell you what. I'll let you make it yourselves."

She brought them to a nook they hadn't seen before, a space with a bench upholstered in red vinyl. Ecclesiastical cuisine design. Jeremy squeezed in, and Sister Felicity, Mother Clare du Plessix, and Sister Clothilde followed. Marty fussed about making a fabulous pot of tea. "*Ta-da*," he said. The tray looked splendid, a yellow napkin folded just so, cookies angled daringly in a glass butter dish, a sprig of rosemary providing just the right color contrast.

"Nuns have no style," said Sister Clothilde, sighing. "I didn't think men did either, but I see I'm wrong." She fingered a crumb of cookie.

"Don't be maudlin, Sister Clothilde," said Mother Clare du Plessix, mildly.

They munched and nibbled for a while. The rain on the window crinkled the view of a dead garden, supervised by a supremely indifferent concrete statue of Saint Francis of Assisi. "So," said Jeremy, "I'm surprised you're working on a leaking roof on a Holy Day of Obligation."

Mother Clare du Plessix's response was automatic. "Obligation before devotion. This home is our responsibility, and we must keep it up as we can."

"I love this holiday, though," said Sister Clothilde. "Without the perfection of Mary, there'd have been no suitable vessel for Christ. He couldn't have been born. We'd all be lost."

"That's nonsense," said Marty. "You'd all be grandmothers. Some of you would be widows. You'd be retired from public office maybe, or having late-in-life professional careers as doctors or lawyers. You'd be managing Hillary's campaign for the Senate. Or challenging her. You'd have found a way to uncover meaning in your lives."

"The young are so naive, one forgets sometimes." Sister Felicity beamed at the boys. "You things imagine that what's available to you—or to young women of your generation—was also available to us. You can't see how the world has changed; you have no perspective."

"People of drive could always find their way," said Marty. "Look at, um, Emma Goldman. Madame Curie. Um. Lucrezia Borgia. Not to mention Madonna."

"There are as many different walls to fence one in as there are people in the world," replied Sister Felicity. "You can have no idea what someone of my generation faced. I was born the seventh of nine children on a farm in New Brunswick, in 1912. After six boys my parents didn't think the farm could support a child who couldn't haul milk—I was small and my leg was twisted as it still is. So I was given to a cousin to be raised, and brought to the convent when I was thirteen. No one could afford to feed me. They were hard times, and I was an offering to the Church. I was holy barter. My parents kept the other two boys they had after I was born, and once a year they came to visit me, as long as they were alive."

"Surely you could have left—"

"At thirteen? You think so? At fifteen, at sixteen, at nineteen? I'd taken vows, I'd been raised to believe that one kept vows. It's an outdated notion, I know."

"So you were brainwashed—"

"I found a family," said Sister Felicity. Her face was empty of rage or regret, because of intense willpower, or was it a natural state? Jeremy couldn't tell. She went on. "I entered into my formation with a will to know God and serve Him. I was devoted to the notion of service."

"You were an innocent," said Marty.

"Some innocent," said Sister Clothilde. "Did you know Sister Felicity has a doctorate in philosophy from McGill University?"

Sister Felicity looked annoyed at the exposure. "I found my way. And not at the cost of abandoning my vows or my faith. Nor my family."

"But your family abandoned you." Marty looked petulant.

"I mean my chosen family. My sisters."

"As for me," said Sister Clothilde, "I was from the proper side of the tracks. A wealthy Ontario merchant family. I was paraded in Montreal society as a great catch for some rising industrialist or politician. We were too prosperous for me to need to be educated. I entered the Order to focus on divine things and to leave that sort of—oh, a kind of faux-royalty, you might call it—behind."

Mother Clare du Plessix did not reveal her past when eyes turned to her. "We are in the present, we are in our community now, and God provides for us," she said. "I do fear sometimes that making fun of the religious is one of the last acceptable forms of social intolerance in our modern culture. All religious women are not feminists, at least not by the contemporary definition, but we are all feminists by experience."

"Hello. You are directed by male bishops and a pope," said Marty.

"Stone walls do not a cloister make, nor iron bars a cage," Mother Clare du Plessix insisted. "The *regula* of our order"— Jeremy saw that she recognized Marty's incomprehension—"by which I mean the body of rules of daily practice—reminds us what is of value. Daily. Think of it like this: the nutritional significance to a growing child of a daily glass of milk lies far more in the milk than in the glass."

"I would smash that glass," said Marty cheerily.

"And lose the milk. I know. Don't we know this? Where are our young sisters coming along? They want to find milk somewhere else."

"In their own bosoms." Marty couldn't help swiveling his shoulders as if they were padded to Joan Crawford proportions. "How could you live without children, really? Isn't that what gives life meaning?"

"How could *you* live without children?" said Sister Clothilde back at him. "Three single men old enough to have toddlers around their knees. What is it you're finding in life that makes being child-less tolerable?"

"Ah well, that's a different story," said Jeremy. "Is the rain letting up?"

"We're gay men, you know," said Marty. "You must know that, you're not blind."

For an instant Jeremy thought that one of the sisters was going to chirrup a remark about happiness, but he saw them all—one by one—accept the public announcement, and Mother Clare du Plessix said, "Of course we're not blind."

"It hardly makes a difference—" said Sister Clothilde. "Do you think women who live in community all their lives don't know about falling in love with persons of their own gender?"

"Well, it's the hot talk show issue, isn't it—lesbian nuns."

"Friends," said Mother Clare du Plessix, "let us accept that none of us here is either ignorant or stupid, but that all of us value our privacy. Let us keep the conversation to that which concerns all of us—"

Sisters Clothilde and Felicity looked faintly chastised; Marty looked as if he wanted to challenge Mother Clare du Plessix's authority to lay down conversational guidelines. Jeremy said, "We're more alike than we let on. Look at us. In our own ways. Communities of the same sex. Trying to get on in a world that makes us the butt of jokes. Trying to live together communally, sort of, in a world that prizes individual freedom above all."

"Trying to live without children," said Sister Clothilde.

"And some of us close to the end," said Mother Clare du Plessix. At Jeremy's expression she said, "Do you think I can't see Sean's condition, do you think that the cloistered are also clueless?"

"Why do you think we voted to welcome you back?" said Sister Felicity.

"There are never enough ways to be kind, and this was one that presented itself," said Sister Clothilde. "Besides, we get bored with only ourselves. Don't you?"

Mother Clare stood up. She muttered a prayer nearly under her breath and the other sisters answered "Amen." Before turning, she said, "In youth we accepted a life without children, believing that we would not die alone. But the modern times play a trick on us. God asks of us a final sacrifice. Nuns in our seventies and eighties, we find ourselves bereft of a younger generation, our sisters who would also have been our daughters. Sister Alice Coyne, alone in this neck of the province, cannot possibly fill the bill, however good she is. For gay men"—her pronunciation made it sound more French, *gaie*—"who are threatened by AIDS, who are dying young and childless too—it is not such a different situation. Perhaps, perhaps God brought us together."

"I am not going to be a son to any nun," said Marty. "Rosa Leftkowicz Rothbard of Flatbush would *plotz*."

"Be a brother, then," said Mother Clare du Plessix.

"I'm a sister, Sister." But he grinned.

"Small difference," said Mother Clare du Plessix, shrugging. "I'll be your brother, then, your big brother. And nag you to take care of yourselves. You hear?" She wagged a finger in Marty's face. "Take care of each other. That's the *regula*. That's all it is."

As Jeremy drove home under a tormented sky, he felt Marty glance over at him. "That was bizarre," Marty said at last. "I feel entirely too religious. Sort of slimed with it. This is fishing on a moonless night, I know, but I don't suppose you'd like to come home with me and get out of those wet clothes? Get warmed up by getting naked?"

Jeremy thought: It's my talking of Sean's sickness out loud that has pulled up the thought, the need, in Marty. I can feel it too. We're all so damned proficient in reticence.

He thought of admitting—*If I only thought I could!*—but he knew that would uncork the subject of Willem. "I thought Sean was the only one crazy enough to fancy me."

"Don't give yourself airs." Marty was curt. "Happens there are no other gay men in the car besides me. Sorry I mentioned it. Besides, I have to go to work in an hour. Can't call in sick at the Craftique, not with Christmas coming."

So much for brotherhood.

23

TABITHA HAD NEVER had much truck with nuns of any variety. Even during the period that her mom and Daddy Booth had suffered some sort of Catholic madness—later they called it the Roman flu—Tabitha had stayed the hell away from any of those witchy women, even the ones who had left the convent. You could always pick them out. Linda Pearl once made Tabitha choke on a Coke by standing over one of these escaped prisoners and miming giving the poor woman a Sinéad O'Connor scalping. Collaborator! There's no possible camouflage. It shows right down to what kind of pocketbook you carry; you pick whichever one makes you look the most uncomfortable with it.

Therefore, Tabitha's conversation with Sister Alice Coyne after mass had confused her. The woman was possessed with an obsession to comfort Tabitha, and Tabitha didn't want comforting. Nor did she want the phone number of Planned Parenthood, which she kind of thought Sister Alice might have been hinting at, but then Tabitha had always sucked at the game of Clue. "You need to find out for sure," Sister Alice had said.

"I am sure."

"What is the young gentleman going to do about it?"

"He didn't say anything. I suppose he thinks I'm lying, or that it's not his."

Sister Alice kicked a lower vestment drawer closed. "So you want to see Father Mike then. Shall I grab his calendar and make an appointment?"

"No." Tabitha had already changed her mind. The idea of Father Mike was even more upsetting than the idea of Pastor Huyck. Mike and Huyck. What made everyone think that she wanted to talk to men? She only wanted to marry one, not talk to him.

"Look. You are in a bad way." Sister Alice delivered herself of this pronouncement with relish. "Tabitha, I don't know why you came to us instead of to your own pastor, but I'm not going to ask you to explain. I know how things are. The Lord works in mysterious ways His wonders to perform. An outdated notion in this era of the Uncertainty Principle and millennial disgruntledness, but never mind. You've come here because you're in your life up over your head."

Well, yes, perhaps, but wasn't that the point about life? She didn't say anything.

"You've got a possible pregnancy, you're unmarried, and your mother is suffering some sort of confusion of the brain. I can see that your two younger brothers are not much help these days. Hogan and—is it Kurt?"

"Kirk, like in *Star Trek*."

"Yes." Sister Alice didn't look as if she knew much about *Star Trek*. "Tabitha, you've got to get to the root of your problems. You shouldn't be going through this alone. Do I understand you have a series of Deadbeat Dads who were married to your mother? They should step up and help you with her, so you can concentrate on your own problem."

"I already tried them."

"Then when you get home, call me with their phone numbers. I'll do a little advocacy work on my lunch hour today. No, don't thank me, I feel like it," she said, grinning like a bulldog that has cornered a chihuahua. "Nothing gives me a rush like doing works of mercy or menace." But she was laughing at herself. "Share this burden. You needn't carry it all alone, Tabitha."

"If only I knew what my mother wanted," said Tabitha.

"She wants to go back to her roots. Isn't that what we all want?"

"I'm not sure Grandma Prelutski was a barrel of fun for Mom."

"Your mom can't take nourishment from her present day, she can't help abusing her kids. She just can't help it. She wants *something* in her past. One of her husbands might help. They ought to. Look, I know this, Tabitha. I was an adopted child myself. I spent twelve years in an orphanage in Troy, New York, run by nuns. Then I lived with my adoptive parents for nine years. I loved them and still do, but in the end the nuns were my first home. I needed to go back. We all do, especially in times of crisis."

What do I go back to, thought Tabitha, but didn't say anything. She just thanked Sister Alice and left the parish house, and did as she was told: called Sister Alice with the dads' phone numbers. What a peculiar feeling to do as she was told. She didn't actually mind it.

After homeroom and first period next day, she cut out. She tried to look as if she was running to vomit in the gutter, just in case Principal Jack Reeves was glancing out his window. In fact, she felt like throwing up, just a little, and she might have been able to produce something if apprehended. But if Reeves saw her, he just let her go. She wasn't worth the chase. She knew it herself.

She'd spent some time last night on the sofa thinking about roots, about her earliest memories. They seemed blank of mood, like stills from someone else's childhood. Near as she could figure, her oldest memory was of Mom giving her a Cabbage Patch doll one birthday and then taking it back after Tabitha had ruined it by soaking its head in bleach trying to dye its hair. Mom had hung the doll upside down by clothespins to the clothesline in the backyard. Bald, glassy-eyed, rained on, swarmed by little red ants, the doll endured. Tabitha had camped out beneath, too small to reach, too stupid to think of a chair. By the time Mrs. Scales had surrendered the creature, Tabitha had lost interest in it.

The curious thing is that she could see the picture in her head like a snapshot used in a Christmas card to summon up a year in the life of the family. But she couldn't remember feeling guilty about her misbehavior, or angry at her mother, or sad for the doll. What kind of sorry oldest memory was that? Admitting the feebleness of her response made her feel kind of pukey.

Bijou Motor Supply. She stood in front of the door-sized glass case that had once displayed movie posters. Now there was a hand-lettered sign that said:

DID YOU KNOW?
We Stock:
V BELTS
SHEAVES   PULLEYS
ROLLER CHAIN
SPROCKETS   DRILL BITS
BAC-A-LARMS
S-K TOOLS   DUPONT PAINT
EMERGENCY BEACONS
We Make:
HYDRAULIC HOSES
We Press:
50 TON HYDRAULIC PRESS
We Turn:
DRUMS AND ROTORS

What the sign didn't say was:

We Supply:
IMPLEMENTS FOR WHACKING YOUR MOM

But Tabitha supposed that they did, and so she went in and found something suitable, a heavy-duty staple gun with convenient handle. Tape a couple of Pampers around it and wrap that up in a towel. You got maximum grip, considerable weight, padding for safety. And, Tabitha thought a bit uneasily, if there was bleeding you could just dispose of the Pampers in the traditional manner. Jack Reeves wouldn't dig up the septic system looking for a couple of bloody Pampers, would he?

She spent the rest of the day hanging out at the Crosswinds Shopping Center, shoplifting a little lunch and thinking of other unpleasant moments of childhood in which she might have wept, or cursed, or snuggled, or run away. Why had she been so passive? She felt increasingly disgusted at herself. When she got home that afternoon, Kirk wasn't there. "Where is he, I thought it was his turn to babysit?" she said irritably to Hogan.

"He came home at lunch and was practicing scales. I think he's converting so he can sing in the Catholic choir. I think he's fallen in love with that faggot music director."

From her bedroom, Mrs. Leontina Scales began a wail, like the noon siren. "What, she's going to join the choir too?" said Tabitha darkly.

"You know, it's all these Catholics' fault."

It was so rare for Hog actually to converse that Tabitha stopped in her tracks. "Mom, cut it out," she yelled, and turned and looked at her brother. Scarfing down a plate of cold beans, he stood against a metal folding chair he'd stolen from some community function or other. His butt bunched up over the back of it. He hadn't shaved in a week and he looked like a high school graduation portrait of Fred Flintstone.

The bag with the staple gun was heavy but if she set it down it might clunk, and she didn't want Hogan to guess what she was up to. "What do you mean, it's the Catholics' fault?"

"If the stupid bitch hadn't gone over there, that Catholic statue wouldn't have clobbered her."

"Yeah but, I mean, statues aren't like responsible parties."

"Duhh. But she's obsessed, she's going there all the time. She's possessed."

The Radical Radiant Pentecostals believed more in being possessed by the Holy Spirit than by anyone else; they were sort of snooty about Satan, as if Satan needed to be discussed only in lower-class churches.

"Daddy Booth called today," said Hogan.

"You talked to him?" Hogan wasn't much on the phone. Daddy Booth's fluctuating delight and disgust in his son Kirk usually made Hogan indifferent to him. But Hogan was indifferent to everyone.

He shrugged. "Said some stormtrooper nun called him up and told him he had to come see Mom and take care of her."

Tabitha put the shopping bag with the staple gun down on the floor gently. If she didn't use it, could she bring it back for a refund? (Come to that, could she clonk Mom over the head with it and then bring it back for a refund?) "Yeah?"

"He said he wasn't answerable to any stupid nun and he hadn't been a Catholic in ten years or more and she should mind her own fucking business, in those exact words."

And Daddy Booth was the educated one among them. "So I take it he's not coming?"

"He said he'd call Daddy Wally and Daddy Casey himself, and to tell you to tell the nun to get off his case or he'd get a court order restraining her."

"I don't think you can restrain a nun."

Hogan shrugged. "Daddy Wally seems to have escaped." He began to shove beans in his mouth forkful after forkful, even before he could swallow what he already had in there. It was as if he was trying to choke his own words. Well, Daddy Wally was his father. "His phone is out and his landlady said he moved without paying the last four months, and no forwarding address, and we're supposed to pay it."

"Daddy Booth called to tell you that?" Tabitha was irate. "Mom, shut up!" The siren again. "You know, it makes him look good to make Daddy Wally look bad."

"I don't care, don't give a fuck how anyone looks. No stupid nun should be riling up the Daddies, however lousy they are. It's those Catholics, they think they own the universe."

"They do," said Tabitha. Hogan looked at her hatefully. "I mean, they do think that," she said.

"Mom's off her rocker and goes playing the Curse of the Mummy every Sunday in the Catholic church. Kirk's gonna slice off his nuts so he can sing the high notes in Catholic hymns for his new boyfriend, and you're giving out our family phone numbers to some Catholic nun? What the fuck is wrong with everybody?"

"Chill pill. Don't get on my case. That nun said Mom needed to get back to her roots, since she's sort of brainwashed about the present and isn't really here. I thought it made sense, so I gave Sister Alice the phone numbers. Look, Hog, I can't help it if Daddy Wally isn't answering his phone."

"This is not about Daddy Wally, you cretin." He went to the doorway and screamed, "Mom, will you cut out that racket before

I strangle you." His voice had wobbled with its own treble panic, matching her own. There was a moment of strange, curious silence. Then Mrs. Scales began again, down in the lower register.

"This is called going back to her roots? Do you mean going back to baby talk? She hasn't said a word in English for three days."

Tabitha picked up the bag again. "Let me go talk to her."

"Something's gotta break here," said Hogan.

Her skull, thought Tabitha.

"I'm gonna go assassinate that nun, first off, and then I have the evening shift," said Hogan. "Don't wait up."

"Mind yourself." It just slipped out.

"Mind myself?" said Hogan. "You want me to mind myself?"

"I mean, I'll mind Mom, leave me alone, will you?" And what, she thought, what will it do to my baby if I accidentally hit Mom too hard and kill her? They talk about original sin, does that mean anything to this baby, being part of me now, no larger than a—oh, how do I know, a lipstick maybe? Is this little baby going to have to share in the blame?

She was glad Hogan was getting ready to go out. She didn't want to have to explain the box of Pampers to him. She started to work it out. She could use two diapers for the gentle application of force, and if they didn't rip or tear under stress she could put them back in the box and save them for applying to the baby when necessary. Having a project gave her a kind of rush she liked.

Working in her room with the diapers and the staple gun, she could hear Hogan in the garage, cursing because the dryer had stopped mid-cycle again and his grease-suit was still mostly damp. A string of unimaginative profanities issued, at a volume to challenge their mother's, from where Hog was no doubt standing in his grimy jockey shorts, his stomach pouching forward like his own pregnancy. He'd be wanting to beat the crap out of the dryer.

She knew exactly how he felt, and she secured the Pampers with extra adhesive tape. She murmured "Holy, holy, holy," under her voice just to be contrary as she tiptoed into her mother's room.

Sitting up in bed, Mrs. Scales was dressed in a housecoat that dated from the dark ages. It had pictures of a hundred identical dusky Jamaican women with big bee-stung lips the color of cranberry sauce; each woman stood beneath a palm tree and slung her hips at an angle. On each turbaned head balanced a tray with a whole produce section of tropical fruits. The housecoat had been washed so often that the lime green piping was reduced to a white frayed coil. On her head, perhaps in sympathy with the tribe of fruit ladies, Leontina Scales had wrapped a bath towel. Had she had some sort of premonition about what Tabitha intended to do? Or had she merely washed her hair? If the latter, Tabitha could look on this as a sign of improvement, maybe, and abandon the current campaign. She skootched the paper bag with the padded staple gun in it along the floor with her feet so that her mom wouldn't see it. "Hi there, Mom," she said, as brightly as she could, which wasn't very.

Her mother didn't look over. She did, however, reduce the volume of her wails. She had two hands up to her face, one at each cheek, as if feigning an expression of abject surprise. Her feet, in bunny slippers that had once been pink but now were gray with old age, were tucked one on top of the other, as if the bunnies were comforting each other before being butchered. "Sheez," murmured Tabitha. Her mom wasn't going to make this any easier for her, was she. "What, you got a mess of hair there, Mom? You're going to catch your death of cold." Or of something.

Tabitha pulled a bit of toweling away and felt at her mom's scalp. This felt halfway between assisting Linda Pearl at an unwrap and testing a diaper. The hair was dry but there was a funny crinkle, a feel of dry raspy coolness. "What the hell you got up here?"

A loaf of bread in its wrapper, bundled up in the towel. Two slices were gone and the twistie replaced like a topknot. "God almighty, Mom, you're wearing day-old baked goods now? I can't take this anymore." Tabitha removed the loaf of bread and brought it to the kitchen. Her mom began to wail again, louder.

"What're you doing to her, she was settling down," snarled Hogan from the garage. He was trying to iron his uniform dry, and he was farting in his underpants loud enough to be heard over their mother's ululations.

"I'm going to read the Bible to her, leave me alone," said Tabitha. "I thought you were gone already." She scooped up the Bible from the folding table in the living room. Something long and boring. Mom might fall asleep and then, clonko. Tabitha could arrange a broken lamp on the bedclothes and concoct some story about a housecleaning accident.

And then? And then what? Mom could sleep in heavenly peace. They'd ask for a Catholic funeral. And Tabitha could have her child without fear that her mother would sniff it down and ruin it too.

"You want a story?" said Tabitha. "Something to listen to. Shut up and listen."

She snatched up the stool from her mother's kidney-shaped makeup table and dragged it next to the bed. Then she balanced the Bible on her lap with her left hand and let her right hand fall into the paper bag. She had to stoop a little to graze her fingers against what she was beginning to think of as Mother's Little Helper. "Let's see," she said, looking in the table of contents for the shortest chapter of the Bible. She settled on something called Tobit and began to read.

Mrs. Scales dropped her hands from her face and plumped up her pillow and lifted her head a little bit, and only then did Tabitha realize that her mother could probably see her in the mirror of the makeup table. Damn. She'd have to read until her mom actually nodded off.

But the section—accidentally, of course, for God hadn't inspired the Bible to be interesting—the section wasn't too bad. It was sort of like a fairy tale. A magic fish in it, if she was getting the point, and a guardian angel.

The story was too good. Her mom's eyes looked bright and gummy, like coffee candies after they've been sucked for the first couple of minutes. She was training her gaze on her daughter like a hawk. Double damn. Tabitha tried to make her voice sound boring, but Mrs. Scales just seemed to listen all the harder.

Tabitha had picked too compelling a section. She purposely flipped over a couple of pages and began to read from something more suitably dreadful—the top of the page said KINGS—but her mom began to moan and paw at the book. She was actually following the story of Tobit, then. Tabitha had to turn back and find out where she'd left off.

When the story was done, her mom closed her eyes in satisfaction. She wasn't asleep, but at least she wasn't looking. Tabitha reached down and gripped the staple gun. On your mark. Get set.

The phone rang. Triple damn! Mrs. Scales's eyes flew open. "Waaaaaaah," she said, like I Love Loooosy screwing up again.

"Tabitha!" It was Hogan. Goddamn it, wasn't he gone yet? "Tabitha, it's for you. It's Daddy Casey."

She dropped the Bible. She pulled the towel down over her mother's eyes, and ran out of the room, hugging the paper bag with the staple gun to her belly. Before she got to the phone she knew already that Daddy Casey was going to be no help. Dads didn't do *help*. Ask Jesus Christ himself. Hanging on the cross, hung out to dry, he must have waited and waited for his Heavenly Father to come in the nick of time. *Ha.*

24

AFTER MASS ON the Sunday following the Feast of the Immaculate Conception, Jeremy headed across the parking lot. It had snowed the night before, three powdery inches, and the old geezers were being cautious on the blacktop. Polly Osterhaus and Peggy Mueller caught up with Jeremy as he waited in the line snaking toward the doors leading into the downstairs Assembly Room of the Radical Radiants.

"If Thebes had anything that approximated a real mall, instead of that strip mall wannabe called Crosswinds, we hard-boiled holiday shoppers wouldn't have to make do with Radical Radiant handicrafts," muttered Peggy. "Ames is all well and good, but a trip to Syracuse and Watertown can be treacherous this time of year."

"Face it," whispered Polly, "the Radiantics have better small muscle coordination. Their potholders are in peppier colors. More fringe on their afghans."

"Hey there, we Catholics do better macramé remote sleeves," objected Jeremy.

"Yes. And just who needs a remote sleeve? You can't see through them to change the channels."

"Then you use them to store your extra bacon. Of a Sunday morning."

The atmosphere was one of manufactured mirth. Jeremy thought the Catholic husbands, trailing behind their wives, were looking dubious. Probably, he guessed, their Catholic wives spent money in the name of ecumenism and because this was a better grade of goods. The Pentecostal wives seem to have perfected a semblance of shyness and even indifference—"Oh, do you really want that old thing? Mercy, you're being charitable again; let me wrap it up for you 'cause I just can't stand even to look at it anymore." Jeremy heard one Catholic woman say to her husband, "You old grouch. They send all their kids to Our Lady's June Fair. It evens out."

"So," said Peggy Mueller, "I hear that someone else is doing the music for your wedding, Polly."

"An old friend," replied Polly with, thought Jeremy, supremely well-calibrated nonchalance. "Irene Menengest. You don't know her, I think?"

"Does she go to Our Lady's?" said Peggy, who must know that if Irene Menengest went to Our Lady's and had a singing voice she'd be in the choir already. Jeremy would have insisted on it.

"No, she's not a Catholic."

"Oh is that so. Jeremy, is that allowed?"

"Of course it's allowed," said Jeremy. "Really, Peggy. Polly can have the Village People if she wants. The only restriction comes in the choice of material, and Polly's chosen some nice stuff."

"I hope you're coming, Peggy," continued Polly. "We're still waiting for your RSVP."

"Wild horses couldn't keep me away, but unfortunately I didn't marry into a family of wild horses. I married into the Mueller clan. There's talk of a post-Christmas Christmas party that weekend."

"I figured there'd be lots of that type of complication. Which is one reason I didn't try to engage the choir for the wedding. After all the holiday rehearsals, the concert material leading up to the midnight mass, and so on—who needs another obligation?"

Peggy said, "How thoughtful you are. Now Caleb—it is Caleb Briggs, isn't it?—he's not Catholic, is he?"

"He's thinking of converting, but we're not waiting for that."

"In the old days you'd have needed a dispensation to marry outside the faith."

"You aren't old enough to know the old days," said Jeremy. "Really, Peggy."

"My mother needed a dispensation to marry my father because he hadn't made his Easter Duty the year before."

"Shocking," said Jeremy, "I didn't know you were a child of sin."

"He was in a wheelchair for eighteen months following an industrial accident at the paper mill. Don't change the subject. I want to hear more about Caleb. How'd you meet him, Polly?"

The line moved forward bit by bit. "All the good stuff is going to be snapped up by these sharp old ladies," replied Polly. "Oh, I met him around town. You know, he's not even religious. He's . . . he's sort of nothing." As if eager to change the subject, she swiveled to Jeremy. "How're the rehearsals going with Irene?"

"She's got a nice voice," he answered. "I can see why you trust her. She's a little tentative in the upper registers, but she's got decent volume and a pretty sure pitch."

"Sounds lovely," said Peggy. "You should sign her up, Jeremy,"

"I don't know, we don't see eye to eye." And besides, he thought, maybe pretty soon it'll be someone else's problem.

They were in at last. The queue snaked at the pace of a buffet line. It was embarrassing to spend five minutes in front of a card table selling old Barbie dolls with crocheted hoop skirts *à la* Scarlett O'Hara, beneath which you were intended to store an extra roll of toilet paper. "Bathroom Barbies," they were called. Their legs fit right in the cardboard tube. But Jeremy didn't want to spend eight dollars on a Bathroom Barbie, and he didn't want to meet the eye of the clever Radical Radiant Pentecostal craftswoman who had spent all year buying old Barbies at Catholic yard sales and turning them into moneymakers for the Cliffs of Zion.

"Are you still rehearsing with Irene?" said Polly after a while, considering a sad little potholder that looked pre-scorched.

"One time more, maybe two," said Jeremy. "I had to order some sheet music from Iowa City, and it hasn't come in yet. So we've got stuff to work on still."

The line advanced along a display of potted cacti made out of stuffed denim. "Pin cushions," said the saleswoman. "Cacti are already prickly, you see, so they don't mind being pricked some more."

"Me either," said Jeremy. "But I don't sew much, myself."

"Your wife?"

"Well, I don't have a wife."

"I should get it for you and show you how to sew," said Peggy, leaning forward. "Someone without a wife shouldn't suffer so."

"I'm not exactly *suffering*," said Jeremy, but thought, Really, what other word would I use?

"Hi, hey, it's you," said someone, in his face almost, and Jeremy reared back to register the kid brother in that basket case of a family.

"Oh, hi," said Jeremy, "um, Kirk."

"*Hi*. Whatcha doing here?"

"Well, um, realizing I don't have enough money for a stuffed cactus," said Jeremy, glancing at the saleswoman, who had arbitrarily picked one up and was poised to wrap it in a sheet of newspaper.

"He doesn't have a wife," explained the saleswoman.

"Oh, you don't?" said Kirk. "That's too bad." He looked thrilled.

Polly pushed from behind. Jeremy was trapped and uneasy. The kid stood inches from him, their belt buckles were almost touching, and though he was cute in that sort of coltish way Jeremy didn't want either Kirk's attention or his warm breath so near. Jeremy's glasses were fogging up. "It's nice to have some Catholics here," said Kirk. "You should come more often."

Jeremy glanced around for an escape route. "How's your mom?"

The boy's face clouded over. Jeremy relented. "I hope she's feeling okay. I liked meeting your family."

"We liked you, all of us did. You should come back. I could show you the song for the high school Shakespeare and maybe you could tutor me. I need help at the singing part. I'm being the Fool. I have to wear diagonal colors, and jingles on my feet. I have to prance."

"Jeremy could tutor you at that," said Peggy, "or I'm available. We're all fools here. I've had a lot of practice."

Kirk turned pink and put both his hands on Jeremy's chest, like a dog about to lick his master's nose. "Would you, do you think? I need a teacher."

Jeremy backed up into Peggy Mueller's bosom.

"Steady," said Peggy.

"Please," said Jeremy, "can we put it off? The Christmas season is so busy, and there's so much going on—"

But this was the kid with the crazy mother, and there was no subtlety of expectation in his eyes; it was all or nothing, and *nothing* was beginning to show on his face. "I'll see," said Jeremy, panicking, "maybe. I'm sure you're better than you think. Isn't there a music coach in the high school?"

"Oh well, if you call that music." Kirk backed off, and looked hurt, and managed, being a slender kid and a Radical Radiant, to slip off through the crowd. He paused halfway up some steps to the stage area and looked back over his shoulder balefully at Jeremy. His jeans were so tight his bum looked inflated, as if it would squeak like a bathtub toy if you pinched it.

"All things to all people," singsonged Polly Osterhaus. "That's our Jeremy."

"I can't take this, I'm not giving any Christmas presents this year," said Jeremy, "so help me God, it isn't worth it. All that unfettered—enthusiasm—"

"There you are," said Sister Alice Coyne. "Mercy, this is a mob scene. What, you're not buying? That's not very ecumenical of you."

"You think the Sisters of the Sorrowful Mysteries want a Bathroom Barbie for Christmas?"

"Probably not. Jeremy, I've a phone message for you, it just came in at the parish house, and I thought I might find you here." Sister Alice consulted a scrap of paper in her hand. "It was from Martin Rothbard. He said to tell you something about Sean; he's got an infection or something."

Jeremy was halfway across the parking lot to the rectory when Kirk Scales showed up at his side. "I thought you were maybe looking for me," he said.

"I wasn't," said Jeremy.

"You can call me. I am free on Tuesdays. I need help."

"Yes," said Jeremy. You sure do. He sprinted to the parish house steps.

At the office Jeremy called the Riley house, but Sean's mother sounded calm and undistressed. "Oh, Sean," she said, "himself spent the night out with one of his boyfriends, don't you know. Probably drunk and disorderly. That's lads for ye." She had that old Irish way of stressing the gender to indicate, not so subtly, that he wasn't sleeping around. "Who's this?"

"Jeremy Carr."

"Oh, yes, the music fellow. Sure and I don't know what to tell you, Jeremy, but I'll let him know you rang."

Jeremy hung up. Sean must be at Marty's if he didn't spend the night at home. With some difficulty Jeremy extracted his car from the parking lot, eager not to encounter anyone else.

Marty Rothbard lived a quarter mile from the I-81 exit ramp about three miles south of Thebes. His apartment had been something of an afterthought, and done with economy or tightfisted stupidity. It was basically a one room tent-shaped space built over a garage that the county used for storing highway lawnmowers; you could only stand up straight in the center of the room, a square of about ten feet in each direction. Beyond that the roof slanted to meet the floor, and you had to stoop, or crouch, or slide yourself on your belly. The difficult part was the toilet. It was tucked under the eaves; you had to use it with your chest pressed up against the tops of your thighs. Given that there was only a cardboard screen around the toilet, made of refrigerator packaging, the indignity was immense, and Marty didn't entertain often.

So Jeremy wasn't used to seeing Sean there, stretched out on Marty's futon. Sean was fully clothed, and had a scarf wrapped around his neck beside, and several greasy looking blankets were half kicked away. "Got your message," said Jeremy to Marty, who looked grim and tired like a vet of some secret war. "What is all this?"

"Oh, the saints come marching in," said Sean from the bed. "How was church? See my folks there?—" He interrupted himself with a low, rumbling cough.

"We ate last night over at Bozo Joe's," said Marty. "Sean had a milkshake and it was too thick or something, he started coughing and couldn't stop. It was disgusting. I took him back here because he didn't want to go home."

"Why didn't you take him to the hospital?"

"This isn't hospital-worthy gunk I'm expectorating," said Sean. "It's your standard issue thoracic snot—" He demonstrated, filthily; then he grabbed for a bath towel.

"So Marty—we're going to take him bodily to the hospital whether he wants to go or not? I'm ready."

"I wanted you to come over and make sure he didn't choke on his own fluids while I go out and grab some coffee," Marty replied. "I wasn't exactly expecting company so I didn't get things in."

"How bad *is* this?" said Jeremy. He sat down on a footstool and didn't judge correctly, and bumped his head against the ceiling. But when he turned and glared, he saw that there were smudge marks from Marty's oily scalp as a sort of high-water mark all around the room. "Sean, are you being stupid or are you just being idiotic?"

"Glad to know you've just come from church, it makes you that much more sympathetic. Just for that, I'm going to let you help me get to the crapper. Can you pull me up?"

"I'm outa here. Three coffees?" said Marty, and split.

"Marty's such a good friend to you, Sean. Now please don't tell me you're feeling liquid at the other end, too."

"Feel me yourself and let me know," said Sean. "You fucktard. This isn't exactly fun for me, you know."

Jeremy got him to the toilet and then stood as far away as he could and called, "You're okay, right?" and there was an answering blat.

"Name that tune," called Sean.

Jeremy began to sing one of his songs, the one that still required a little work on the bridge. "You don't need help?" he called hopefully.

"The kind of help I need you can't give."

"Did you tell your folks you were feeling under the weather?" said Jeremy, knowing the answer.

"What business is it of theirs?"

"I think it's some business of theirs. You might need a doctor."

"I'm not a kid, Germy." The toilet flushed. "Would you mind opening a window? I have some pride, you know."

"It's freezing out. That's the worst thing for you, that air."

"Do as I say."

Jeremy obeyed, but he closed the window after only a minute. "You're going to wait until the absolute last possible minute to tell anyone? Don't you think you should get some advice about this, Sean? They are your family. You've got to prepare them."

"There's no fairness in any of this, why should I try to introduce any? Don't make me mad, I'll cough my lungs out. You know my folks. You see them at church. Come on. Mr. and Mrs. Sanctum Sanctorum. They're Catholic Nazis and homophobic Irish mafia and the Judgment of Santa Claus all rolled up in one. If they can keep themselves in the dark about me despite all evidence to the contrary, why should I disabuse them of it? Why should I help them out one fucking bit?"

"Well, for one reason, you live with them." It was a relief to try sounding abrasive. "They could be Genghis Khan and the Queen of the Night, but they're still your kin, and even the wicked are capable of suffering."

"I consider it a spectator sport to watch them slip around any difficult subject. They'd rephrase the truth to make me—inert—irresponsible—a victim. They'd rather suspect my dentist of infecting me with a contaminated toothpick than accept the fact that I'm gay. Why are you making me talk this all out again?"

"So you're going to stay here until exactly when?"

"You heard about the Hawaii Supreme Court ruling this week?

Upholding some legalized oppression that the legislators added to the state constitution to forbid gay marriage? Who do you think was out there leading the rally?"

"You're joking."

"They would've been if they weren't so cheap, I bet. Anyway, I'm sure they sent their prayers winging to support the bigots."

"Must be fun to have dinner at your house."

"You're welcome to stay here, of course," said Marty halfheartedly, coming in with three coffee cups steadied in a takeout tray.

"I'm going to stay until I'm ready to go. A day, or two," said Sean.

"What if I stop by your house and chat with your folks," said Jeremy. "Listen. I could just tell them you're not feeling great and that's all. At least it'll be the beginning of telling them, Sean. Come on."

"You do that," said Sean, "and I'll back out of singing with you in New York."

As if, Jeremy thought, looking at the exhausted, yellow-skinned figure letting himself back down on the mattress, as if you're ever going to be able to make it to Manhattan at this rate. But that was a fiction of survival, it was something Sean was aiming for, and Jeremy didn't have the heart to contradict him. He just shook his head—trapped again by people he loved—and fiddled with the lid of the coffee, burning his fingers.

25

PASTOR JAKOB HUYCK wanted nothing other than to make a nuisance of himself. A good fundamentalist pastor should pester everyone with the fundamentals, he reasoned. You're not a high school kid. So what are you doing creeping your car along Papermill Road like some sort of criminal casing the joint? Just park and march up to the house and ring the bell. You have as much right as anyone.

Sadly, it was Kirk rather than Tabitha Scales who opened the door.

"Oh, hi," said Kirk. He was panting slightly and looking a little disheveled. Huyck couldn't help wondering if the boy had been indulging in self-abuse, but then he saw a couple of bite-size barbells lying on top of the newspapers on the radiator. "I thought you were someone else," said Kirk. "Do you need to come in? Nobody else is here."

Perhaps Jesus had led Huyck here to do some holy work or other. Or maybe he could find out more about Tabitha. "I'd love to, thanks," he said, and shouldered his way in.

The boy was ill-clad for the season—a family trait, Huyck was deciding—and when Kirk sprawled in a sort of disconsolate longueur on the sofa, legs akimbo out of those white moiré running shorts, Huyck was given to think of Tabitha in a gratifying if unsettling way. Unsettling because this was a lad, more or less, shaking his crop of ash brown hair like some kind of female film star of the Forties, and though Huyck was modern for his church and judged not lest he be judged, the idea of finding a boy sexy, even for a misbegotten brief moment of mistaken identity, was repugnant not to say disgusting. "Put something on, you'll catch your death of cold," said Huyck. *In loco parentis* when needed, and Lord knows the only parentis around here was certifiably loco.

Kirk sneered and put on an oversized sweatshirt that, in its voluminous folds and low hem, made him look even more like an anorexic female posing for one of those ads for bisexual cologne, the point of which escaped Huyck except to drag the young to perdition. What a refreshing concept, perdition.

"Tell me about Mother," he said. "Might I hope that she's off someplace being rehabilitated?"

"She's off someplace, is right." Kirk's was a mumbly, sideways voice. "A nun gave my sister Tabitha some advice about Mom needing to connect with the past, with her roots or something—don't ask me."

"A nun?" Huyck smelled betrayal. He smelled conversion. He smelled the faint acrid undertone of male sweat emanating from the boy on the couch, and considered telling him to go wash under his armpits, but decided that was beyond the scope of his ministry. Besides, the boy would probably return shirtless. Please. "You must mean Sister Alice Coyne, I presume, of Our Lady's."

"Yeah, her. She's been talking to Tabitha and trying to help."

Huyck wondered if his reticence about not beleaguering the Scales family in general, and Tabitha particularly, was about to backfire in his face. "So where are your mother and Tabitha—I'm assuming they're together."

"Tabitha took her out in the car for a drive. Tabitha said she couldn't get anything done here, there were too many interruptions."

"She's left you all alone in your exercises."

"I didn't want to go. Besides, I'm expecting company."

"You hardly look dressed for company."

"I wasn't expecting you," said Kirk pointedly. Huyck wondered if that was a subtle message that he was to move on and leave Kirk alone, but he decided not to abandon the boy yet. "So what's this roots business again? Sort of like that television show?"

"Oh, it doesn't make any sense to me. You know for a while Mom couldn't say the beginnings of her words. It was kind of funny at first, as if there were other meanings behind everything she was trying to say. As if they'd been there all along, but she'd been too good and churchy to say them. The day we brought her home from the clinic, we passed our neighbor up the street—Ann Bletheroe. She was eating a piece of pizza at the curb while waiting for her ride to work. Mom looked at her and said, *Ann does not live by bread alone.* Well, she's pleasingly plump, you know, and then Mom said, *Oy, her cup is overflowing.* I mean, it was almost cool at first. The Dark Side of Mom. But she's seemed to get lost in it. Well, you've seen her. Sister Alice says that Mom losing the beginning of her words means that she's lost the sense of the beginning of her life—where her life has meaning, or where meaning begins, or began, something like that—so Tabitha is taking Mom out for a drive to look at the places she lived when she was a little girl with her own mother, who is dead a long time now."

"And Sister Alice is trained in this sort of mumbo-jumbo medicine?"

"She helps take care of a lot of old nuns somewhere, I think."

"Your mother and Tabitha both should beware the blandishments of the Catholics among us. Of course I like Father Mike Sheehy and it's a great convenience to share a parking lot with the faithful of Our Lady's, but one has to understand the difference between being neighborly and poaching on someone else's territory." He thought he had said that pretty well, and allowed himself a smile. "I haven't seen you at Sunday services lately, Kirk."

"Mom is quite a handful, and you know she goes down in the basement of the Catholic church. Do you think it's something like being Slain in the Spirit? I mean I've seen folks roll and tumble when you do a Call to the Lord. Do you think Mom is rolling and tumbling in answer to her own Call?"

"Answering the Call of a Roman Catholic refrigerator? I think not. Don't make fun of things you don't understand, Kirk. You're not fully formed in your attitudes."

"Mom used to say that to Tabitha when she wanted to see R-rated films at the age of twelve. We all thought she meant that Tabitha's breasts weren't fully formed yet."

The thought of Tabitha's breasts was a bit overwhelming, and Huyck concentrated on the glossy reproduction of a painting of cows in a millstream that hung over the TV. At some point in the history of the print it had been set flat, and a cup of coffee placed on it, for a mug-sized brown ring hovered in the air around the head of the nearest cow. It looked something like a halo. Well, he thought. Holy cow.

"Where did Mother grow up? Nearby? Perhaps I'll run into Tabitha and Mother. I can't abide the notion that they're taking advice from Sister Alice when I'm available to help. I am your family's spiritual adviser."

"Mom lived here and there, mostly on the mill slope," said Kirk vaguely. "She used to point out the houses when we were little, but I never paid attention."

"I assume your brother is with them?"

"No, he's at work at the gas station."

The phone rang. Huyck prepared his closing remarks while Kirk scrambled across the sofa to grab the receiver. There was no point in Huyck's trying to pretend he couldn't hear Kirk's remarks, nor see the sudden slump of his shoulders. The conversation was brief and Kirk spoke in a monotone after the initial flare-up of pleasure.

"Nothing too too troubling, I hope," said Huyck mildly.

"Nah. This guy was going to come over and help me learn my vocal parts for the school holiday *musicale*, but he's busy and can't make it."

"I'm quite a singer myself, as you know. I've done *Pirates* and *Mikado*. Perhaps I can assist."

"I don't think so."

"Was it Jeremy Carr?"

Kirk blushed. "I'm being a fool. I mean in the school play, the fool, the one who says and does all the dumb things, only they're really the things that matter. We can't do anything religious, of course; it's a public school."

"Don't get me started. Ah, but you can be a fool for God whether they know it or not. Saint Paul called himself one. Second Corinthians, Chapter Eleven—and he admonished the faithful to accept him: 'For you suffer fools gladly, whereas you yourself are wise.'"

"I'm not that kind of fool. More like a jester or a joker, I think."

"'For you suffer if a man bring you into bondage, if a man devour you,'" continued Huyck. "And so on."

"You want to see my costume? I was going to show it to Jeremy." He looked dejected.

"The Catholics will let you down, and they will let you down. They can't help it. Why are you doing this to yourself? Your whole family is wobbling in its faith. This is a very dangerous time for you all. Kirk," said Huyck, "get down on your knees and pray with me for your faith to be revitalized."

"I don't think so."

"The Lord is calling you."

Kirk just shook his head.

Things were worse than Huyck had realized. He was beginning to lose his grip. "Well, I will keep you in my prayers," he said. When he stood to take his leave, Kirk threw himself on the sofa and buried his face in a pillow. He didn't give the Pastor a proper goodbye. "Peace be with you," muttered Huyck, dubiously. He was glad to get back to his car, even if it did smell of spoiled milk.

The hills were covered with snow, and the houses too. In the daylight the strings of Christmas lights looked like tassels on the lot of a used car showplace. People of Thebes who couldn't afford pizza would spend ungodly amounts of money on colored lights in the winter. It was on the edge of blasphemy, somehow, and it always set Huyck off.

Now where was Mrs. Scales amid all this Christmas garbage, where was Tabitha?

26

TABITHA HAD SPENT a half an hour that morning sitting alone behind the steering wheel, practicing pulling out the Object of Healing from behind the passenger's seat and clunking the headrest with it. The headrest was nicely padded and so the instant of contact was blunted; the staple gun bounced in an easygoing way. It gave Tabitha courage.

And who knew, maybe Sister Alice Coyne was right. Perhaps in revisiting her childhood haunts, Mrs. Scales would respond nicely to a tender clunk on the head, reclaim her origins or whatever it was that was supposed to happen, sit up firmly and chastise Tabitha for taking the car without permission, and go back to being the annoying, overbearing, sanctimonious mother that Tabitha needed to get away from.

Or maybe her mother would just die. Tabitha was willing to be flexible.

The habit of wailing had faded—thank heavens. Between Mrs. Scales doing the banshee routine and Kirk warbling "Hey Nonny Nonny" in the shower, the house had become intolerably musical. But Mrs. Scales had begun to shut down even more than before. Reading the Bible had been a solace that one afternoon, but after that Tabitha couldn't seem to get her mother's eyes to focus in any kind of comprehension. And Mrs. Scales was beginning to reek of hydrangeas past their pink, that old person's odor of drying flowers.

But she was proving as capable of thwarting Tabitha's intentions as she ever had been. Tabitha settled her in the passenger seat and fastened the seat belt. She rotated the passenger door rearview mirror upward so that her mother wouldn't notice Tabitha reaching to grab the staple gun from its hiding place behind the passenger seat. She pulled out of the driveway, growling, "We're going to go look at where you grew up with Grandma. Isn't this going to be fun." Mrs. Scales responded by gripping the lever and tilting the seatback almost horizontal. It blocked the staple gun on the floor of the backseat. "Fun," swore Tabitha.

Mrs. Scales put her thumb in her mouth and curled away from her daughter. She stroked the ribbed cord of the upholstery, some kind of animal plea bargain.

Tabitha began a glancing tour of Famous Sites in the Life of Leontina Eleanor Prelutski Scales Hauenstein Garrison, default to Scales. "There's your old house from when you were a girl. Looking kinda white trash these days, isn't it."

Mrs. Scales roused herself on an elbow to peer out the windshield. A maple tree was growing up through the front porch roof. Any former lawn or garden had given up. Only a snowy patch remained, in which locals were abandoning stripped automobiles. "No one owns it now, looks like. Though it was a mighty pretty house once upon a time," said Tabitha. Her mother grunted noncommittally and went back to her thumb. Tabitha pulled up behind the garage.

"Are you up for a little walking?" said Tabitha. "We could look around. Wasn't there a doghouse out back? Your little Bowser, remember?"

Leaving the car turned on in case she had to make a quick get-away, Tabitha had to go around to the passenger door and poke her mother to get her to budge. Her mom got herself up on her elbows and her feet swung out the door onto the unplowed driveway, but then she changed her mind and with an agility and strength she hadn't yet shown today, she pulled herself back in the car, closed the door and locked it. Then she reached over and locked Tabitha's side.

"Oh, this is fun. This is really fun. Open up the door, Mom."

Mrs. Scales opened her mouth, and pulled on her thumb with satisfaction.

"Mom, it's cold out here."

Mrs. Scales closed her eyes and turned her head away from the car window.

"I don't know why I bother." Tabitha's voice was spiraling into a scream. "Why do you drag me through all this shit!"

Mrs. Scales turned up the car radio as loud as it would go.

Tabitha looked around for something to smash the window with. There was a stone wall a half mile away on the crossroad. She would cut across the field and get a boulder and come back and bash her way into the car. Then she would do the job on her mother and Lord save her if he would.

She had only taken the first two or three steps with a boulder the size of a Mrs. Chanarinjee Pyrex casserole when a car pulled up alongside her. "Let me help you carry that wherever you're going."

It was Pastor Jakob Huyck. Fuck.

He leaned across the passenger's seat and opened the door, and smiled up at her inanely. She had a notion to brain him instead, he was angled just right, but she controlled herself with that maturity she was beginning to cherish, and dropped the boulder on the floor of the passenger's side. "I shouldn't be carrying such heavy loads in my condition," she heard herself say.

"Where are you going with that thing?" said Pastor Huyck.

"It's a long story."

He looked as if he were ready for a long story. "Get in."

"What stinks in here? Go straight ahead, turn at the grange. What're you doing out this way?"

"A meditative drive. Thinking on the Advent season."

"Oh."

"And the rock?"

"I wanted to brain my mother and put her out of her misery."

He laughed. "I like you, Tabitha, I like your style. If your son shall ask for bread, would you give him a stone?"

"Depends on the size of it. You want to help?" She was sinking down in her seat. "Left. There she is."

"Oh my." Of course there had to be a car involved; Tabitha wouldn't have been out wandering alone. And there was Mrs. Scales, looking happily fetal, rocking her head back and forth to some satanic melody blaring through the car windows.

"She's locked inside. I was only kidding about braining her." Tabitha tried to rouse herself. Maybe she could get the Pastor to break a window and think he had accidentally knocked her mother on the head. Maybe if a Pastor with holy intentions did the deed, it would be more likely to work? How could she arrange this?

"You haven't got an extra set of keys," said Pastor Huyck, getting out his car and staring down at Mrs. Scales through the front windshield.

"No. Of course she might be being asphyxiated in there. Hog says that there's a slow leak in the exhaust, and he usually doesn't let us drive unless the windows are open. Mom was being stubborn."

"Is that so."

"So the boulder is for breaking her out of there."

"I see. Should I try to reason with her first?"

"Oh, well, reason," said Tabitha, shrugging. "If reason works, why not?"

"Hello, Mrs. Scales." Pastor Huyck wiggled his fingers as if talking to a deaf person. "It's Pastor Huyck from the Radical Radiant Pentecostals. How are you today. I'm here with Tabitha," he yelled. Well, *duh*, thought Tabitha. "I guess you could help us by opening the doors. Would you do that?"

Mrs. Scales didn't respond.

"In the name of Jesus and the Blood of the Lamb, I encourage you to follow your conscience."

She was either ignoring him or her conscience was fucked.

"Don't be alarmed if you hear a loud noise, Mrs. Scales. I'm going to have to smash one of the back windows to get you out of there alive."

"You're so good," said Tabitha. "Here's the boulder. Ready?"

"I don't know how much force it takes to break a car window."

"It's hard to figure these things out. You have to do the best you can. You're being a big help."

She smiled at him suddenly. He smashed the rear window on the driver's side. Mrs. Scales hopped and scrabbled and shrieked a stream of falsetto vowels, but she calmed down when Tabitha reached in and plucked the keys from the steering column.

"You are having a very hard time of this," said Pastor Jakob Huyck.

"You don't know," said Tabitha. Her head went down on the lapel of his camel-colored car coat.

"I would like to be more help than I've been. I fear you are all slouching toward Rome to be born."

"How many times can you be born again?"

"From a Radical Radiant Pentecostal perspective," he said, putting his hands on her shoulders, "as many times as you sin. From a Roman Catholic perspective, I couldn't say, but I certainly wouldn't stake my immortal soul on anything they tell me."

Mrs. Scales looked as if she was settling down nicely in the passenger seat, waiting to be born again. Then, her eyelids flickering, she seemed to notice the Pastor with his arms around her daughter. She brought herself forward again and leaned over on the horn. Leaned, leaned. It blared like a curse all over the hillside.

"She does need help," said Pastor Huyck sadly.

"You take her home in your own car," said Tabitha. "Kirk should be there to sign for her. I've had enough of this old lady for one day. I'll walk."

27

"I KNOW IT'S going to be cold," said Irene Menengest. "I just want to have a little sense of the place. Surely you have a key to the church building itself? You gatekeeper of the faith, you?"

"I do," said Jeremy. "But can't we do this another time? I was hoping to keep this brief tonight. I have a friend who's under the weather and I promised to look in on him."

"This won't take long. Let me run through one or two things from where I'll be standing. It comforts the afflicted, Mr. Catholic Hot Pants. I once had to sing for a high school awards ceremony and they had the microphone set up in a bank of ferns. I looked like the Warbling Ficus of Malone, New York."

"We've got three weeks yet. I just can't do it today, Irene. Give me a break."

"Fine. Leave me to suffer in my anxiety. *Men*. So to speak."

From the parlor in the parish house, Father Mike Sheehy gave them a weary nod over the top of his Sunday *New York Times* of several weeks ago. "Sounds divine," he called.

"Too, too kind, Father," said Irene. "I sound like a whale on steroids."

"If you insist," he murmured, turning a page. "But a divine whale."

They were angling their keys into the doors of their cars when a third car pulled into the parking lot. "Expecting anyone?" Jeremy said to Irene. "Oh. It's Willem."

"Imagine that." Irene waited for her brother-in-law to roll down his window. But instead Willem Handelaers cut the engine and got out.

"Irene—just in time. I hoped I'd catch you. Francesca said you'd be rehearsing in the church, so she couldn't phone."

"No such luck," said Irene. "Your mean old buddy denied me sanctuary."

"Francesca's over at that fancy store in Aberton—you know the place? Pepperdine's? Pappadum's?"

"I forget the name, but I know the one you mean. Popsicle's, maybe. Potpourri's."

"She's found something to wear to Polly's wedding and she wants you to come over and look at it. Someone else put a deposit down but hasn't come back, and they're willing to sell it to Francesca if she buys it tonight, so she needs your opinion. They're open till nine on Wednesdays, luckily."

"I've got other things to do myself, but hell, clothes come first. Where're the kids, anyway?"

"My mom is visiting. She's reading them *Curious George* or something."

"Essential reading for future anarchists. Where do you think that monkey got his curiosity from? His mother. She was Fay Wray, did you know that? His father was King Kong. His autobiography is *I am Curious, George*." Irene got in her car. "Well, thanks a lot, Willem." She turned the ignition key and waited a moment, as if to let the car warm up. Probably snooping to make sure Willem took off now that he'd delivered his message. But Jeremy didn't really care what Irene thought anymore.

"So you're going to this wedding of Polly's?" he said. Pointless and floundering as usual.

"Couldn't let Francesca go alone. Who knows what trouble she might get up to. I don't have the need for new clothes, though. I have the one good jacket I wear all winter. It's a kind of forest-green corduroy with faggy styling. Sets off my jewel-like eyes." He batted his lashes and grinned.

"Don't forget your visit to the *sick*, Jeremy," Irene called as she circled out of the parking lot and disappeared.

"Who's sick?" said Willem. The temperature hovered near freezing, and snow was predicted, but he leaned against his car and folded his arms as if it were summer and he was about to jump into a lake. Jeremy felt warmer, or said to himself he did. He could linger a moment before taking refuge in the car.

"Sean. Sean Riley? Chesty thing."

"He's, uh, HIV—?"

"Very. I've told you that. His viral load is pretty hefty."

"Not sure what that means. Sounds bad?"

"He's been up and down with this respiratory stuff for months. The side effects of the treatment are a whole category of punishment in themselves. He's staying with Marty Rothbard—do you know Marty?—who has a really small place, and Marty works in the evenings over at the Craftique, so I've been stopping by and having a sandwich or some soup with Sean, who gets pretty bored."

"Sorry to hear about it." Willem cracked his knuckles. "So how are you doing?"

Behind Willem, the light in the parlor of the rectory went out. Even if Father Mike was standing there in the dark, looking out, he would only see two guys chatting, and Father Mike wasn't nosy. He was probably on his way to bed. Then the light in the parking lot dimmed, which meant Father Mike had flipped the switch, not realizing that Jeremy was still there. The shadows rushed in, warm purples and bluish grays; the more distant sodium street-lights down the block filtered the frosty background with a urin-esque yellow. "How am I doing? Do you mean, am I infected? Or do you mean, like, have I gotten involved with Sean? Or am I oblivi-ous? No, no, no."

Willem waited without speaking, just looking at him.

Those four songs Jeremy'd been rehearsing with the guys this month, a full twenty-minute set; the songs came rushing up into the back of Jeremy's mind all in tatters and interwoven like a cor-rupted music file. In some way everything he wrote was about Wil-lem, and had been ever since. A crime and a punishment both, except to sing about it helped, sometimes. But Willem wasn't standing there in the December darkness waiting for Jeremy to sing. He didn't even speak the same language as Jeremy. That had always been their problem. They were of two different species en-tirely. You might as well fall in love with a porn star in a stroke magazine, or a painting of a nymph cavorting as Daylight or Mel-ody. When the real Willem shows up again you can hardly see him for the trash in your eyes.

"How am I doing?" Jeremy said again. "I'm doing okay. It's been a hard year."

"You look like it. What's up." Willem rested his hand on Jere-my's shoulder; the palm's furnace burned through fibers and skin and scorched Jeremy's clavicle. "Boyfriend trouble?"

"Who, me? What's a boyfriend?"

"Your health—?"

"I've told you. It's okay. I wish I could say the same about Sean, but I can't rework his wiring or his history." As much to escape scrutiny as to know the answer, he continued, "How about you?"

"Oh," said Willem. "Kids. Well, they do crawl all over you."

"Tell me about it. I live part-time in an elementary school, re-member. Francesca's fine?"

"Of course. Are you playing this wedding of Polly's, or just do-ing the rehearsal for Irene?"

"Irene. Now there's a piece of work." Jeremy slid a sidelong look. "Better not go there, verboten family territory. Yeah, well, I'm try-ing to work it out. I have a trip planned to New York that week but I'll probably be able to arrange to leave after the wedding." He'd just tossed it off in the middle of a line—*to New York*—to see if Wil-lem would flinch, even a little, would guess at Jeremy's motivation.

"Come to the reception, it'll be fun," said Willem. "You wouldn't come to my wedding."

"Right, I was supposed to dance with the groom? Please. This isn't Provincetown. Or Amsterdam. Or Greenwich Village."

"Or Larch Lake. Don't I know." Willem's head went down and his eyes looked out from beneath bangs that were unnaturally flat-tened due to the ski cap. Made of some sort of priceless Peruvian wool, no doubt, from an original *Design by Francesca*. "I remember. Didn't we dance naked on that balcony? To the music from down the lake. You held my waist and I held your—"

"Hey, you gotta remember something. You got a good head on your shoulders." This was the thing Willem wasn't supposed to do. Jeremy twitched out from under Willem's hand.

"Isn't it good to have that there?" said Willem, looking a lit-tle doubtful for perhaps the first time in his thirty-some years. "I mean to have that between us, in the past? Aren't you glad? Isn't it better than—not to have it?"

Jeremy had to wait to answer. "Hard to respond to that."

"How hard?" Willem came in closer.

"Hard enough."

They stood near for a few minutes, almost touching, looking

over one another's shoulders. Despite the combustion it began to snow. "Do you want to dance?" Willem half whispered. Then there was a cough, in the shadows, and Willem pulled away, and Jeremy was fussing with the music that, he was surprised to remember, he was still holding. Father Mike? Not likely. A pair of thugs, or more, going to pulverize them for being faggots in a church parking lot? "Get in your car," said Jeremy quietly, evenly.

"You jump in too," said Willem. "We'll split—"

"Who's there?" Jeremy wheeled away from Willem. *We'll split.* They had already done that, hadn't they? Willem had jerked himself apart out of fear of discovery, which was hateful and legitimate, too. Willem had kids and a wife. Let him leave. "Just go," said Jeremy, and then louder again, "I said, who is it?"

"Oh, sorry." A figure came stumbling out from behind the corner of the Cliffs of Zion. "I was just out walking—"

"Oh, it's you," said Jeremy. "Great."

"You know him?" said Willem.

"Yes. Look, it's okay. Just go. Just go, will you?" You've split already. Act your age.

Willem looked Kirk Scales up and down, an appraising if neutral expression taking hold. "I've interrupted your evening. See you at the wedding, then. And look, Jeremy, take it easy, will you?"

Jeremy waited for Willem's car to leave. Then he turned to face Kirk Scales, who was sloping across the parking lot with an expression that looked askew.

"I know you're in Drama 101 and believe me, your timing couldn't be more theatrical. Have you been drinking? Is that it?"

"Oh, a drop. Found a little drop somewhere and had a little drink. What's the big deal?"

"Liquoring yourself up so you can spy around the church? Waiting for me? Hanging out in the shadows here? That's just not going to do any good, you. Come on. You need to sit down? You look pretty bad."

"Oh I look better than I am—"

"You're wobbling. Sit down here." Jeremy led Kirk to a free-standing air-conditioning unit mounted on a concrete slab at the edge of the parking lot. He gripped Kirk's shoulders and made him sit. Jeremy perched next to him, a good nine inches away, far as he could get. "You're not dressed for this weather. Where's your hat? You need me to take you home?"

"I need you—" Kirk began to inhale gustily as if a sneeze was inevitable.

"You don't need me. Christ. You don't even know me. I'm old enough to be your—your older brother. You're just having a bad time with your mother so wacko. You'll get over it. Don't embarrass yourself—"

"There's nothing in me to embarrass, I'm nothing, I'm worth nothing." He began to sob.

"You know this is very upsetting but frankly I have to be someplace else . . . Stop, this is crazy. Isn't your sister any help?"

"She's a bitch—"

"Well, so?"

"And Hog calls me names. Everyone calls me names—"

"Look, we all go through this. It gets better," he lied. But Kirk turned and threw himself against Jeremy's chest. "Holy Mary, Mother of God," said Jeremy. "Come on, it's okay. Get a hold of yourself." Leave me alone, he wanted to say. What do I want with a frail teenage Adonis in a slightly smelly quilted vest, probably from the Salvation Army, sobbing in my arms? If this was a temptation, the Powers that Be had better work harder. But he was conscious of the backbone beneath Kirk's rocking, the cheek so soft it could be a woman's. Kirk was letting himself go; he rolled from the pelvis up in sinuous contortions as if he were in extremis. His sobbing voice, thought Jeremy a bit guiltily, actually has a nice airy quality, as if his sinuses are generous; he might be a capable singer if he has any control of pitch.

"Come on, thataboy," said Jeremy when the worst seemed to have passed. "You need a handkerchief? Ah, come on. It breaks my heart. There must be a counselor at the high school, isn't there? How about your pastor? Not sure what the Cliffs of Zion Pentecostals think about the hormonally homo. Is he cool about things like that?"

Kirk clenched Jeremy more tightly around the waist and mumbled something into his neck.

"What?" said Jeremy.

"I said, I'm not gay."

"Oh, God. Is that so. Then why are you just about sitting in my lap?"

Kirk pulled back a half an inch. "You don't understand."

"Of course I don't. Sure I do. Why are you drunk then?"

"You didn't come to help me with my singing. You said you would."

"I said I might. I had a crisis to attend to. Kirk, let go. Come *on*, you're okay now. Pay attention. This isn't about singing. Look, it's not my business to talk you into anything or out of anything. How old are you? Fifteen?"

"Almost sixteen." The sullenness was proof fiercer than an ID.

"Great. Well, you're too young to know who you are yet, especially in this town. What with the year you're having. Just give it a rest, will you? Relax a little. Wait till you go away to college. It's safer. And there's plenty of time to figure out if you're gay. Have you ever dated girls?"

"I don't want to go on dates, I want to learn how to sing 'Hey

Nonny Nonny!' I haven't come here to be molested by some queer old guy, you jerk, I need your *help*!" He bunched up Jeremy's anorak, and he drilled Jeremy with a wide-eyed look, and kissed him, briefly but very wetly.

"Look." Jeremy pulled away, falling off the side of the housing. "I don't know that song. You have to talk to someone else, not me. You need to lie down and get over this. You'll feel better in the morning. I'll bring you home—"

"You're not bringing him anywhere," said another voice. Jeremy thought wearily: What—now it's Father Mike? How embarrassing. I'm going to get fired before I can even quit. "Get your fucking hands off him." Not Father Mike, then.

"What is with everyone tonight? It's like a Buster Keaton film," cried Jeremy. "Doesn't anyone notice it's freezing out?"

Kirk's brother Hogan came walking through the snow carrying a wrench that looked like fifteen pounds of Kryptonite. "I catch you near my brother again, you butt-surfer, I'll beat the crap outa you."

"Oh god oh god. Hog, what're you doing here?" said Kirk. "You never come to church."

"You steal two beers from my room and leave the cans on the kitchen counter? You want me to think *Mom* has taken up drinking now? You're outa here, Kirk. In the car before you get hurt. Now. It's out on the street. Tabitha said you were going to church. Their church, right? His church." Hogan's face through the snow looked like some sort of puppet mask; he was glowering with excitement and menace. His hand was rigid on the wrench and he took three little hops like a javelin thrower, focusing on Jeremy.

"You have got this *so* wrong," said Jeremy. "I don't have the slightest interest in your brother—"

"Bringing him home?" Hogan began to swell, his arm to wind

up. "You're not getting your mitts on him, you cocksucking bas-tard—"

"Don't, Hogan, you're ruining everything," shouted Kirk, "as per usual!" He headed for his brother but slid in the snow and landed on one knee. "Ow, that's—I said major OW."

"Let's calm down—" said Jeremy.

"You sniff around for boy pussy, you come right into our house to hunt for an innocent kid, pretending to be kind—"

"That'll do now," said Father Mike Sheehy, in the bright light of the open door to the rectory. He was wearing a bathrobe and he had a baseball bat in his hand. "We can't have language like this in the church parking lot, fellows. Just won't do. Anyone want to come in here and sort this out like gentlemen?" He advanced, and cracked his bat hard on the top of the concrete steps. "Or not?"

28

BY THE TIME Jeremy got there, Marty was already home. He met Jeremy at the door. "Sean's asleep, first time in twenty-four hours, so let's go sit in your car and chat."

"It's freezing out there, no way," said Jeremy, as Marty pushed him down the stairs. "You won't believe the evening I just had. A night of temptations and punishments and humiliations. I don't deserve any of it."

"You're that kind of sick individual that life likes to abuse. It's your own fault for never saying *Fuck you* to anyone. Can we manage not to talk about you for just this once?"

"Nothing would give me greater joy."

"The thing is," said Marty, when they settled in the front seat, "I think Sean is going downhill. The last twenty-four hours have been really bad. You don't want to see the gunk he's bringing up."

"No and I don't want to hear about it either. You shouldn't be dealing with this, Marty."

"Tell me about it. I don't know what the hell to do. Mrs. Riley has called several times wanting to talk to Sean. He won't get on the phone with her. Everyone's getting jittery, and Sean's got us in this bind. But the time has come to get unstuck, because he needs medical treatment. He's not well enough for you to bring him back to Syracuse, Germy."

"And you're thinking we should just bundle him into my car and dump him home?"

"Or to the clinic on Morse Hill Road."

"Maybe tomorrow," said Jeremy at last. "If he's finally sleeping now, he might feel more himself when he wakes up. And anyway, even if he doesn't, morning's a better time to show up at the clinic. Less scary. Also his parents won't be so frantic."

"They'll be frantic enough."

"Well, for Christ's sake. That's not our fault, is it?"

"Keep your hairshirt on. I'm sure it's your fault one way or the other, you just aren't concentrating. You want to go get a beer while Sleeping Beauty tosses in her bed of pain up there?"

"I'm going home, I'll come back in the morning. Call me if there's a crisis."

"I don't know why you're mad at me all of a sudden," said Marty, without rancor. "But knowing you, there must be some odd twisted rationale behind it. It's so comforting to have you as a friend, even when you've got PMS."

On the phone next morning, Marty sounded a lot less jocular. "I'm hauling Sean down the stairs and into the car whether he wants to go or not. Why don't you just meet us at the clinic in an hour? Can you do that?"

"I guess," said Jeremy.

"Here's the hard part. Would you call his folks?"

"Does he know I'm going to do that?"

"He's not knowing a whole lot this morning. High fever or something."

Jeremy futzed around with a cup of instant coffee and, trying to stall, he remembered he had an appointment about plans for decorating the church at Christmas. He called to postpone the meeting. "Taking one of my friends to the clinic on Morse Hill Road," he told Sister Alice.

"Oh. I see. Is it one of the singers?"

"Yes."

"And it's serious. Is it Sean Riley?"

"Uh-huh. I don't know how serious it is. I think very. How should I know?"

"You'll keep me posted this afternoon?"

"I will."

He hung up, said an Our Father, a Hail Mary, a Glory Be, and another Our Father. When he started in on "Bless us O Lord, and these Thy gifts," he knew he was stalling. So he took a deep breath and dialed Sean's home.

"Hi, Mrs. Riley? This is Jeremy Carr. The choir director from Our Lady's. Hi. Look, I have some news for you—kind of serious. Sean isn't feeling so hot and so we're taking him over to the clinic on Morse Hill Road." He was talking as fast as he could to keep Sean's mother from having a chance to explode, but there was only an editorial silence on the other end of the line. "Mrs. Riley? You there?"

"This is Colum Riley," said a new voice after a moment. "What is it?"

The dad. Jeremy drew in a breath and began again. "He doesn't know I'm telling you this, but I thought you should know."

"Well, run that by me again." Mr. Riley's voice sounded as if he'd been following something on the TV while Jeremy had been speaking. Jeremy obliged. "I don't like the look of it, actually," he finished.

"He's been poorly this year, we noticed. Well, we'll get ourselves down there and see what's what. Thanks a lot, young man." Mr. Riley didn't sound exercised over the whole thing. As he was hanging up the phone, though, Jeremy heard him saying to his wife, "Don't break a hip, Deirdre, he'll keep—"

The air was fine, choked with a dusty sort of snow that the wind kept beating off the tops of the paper-thin drifts. Cloudy bright. The combed fields on either side of Morse Hill Road stood suddenly yellow, gold, like something from Breughel, and then went back to being brown, like something from Sears. The road was busy, all that northbound traffic still being diverted due to the stalled construction. At East Tupham, a school bus had stopped, perhaps engine trouble, and a flock of children in candy-colored snowsuits and hats and red plastic boots were making of some dark ravaged cornfield a cheery board game.

He had only been to the clinic on Morse Hill Road once, though he had heard Tabitha Scales talk about it with a great deal of scorn. It didn't seem so terrible to him. The Oswego County Clinic was a couple of prefab buildings joined by an airy elbow corridor, glass on both sides and rangy geraniums perched on spray-painted overturned milk crates. More like an animal hospital than anything else; he expected to hear yipping.

He found Marty in the waiting room. "Told me to stay out here. I'm not family."

Jeremy stood near the double doors. A sign said NO UNAUTHORIZED PERSONNEL BEYOND THIS POINT. Every time the doors opened, he glared at the nurse behind the desk just beyond, but she was gifted at ignoring visitors. Once he entered anyway, and she said, without looking up, "Out. Out." She pointed back the way he'd come.

"But you don't even know who I've come to find out about."

"It's Sean Riley, and someone will be out when there's something to say. He's still in examination, and it'll be a while yet. You might go get some lunch."

"It's only eleven o'clock."

"Have a long lunch and come back at two," she said. "Cafeteria downstairs, or you can go get the regrettable coffee at the International House of Pancakes." Her name was Nurse Gompers, Marilee Gompers. Jeremy thought she looked as if she chewed on thermometers to relieve her sexual tension. Marty and Jeremy took her advice, though, and went and ordered pancakes and lingered over the endless cup of coffee until the lunch rush was done. It was ten after two when they returned.

Nurse Gompers pointed them upstairs. The Riley parents stood in the hallway, several yards apart from each other. "Look who's here," said Marty. "Us."

Deirdre Riley was a small woman with a bird-like pelvis; her thighs seemed bowed to the front somehow. She wore a blue Windbreaker that said OUR LADY'S SODALITY in white shadow-box letters, and she carried a canvas satchel of needles and yarn. She looked prepared for a stay. Colum Riley was bald and silent.

"Hi," said Jeremy. Mrs. Riley looked suspicious, but since she also had this expression as she approached the altar for communion Jeremy wasn't alarmed. "You know me from church."

"I realize that," said Mrs. Riley.

"Does he know you're here?" asked Jeremy.

They didn't answer.

"When can we go in?" asked Marty.

"In good time. They're taking care of some business just now," said Mr. Riley. A muffled sound behind the door, and Sean's voice, distinctly: "*Fuck*." Mrs. Riley pursed her lips and Mr. Riley's face registered no particular expression. He might have been waiting for an elevator. Jeremy recognized the strategy from his own dad.

When a couple of blue-clad male orderlies left the room, one pointed to the parents and said, "You. Only the two of you. Fifteen minutes. Nurse Gompers will come up and check. Watch it." The parents pushed in without evidence of having heard, but the door shut in Jeremy's face as he tried to follow them.

"I like the Puerto Rican," Marty said. "A bedside manner to stiffen my—resolve. He can take my rectal temperature any time."

"How about you shut up."

"God, his folks are just like he said. I always thought he must be exaggerating."

"They didn't seem so bad. They aren't in a good mood."

"Well, they were a matched pair of grouches. They're like, like Ernest Borgnine and that little Exorcist kid. Linda Hunt."

"It was Linda Blair."

"Right. Linda Hunt is what happened to Linda Blair after she was possessed. That explains a lot."

"Let's not talk about being possessed in the company of a virus."

Marty ignored Jeremy. "What're we doing, leaving him alone with them? They don't get to make the rules. We must be crazy." Marty pushed past Jeremy, threw open the door, and sang out, "Honey, we're home."

"This is not a farce. This is a nightmare," said Jeremy, following.

Sean was sitting up in bed halfway, with a paper mask hanging from one ear. "Thrush," he said in a croaky voice. "On top of everything else. You can't believe the sore throat."

"We want some privacy here," said Mrs. Riley, turning on the boys.

"Don't mind me mam," Sean said to them, an Irish softness in his voice they'd rarely heard. "Mam, don't get your knickers in a twist. It's too late for privacy. Come on." It was a patois to calm them down, Jeremy thought.

"Don't talk," said Mr. Riley.

"You better talk," said Mrs. Riley. "You've got some explain-ing to do." She wrestled a crucifix out of the knitting and looked around the room. There was a faded print of some daisies, 1970s style, in a frame without glass; she took it down and slapped the crucifix in its place against the wall.

"Saints and begorrah, is this the wee magic portable confes-sional? I never dreamed I'd catch sight of one," said Marty.

Sean's head fell back on the pillow as if unable to imagine he was present, at last, at a meeting of his parents and his gay compa-ñeros. His face looked bluish-gray. Worse than last night.

"This is a hell of a way to learn about this," said Mrs. Riley, though it wasn't clear if she meant her son's homosexuality or his illness, or if she had quite yet put the two together. "I would like to know what you actually thought you were up to?" Was she talking to her son or to all of them?

"Sweet Jaysus of Nazareth, Deirdre," said her husband, "'tis neither the time nor the place." They were all turning into paro-dies of Frank McCourt, thought Jeremy. Anxiety does weird things to a family. Pretty soon they're going to start singing "Danny Boy."

"Coughing up blood for several days and nobody thinks to call his mither? What's wrong with you? What's wrong with you all?" She answered her own question. "I know what's wrong with you. You're bloody selfish."

"Mam," said Sean. "Don't do the Mam thing with quite such accuracy—"

"Don't talk. Save your breath. You'll be needing it. I know what we're talking about here. I'm not stupid. You're not lying here be-cause of—of—an ingrown toenail, for the love of Pete!"

"That's just about the size of it," said Marty. He turned to Sean. "You dog, you never told me about Pete. Pete who? Is he cute? Taken? Well, let's not be fussy. Is he free for an hour?"

"Oh Christ," said Sean. "Oh Jesus McGillicuddy Christ. Oh Christ. Christ on a crutch in the foothills."

Mrs. Riley's tears were hasty and plenty. "And the mercy of God be on you, you selfish boys, keeping yourselves for yourselves, and the unnamable sins you suffer for now."

"Little Bird," said Mr. Riley, reaching out his hand and moving it in the air as if patting an invisible deer somewhere between his wife and the bed. "Little Bird, don't."

Jeremy, catching Sean's eye, handed over the shiny aluminum spit pan and they all averted their eyes. Mrs. Riley closed her eyes and her shoulders shook. "Bad enough you should turn your back on your faith, and the tabernacle light was burning for you all those years and you never looked in on your Friend; but that you should be so aloof and engage in the sin of selfishness—"

"I've never heard it called that before," said Marty.

"I'll rinse that out," said Sean's father.

The door opened. "Get her some Kleenex," said Jeremy. "Come on, Marty, I think we better go—"

"—just when you need the faith of your fathers the most!" she said. "And you don't turn to your parents, you can't turn to your church, you have none to take you in but your so-called *buddies*—"

They all turned, expecting Nurse Marilee Gompers. "Here we are, right as rain," said Mother Clare du Plessix. "Goodness, a little family party already?"

Mrs. Riley's jaw couldn't quite drop, as it was already opened ajar as it could go, but it wobbled on its hinge a bit. Mr. Riley stood up a little straighter.

Mother Clare was followed by Sister Jeanne d'Arc, Sister Felicity, Sister Perpetua, and Sister Clothilde, who was having a hard time squeezing through the doorway with everyone else already there. "How are you, dear boy?" said Mother Clare.

She approached the bedside in the quiet caesura of implacable intention, broken by Sister Clothilde's stage whisper to the room at large. "Sister Alice called us to tell us, and it sounded serious enough to hire a cab. Sister Maria Goretti is still down with pneumonia, poor thing, and we thought her germs in this instance would be a real no-no."

The old nuns stood on one side of the bed, taking little notice of Mr. and Mrs. Riley, and nodding only perfunctorily to the boys. "Sister Alice will be along a bit later," said Mother Clare du Plessix. "Don't worry, dear child, we're not going to stay long."

"I have no idea who you are," said Mrs. Riley at last.

"We are the friends of Sean," said Mother Clare du Plessix. "Shall we take a moment of silence?" They all closed their eyes. Sean did as well.

"This is a private family matter. I don't believe I know you—" said Mrs. Riley.

"Silence," Mother Clare du Plessix reminded her, gently. "Silence."

29

THE NUNS IN their hired car and Jeremy in his were both caught in a slowdown beyond the I-81 traffic diversion. The pulsing ruby light of emergency vehicles had a weird Christmassy aspect, but by the time Jeremy breasted the wreck the rescue squads had left the scene. When he got home, the crummy old phone machine showed twelve calls. Sean, he thought. A turn for the worse this soon? Or hate phone mail from Mrs. Riley? Anonymous heavy breathing from his stalker, Kirk Scales? Before he could press the button to retrieve the messages, the phone rang again.

Peggy Mueller in high weepy mode. He couldn't make it out at first. "Sister Alice what?" he said.

———

THE FUNERAL HAD the feel of a dress rehearsal, a quick run-through before the actual eminences would arrive to make witness to Sister Alice's life. But, thought Jeremy, what eminences would that be? The shivering Theban souls in their winter garb were it. If something like the Holy Spirit—the Holy Ghost, he was enough of a romantic to prefer that outdated terminology—were to arrive, who would notice? Would the balsawood angels in the ceiling begin to sing in reedy voices? In their skeletal leading, would the figures in the stained glass windows add their hosannas through throats of sanguine pink glass?

Jeremy had been asked to lead the congregation in a couple of anthems and some hymns. His choir sat on folding chairs in front of the right side altar. Peggy Mueller, her face contorted with desolation. Polly Osterhaus, who must be thinking of her own wedding in three weeks' time. Marty, who had asked to join the singers, was the most skeptical among them, but he wore the most devout expression, and he kept his head bowed during the entire ceremony.

Jeremy's small chair perched on the grating above the crypt. He couldn't overcome a feeling that the grille was loose in its marble framework, and it shifted incrementally as he rose from his seat or sat down again. Or was it just the world that was unsteady? Coming loose from its moorings at the millennium, ready to split its husk, convert, evolve, metastasize? He looked out over the faces of familiar people, faces rosy with grief or blank with grief, or faces that betrayed the exhaustion of the Christmas season, and the inconvenience of a funeral five days before the holiday. For most of the parishioners of Our Lady's this must be their first visit to the chapel of the Motherhouse of the Sisters of the Sorrowful Mysteries. Even finding it would have been a pain.

Facing out from the dais, Jeremy turned to look at the other side of the chapel. The Sisters seemed arrested in demonstrations of palsy. A hobbled band of ancient tuberculars. So many of them were too old to be alive. They couldn't even sit up straight in the pews, but leaned and tilted like untended gravestones. It was the most of them he had seen at one time—he counted fifteen, and could name six of them. Sister Clothilde and Sister Jeanne d'Arc flanked Mother Clare du Plessix in the front row, and other familiar faces were slotted in among the new ones. Sister Maria Goretti apparently was still too sick with pneumonia to be released from the infirmary. Still, the representation was impressive. Impressive, and upsetting: Everyone knew this should be a funeral for an antique nun, one who had been letting go, or trying to let go, for decades now.

Father Mike Sheehy was the principal celebrant, and a couple of priests from Syracuse and one from Montreal had come to crowd the altar with their communal effort to attract the attention of God and to thank Him for the life of Sister Alice Coyne. Why it was thanks and not recrimination was one of the central mysteries of the faith, as far as Jeremy was concerned. Thank you, Forces of the Almighty, for giving Sister Alice Coyne to us all; You give and You take away; it is not ours to question why You allowed the truck of Christmas trees heading into the intersection to skid sideways into the driver's side of Sister Alice's Nissan. If Sean Casey hadn't been in the clinic, Sister Alice wouldn't have been heading west on Morse Hill Road at exactly that moment. If the repairs on I-81 had been finished as scheduled the Christmas tree truck would have been on the interstate, not on Morse Hill Road. If the German immigrants hadn't deeply rooted the notion of Christmas trees onto the American celebration of Your Nativity, mirabile dictu, there might have been no truck there that particular moment. Amen. Your kingdom come. Your rotten kingdom come.

The nuns looked rheumy and disgruntled at the choir's efforts. Only when he heard the noses being blown did Jeremy realize that they were affected. Next to Mother Clare du Plessix was a woman with blond hair, most likely a sibling of Sister Alice; she resembled her enough maybe even to be a twin. She looked grim, and as if her life had been hard; Mother Clare reached over and pressed her old claw over the woman's clenched hands. Maybe at a time like this the call wasn't for music, but silence.

They sat with the prospects of their own funerals in their laps. They would be back in church again before long for Sean's funeral, and for Mother Clare du Plessix's, and maybe some of them would be at the Cliffs of Zion Radical Radiant Pentecostal Church for the funeral of Mrs. Scales. Jeremy could see Tabitha Scales in the back of the chapel, squeezed in between her brother Kirk and Old Lady Scarcese. Tabitha looked pale, and Kirk was ruddy and bleary beneath his to-die perfect coif.

They had hardly known Sister Alice at all.

The procession to the graveyard was brief; a sanctified spot waited behind the chapel where other sisters were already at rest. The entire congregation squeezed out the side door of the chapel and stood amid the stones, and Father Mike led them in the final round of prayers. Some of the more infirm nuns did not come out, for the wind was high and the temperature dropping. More snow expected before the week was out. The sound of the wind in the arborvitae blocked out the few words that Mother Clare du Plessix was trying to say about Sister Alice; Jeremy had to move forward to hear. He didn't catch much, though there was a moment when the wind rested, and he heard Mother Clare's voice reach out, "It used to be said that when a nun died, God put another in her place, much as you replace a pane of glass—" Jeremy shifted to see how Mother Clare would update this thought, since Sister Alice had already been the last replacement pane. But suddenly Mother Clare had no more words, and bowed her head. Her veil wavered in the strengthening wind and hid her face.

30

TABITHA AND KIRK drove home from the funeral in silence. Tabitha was thinking about God's plan: Number One, was there such a thing, and Number Two, who cares, if it's so full of pitfalls and potholes?

However thick God might have made her, was it possible that fate was infested with meaning whether or not she was clever enough to notice it?

She had resented Sister Alice Coyne, but now that she was gone, Tabitha missed her. The last conversation they had had was about historical pregnancies, by which Tabitha had thought Sister Alice was referring to Mary the Mother of God until she realized she was misunderstanding and the pregnancies were *hysterical.* "Hardly hysterical," said Tabitha, "I haven't had a good laugh all month. Do you know what I feel like in the morning? I can't keep anything down." Sister Alice Coyne had talked about the cleverness of the womb and the secrets of the human heart, and the possibility of imagining symptoms of pregnancy. Tabitha had had to excuse herself to go imagine some morning sickness, even though it was already two p.m.

And then Sister Alice had been creamed by a truck full of Christmas trees, so was Tabitha to take it that the notion of a hysterical pregnancy was thereby obliterated? Would God speak to her in such crude language? Perhaps He would need to, especially if she wasn't listening closely enough. What was it exactly that He was trying to say? "Spit it out," she mumbled out loud without realizing it, and it sounded in her own ears as if she were talking to her Goddamned earthly mother instead of her heavenly father.

"I can't stand all that Catholic crap," said Kirk, apparently thinking that she'd been talking to him. As if.

"What did you expect? Sister Alice was a nun. You didn't have to come. You should have your seat belt on, by the way."

"And I hate that guy."

"Father Mike?"

"No, the music leader."

"Jeremy Carr? Like hell you do."

"I do. He makes me sick."

Tabitha felt the baby kick. Or something. Did babies have feet by seven weeks? It made her feel mean. Kick me, will you, she thought. You too? Already? "Hog says you have a crush on Jeremy."

"I don't have a crush on him or any other guy. You make me sick."

"Oh, grow up," said Tabitha. "I'm not blind, you know. You're not exactly watching reruns of *Baywatch* for the babes. You wouldn't recognize a tit if it popped out of a bikini and bit you."

"What is wrong with you? Just what have I done in this family to make you and Hogan so contemptuous? You act like some martyr, as if Hogan isn't doing what he can, as if I'm not. I help with Mom too, you know."

"Change the subject. It's your favorite strategy. Okay by me. I don't care if I have a faggot for a baby brother. You're the one who brought up Jeremy Carr."

"I said he made me sick."

"Yeah. Hog told me he caught him making a pass at you. He said you were not exactly resisting. He said he threatened to beat the shit out of him."

Kirk took in several deep breaths.

"I think you're scared of the whole business," said Tabitha. "You're having a hysterical reaction to the truth." She watched him out of the corner of her eye, and wondered—briefly—if she was enjoying how he crumpled up against the door. "The truth shall set you free." It was a quote from somewhere. *Star Trek?*

"I know what'll set me free. For one thing, you can drop me off at the corner."

"You have to go to school."

"The hell I do. Everybody else gets to be a juvenile offender. Let me try."

She was so surprised at his language that she did what he asked, and turned the car around to go home to relieve Hogan, who had to get ready for work. She guessed Kirk wasn't about to hire out as a guy whore, but would only go to the library. Still, this was a start. She was almost proud of him.

———————

THE AFTERNOON WAS endless. Mrs. Scales was curled up like a baby on the braided rug. She had her thumb in her mouth and her dentures beside her, set upon a piece of toast. Tabitha sat down and watched *One Life to Live* over her, and during the commercials wondered if she would have a chance to try another nonk-nonk on her mother's head after Hogan went to work. But someone called from the station and Hogan talked for a while, and when he hung up he told Tabitha that he had switched shifts and was going in later. So they watched Maury Povich for an hour while Mrs. Scales stared, unblinkingly, at the dust under the sofa. "Do you think we should call someone?" said Hogan.

"About what?" Tabitha wondered if he was going to suggest electro-jolt antigay therapy for Kirk.

"About Mom." They checked to see if she was perking up at the sound of her name. She wasn't. She showed no sign of apprehending their presence or, indeed, her own. "She said *no fucking doctors*. But at this point she can't tell a doctor from a tow truck. I mean, how much does our promise mean if she's going to die?"

Tabitha had an uneasy feeling that Hogan knew that she had a padded wrench hidden between the sofa cushions. "She's resting, she's not dying." She resisted an urge to prod her mother with the toe of her sneaker, like poking a fish on a dock to see if it could be goaded into flapping around some more.

"I mean, is she still our mother if she's dead?"

Tabitha shrugged and made loopy-loopy circles in the air with her fingers. "Want a fluffernutter? I'm just hungry all the time." She stepped around her mother and headed for the kitchen. She was there when the phone rang. "What," she said, her mouth gluey with marshmallow.

"Hi, is that Tabitha?" Caleb? Caleb! thought Tabitha, her heart leaping up.

"Yeah," she said.

"Jeremy Carr."

"Oh. What?"

"I just got back from the funeral and there was a message from your brother on my machine. Is he there?"

"You don't mean Hogan," she guessed.

"Right. I mean Kirk."

She wasn't sure how she felt about this. She thought that guys being gay was a waste of good cock, but maybe they didn't have good cocks and that was why they were gay. She didn't care one way or the other. If everybody on TV was cool about it these days, she was, too. But Kirk was more than just some gay kid, he was her annoying baby brother and her responsibility, at least until Mom kicked the bucket and Family Services waded in. "What do you want him for?"

"Nothing," said the choir dude. "Absolutely nothing. But he called me and asked to meet me this evening. I can't. Would you tell him I can't? I have a music rehearsal in the church tonight. For a wedding."

"Oh," said Tabitha, licking the back of the spoon. "Whose wedding?"

"Someone in our choir."

She said, "Polly?"

"Yeah. Polly's wedding. You know Polly?"

"Nah. Well, I'll tell him."

"Tell him I'm sorry," said Jeremy, but he didn't sound sorry.

"Sorry for what?" said Tabitha, and hung up.

She went back in the living room, the jar in one hand and the spoon in the other. "This is like marshmallow mucous," she said.

"Who was that?" said Hogan, eyes trained on the TV. It was a rerun of *Gilligan's Island*.

"It was Kirk's boyfriend. Would you tell Kirk when he comes home that Jeremy has a wedding rehearsal tonight in the church and he can't make their date?"

"Goddamn it." Hogan threw the channel changer at the TV screen so hard the glass spit, but Gilligan didn't notice. "That faggot's gonna get his ass handed to him. Where are you going?"

"Out. I need to see Linda Pearl about something very important to me."

"I'm leaving at seven. I got the evening shift, the seven to eleven tonight."

"Kirk'll be home."

"What if he's not?"

"Just put a blanket on her and turn out the lights, how do I know? Really, Hogan, I'm only two years older than you, you expect me to figure out everything?"

"Should I get her some food? That toast is two days old."

"She gets hungry enough, she eats it."

Tabitha didn't really need to see Linda Pearl. She didn't want to go to the House of Beauty. She didn't know what she wanted. There was a sense of things hinging within her, swinging this way and that. She was broad as a barge, full, capable, monstrous, thunderous, generous, judgmental. She walked along the side of the road and felt the world sink back to make room for her. Physically she wasn't any larger, she knew; she might even, with all that nausea, have lost a few pounds. (Never a bad thing.) It was inside herself that she was larger.

Once, on the only family field trip they had ever taken, Mrs. Scales had bundled up Tabitha, Hogan, and Kirk, and brought them all the way to Boston. It was a celebration of some kind; maybe Hogan's getting off of junior parole. They had stared with slack jaws at how large and specific the world was—all that green particularity between Thebes and Boston—almost six driving hours of it. TV served the world in very flat slices, like an animated placemat. Whereas in reality the world had a lot more chunk to it.

In Boston they had gone to the top of some skyscraper and Hogan had done some projectile snot-blowing out of his nose. They had seen that place that Paul Lynde had lived in before he shouted "The British are coming! The British are coming." Not Paul Lynde—Paul Revere. Kirk had stolen nine packages of oyster crackers at some fish chowder place and put them on the tracks of the trolley to make crumbs. Then their mother had brought them to the Mothership of the Christian Scientists. It was a modern all-concrete plaza that still looked like its architectural drawing; nothing in it had gotten spray-painted with graffiti yet. Inside one of the older buildings, after they had listened to some lecture about the total stultifying boringness of Christian Science, they had been kidnapped and forced to take a tour. Deep inside one building they had come to a place called the Mapparium.

"It looks very Catholic," said Mrs. Scales doubtfully, and at first she wouldn't let her children go in.

"That's just the stained glass," said the guide. "Don't mention Catholics to *us*." So Mrs. Scales had relented.

The Mapparium was a stained glass globe, about two stories high and two rooms wide, too. A map of the world in some year like 1936 or something. Every country in the world and all the oceans and seas between were made of curved stained glass puzzle pieces and fitted into place, and things were marked so you could find them if you knew what to look for. All the states were there, except Alaska, Hawaii, and Mexico weren't states yet. You walked in a bridge across the dead middle space right inside the globe, and the outer skin was the glass, framed in lead, and lit by bulbs on the other side of the glass. It was weird, like the world was kind of like church, or church was kind of like the world. And either way, you were inside it.

Now Tabitha was walking along with the whole globe inside *her*, the whole brightly colored existence, all its impossible skins and layers and transparencies. It was hard to think about it. If she could only look in her own mouth she would see the universe and the stars, like the beginning of most movies, black night and white speckles; then zoom in to the galaxy, the solar system, the sun, the

Milky Way, in some order or another, like nesting boxes, and the whole globe was in her, and in the globe was the eensy little baby with its little kicking feet, and the whole baby's whole life was in there with it, and the whole world it would experience, it was all right there, all inside her. It made her feel a little queasy, to tell the truth, and as if the House of Beauty was really the place she should be going, if for the name alone. But she didn't think that Linda Pearl Wasserman would make a very good godmother to a whole new galaxy cooking away inside her, even if Linda Pearl was first home with any new gossip and a fucking genius at feathering and layering.

She walked past Pastor Jakob Huyck, who with his usual timing just happened to be driving by. He rolled down his window and said, "Going somewhere?"

"Not going," she called, "coming. I'm coming." In an earlier month she would have said this sexily, but the sound in her own voice was more than sexy. It was godly.

She waved him by and kept walking, loving herself almost for the first time. She walked all the way to the gas station, thinking about everything and nothing at once.

31

JEREMY STOPPED BY the clinic to see Sean again. The argument about whether to tell Sean about Sister Alice hadn't been won or lost before one of the old nuns had spilled the beans. Sean had plunged into a gummier somnolence and the medics pumped into him an increased dosage of whatever it was. Tonight he lay groggily in his pillows, scarecrow's limbs in place of his own. His eyes were closed.

Jeremy sat by him and hummed quietly. His mind wandered to all the usual haunts. He lost track of the time, eyes on Sean's eroding face. He may even have dozed off for a minute or two. When he looked again, Sean's eyes were open but his attention unsteady.

"You could read to him," said a night nurse. "His folks brought by some paperbacks."

Jeremy didn't want to touch them, but he had to do something since Sean was so unresponsive. A bunch of dog-eared children's novels. These were the things that Sean's parents knew of their son. No *Honcho*, no *Blueboy*, but *The Wind in the Willows*, and *Charlotte's Web*, and *Half Magic*, and some of the Narnia books. Sean's name claimed them in an endearingly round, uneven attempt at the Palmer Method. Sean Kevin Riley. S. K. Riley. Father Sean Riley.

He opened a book and read aloud at random, but he couldn't

follow the words, and neither apparently could Sean, but at least it brought him around enough to croak, "Will you shut the fuck up?"

"The power of literature. Works every time. You're up just in time for a quick hello and goodnight. I have to dash out soon to do a rehearsal. The dread Irene Menengest. Again."

"Sing for me," said Sean. So Jeremy obliged, lightly, faintly. Sean closed his eyes but when Jeremy stopped he said, "I'll be out in time to make the New York trip, you know."

"Counting on it." He hoped the huskiness in his voice didn't betray him.

"Don't cancel because of me. Even if that's the day they dust-to-dust me."

"You're insane. You're raving. You're nowhere near that."

"It's called dementia, sweetheart. Listen to me. We both know that Jeremy Carr can come up with a hundred and six reasons to cancel. That's your special blessing. But don't. I forbid it. I'll come back and haunt you. You know the only thing I regret is that we never slept together. It would have been so sweet."

"Dementia, got it."

"It's all Willem, I know. Get yourself out of his poison shadow, will you? You're sicker than I am but you could recover. I'd feel better going down the crapper if I knew you were going to do this."

"I'm going to New York," said Jeremy. "I am. Do you want me to swear to you on a stack of Bibles?"

"I don't believe in the Bible. But you do. So yes."

"I don't have a stack."

"You work in a church and consort with that coven of nuns. I'm holding you to it."

"He isn't trouble, Sean. You always imagine I'm sneaking around behind everyone's backs—"

"No," said Sean, "*you* always imagine it. Everyone can see it in your face. Including him. Either fuck with him good and hard one last time or get out of here. I mean it."

"I take your point."

"No you don't. Mr. Fortitude, Piety and Fear of the Lord. Get out of here. Now. I don't want to see that pity on your weak-ass face. Visiting time is over."

Jeremy stood. "You, umm, want this book to read?"

Sean turned his face to the wall.

"I'm counting on you to come with me to New York, you hear," said Jeremy.

"If I can't make it, audition that high school kid Marty's been telling me about."

"You'll make it. You're too stubborn to trust me to do it without you." He hoped that would bring some sort of grizzled smile to Sean's face, to end on a convivial note, but Sean didn't turn his head back to reveal anything.

Jeremy checked his watch, and cursed mildly. 7:40. He was supposed to meet Irene Menengest and her sister at 7:15. Irene insisted on a vocal run-through in the actual church building, and Francesca was coming to give feedback about enunciation, even though Jeremy had explained that the acoustics when the building was empty would be nothing like those on the day of the wedding. But Irene had bullied and Jeremy had given in.

Lucky that Father Mike agreed to leave the building unlocked following the Christmas-decorating committee meeting, Jeremy thought. But holy shit. Was I asleep in that chair for an *hour*? What, he berated himself, more avoidance? Sleeping rather than facing the hard fact—that seeing Francesca Handelaers always puts in me the most toxic feeling of worthlessness? And not because she's smug, or superior, or monstrous—but because she's none of those things. Because she's generous, and talented, and attractive in a womanly way that even someone with homo-wiring can admire. Because she's secure enough not to be threatened by me. Who? Jeremy Carr? That dear? Oh yes, the object of Willem's amusing little diversion—we giggle about it all the time.

At least he wouldn't be stuck alone with Irene, that vivisectionist.

Jeremy blinked. What a day. Sister Alice's funeral in the morning, then the long drawn out business of the reception, a quick drop-by for some after-school tutoring of Ginnie Presley, a visit to Sean. No wonder he'd fallen asleep in the chair. Wasn't enough enough?

He took a detour down Coeyman Street, since there was an ambulance siren bearing down on him from the north, and parked in the street behind the church, cutting through the parking lot on foot. A lot of folks hustling along the sidewalks; prayer night for the Pentecostals, maybe. Folks stood near the entrance of Cliffs of Zion, but looked westward, away from their own church. The light in the sky, the sense of atmospheric activity. How sleepy had he been? The air crackled as if with canvas sails. Our Lady's was on fire, burning from the sanctuary forward. The siren wasn't an ambulance, it was a fire engine coming, and it wasn't even here yet.

The people gathered weren't Radical Radiants, they were local residents, crowding around the front door of the church, beating on it. "He's here, he's got keys," called Old Lady Scarcese, seeing Jeremy. She was shivering in a house dress with a sweater tied around her waist. "Jeremy, someone's in there, for the love of Jesus! Locked in there, maybe."

"God God God God God—" He hit the door running, ran into it again. "Oh God Oh God. Oh God."

"Use your keys, don't you have keys!" screamed Old Lady Scarcese.

"No, Father Mike was going to leave the door open—"

"They were here doing Christmas decorating, I saw them a while ago. I thought they left but someone else said they saw someone go in—"

What had he been thinking? Father Mike never left the front door open. He ran around the back of the church. But the sanctuary door was framed in flames; he couldn't even get near it. "Tell the fire guys," he called to no one in particular. The third door was on the parking lot side; that one led down to the kitchen and up to the nave and the Reconciliation Room. On the ice, one foot went out from under him; he fell, ripping the knees open in his trousers; he scrambled up, flailing at the edge of a bush. A canister shoved under that bush, a nozzled metal canister for carrying gasoline.

"Jesus Mary and Joseph." Old Lady Scarcese was moving faster than Jeremy; she had shuffled past, skating on the frosty sidewalk in her house-socks with the rubbery treads. She hobbled to the door, tugged at it. It opened.

Jeremy yelled, "You stay here," and barreled past her. The light switch didn't work; the blaze must have got at the fuse boxes in the back basement already. But the illumination from above was intense and glorious. If he were Francesca and Irene, he would go downstairs—would he? Because smoke rose, didn't it? He couldn't keep the rules of the natural world straight. Smoke rose, heat rose; oxygen fell. But the floor could cave in. He tumbled down the stairs into the kitchen. "Where are you?" he cried. He didn't sound like himself; his voice came late to his ears, like a sound track out of sync.

He hit against the refrigerator and opened the door. For some reason the power was on here; the bulb in the ceiling of the fridge cavity shed enough light for Jeremy to see that there was no one in the front two rooms. He left the refrigerator open and tried the doors to the furnace room and the storage rooms beyond, where outdated statuary stood gathering dust. The basement doors were all locked, as usual. No one could be in there.

So it was up the stairs, now, and into the nave of Our Lady's.

The stench was bestial. The chemically combed carpeting with which the altar area had been redone four years ago gave off a smell of sweet sewage and burnt hair; the parish council should have gone for the all-wool blend, but the synthetic had been 30 percent cheaper. The flames pulsed up the back wall of the church, a kind of three-dimensional wallpaper. The grand piano, chief treasure derived from Old Lady Donegan's bequest to benefit the music ministry, was lidded with fire, and Jeremy imagined he could hear strings popping in treble twangs beneath the incoming-tide roar of the inferno.

He ran back and forth looking for Francesca or Irene in all the pews, in case they had laid down to avoid the smoke. He couldn't get into the front third of the church. The heat was too immense, and the fire climbed steadily, even in the few minutes that he witnessed it. The choir loft? The music group didn't use it, but would the Menengest sisters have gone there? He turned, and for an instant he saw them, waving in panic, but it was the gyrating shadow of the crucifix suspended on its chains above the altar, a crazed marionette of a holy ghost.

He saw the ax even before he heard it, and went to throw the front doors of the church open so that the volunteer firemen wouldn't destroy any more than they had to. Old Lady Scarcese must have kept screeching that someone was inside, for the firemen weren't surprised to see the door open. "Are you the only one here," said Turk Schaeffer.

"Old Lady Scarcese said someone was trapped in here, and I was supposed to meet the Menengest sisters—"

"They could've opened the door from the inside as easily as

you did," said Turk conversationally. He crossed himself. The crucifix had caught on fire. "Better get out. If someone's up there in the apse, it's too late for them now." Several other firemen in their oversize garb crowded behind Turk. Jeremy left the church. The church is burning down and this feels like an anticlimax, he thought. What's scheduled for 9 p.m. tonight? An asteroid hitting Lake Ontario and tidal-waving and drowning half of upstate New York? It would be a vacation.

Sometimes the world gets punched in the face, it's the world that's the victim, and the ordinary folk who expect to take the damage stand on the sidelines, overlooked. Can't easily take in what has happened. The crowd around the church, any one of them who might have lost their wives or sisters in a burning building, shivered in a shock so deep it might have been peaceful. What could he ever do or say to Willem ever again. Then a second truck arrived, and a new hose unrolled, and the crowd pushed back, and he saw through swimming eyes. In the front seat of a car on the far side of Union Street sat Francesca and Irene. Irene rolled her window down. "I was annoyed to be stood up by you, Jeremy, but I didn't burn the church down to protest. I'm not that type."

"I thought you were inside." Jeremy reached past Irene and clawed at Francesca's shoulder; she lifted up her hands and took his hand between them. "I thought you were inside."

"We weren't going to wait in there, it was cold as Siberia," said Irene. "Get in the car, it's freezing. We came out here and turned the heat on. You want me to ruin my pipes with laryngitis, singing in a cold church?"

"It's not cold now," said Jeremy.

"Surely you couldn't have been worried about me? I never give you the time of day," said Irene. "Don't go all sensitive on me now. Your voice is shaking."

"I'm applying to be a countertenor."

"Good. Shave off your balls. You don't use them much anyway, I hear."

Francesca didn't look at him; her head was turned away from the illuminated church, away from him. No one ever looked at him. He could feel the edge of her wedding ring, though, as she clasped his hands tighter and didn't let go.

32

JACK REEVES CALLED Jeremy down to the police and fire department the next day, and with some trepidation he went. He had never been in the building before, and was hoping to catch sight of the jail cell that Tabitha Scales boasted was reserved for her. Or was that apocrypha? But nobody offered him a tour. He was handed a Styrofoam cup of motor-oil coffee and settled in Jack's office, which had some metallic Christmas garland drooping half-heartedly over a bulletin board shingled layers deep with county law enforcement directives.

"We're going to do a little character profiling of the suspect, like Hannibal Lecter did in *The Silence of the Lambs*," said Jack. "Turk Schaeffer is here as an ad-hoc deputy, because he knows a lot of the folks at your church."

"Shouldn't you be doing this with Father Mike?" said Jeremy.

"He said talk to you first," explained Turk. "Christmas coming up, what's to be done about the services, and Sister Alice, you know, not available to help. So on and so forth, amen. He's got his hands full. He said to trust you."

"Which of course we do," said Jack. "So, straight to it. Our primary lead is the gas can found on the scene of the crime."

"Yeah. I saw that. Under the cedar outside the sanctuary."

"The only clear fingerprints on it belong to the guys at Scarcese's Budget Gas," said Jack. "Which isn't so surprising as it's their can. They loan it to people who come in for gas for their power mowers or snowblowers or idiots who run out of gas on the highway. The clearest prints are of one of the pump boys. Hogan Scales."

"The son of that cracked lady, the one we found downstairs. Mrs. Loony Tunes," interjected Turk. "You know this Scales fellow?"

"Well." How cautious to be—and why be cautious? "I know who he is. I don't *know* him."

"I got this article from *USA Today*," said Jack. "I cut it out when they were having all those church fires down South and I put it in my arson file. Couple of interesting statistics might jog your memory."

"Jog my memory? You think I know who did this and that I just plumb forgot? What exactly am I in here for, anyway? Are you going to arrest me?" Is my sad little affection for Willem Handelaers such common knowledge that I'm the prime suspect in the attempted murder of his wife? Please.

"Sorry, slip of the tongue. Look, I'm tired, we're all tired. I just mean maybe we can brainstorm and come up with a list of suspects. I don't want to go arresting Pastor Huyck for torching the competition!" He threw back his head and laughed, a little too long. "Well, what I mean is, here's the scoop. *USA Today*. About a third of the suspects arrested in arsons at black churches have been black. At mosques, synagogues and stuff, and white churches, they tend to be white."

"Well, we have only one black family in the congregation, and they're new," said Jeremy coldly. "They came from Scranton, Pennsylvania, which isn't south but it's south of *here*. Maybe they didn't like the sermon last week and, you know, old habits die hard."

"You're making fun of me, and I want your help," said Jack Reeves, the most like a cop Jeremy had ever seen him be. "I'm saying that *USA Today* suggests it's probably a white criminal."

"Most of the county is white, isn't it? If we had more of a race problem, maybe we wouldn't all be so caught up in these church skirmishes."

"Mind your mouth. This is a serious offense even if there are no fatalities."

This must be sort of fun for him, thought Jeremy. "Look, it's my church that burned down, too, you know. I'm not exactly happy about it. If I had any good leads don't you think I would have called you up and told you?"

"Jack," said Turk Schaeffer, "Jeremy's right. We don't have any black churches here."

"Juveniles have accounted for forty-four percent of the arrests," said Jack.

"So that means sixty-six percent of the arrests have been adults," said Jeremy.

"Fifty-six," said Turk. "You forget to carry the one to the tens column."

"Does this mean you're trying to hunt down adults or juveniles?"

"The question's interestingly open, wouldn't you say?" said Jack. "Though the way *USA Today* words it, better we focus on juveniles."

"I thought we were supposed to be trying to close down some possibilities."

"At least half the arrests in the South had racial implications," said Jack. "The South with its history, you know, and all that."

"Do you have any suspects?" said Jeremy. "I really think it doesn't work to play the race card."

"I'm not an idiot. There's a pattern to these findings, don't you see? I know we don't have a very multiracial society in Thebes. That doesn't mean we're lacking, uh, other stereotyped notions that cause people to not get along so well with each other. It really could be what church you go to. Frankly. Or it could be other things. You know, alternate lifestyle things." He looked at the floor.

Then Jeremy knew why Turk was there. Both as a witness and to make Jeremy feel he wasn't about to be bullied. It was actually a civilized gesture. Almost good cop, bad cop. Still, it wasn't easy for Jeremy to bring it up. Though that's what both men were waiting for him to do. This was awkward for all of them. Why didn't they have a plump, motherly cop on hand for this kind of interview? Or a nice winking hunk just out of the Police Academy showers, with his blue shirt open three buttons to reveal his manly holster?

"You mean *my* alternate lifestyle?" Jeremy hated to help them out but he didn't have all day. He was meeting Marty at the convent for an emergency rehearsal.

"Well, do you know anyone who might've wanted to hurt you? You were supposed to be in the building at that hour, Father Mike said. You had an appointment."

"This is crazy."

"A juvenile, probably white, who had it in for you because you're, you know—"

"Sensitive?" He couldn't help it. "Artistic? Soft-spoken?"

"Come on, Jeremy, this isn't about you." Turk was turning a sort of gravy color. "This is about who burned the church."

"The guys at Scarcese's would know who came to get gas recently. Ask that Hogan Scales."

"We did. He said that the gas thing was stolen. Someone walked off with it. But that happens fairly regularly, he says."

Jeremy wanted to get up and leave. But what if Francesca and

Irene actually *had* been caught inside, and been burned, or even killed? Law enforcement had a right to do its job. "You know, there are a number of parishioners who have been sour since Vatican II, waiting for us to go back to the Latin mass and Gregorian chant. I've heard I sound too much like Neil Sedaka to sing in church. But I don't think anyone I know has gone over the edge enough to try to burn down the church with me in it. So if I were you, I'd go back to the gas station. Hogan Scales and his friends, if he has any. I'm not saying he had anything to do with it—*anything*—how do I know? But the clues would come from there."

"But we talked to Pastor Huyck," added Jack, "who ministers to the Scales family when they're in a church-going mood. And he says he thinks that the younger Scales son is a bit off."

"Off?" said Jeremy.

"Sheez, Jeremy," said Turk. "You know what he means. Give us a break."

"I plead the sanctity of the confessional," said Jeremy.

"You're not allowed. You're not ordained," said Turk.

"I'm just asking for general advice," said Jack Reeves. "Are you purposely changing the subject? I want to know if you think that Scales boy is a little cockeyed."

"Cockeyed. That's a good one. Then what do you want me to do? Defend him out of some brotherhood of gay men thing? Accuse him of stalking me? Oh. Or do you want me to provide a model for how a young gay outlaw thinks? Is that why I'm here? A local Jean Genet?" He felt obscurely flattered and considered trying to slouch a little.

"Could you think of a motive?" said Jack. Now they were onto it, and he was sitting forward in his chair. He absentmindedly reached for a cookie in an open box of Freihofer's.

"I can't do this," said Jeremy. He stood up. "Maybe there is a motive and maybe there's not, but I don't know anything about how that kid thinks. I hardly know how *I* think. You want me to lead the Police Precinct in Christmas carols, call me; that's the work I do."

He wasn't a flouncer by nature but he had to resist the urge to sashay when he left the room. He wouldn't obstruct justice, but he wouldn't take part in some sort of smear campaign, either. Of course Kirk Scales really *could* have tried to do such a thing. So could Irene Menengest, who despised Jeremy. Or Sean's freaked-out parents. Or Kirk's brother. Why focus on Kirk? The most obviously aberrant because of his effeminacy? Sure, Kirk seemed to have fastened on Jeremy. But that's not such a crime in itself.

At the convent, Jeremy didn't mention the conversation with Jack and Turk about Kirk Scales. County law enforcement might not accept the notion of the sanctity of the confessional, but Jeremy did. What Marty gaped at was Jeremy's reaction to the fire. He said, "You mean you didn't think *for a moment*, 'Hey, this is okay. Farewell Francesca and Irene, Goodnight? This leaves Willem, sweet Willem free and unattached, and he's going to be in need of a very special kind of comforting?'"

"You're sick. Of course not."

"Well, but the idea occurred to you later, and you cursed yourself for the lost opportunity—"

"You don't know who I am. Even after all this time."

"You are one sick puppy, if even your fantasy life is circumscribed by morals."

"We have stuff to do. With Sean out of commission, we have to reduce all these trios to duets. I can't talk about this now."

"I should give you a going-away present. Assuming you're really going to go through with this New York gambit, which I doubt. How about I just sort of hijack Willem for a night? There's two of us and only one of him. Hire a van, hustle him inside, rent a motel room, tie him up a little—just for fun—give you both a bottle of bourbon and a boombox with something romantic on it. Maybe I could find some amyl nitrate for old time's sake. I'd leave you alone, and I wouldn't peek. He owes you. You saved his wife."

"Stop. I don't even like this kind of kidding. *Stop it*."

"Well, what do you want? What the hell do you *want*?"

Sister Clothilde came to the door, ushering a seriously frailer Mother Clare du Plessix. As they made their way across the sunroom, the guys fell silent. But Jeremy wouldn't have said aloud, even to his friends, what he really wanted. He wanted Willem, who was one of the lucky ones bisexual enough to have a choice—he wanted Willem to have wanted him. And since Willem hadn't—or not enough—there was no going forward.

Since possessing him is impossible, I want to love Willem without possessing him. I want to have him without holding him, or to hold him without having him, for better and for worse, for richer and for poorer, with our other partners and lovers and parents and children in tow, till—till whenever.

And since that's not likely, not now, not yet, what I want, thought Jeremy, is a life free of him.

Mother Clare du Plessix sat down and said, "Let me catch my breath. Sing for me."

Jeremy picked up the guitar and began; Marty joined at the bridge.

They were missing Sean's nasal, pitch-perfect high A on the end. But the sound was good, anyway; the rehearsals had been paying off. Mother Clare du Plessix smiled distractedly, and Jeremy waited for a benediction. "An awful lot of words, aren't there?" she said.

"Well," said Jeremy. "It's supposed to build."

"Oh, that it does," said Mother Clare. "I suppose I should hear it again. Not just now—" she protested. "I have come along to get your opinion on something. I just had a phone call from Father Sheehy at your parish. Sweet man. Distraught—Sister Alice and the church in the same week. Horrible, really. It makes you wonder."

"The chapel," said Sister Clothilde, nudging Mother Clare gently.

"Father Sheehy called and we discussed the possibility of having your midnight mass Christmas service at our chapel," she continued. "The only other option that seems viable is some gymnasium at the local secondary school, he said. You know the chapel better than he does, having seen it several times this fall. He asked you to make the decision and for me to call him back with it."

"Well, the chapel is small," replied Jeremy. "I mean, smaller than Our Lady's. But I suspect a fair number of parishioners wouldn't come this far for midnight mass if it wasn't what they were used to. Does he propose having all the Sunday services here, too?"

"No, no. I believe the Pastor from that start-up next door to Our Lady's is being very generous. But of course Christmas Eve is special and the other church requires their space, too. Apparently there needs to be some decorating and so on. Father Sheehy is going to rely on you to help set things up."

"Rig them up," said Jeremy. "I hope he's not going to bring the Magical Flying Baby Jesus here."

Mother Clare's face folded, like an old-fashioned accordion camera. There were things she did not have the reserves to consider, and she looked as if she hoped she hadn't heard Jeremy correctly. "If you approve, then, I shall have Sister Clothilde place a telephone call to the Rectory of Our Lady's," she said, rising. "I do hope he's not doing this just to make us old nuns feel—included."

"Well, what if he is?" said Jeremy, thinking of his need to be in-cluded in Willem's life.

"The whole notion of the cloister still escapes you, doesn't it? At least one of the many reasons one enters is not to escape the world because it is too painful, but because it is too beautiful to bear."

Marty said, "Hey, sister, there's the answer to your problem of attrition. You should start accepting men. I nominate Jeremy. He's, like, totally qualified. Can't deal with the beauty of the world. The first male nun. It's a win-win, don't you think?"

"I believe my being hard-of-hearing is serving me very well just now," said Mother Clare, "for which be praised Jesus and all the saints. Saint Marty of Flatbush among them."

33

THE NURSE'S STATION, strung round with hard-boiled colored lights, was empty except for Marilee Gompers, an alien on the command deck of an enemy spacecraft. Jeremy flashed her a smile as she glanced up from the folded strips of paper candy canes she'd been snipping out of gift wrap. "Season's greetings," he offered, nondenominationally.

"Hey you," she said. "Come here." He did. "His folks had to step out to do some last-minute shopping. They must be caught in traffic. They don't want you left alone with him but I figure, now's your chance."

"You want me to—kidnap him?"

She wasn't amused.

He shrugged. "They won't tell me anything."

"I put it at six weeks."

"Six *weeks*? Till he gets out?"

"Six weeks, honey." Her voice was cool and soft and her eyes followed her scissors, which angled more slowly, deliberately. "Six weeks. You know what I'm saying to you?"

He nodded, more surprised than aghast. "Is he comfortable?"

"I know how this happens. At a certain point it can get kind of peaceful." She looked up from under her horrible bangs. Her eyes had the glint of scissors in them. "You can take it on faith. He's not that peaceful yet, but he's on his way."

Jeremy dropped his gaze to the pleated candy canes.

"I believe it comes down to something simple. It's pretty basic. It's not that he's happy to leave you. He just wants to go home. It's the same for everyone."

"What *are* you saying to me?"

"He's sleeping a lot. Here. Make some decorations for me, will you? Brighten up that room with some nice stars." She handed him the supplies. "Say what you need to. This might be your last chance before the ogres return."

Sean was too doped up to talk. His eyes were open, though. "Hey there, big boy," said Jeremy. "Anything special you want for Christmas?"

The radiators clanked. Antiseptic holiday ditties from the hallway corrupted the evening. A new roommate in the next bed wheezed, courtesy of an oxygen machine. Sean raised his left arm and gestured toward the roommate, the window, the falling dark. Jeremy wondered. Oxygen?

Sean's arm fell against the copy of *Redbook* boasting *Christmas Plum Pudding Even a Scrooge Could Love!* The pulmonary appliance made a sound as of faraway raveling, like a train on a horizon.

34

ON THE DAY before Christmas Eve, Peggy Mueller arrived to help Jeremy and Father Mike set up the chapel at the convent of the Sisters of the Sorrowful Mysteries. She brandished new-cut branches, decorations and tools, and a can of spray-on pine scent in case the balsam gave up the ghost too quickly. The sap was redolent enough; Sister Perpetua got to sneezing and had to abandon her devotions and run for cover.

Jeremy thought: Peggy's throwing herself into the service of the Church with more fervor than usual; she hadn't approved of Sister Alice's managerial clout, so Father Mike's need provides her an occasion to ambush him with her efficiency. Rushing in where angels fear to tread. I might take lessons.

Father Mike and Jeremy carted in the crèche, a good-size set turned out of plaster molds sometime in the early part of the century. The Virgin and Joseph knelt a good three feet high. The shepherds and wise men stood smaller—a tautological distinction, wondered Jeremy, or had they come from a smaller set to save some money? A cute lamb looked somewhat devilish due to an extra flourish of dark eyebrows, though do lambs actually have eyebrows? The lone cow, any way they turned it, appeared about to belch. The camel had lost most of its nose, perhaps to syphilis.

The wise men were bracingly multiracial. One of them glared with ovoid eyes, a cross between Krishna and Dracula; another was black and shiny as a Steinway; the third resembled an anthropomorphized aubergine. The shepherds were dressed in bathrobes like grade school boys at Christmas pageants; Jeremy got the feeling that beneath the robes, the shepherds were wearing ceramic pajamas printed all over with Bart Simpson.

He had no desire to stand again on that wobbly grate over the crypt while he was leading the congregation in Christmas music. The world was shaky enough. Instead, he staked out the left side of the chapel for the music ministry. (What he called privately "altar right," as in "stage right"—the altar being the proper point of coordinates from which to determine the room's orientation. But only privately.) So Father Mike and Peggy set up the manger on the church right (altar left). The plaster crèche came with removable plaster straw, so they removed it, and Peggy arranged some extra balsam boughs there. "Tomorrow night I'll give them a good spritz of Pine Fresh to remind them of their duty," she said, apparently to Jesus on the cross above the altar, as Jeremy and Father Mike were heading to the choir loft.

"I hate the Incredible Flying Baby Jesus," said Jeremy. "Do we have to?"

"Jeremy, don't be a wet blanket. Father Orsini brought this local custom from Sicily home when he was returned from his wartime posting. It's remained a staple of the Christmas Eve service of Our Lady's ever since. We're not giving up on it at this point. Please."

In the vestibule of Our Lady's, and therefore saved from fire and smoke damage, the crèche had been set up since the First Sunday of Advent. The whole kit and caboodle except the Holy Family. "It's parish tradition to introduce Joseph and Mary on the fourth Sunday of Advent, and leave the crèche gaping empty as they kneel, staring expectantly into it. I love that porcelain expectation," said Father Mike, going a little teary on him. "And you just watch the tithing drop if we were to retire this bit. They wait all year for it."

"I know, never mind," said Jeremy. He knew the drill. On Christmas Eve his program of music would kick off at 11:15 p.m. Partly a concert, partly a community sing to entertain hearty souls who came early to midnight mass to get seats and avoid having to stand in the back. At 11:55, the lights would dim, and the soprano on call would launch into "O Holy Night." At the minor key bridge—"Fall on your knees, oh hear the angels singing"—the sacristan, waiting in the choir loft, would hook the Incredible Flying Baby Jesus onto the guy cable with a twist of copper wiring. A little nudge—the cords were lightly greased—and the Baby Jesus would come sailing slantways through the incredible darkness. The other end of the cable hooked precisely to the head of the crib, where the Baby Jesus arrived by the close of the verse. Some years at a zippy speed, so the pine boughs on the receiving end needed to be arranged carefully to cushion the landing.

"It's just that it's so obvious," said Jeremy.

"What's wrong with obvious?" asked Father Mike. "Obvious is consoling. It's bad enough that our own space is off-limits until we can schedule the county inspectors and get the insurance papers filed. Something Sister Alice could have done with her hands tied behind her back. But the death of Sister Alice, her funeral, the whole nine yards—everyone will think of that when they come back to this chapel. So we need these figures, we need this arrival. It's a different moment. We need this child more than ever."

"The millennial Christ."

"Don't be snarky."

They worked for seventy minutes tightening the guy wire, loosening it, sending the Baby for a couple of trial runs. The angle was steeper here than in Our Lady's, so Father Mike had to catch the child headfirst, as if it had been evacuated out of a heavenly womb like a projectile missile. "Gotta slow this Baby down. Any suggestions?"

"We could go to the IGA-Plus and get some of those twisties they put around the base of lettuces," suggested Jeremy. "We could fray the paper and fringe it, and wrap it around the connecting wire. The friction should provide some drag."

"Black yarn," called Peggy, washing the face of the donkey lovingly. "If the nuns don't have black yarn around this place, I'll convert to Buddhism. Doesn't this donkey look as if it has put on a little weight since last year? I wonder if she's pregnant."

35

TABITHA WAS STUCK. She couldn't carry out her vague plan of clonking her mother now, not with the police having shown up several times to talk to her about Hogan and Kirk. Her mother dying the same week as the Catholic church catching on fire wouldn't look like an accident. Pity the goddamn church hadn't burned to the ground; everybody said it was mostly cosmetic damage, which made Linda Pearl snort and say, "Honey, you ain't *seen* cosmetic damage till you get a load of what I'm going to do to Polly Osterhaus on the day before her wedding."

"Oh, Linda Pearl," said Tabitha, "grow up."

Linda Pearl looked at Tabitha sullenly. "You're giving up? Is that it? You're letting your man walk out of your life? You're not going to put up a fight?"

"You're not making this any easier," said Tabitha. She was majorly flipping out. She'd rather be home, but she was trying to duck the police. She didn't know anything about the church fire. Maybe Kirk had set it, pissed off at Jeremy for some sicko reason or other. Maybe Hog had set it. She wasn't asking because she didn't want to know. She needed to be blameless in all things from now on, and sometimes that meant keeping your eyes closed. An act of willpower.

Willpower was an old-fashioned mom-whip that Tabitha was thinking about a lot these days. Maybe there was something to it. If Tabitha had a son, maybe she should name him Will. Or Power: was that too corny? But Power Scales sounded like something used over at the paper mill.

She was trying to be good, somehow, and Linda Pearl made her feel sullied and sour. "Just you do Polly up the way she wants," said Tabitha. "I gotta go. Hair spray and doughnuts are making me yucko."

"I got a constitutional right to express my rage," said Linda Pearl. "No one can take that away from me. I'm your loyal friend even if you're being Miss Wimpella, the Pagan Queen of Christian Martyrs."

Tabitha walked home, one step after the other, watching her feet. Step on a crack, you break your mother's back. Step on a crack, you break the devil's back. Which crack was which—or *were they the same?* Spooky. She shattered dozens of unidentified vertebrae before she reached the corner.

No police cars loitered in front of the Scales house, but Pastor Huyck's car squatted there. Shit. The more forcefully tender he got, the more he gave her the willies. She couldn't stand that pious gaze. She pictured smashing his face with a baseball bat, but realized that maybe her thoughts of braining her mother were becoming a habit. Watch it, baby, she said to herself. There is a beginning and an ending cooking up, so mind your step.

She and the unknown universe trudged through the unshoveled walk up to the front door and pushed in.

She was glad to see that her mother wasn't sacked out on the floor of the living room. Kirk must have dragged her into her bedroom in case the cops came back. Pastor Huyck weighed down the middle of the sofa, the far ends of both seat cushions elevating three or four inches. Tabitha suppressed the urge to push right by him without a hello. He could be undercover for the cops. "The gifts of the season!" said Pastor Huyck, eyeing her breasts.

"Who let you in?" she said, as graciously as she could.

"I'd say that Mother did." For an instant she thought he meant it, and her heart lilted even though she'd been readying to ice her mother. "She came to me in a dream just as she came to me in real life, and said, Be my pastor. Take care of my little girl."

"Oh, dreams. That figures. She doesn't get around much in real life."

"I'm not one for dream visitations," said Pastor Huyck, a holiday ruddiness on his face. "This was however a potent experience. You were in it."

"Oooh." Tabitha felt as if she'd just found ants in the sugar.

"This is a very holy time. I've come to see if I can help getting Mother to services tomorrow night."

"She might come to you in a dream, but she's pretty useless on her legs now. Hell in a handbasket, maybe, but you'd need a pretty hefty handbasket. She's not going anywhere fast."

"The rewards of the holy feast might revive her."

"She has a thing about your church now." Tabitha tried to be as kind as she could. "She bucked and clawed and twisted when we tried to bring her there. You know that."

"You've said she's less mobile. She'd be less resistant now."

"That'd be taking advantage. Why not just let her be."

"You come then. Come in Mother's place. Come home. Come here." He patted the sofa beside him. "You've been carrying this load too long, Tabitha, and I've been a bad pastor to you. You look like you need a holiday hug. Sit down."

"I, um, can't." She looked about. "I got to, got to—" Her eye fell on a dusty photo album that had fallen off a heap of pirated videos of *X-Files* that Hog must've been rooting through. "I've been looking for a picture."

She lunged for the book as Pastor Huyck got up. The sofa cushions sighed. "I'll help you look."

"I can look myself." She put it down on the side table and began to flip pages. Too bad there wasn't a recipe for poison communion bread in here. She felt him enter her airspace, and smelled him, a thunderhead of Old Spice masking a hint of vinegar. Or was that something sweetly alcoholic, like sherry?

"What're you looking for?" He put one set of gorilla knuckles on the tabletop beside the book, and the other set on her shoulder. He massed against the back of her knees to her shoulder blade. She could feel the car keys in his left pocket as he began to rotate his body more centrally to line up with her spine.

"This, here it is." At random she tore out an old snapshot, the kind from beyond time, with rippled white edges, when the world could be remembered only in black and white.

"Who is it?"

She could hardly talk. "It's Grandmother Prelutski, my mom's mother. Don't do that."

He put his chin on her shoulder, squinting. "She looks pretty fierce."

"Mom called her Mother Stalin. She raised Mom alone 'cause her husband took off to shack up with some filthy whore from Hattiesburg, Virginia."

"Yet Mother learned to be a good mother from her."

"Well, that's debatable. Stop that."

His lips were in her hair and his left hand had reached her breast. She couldn't think. But maybe this wasn't the time for thinking. Shy of a wrench, shy of a convenient portable gas can and a match, she reached for the only thing she had, the photo album.

She closed it with both hands and sighed as if remembering the crimes of her family background, and then she heaved it up back-hand right against Pastor Huyck's face. It wasn't heavy enough to hurt much but it scraped his glasses off his face, and as he turned to grab them she ducked out under his left arm.

Then she hit him with a better blow. "If I take Mom to church tomorrow night, we're going to the Catholics. That's where Mom seems to be drawn, and while she's down and out I guess I'm the man of the family. And if you touch me again I'll tell everyone you been hitting on me."

"You're misunderstanding my ministry."

"Take a hike. Huyck." By now she'd got across the room and had armed herself with a real fire poker they kept by the fake fireplace.

He left in a righteous sulk at, she thought of it and laughed, a goodly pace.

"Merry Christmas, by the way," she called after him.

Kirk peered out of the bathroom and whispered, "Is he gone yet?"

"You could've come out. He was pestering me like a pervert."

"I was just about to. After I finished my nails."

"Hog would've cracked his honking skull. He's the only real hero round here."

"I know." Kirk sounded sad. "I've seen him in action."

Can't be easy to be Kirk, she thought. She went in and sat on her mother's bed. Mrs. Scales lay with open eyes facing the closet door. Her knees were drawn closer to her chin, but her breathing seemed calm. The skin on her face was slack and drooped bed-ward.

She was starting to be smaller than Tabitha. She was curling herself together, knitting fingers together, tucking ankles toward her rear end, arching her neck to complete the circle toward her

bent knees. A fossil of herself, but still breathing; fragile and help-
less as a baby. How would Tabitha ever manage both her own new
baby and this old one too?

She wanted to kill it and she wanted to save it—this mother
baby, not her own. How to do both things at once? Her desperate
words to Pastor Huyck rang in her mind. Maybe I'll get Kirk and
Hogan to help. I'll take Mom to the Catholic mass, wherever it's going to be, and leave her there. A baby on the doorstep of the church.
She won't be my responsibility any more. It makes perfect sense.
Look: Mom has been driven to lie in the basement of that Catholic
church, entombed there; she's scrabbled and bit her way there. I'll
give her what she wants. My Christmas present to her.

She called the rectory of Our Lady's. A recording announced
where the midnight mass was being held. Concert starting at 11:15
p.m. Well, she'd get there earlier. She'd have to explain enough to
get her brothers' help. And since they were both looking jittery
these days, she ought to be able to swing it.

In fact, her brothers were oddly compliant. Maybe they had
worked together to set fire to the church? *That* would be a kind
of brotherly cooperation she hadn't seen before. Or maybe it was
merely clear that now they were all in this together, because if the
police came and put one of them in juvenile court, it would be bad
for them all. If she could only lift the burden of their mother off
her shoulders, she could begin to take care of her brothers. It would
be good practice for when her own baby became a satanic teenager.

AT ABOUT 9:30 p.m. on Christmas Eve the Scales children went
into their mother's bedroom. First they propped her into a sitting
position. Tabitha washed her mother and cleaned her up, top to

bottom. Her mother offered no resistance. The boys looked the
other way during the worst of it, and Tabitha wished she could too,
but this was the last indignity, she hoped. She lifted her mother's
breasts and set them gently in place in the bra to avoid pinching,
and latched the bra behind. Doing the panties and the slip was going to be, she feared, unforgettable. Then the boys turned around
to help with the blouse and the skirt, elephantine red flowers with
avaricious black interiors. "Boy, isn't there such a thing as enough
with Georgia O'Keeffe already?" said Kirk.

Tabitha didn't get it, didn't try. "Jewelry?"

"Skip it, why bother?" said Hogan.

"The black jet beads, in a double loop," Kirk declared without
going over to the jewelry box to find out what was there. Guess he
knew.

"I was thinking something Christmas-y," said Tabitha.

"We can stick holly in her fucking ears," said Hogan. "Let's get
this over with."

"All right then," said Tabitha, "on the count of three."

They hoisted her up. With coaxing, her legs straightened out,
which was something of a relief; Tabitha had been afraid they were
going to be stuck in that pretzel position. Mrs. Scales was unsteady,
though. Hogan and Tabitha kept on either side of her. Kirk darted
ahead to kick the footstool out of the way, turn off the TV, and open
the front door. It was a snowy night; a Bing Crosby white Christmas with Lake Ontario wind. They couldn't even see the car until
they were halfway down the walk. Snow had fallen in the smashed
rear window.

"Going to church, Mom," said Tabitha. "Just where you like it."

They put her in the front seat and arranged the seat belt carefully. Suddenly, caution at every turn. Fold the skirt neatly under
her; settle her hands together. Are you all right? Comfy? Odd how
you could change, or was it just a Christmas mood? She couldn't

believe she'd considered hitting her mother with a wrench. What if she'd hurt her? The dear thing. The dear, knotted, gnarled, hateful thing.

They'd be there in what, thirty minutes maybe, going slowly because of the blowing snow.

Tabitha hadn't figured on the choir. If the concert was going to start at 11:15, she guessed that getting there by 10:30 would allow plenty of time to set her mother down and disappear. Someone would find the old bat within forty-five minutes. But when Tabitha pulled the car up to the convent, old nuns in their witchy drag were propped up against the front doors, welcoming people.

Bravely she got out and ducked inside to case the joint. The vestibule and front hall of the convent were busy with violins tuning and a flutist trilling like a demented parakeet. The doors to the chapel, across the corridor and opposite the front door, were flung open, so Tabitha peered inside. The choir was augmented by a trumpet and a clarinet and a set of snare drums that read "The Harmony Brothers" on its face, and Jeremy Carr was leading a bunch of giddily dressed choir members in warm-up vocal calisthenics. Shit. She should have come an hour earlier.

Think, think. If the nuns were gathered in a black cotton flurry in the front, maybe the back of the convent was deserted. Mom didn't actually have to be on the doorstep of the church, did she? She could be left at the kitchen entrance. New supplies. Jeremy had said that this was a place that old nuns went to die. Maybe Mom could become a nun in order to qualify for the retirement benefits. "Where are you going?" said Hogan irritably, but Tabitha started the engine again without answering. She pulled the car along the entrance drive until she saw a service road veer off. She threaded the car through overgrown hedges, which shook fistfuls of grainy snow onto the windshield.

The first door she came to was propped ajar with a music stand.

A couple of cigarette butts had been flicked in the boot-stamped ground. "Here, Hog. Smoking nuns left the door open. A Christmas miracle."

The lighted doorway revealed, inside, a landing and a set of steps. One flight led up to the chapel and a glorious misshapen noise of music. Another flight led down.

"Near enough," said Tabitha. "Let's just spread out Mom's coat and set her here on the landing. She can listen to the music and she'll be perfectly happy."

"She'll fall down the stairs," said Kirk.

"She can't stand by herself, she's not competent enough to fall."

But their mother made a motion with her chin—the first sign of expression in eight or ten days—toward the stairs leading down into the dark.

"She's looking for that refrigerator again," said Kirk. "This is a different place, Mom."

"Unngh," said their mother.

"Oh, Lord," said Tabitha. She didn't want her mother to go suddenly vocal on her, not just when they were trying to tiptoe away. "Okay, come on, downstairs then. Just take it easy."

The light from the stairwell went only so far. Once they were at the bottom of the stairs, though, they could see the low space ahead, because a grate in the ceiling let down some light and music from the chapel upstairs. "Look, it's a kind of shelf, right underneath," said Tabitha. "Perfect. We can let Momster lie down right here."

"It looks like an autopsy table," said Hogan, approvingly.

"She'll fall off it," said Kirk.

"Come on. She can't even get her thumb into her mouth to suck it, she's not going to start rolling around like some fourteen-year-old Russian gymnast at the fucking Olympics."

The time had come to leave her. They could go upstairs and

listen to some music for a while, and Tabitha would find a pencil and a paper somewhere and drop a note in the collection basket. They were making an offering of their mother. Take her with all our best wishes, XXX OOO. She's in the cellar on the stone table. Merry X-mas. Merry XXX-mas.

They stood at the door and looked back. The light fell upon her face, which was facing the ceiling. Her eyes were closed. Hogan had folded her hands in a religious way on her stomach. She looked like a stone carving of a knight in some old English church, except for the black jet beads. "Sorry there's no refrigerator," said Tabitha. Really, it was the only thing missing.

"Wait," said Kirk. He pulled something from his pocket. "I found this picture of Grandma Prelutski on the living room floor the other day. Remember how she was rooting through those boxes in the cellar? I think she was looking for photos; that's why I brought the albums up. She might want to keep this with her." He tucked it between her hands.

This isn't good-bye, Tabitha said to herself, as they hurried back to the car, to sneak into the chapel from the front without anyone seeing. This is something else.

"You're not expecting me to go into a Catholic voodoo cannibal service, are you?" said Hogan, when Tabitha had parked the car around front.

"Hogan," said Tabitha, "I'm going to say one thing to you."

"Promise? Only one?"

"Turk Schaeffer is a Catholic, and he's helping Jack Reeves. And it won't hurt any of us to be seen together at a service. Especially if someone is prying for clues about the fire at Our Lady's. And I'm taking the keys so you can't drive away and abandon us here out in the woods with *Mother.*" It felt good to take Pastor Huyck's word from him.

Even Tabitha could see that there were lots of ways to argue against this, but Hogan sure as hell wasn't going to sit in a cold car while Tabitha and Kirk went inside. The wind was strong and the snow stronger. "You are a regular Christmas bitch," muttered Hogan, somewhat appreciatively, and he followed them into the chapel.

The place was warm and dark. Something different here, as far as Tabitha could tell. It wasn't the talk show self-i-ness that hovered like a faint stink in Catholic mass during the daylight. It was something older and more secret. Something kinder, richer, harsher. Something farther away. Darker, obscurer. The mistake that the Radical Radiants made, and the Catholics made during bright modern Sundays, was trying to get in your face so much. In the middle of the night, with the snow billowing outside, Tabitha could comprehend this more clearly. The candles and their thin, black-chiffon streams of smoke. The glints of gold and the slow-motion gestures in the paintings, the statues. Even the choir up there was sounding decent, wreathed with the tendrils of ancient melody. That nut-job Jeremy Carr was looking distinguished, not frazzled. The instruments were beginning to speak in concert.

"It's a puppet theater," hissed Hogan. "Look at those idols in the front. What happened, somebody kidnap the Baby Jesus for ransom? He's missing."

"Look at the angels in the ceiling," Tabitha said to Hogan, since he hadn't come to Sister Alice's funeral. "So stinking gorgeous."

In this light the angels made a rack of wooden origami, rank upon rank of them, almost hidden in the high shadows. One of them looked darker than the others. Lucifer, maybe? No, Lucifer wouldn't be attending a Catholic mass. Maybe a leak in the roof, and the snow was melting and staining the wood. Yes, that was it, must be, for the room was already filling up, but below that angel the lusty garrulous Catholics were avoiding the pew. Water must be dripping, perhaps into a bucket.

Caleb Briggs would be here somewhere—maybe she'd remembered that deep down, or maybe not, but now she realized it up front and personal—because Polly Osterhaus bobbed perkily in the choir, looking in red and green like a tortured poinsettia. Tabitha could wish peace on earth and goodwill to all men and even all women except P.S. not Polly Osterhaus.

Tabitha put her head down to avoid seeing Caleb—at least, not yet—and, since she appeared to be praying ("You phony," muttered Hogan next to her) she thought, Oh, what the hell.

The only thing she could think of was the Lord's Prayer. But it came out funny. It came out slowly, as if each line needed to be thought about before she could go on. Maybe that was the baby inside; everyone said babies slowed you down and kept you in the present. Could it be happening already?

Our Father, who art in heaven—how did it go?

. . . Forgive us our trespasses

As we forgive those who trespass against us.

Ah. A tricky part. How to work it out? It was like algebra, at which she'd tanked. The equation was about God forgiving us the way we forgive others—like, say, if she forgave Caleb Briggs. Or Pastor Huyck if she could ever manage it. The equation didn't say anything about being forgiven by other humans like, say, Mom. Maybe God's forgiveness was supposed to supersede your own mother's, so you didn't need to wait around for her forgiveness. You could pick up and walk out without it.

Wait'll Mom gets a load of *that*.

The choir was starting. A sprightly rhythm to it, as if goats and shepherd boys were going to do a folk dance across the altar. After a few verses Tabitha glanced sideways at Kirk. She had kind of forgotten about him. If he was really stuck on Jeremy Carr, this stuff must be hard for him to sit through.

"You okay?" she said.

"Oh, yeah." A dour mood that sounded as if it was going to take about ten years to lift.

"Cheer up. It's Christmas."

"Christmas in hell."

"Well, I can understand. He is kind of cute."

Kirk slanted his eyes at her without moving his head. A cautious expression of surprise. But not, she thought sadly, surprise at her admitting Jeremy's appealing manner and looks. Kirk was surprised that Tabbers could understand her baby brother. Or anything at all.

Luckily, a greatest hits carol began—"The First Nowell"—that everyone in the chapel sang. Kirk went liltingly up at the end of each chorus, which caused Catholics to turn around and smile convertingly at him. He did have a nice voice, she had to admit it.

She dozed on and off. Well, it was late, and she was always so tired these days. She managed to avoid peering around for Caleb. Jack Reeves and his wife entered; she hadn't known he was Catholic too. Father Mike Sheehy flapped about in his costume, greeting people. Crippled old nuns hobbled up and down the aisles passing out music sheets. A blond soprano with an expression like a Nazi stormtrooper began a glorious hymn, and the lights went down except for the candles in sconces along the wall. "Oh, holy night," sang the lady, over-articulating as if she were singing on a language tape for immigrants. The program advertised her as Mrs. Leonard (Peggy Moynihan) Mueller.

Everyone turned in their pews and looked at the choir loft, and so did the Scales kids. "Oh Jesus," said Hogan. "Duck. It's a little bundle from heaven."

"Long lay the world, in sin and error pining," sang the Mueller.

"Is this like New Year's on TV?" whispered Hogan. "When the Baby hits the manger, it's officially Christmas?"

The hush was reverential. The Baby was suspended and some parishioner wearing black gloves gripped the Baby's feet. For a second Tabitha thought it was a real baby and she had to fight an uprising of panic, but she took a chill pill. It's only a Christmas pageant and you sat through a hell of a lot of those while Kirk was into it.

"Till He appeared, and the soul had its birth," sang the soprano.

The black-clad midwife let go of the Baby's feet, and the Infant began to sink, headfirst, through the gloom of the chapel. Everyone said "Oooooh!" softly, as if the Baby had just burst into cartwheels of sparkles, like the Fourth of July.

"Fall on your knees," the soprano commanded, and most of the congregation obeyed. "Oh hear the angels' voices."

The Baby made a dignified approach toward the waiting plaster family below. His sacred parents weren't looking up, but the cow seemed to be guiding Him in with a filmy, dyspeptic expression. The Baby wobbled head to toe in mid-air, rocking like a football as He descended. Then He got stuck, and stopped about twelve or fourteen feet up in the air.

Stuck in a holding pattern just underneath the leaky angel. A murmur of dismay, the way people sound when a dog comes through the open doors during a summer service and parades with evil ignorance around the room. Tabitha whispered to Kirk, "Maybe the angel has dripped some roof tar or something sticky onto that wire. That Baby's not going nowhere." The soprano kept on but no one was listening to the words any more.

A man sitting nearby, with an apologetic look at his neighbors, got up and stood on the pew. He reached up, trying to tap the Baby past the speed bump, but he was too short by a yard or so.

One of the altar boys, apparently at Father Mike's calm

instruction, waffled in his crimson robes to the front of the chapel, and knelt down by the crib. He gently shook the guy wire, trying to jostle the Baby loose.

"O holy night," began the soprano again. "The stars are brightly shining."

Maybe they were, but between the stars and the Baby an awful lot of stormy wind was bringing snow onto the roof, and some of that snow melted down through the angel's wings. The knot of black yarn fastening the Baby to his high wire was visibly dripping. The Baby was getting wet, too; drops splashed on His head and ran, with terrible accuracy, down His perfect stomach, where they collected in the folds of His plaster diaper and dripped off of His holy bottom. He looked like a Baby who badly needed a change.

"Fall on your knees," sang the soprano again, and the kneeling people took this as a sign they could get up and sit down now.

The man nearest—it was Turk Schaeffer—was being helped to climb even higher. He balanced his feet on the backs of adjacent pews. This gave him another eighteen inches or so, which was still too low. Loyal parishioners leaned against his knees but propriety forbade them from shoving their hands against his behind. Without that tripod sort of support, he couldn't swing with any assurance.

"O night divine." Then she hit the famous high note—"O night di-viiiiine"—and Tabitha thought the reverberations might be enough to spring that Baby free. Most of the old nuns had remained on their knees with their heads in the hands. Their shoulders shook.

"O holy night," began the Mueller again. The choir, out of boredom or maybe solidarity, began to *ooh* in the background. Lots of *oohs* oozed out. Jeremy Carr was looking frantic, gesturing to the two violinists, who began doing something with long drawn out notes. Someone else whipped out a harmonica and it was O Holy Night on the Range, where the deer and the antelope play with the syphilitic camels.

Solange Lefebvre's grandmother handed Turk Schaeffer a folding umbrella. Other parishioners were lifting up umbrellas and a couple of crook-handled aluminum canes. "A Jesus piñata!" whispered Kirk, delighted. "Is He stuffed with candy?"

"This is a goddamned zoo," muttered Hogan.

"I hope they don't break Him," said Tabitha.

"Fall on your knees," pleaded the choir.

The song was nearing that stratospheric note again. Tabitha wondered: Was the emotion of the moment going to inspire *every member of the choir* to try to reach that high note? It looked as if Jeremy was afraid of the same thing: he began to wheel his arms about like a teacher trying to keep a bunch of kindergartners from dashing across the street without looking. The altar boy, meanwhile, had reached Turk Schaeffer's side, and whispered in his ear. Turk hoisted the kid onto his shoulders in a piggyback. Someone handed the kid an umbrella.

The choir hit the high note with recklessness. The altar boy took aim, and let fly with a mighty wallop. His whack was heard all over the church. The congregation allowed itself a soccer goal cheer. But the Baby kept its sleeping eyes shut and barreled toward its destination. Tabitha thought, wow, isn't that too fast? There's no one at the end of the incline to slow it down. It's going to smash to bits in the cradle.

She wasn't the only mother who stood, fearful for any baby, even a holy plaster one. She saw the crib shift an instant before the Baby made touchdown. It hopped, then tipped over, and the grille it was sitting on opened like a trapdoor. Mary and Joseph looked down devotedly to see what child is this. Up popped the head of Mrs. Leontina Scales, eyes blinking in the light, as if the choir's exertions had woken her at last. Several people in the front pew screamed. The Baby caught Mrs. Scales in the forehead and smashed into a thousand holy pieces. Tabitha's mother juddered backward, hitting her head on the floor-level iron housing of the grille behind her, but she didn't lose her balance.

"What the hell is going *on* here?" she said into the fading echo of the choir's final, divine word.

36

"YOU'RE NOT WELL enough to go," said Tabitha.

"Don't you take that tone to your mother," said Mrs. Leontina Scales. "I may have been under the weather, but now I'm peppy as the first cup of Folgers. Do you think the green or the pink?" She held up a lime-colored spaghetti-strap straitjacket poxed with sequins. The pink was cut more matronly, a twin-set with shoulder pads.

Tabitha thought that with her new close-cropped haircut, dear Mother would resemble a walking bottle of Pepto-Bismol. "The pink looks sucky. I don't even know why you're invited."

"The pink it is, then. If you disapprove, that makes it respectable. Listen, honey. I work on the Republican voter registration committee with Caleb's mother, Betty. And there was a time when their marriage wasn't doing so well that I considered becoming Mrs. Leontina Prelutski Scales Hauenstein Garrison Briggs. So Caleb could almost have been your stepbrother. What do you think of that?"

The notion made Tabitha feel sick, but everything made her feel sick these days. "You have some history, Momster. Is there any man in town you *didn't* almost marry?"

"I preferred the married life, actually. Father, mother, and babies. Like the holy family."

"So you divorce three husbands in a row?"

"I'm a slow learner." She pointed a finger. "Like you. I found out by going through them that none of those guys were competent to be father to you kids."

"I'd say they were *competent*. I mean, ta-da: here we are."

"No. They didn't buy into it. They were too much of this world."

"So you walked away from them? It's holier to raise your children without fathers than with them? What if Mary had said to Jesus, Come on, Jesus, we don't need that schmuck Joseph. He's not *competent*."

Her mother paused. "Of course, Joseph wasn't Jesus's real father. So I wouldn't really have blamed Mary. She always had God the Father as backup. No walking way from *Him*."

"Bullshit. Who gave you the right to interpret the world?"

"What else is a mother but the focal depth for her children?" She pursed her lips. "Betty Briggs is inviting me to her son's wedding to point out her marriage was never threatened by me. Even though Eli Briggs, bless his triple-bypassed heart, is dead and gone. The least I can do is show up and prove her point. What are you wearing?"

"I'm not going."

"I accepted for the whole family." Mrs. Scales hadn't forgotten how to be firm, Tabitha noted. "I need you. I don't want neighbors pointing at me and remembering that little flirtation with Eli Briggs. I need my children around me to prove *my* point: I got on with things. Understand?"

"Don't I ever get off the hook?"

"Any hook you're on, you put yourself there. Don't I know that full well?"

And, within reason, Leontina Scales felt she did. The world was solidifying every day, and the lost months of November and

December, mothy enough while they were happening, were taking on a further quality of dream. Evaporating under inspection. The physical therapy seemed to be helping, though Nurse Marilee Gompers said there was a good deal yet to be accomplished. "It's all up to you, Mrs. Scales, how fast you're going to come back." An unspoken implication signaled in the eyes of Nurse Gompers: You revolting couch potato. You disgust me.

But Mrs. Leontina Prelutski Scales had already come back, she wanted to say. She had drifted into a place of masks and disguises, where no one had eyes, where voices were insistent but devoid of language. Everything unfamiliar. She remembered a sense of being with someone like her mother, someone who disapproved of her every tentative step—though her mother was long dead. But this mother entity, not Mrs. Ida Prelutski but some faint simulacrum—this maternal vapor had not interfered. Reticent, shadowy, constant. As always dubious to claim a genuine religious reveal, Leontina Scales was hesitant to name it Friend Jesus. But its presence had been a big relief.

She hadn't yet told Tabitha—and perhaps she wouldn't—how she had wakened up at last to the sound of angels in need of a tune-up. She'd become aware of mustiness, dankness, yet light fell from above. She'd wondered if she was entering the afterlife. Wouldn't Jesus have sent her a guide? Someone who had gone before, a kind of Orientation Day Big Sister?

She had sat up and found the photo in her lap. Old technology, but there was no gainsaying heaven. Her mentor, her welcomer. She couldn't make it out until she'd stood on the bier. When she saw Mother Stalin, she'd screamed. In hell no one can hear you scream.

Leontina had run away from Ida Prelutski once, when she was nineteen. Wasn't once enough? If her own mother was waiting in the afterlife to take up the cudgel of motherhood again, then Leontina wasn't going. Amen, end of story. And she'd tried to escape by the only route she saw, through the grille in the ceiling.

I never asked for much in the way of grace, she reminded herself, and I have not deserved much. I merely asked that my spiritual incompetence not be found out. To be spared having to walk out of a church service because of exposure and humiliation. And yet there I am, being ushered by my weeping children down the center aisle of some foreign chapel stiff with Catholic froufrou.

At first, coming back from the dead hardly seemed worth it.

She still hadn't figured out why her children had brought her to a midnight mass in a Catholic chapel. It was like trying to Center Your Breathing in a pit of demons. But then, she reconsidered, maybe if you could do it here, you had passed the test at last and could hold your head up high. "Are you out of your minds?" she had said to them, coming up from the netherworld and shaking the shards of porcelain from her clothes and her hair. "What is this, the All-New Candid Camera?" She hadn't known it was Christmas. She'd thought it was All Saints Day.

"Wear your plaid skirt and the mock angora with cowl neck," said Mrs. Scales. "That's darling on you."

"I'm not going."

"How about the ivory with the blue piping? Memo to Daughter: While we're here—while we're here together in this life, Tabitha Scales, we're sticking together. You are going and that's the last of it."

"I was better off with a staple gun in my hand."

"What's that?"

Tabitha didn't reply, and she did knuckle under, but she chose an old-fashioned full-skirted white dress she found in a garment bag in the crawlspace. Over a stain on the bodice she pinned a

rusty pin from the promo campaign of one of the ancient Madonna recordings—it said Like a Virgin. "Really," said Mrs. Scales.
"Doubt it very highly."

"Call up the feds, we got a Truth in Advertising felony here,"
said Hogan.

"It doesn't say A Virgin, it says *Like* a Virgin," said Tabitha.

"It's a great dress." Kirk held up the skirt and swished it around
his own knees. "It's got about nine yards of tulle underneath."

Mrs. Scales recognized it. The very dress she had worn to
the Spring Fling mixer where she had met Wally Scales. She
hadn't remembered saving it. All Tabitha needed was a pointy little hat chugging along the swells of her heavily-sprayed hairdo.
"You're not allowed to wear white to a wedding unless you're the
bride."

"I can wear whatever the fuck I want."

Mrs. Scales conceded the point. So much lost time to make up
for. "Well, at least your hair is divine."

"I can't believe you'd attend a Catholic wedding, Mom," said
Kirk, as they headed toward the car. Tabitha itched to twist the key
in the ignition, but Mrs. Scales drove. Tabitha was stuck in the
backseat with Hogan. So much taken away from her. Why didn't
she feel more relieved?

"It is troubling to me, you bet," said their mother, "but at least
the service isn't *in* the Catholic Church. I'm so glad that Pastor
Huyck permitted the families to use Cliffs of Zion. True Christian fellowship, wouldn't you say?" She turned to beam at Kirk sitting in the passenger seat. "Pastor Huyck signed my release forms,
I see. The dear man. He took some responsibility, which is more
than I can say for some. When I was lost and a lamb astray. And I
never knew. So I intend to stand by him."

"Watch the road, Mom," said Kirk.

Hogan picked his nose and flicked it at Kirk's bouffant, where it stuck and hung like a little worm.

Don't bother watching the road, thought Tabitha. No one's going anywhere.

———————

THAT LINDA PEARL is all talk and no action. Here comes Polly Osterhaus up the aisle in a warm front of white winds and the aroma of orange blossoms. When she threw back her veil, Tabitha saw Polly's clear skin, her bumblebee nose, her perfect volumized updo, her carmine plastic lips. Caleb stood, rooted in shock, as if a truck packed with explosives was coming up the aisle at him 100 miles an hour and Timothy McVeigh at the wheel. Thank God the usual choir from Our Lady's was on break or something, for the music was thinly provided by Jeremy Carr and a soloist. "Irene Menengest, alto." She was okay. At least it wasn't "O Holy Night."

Tabitha tuned out. A couple of weeks ago she had been jumpy, jittery, feeling everything, and now all that had vanished. Here, look, Mom standing next to me, beaming like an idiot, weeping from her nose, for Christ's sake, and she doesn't even know what this marriage is doing to her own daughter. How can people be so blind? What, am I going to accept blindness too, she thought, accept dullness, accept wrapping my fingertips and all my lips in layers of padding, like Pampers? Am I going to stick with being the resentful daughter, plodding in the wake of Mom's pitiless climb toward grace? Or is my devotion to Caleb asserting itself once again, and am I shutting down to keep from breaking down?

Linda Pearl Wasserman had told Tabitha that Catholics didn't believe in saying "If there's anyone here who knows why this

marriage should not proceed, speak up or forever hold your peace."
What might Tabitha have offered as protest? That Caleb had gotten
her pregnant? Without having gone to the formalities of taking the
easy 1-2-3 test, she couldn't prove it to anyone yet.

Anyway, what had Caleb done with the news that Tabitha was
pregnant? Flushed it farther away from himself than she had done.
Acted as if she hadn't even spoken.

She didn't have the stomach for that kind of scene, anymore.

Or for any of this. But what kind of scene would she prefer?

The bride blushed. The groom kissed the bride. The audience
clapped as if this were *Wheel of Fortune*. Maybe it was.

———————

THE RECEPTION WAS in the assembly room underneath the worship space—the same room in which the annual Christmas sale
was held. Polly's friends had decorated it with trails of white and
pink crepe paper. Caleb's friends were making farting noises with
their hands; Tabitha saw them passing a bottle around in a paper
bag. Caleb's brother was plastered. The punch, thick with soggy
sherbet, resembled Lake Ontario in March, melting industrial run-
off. The room overheated so Pastor Huyck, who was going out of
his way to avoid Tabitha, smart man, opened the windows near the
ceiling.

"Look at that, cunning little *sandwiches*," said Mrs. Scales
loudly, as if she'd never seen anything like it before. On aluminum
rounds sat treacherously arranged ziggurats of bread triangles: cu-
cumber, tuna, some kind of paste that looked suitable for sizing
particle board.

"Cheapest excuse for refreshments I ever saw," said Hogan.

"Shhh, she's probably paying for it herself. I don't see anybody who looks like wealthy parents," said Mrs. Scales. "Where's Kirk gone off to?"

"Over trying to locate the organ on the organist," said Hogan, under his breath so Mrs. Scales couldn't hear, or could pretend not to have heard.

37

DURING THE WEDDING Jeremy hadn't looked once at Willem, who sat in the fifth row on the left with Francesca and their preternaturally clean and orderly children. What a relief to concentrate on organ pedals, keyboards and stops, and, for one number, the neck of the guitar. He wouldn't have wanted to try to sing. He had only sung before Willem once, that first night in the Adirondacks, when the melody seemed capable of swallowing them up whole as the warm black water had done.

Jeremy's car was packed; he was leaving tonight. He just wanted to say a good-bye to Willem—not a loud good-bye, not a demonstrative one, but one that would serve to launch Jeremy toward whatever this new year held. The only thing he was sure of was that he didn't know what was coming next. They'd made it through Y2K without a hitch or a hassle. One thing at a time.

Weddings are occasions of brutal separation as well as of union, he thought. The precious couple gets married and everyone else doesn't. Last night at Bozo Joe's, Jeremy had had a fight with Marty over his intention to show up at the reception. "Why do you abuse yourself like this?" snorted Marty. "Using someone else's wedding for your refresher course in masochism."

"It's called closure."

"It's called sick."

"Let's change the subject. Are you sure your brother's okay with my staying with him for the first week or so?" Everyone so jittery in the nervous new millennium, thought Jeremy, watching Marty work for access to a civil tongue.

"Ben's an angel. You're good for about a week, tops. He works four afternoons at one of those restaurants on the top of the World Trade Center. You know, the twin towers downtown. If you really think you can stick it out and you're not going to fold on him, he told me he'd be willing to introduce you to Human Resources. Maybe you can get a job waiting tables, or kitchen work. Make ends meet until you find something else. Ben won't be much company, though. He'll be out most nights doing gigs. A good saxophonist gets a lot of work. At least the place will be free if you want to bring some subway saint home for an hour."

"I'll send you a telegram the day it happens."

"Look, but the timing of this has gotten really dicey. What're you going to do if Sean starts fading the day before the competition?"

He had thought of this. "Sean told me what he wanted me to do. But how about you?"

"Germy, you know the answer. If it comes to that, you'll have to wing it in Manhattan on your own. Even if this is your once-in-a-lifetime."

"I get it." Jeremy dangled the spoon over his coffee. "Maybe he'll hold on till after the twenty-first."

Marty started humming "New York, New York."

"If you begin to croon I will pitch this scalding coffee in your face."

"You sound as if you've been taking correspondence courses in New Yawk courtesy." Singing. "Start spreading the shit.

Fuhgeddaboudit. You'll make a great big fart of it—hey, don't take it personally, Jeremy. Come back."

At least someone's going to miss me, thought Jeremy, not turning back.

He'd gone home, finished his resignation letters to Father Mike and the school, taken an hour to get up the nerve to post them, and then, Willem in his thoughts, had not been able to sleep and find Willem in his dreams.

He was glad that the reception was in a church basement where the wine wasn't expected to flow liberally, if at all. Though that punch might be many-colored, none of the colors was spiked. He couldn't have dared a tipsy farewell. One stray tear and he'd have to kill himself.

At least Polly and Caleb appeared to agree about avoiding the hokeypokey and the tossed bouquet and newlyweds cramming cake into each other's mouths the way, presumably, they were expected to cram themselves in a matter of hours. None of that seemed in the cards. Still, Jeremy stayed on high alert, poised to escape to the men's room if all bachelors were conscripted to vie for the honor of catching a flung garter.

He felt rather than saw the lanky electricity of Kirk Scales seated at the other end of the long folding table, but Kirk was making no attempt to come closer. Kirk's fixation would begin to fizzle out the moment Jeremy's getaway actually took—if without turning back Jeremy made it to his friends who lived in the Albany area tonight, and to New York City tomorrow. If, if. If, on January 21st, the cabaret showcase went well and there was one, at least one, only one little crumb of encouragement—then last night had been his last night in Thebes, and the wedding marked his divorce from Willem, whether Willem knew it or not. Kirk would just have to deal.

Francesca and Irene came along, laughing, plastic cups of

sherbet sludge in their hands; Willem followed. He'd shucked his jacket but wore his daughter Charlotte sitting atop his shoulders, and he carried Bartholomew in his arms. The perfect Handelaers stopped and parked themselves at Jeremy's end of the table. Irene blocked Kirk out. Kirk shifted to watch. "The man of the hour," said Willem. "Music sounded great, Jeremy."

"That's Irene for you, a pro," said Jeremy. Irene flashed him a hateful smile. Jeremy knew she hadn't admired her own middle tone, and was just a good enough singer to find herself wanting.

"Polly liked it, or said she did," Irene said.

"Trust her. Catholic brides aren't allowed to lie on their wedding day."

"Tripe and nonsense. I'm sure even Catholic virgins say, Darling, it was everything I ever dreamed of, while really dreaming of Antonio Banderas a third of the way out of his 2(x)ists."

"Say hi to Jeremy," said Willem to Charlotte. "Give him a kiss? Hmmm?"

Surely Willem wasn't going to play this game in front of his wife?

"No," said sensible Charlotte, and drove her gummy chin into her father's dirty blond head. In children, thought Jeremy, remain the last hopes of salvation for the world.

"I'll give you one, Jeremy," said Francesca, and did. "Like it or not."

"I do," he said. "Happy millennium."

"We made it through Y2K, didn't we? Bit of a snooze, all that panic. What are your New Year's resolutions? Hope you've broken them all; it's January 15 already."

"I hate New Year's Eve. One more chance to remember that you haven't yet done what you wanted. And to pretend it doesn't matter."

She wasn't listening. She had taken Bartholomew from Willem and was playing with him. "Well, I'm going to learn to do trapunto stitchery, I think. It's either that or calligraphy."

"Me, I'm going to ski more," said Willem. "Do you ski, Jeremy? They've smartened up the runs at Gore Mountain. We could go for an overnight sometime. A good day on the slopes, then kicking back by the fire." He lifted Charlotte off his back and set her down at a plate.

"And leave me with the kids. You monster. You're already kicked back," said Francesca. "Got that down cold."

"Practice makes perfect."

Charlotte was giggling and mashing a sandwich. Jeremy stole a glance at Willem as he bent his head over his daughter's silver-blond hair. He was so far away, even when he was only four feet over. Willem scent—sweat and soap and laundry powder and a teasing lick of vetiver, a whiff of the past. Willem there and not there, the most heady paradox. Song alone had a chance of presenting The Mystical Body of Desire with any hope of accuracy.

Jeremy blinked and turned away. At the other end of the table Kirk Scales was shaking his head—probably putting two and two together. Even a high school sophomore could find himself appalled by Jeremy.

He excused himself and went to stand by the emergency door that Pastor Huyck had opened for air. Behind him, a fiddle was being tuned, a microphone tapped. Dancing at this do? They'd have to push the tables back. The late afternoon January sky was glowing royal blue two-thirds along, and the west was red carnation and gold. "I'd like to be alone, if you don't mind," said a voice farther out the door—a person partway up the concrete stairwell leading to the parking lot. He hadn't seen her.

"Oh, Tabitha," he said. "Sorry."

She shrugged, but he wasn't going back in there until he found his bearings. She didn't own the place. Across the lot, the blue plastic tarps on the roof of Our Lady's looked like swimming pool liners. A smell of char still lingered, three weeks and several storms regardless. "Glad to see your mom is better," he said. "That was some performance she put on."

"I wouldn't put it past her to have planned the whole stupid thing," said Tabitha. "That's what it was, you know. A big fake-out. She decided to play the baby to teach me something. Well, it backfired, because she got replaced by a better baby." She had a smaller voice, more defensive, than he'd heard before. Wasn't she glad her mom was restored?

"I thought the nuns would have multiple heart attacks. For a moment Mother Clare du Plessix thought it was the Spirit of the Foundress actually coming up from the crypt."

"Maybe it was and maybe it wasn't."

"You're shivering, why are you out here?"

"I want a smoke."

"You're not smoking though."

"I want one, I'm not *having* one. This is the next best thing."

He didn't try to figure her out. "Not a good day, I'm guessing?"

"Good, bad, you lose track what's what."

"Yeah, I know about that."

The band started. A jug band of a sort, Adirondack hillbilly jazz. "You don't want to dance, I guess?" he said.

"Got that right. I hate this kind of crap. Why at weddings does everybody think they're the fucking Waltons."

"Did your brother start the fire?"

"Did you? Just to be able to blame him and get him off your case?"

"Of course not."

"Well then," she said, as if that was conclusive.

"You *are* shivering. Come on in. It's freezing out here."

They peered in. Caleb and Polly were dragging through their first dance. It was that song from *Cats*. "No. They're right there."

"Come around. We can stand in the vestibule and watch from a distance."

They tramped through the snow to the front of the Cliffs of Zion Radical Radiant Pentecostal Church. Polly and Caleb must have broken off their dance early. The caller was hooting and stoking the applause, and rousing up folks to come and do a square dance. In the well-heated vestibule, with a doubtful look Francesca Handelaers was sniffing Bartholomew's diapers. "He's just got the most perfectly incredible schedule of production," she said as Tabitha and Jeremy knocked the snow off their shoes. "Am I in your way?"

"No," said Jeremy. "I'm happy on the margins."

"Me too," said Francesca, eyes on her work, then, "but I never really believed that of you, Jeremy."

"Coming through," said Tabitha, giving the baby a horrified scowl and wrinkling her nose, and darting for the women's room.

Jeremy sat on the stairs, inching back into the shadows. Peculiar that, so much of the time, he found Francesca's company more comfortable than Willem's. She laid a fresh diaper out on the floor and began to undo Bartholomew's purple leggings. She talked about a New Year's party they'd had—why hadn't Jeremy come to it? He'd been visiting Sean? Reading to him? Oh, Sean. Right.

Irene showed up, a pile of squished sandwiches pinched between her thumb and forefinger, and Charlotte in tow with her other hand. "Anything I can do?" she said to her sister.

"Get your niece to eat *something*, this is supper." Francesca grabbed Bartholomew's feet in one hand and lifted his legs like a couple of trout, so his little smeared bottom rose from the messy diaper. "Pee—*ew*, Bartholomew."

A clatter; Willem came bouncing through the door, all angles and cheer. "It's a square dance, they're looking to fill another square, 'Cesca," he said.

"Got my hands full just now, honey," said Francesca. "As you can see."

"Irene, then. Come on, I'm hot to dance."

"Not me. I performed once today. I'm done."

As Irene shifted in the doorway and the light fell further Willem caught sight of Jeremy sitting there. A beat of silence, a fermata, then the yowl of the caller pleading for another pair. Francesca said, "Maybe Jeremy wants to dance."

"Oh, I don't know that he wants it that much," said Willem.

"Maybe I do," said Jeremy. The beginning and the end. "Why not ask?"

"Go mad. I'll be done in a bit," said Francesca.

"Civil unions passed in Vermont," said Jeremy. He felt he was channeling an archangel. Or Sean. "Almost a month ago. In the next door state. It's the new millennium."

Willem looked at Jeremy with a turned head. Willem's fabulous family around him like shackles and safety netting both. "Well," said Willem almost gingerly, "do you want to dance?"

Jeremy levitated across the messy baby and Francesca's deft hands, and Willem caught his elbow and pulled him up the steps. They stood, chests facing, Willem's head turned one way and Jeremy's the other. Two meerkats defending their honor, thought Jeremy. Looking for predators. Avoiding looking in the eye, though their chins were seven inches apart.

Willem braved up first. Grabbed Jeremy by the forearm. "Guess we're about to give this old town a stir." A blush rose from beneath his loosened shirt collar. "I'm going to be the man, though."

"Works for me," said Jeremy. "I'll sing soprano."

They took their place in the final square. Jack Reeves with his wife. Turk Schaeffer was paired up with Svetty Boyle—who knew? Old Man Getchen and his daughter Stephanie. A flurry of snickering round the edges of the room. "Men to the left, ladies to the right, let's walk through these steps first," said the caller. "Gentlemen, take your lady's left in your left hand, squeeze it so she'll understand, Place your right upon her waist, Show her you've got excellent—" The guitarist was doing a fret-thump, to mark the beat, no melody yet. The caller fumbled. "Whoa, Nellie, we got a snafu on our hands. What, no pretty lady available to fill out this figure over here?"

The caller's remark took an interrogative twist into silence; people craned to see. Willem remarked in an uninflected voice, "We're okay as we are; go on."

"Well." The caller was flummoxed. "I've seen everything now. I guess. I'll just call it out. Okay now. Where were we? Swing your gal—I mean swing your *partner*, swing her through . . . Holy cripes." He mopped his brow. "Folks, I can only call this the way I know it. You're gonna be innovative, you're just gonna have to follow as you can."

Willem swung his partner, swung him through; Jeremy bowed and held on and flourished. They caught their eyes together, and grinned, which changed the nature of the sidelines tittering; transformed it into applause, at least as Jeremy heard it.

The dance began in earnest, and the partners set out to follow their steps. Twelve measures in, Jeremy remembered that in square dancing you changed partners; you were swept in recurring waves around the edge of your world, until you came home. With a look of pre-cardiac trauma, Jeremy's landlord, Old Man Getchen, took Jeremy's hand in his own, and handled him as gingerly as he could manage. Turk Schaeffer was more willing to play, as long as he was caught in the joke—"You're a vixen in your danc-ing shoes, you are," he said, and gave Jeremy a pinch on the cheek. The wedding guests cheered, the room whirled as Jeremy circled. Past Polly and Caleb, Polly clapping with surprise and glee, Caleb looking as if he had died. Past Caleb's drunken friends hooting up a storm, Hogan Scales among them now. Past Kirk, his eyes wide with surprise or delight or dismay, it was hard to tell. Past Old Lady Scarcese and Mrs. Chanarinjee, whispering. Past Linda Pearl Was-serman in a Hairdo of Beauty. Past Father Mike looking the other way diplomatically. Past Pastor Jakob Huyck, who stood like a man surprised by sensing a gun in the small of his back, as Leontina Scales cabled her arm through his and tilted into the icebox of his chest.

Past Irene Menengest, looking wary, hauling Bartholomew; past Francesca Handelaers coming along behind, grinning and nodding her head in time to the music and bouncing Charlotte against her, who spotted her dad, and laughed to see such sport. Round to Jack Reeves one last time, round home to Willem, who by now was flushed lobster red under sunrise wheat-sheaf hair, taking his partner, taking him home, no more need to ramble 'n' roam.

————

THE MUSIC WAS still in Jeremy's head several hours later, when he reached out the car window to grab a ticket from the Thruway at-tendant. He hated country music as much as Tabitha had said she did, though for different reasons; yet there had seemed little so wonderful, ever, as that crazy kindergarten rhythm, and Willem—for a moment of reprieve—willing to be in full swim. With him.

Did he know? Had he seen it in Jeremy's eyes? That a wedding was an ending as well as a beginning, that Jeremy was on his way?

Stars out there beyond the windshield. It was late, the traffic thin, and the country was only farmland on either side of the Mohawk River. Not much light pollution. He'd headed out of Thebes under the speed-trap camera, barreled along the ridge road to the entrance for I-81 southbound, and now continued coursing along the Thruway east toward Little Falls, Amsterdam, Schenectady, Albany. The snow under the stars looked like Styrofoam. Diamonds in the headlights. It was almost as if it was *his* honeymoon, driving away from a wedding reception so late, and heading so far.

To clear the froth of pleasure from his head, he sang part of an old song he'd written, years earlier. It was another Willem song. I'm singing it to deliver myself of it, he told himself.

He let the last note hold out, but it wobbled at the end—a bad sign, would he wobble at the competition? A problem for another day. There was something about words and music together that allowed humans to get nearest to honest truth about what was most difficult to say. Paradoxically, only through the essential instantaneity of music could you approach its eternal pertinence.

"It's a weird song," said Tabitha. She'd been thinking about it then. First thing she'd said in a half an hour. He thought she'd been dozing. "I can't tell if it's about God or about someone you care about."

"Neither can I," he answered. "Or both."

"Isn't that super-sincere kind of music kind of, uh, old-fashioned?"

Everyone's a critic. "Maybe," he said.

She sighed. Jeremy guessed she didn't really care about music. She just wanted the ride, and she had to put up with it. "You know what song I like?" she said. "That Frank Sinatra one." She began to hum in a painfully tuneless way. "Da da, da-da da, da da, da-da da . . ." She patted her stomach. "What I like about that song is that it seems like you count. You go to New York to count. To be counted. To add up."

"You don't go to New York to sleep on the street, I hope."

"We'll find something."

"*You'll* find something. I'm only doing this as a favor, you know. We can stop tonight at my friends who live outside Albany. Then tomorrow night in New York City I have a place to stay, but only briefly. You can crash there one night, I bet, but you have to find someplace else after that."

"We'll find something," she said again. "We'll get counted. You, me, and the baby."

"I'm glad you called home and left a message so they wouldn't worry."

"I talked to Kirk. I didn't tell him who I was traveling with."

Kirk would figure it out. Jeremy had been pulling himself together behind the Dumpster—trying to resist those few threatening tears—when Tabitha cornered him and asked him for a ride. Kicked Jeremy into the new millennium. As they were backing out of the parking space, Jeremy had caught sight of Hogan Scales coming to the door and taking it all in. His face registered something dark—Jeremy had seen it as threatening, and split. But thinking back on it now, maybe Hogan was sharper than he seemed. Knowing his sister so well, maybe he'd imagined what Jeremy hadn't yet deciphered: no way that Tabitha would exit the vehicle until they'd cleared the Thebes town limits by several hours.

So that menace on Hogan's face perhaps was really a sharply rising ache. He was her little brother, after all. "Did you tell Kirk when you'd be home?"

"It's my turn to be the mother," she said, in answer to some question he hadn't asked. "I didn't mean to, but there you are. What's going to happen to the church?"

"It'll muddle through. Won't take long to fix, provided the in-surance money comes through. Meanwhile, the parish will have their services out at the Motherhouse. It's not such a bad deal. The sisters out there aren't attached to any parish, but this gives them a big family who needs them. At least for the time being." He grinned. "Turk Schaeffer is heading out there this week to fix the roof properly, for once and for all. Mother Clare du Plessix is thrilled."

She didn't seem to be listening. She didn't care about ancient nuns. She was very, very young. A novice at everything, though perhaps stronger than he was. She'd refused to let him go on snif-fling. In her old-fashioned white dress that rustled like drapery in the snowbanks, she'd announced, "It's time to get out of here."

She rubbed the condensation on the passenger window and looked out over the hills. "I can see the lights of Manhattan."

"Manhattan is at least a hundred fifty miles to the south. You're seeing starlight, that's all."

"Must be a big star up there." She squinted and then fell back against the headrest. Her hand dropped to her lap. "Sing to the baby."

"I don't know any lullabies."

"Make one up."

He couldn't, not on request, not now. "How about a verse of 'O Holy Night'?"

"Maybe we should call him Jesus, too." Or had she said Jesus Two?

The car filled with a profound, even a great silence.

SON OF A WITCH
Volume Two in the Wicked Years

ISBN 978-0-06-074722-0 (paperback) • 978-0-06-171473-3 (mass market)

Gregory Maguire returns to the land of Oz to follow the story of Liir, an adolescent boy left hiding in the shadows of the castle after Dorothy did in the witch.

"Maguire's captivating, fully imagined world of horror and wonder illuminates the links between good and evil, retribution and forgiveness." —*People*

A LION AMONG MEN
Volume Three in the Wicked Years

ISBN 978-0-06-085972-5 (paperback)

A Lion Among Men features *The Wizard of Oz*'s beloved Cowardly Lion, Brrr, whose story offers clues to missing pieces in the Wicked series and probes profound questions of fate and identity—what was Brrr's real role in Elphaba's life?

"Maguire is full of storytelling brio . . . his Oz is meticulously drawn."
—*New York Times*

CONFESSIONS OF AN UGLY STEPSISTER
A Novel

ISBN 978-0-06-098752-7 (paperback) • 978-0-06-196055-0 (paperback)

Far more than a mere fairy tale, *Confessions of an Ugly Stepsister* is a novel of beauty and betrayal, illusion and understanding, reminding us that deception can be unearthed—and love unveiled—in the most unexpected of places.

"An arresting hybrid of mystery, fairy tale, and historical novel."
—*Detroit Free Press*

LOST
A Novel

ISBN 978-0-06-098864-7 (paperback) • 978-0-06-196057-4 (paperback)

In the spirit of A. S. Byatt's *Possession*, with dark echoing overtones of *A Christmas Carol*, *Lost* presents a rich fictional world that will enrapture its readers.

"A brilliant, perceptive, and deeply moving fable about loss and a storyteller's ghosts."
—*Boston Sunday Globe*

MIRROR MIRROR
A Novel

ISBN 978-0-06-098865-4 (paperback) • 978-0-06-196056-7 (paperback)

A lyrical work of stunning creative vision, *Mirror Mirror* gives fresh life to the classic story of Snow White—and has a truth and beauty all its own.

"A brilliant achievement." —*Boston Herald*

HARPER   *wm*
MORROW   **HarperCollins**Publishers

Imprints of HarperCollinsPublishers • www.harpercollins.com • www.gregorymaguire.com